# The Life of
# Byron Jaynes

# The Life of

# BYRON
# JAYNES

A NOVEL

*James Howard Kunstler*

*W. W. Norton & Company*

NEW YORK / LONDON

Library of Congress Cataloging in Publication Data
Kunstler, James Howard.
The life of Byron Jaynes.
I. Title.
PS3561.U55L5 1983    813'.54    82–14267

ISBN 0-393-01721-4

ISBN 0-393-30116-8 {PBK}

W. W. Norton & Company, Inc.,
500 Fifth Avenue, New York, NY 10110
W. W. Norton & Company Ltd.,
37 Great Russell Street, London WC1B 3NU

1 2 3 4 5 6 7 8 9 0

### Credits

*When you awake*

*You will remember everything*

*You will be hanging on a string*

—The Band

*Fall*

# CHAPTER 1

The first time I met Byron Jaynes was in a series of three interview sessions at his home outside the Catskill village of Tamberlane,
New York, in the autumn of 1968. In early 1971, Byron Jaynes was
found dead in his London hotel suite and was buried in St. Clement's Churchyard, Knightsbridge. The next time I saw Byron Jaynes
was ten years later in the pet food section of a Top Shopper supermarket in Cardiff, New Hampshire.

He was one of the prophets of his generation, and when he died
many of us felt suddenly deprived of some vital piece of sensory
equipment, left paralyzed, struck blind or speechless. The news
crackled across the ocean—Byron's dead—and the sun that had lit
the landscape of so many young lives was permanently dimmed. No
catastrophe of nature or politics could have damaged us more.
Remember how it was: we were a procession of beautiful pilgrims,
millions strong, marching toward a bright horizon. Byron's death
darkened that horizon and flattened us as surely as a hurricane or a
sortie of B-52s. And now, more than a decade after that light had
gone out, I was seized by the astonishing conviction that the figure
in drab clothing a few footsteps down the aisle of a back-country
store was him.

The word "changed" is hardly adequate to describe what I saw.
It was an alteration much more profound than that steady, subtle

erosion of the molecules we call getting older. He was transformed. And though he only slightly resembled the Byron I remember, who we all remember—the slender, incandescent young man in the tight jeans and flowing white silk shirts, the pale face that seemed lighted from within beneath his long black hair—I was struck at once with the physical shock of recognition.

He was methodically selecting cans of cat food and placing them in his shopping cart. I was perhaps five steps away, reaching for a box of Liver-Snap dog treats, when I saw the scar on his neck, below his jaw, just inside his collar. Only someone who had been in the same room with him, as I had been years earlier, would have recognized the baguette-shaped, shiny two-inch scar. It was exactly the kind of small physical oddity one's eye might focus on in the course of a long interview, and I had studied it meticulously during those three sessions, while Byron had gazed abstractly into the fireplace quietly answering my questions. In fact (I remember now), one of the few times he actually looked my way was when I asked him how he got the scar. He laughingly called it his "mark of Cain"—taking a potshot at the earnest young rock writers, like me, who made such a big deal of the biblical imagery in his songs. He'd had a cyst removed in the ninth grade, Byron said, and that was all there was to it.

Trembling, I put the Liver-Snaps back on the shelf and reached for a box of Milk Bone biscuits—anything to study him a moment longer. He placed two more cans of cat food in his cart and rolled past me while I put the Milk Bones back, grabbed the Liver-Snaps again, and glanced at him impersonally the way you would glance at anyone who brushes past you in a grocery store. His eyes did not seek mine. I had barely a second to gather an impression.

About five-foot-seven (Byron's height), he was dressed in a grimy dark-green janitor's outfit, pants and matching shirt, open at the neck with a triangular flag of yellowed T-shirt showing. He was stocky and muscular, not at all like the Byron we remember, so slender that another rock journalist, Timothy Peckham I think it was, once described him as "weightless and hollow-boned as a bird." It was his face that was the most radically altered. Byron Jaynes's nose had been a delicate blade, the nostrils always quivering, the skin seemingly transluscent. But the man who passed me in the Top Shopper aisle had a little upturned bulb of a nose with two dark nostrils that drew your attention like a second pair of eyes. His hair, like Byron's had been, was black, but there was considerable gray at the temples. What's more, it was clipped very short, and so thin at the top that a shiny circle of scalp reflected the fluorescent lights overhead. He was beginning to go bald.

I dropped the dog biscuits into my cart, not daring to look back until I was sure he was way down near the end of the aisle. Then I turned. And what I saw seemed to verify my initial impression—the man walked with an obvious limp.

The general facts of the motorcycle crash at Tamberlane in early 1968 are old news to anyone who followed his career and music. What is not generally known is that the accident left him with one leg half an inch shorter than the other. It wasn't the kind of thing you'd publicize. But when I interviewed him for the magazine in October of that year, he was still convalescing, and we stayed indoors by the fire while a brutal rainstorm blew the last leaves off the maple trees outside. Byron had been off his crutches only a few weeks by that time and was getting used to hobbling with a cane. From time to time he would get up from the sofa—I'd offer to throw another log on the fire, but Byron said he was under doctor's orders to use the leg—and you could see what the crash had done to him. He even joked about it, calling himself "a lousy, good-for-nothin' cripple," saying he was going to get a tin cup and wheelchair and play all his future concerts under the name "Crazy Legs Jaynes."

For the next quarter of an hour I followed him around the store, always careful to keep my distance and stay behind him. He picked up a bag of onions, a package of dates, wheat germ, cooking oil, many cartons of yogurt, a can of Comet cleanser, a jar of peanut butter, at least a dozen cans of Campbell's soup, two cans of insecticide, a loaf of whole-wheat bread, and a bag of Oreos. I was so unstrung that I began to grab items at random—tampons, clam juice, Fruit Loops, all kinds of rubbish. It was after seven o'clock in the evening and we were the only two customers in the place.

Finally, he wheeled up to the checkout counter and transferred his groceries to the rubber belt which moves it all forward. I skulked behind a display of canned tomatoes and lit a cigarette. Unfortunately, a spark from the match-head ignited the whole book. I flung it down on the linoleum and stomped the stupid thing out. The man at the checkout looked my way without expression. I turned up the nearest aisle. When I came down the adjacent aisle, the lone checkout girl—a teenager who probably wouldn't have known Byron

Jaynes from Francis the Talking Mule—was bagging his purchases. He put the three sacks into a cart and wheeled it through the automatic door. I hurried up to the counter.

Through the window I could see him putting the bags into the rear of a dark-green station wagon. I mindlessly unloaded my own cart, meanwhile realizing that not only did I not want most of the items I'd picked up, but that I was suddenly quite anxious to get out of there.

"I'm in an awful rush," I told the cashier. "Would it be all right if I leave this stuff and just take the dog biscuits for now?"

She looked at me like I was crazy, which was perfectly understandable. She had already rung up several items.

"Really, these are all I need today," I assured her, holding up the Liver-Snaps. She started craning her neck around the register, looking for the store manager, I assumed.

"Here." I took two dollars out of my wallet and pressed them into her hands. "Keep the change." I jammed the box under my arm and rushed out the door. The dark-green station wagon was turning out of the parking lot.

Stepping quickly over to my Saab, I tried not to break into a run, and fumbled so badly starting it up that it bucked forward in third gear and stalled. The strange thing was that up to this point I hadn't consciously *decided* to tail him, though this was precisely what I was about to do. I felt, rather, like I was following some glandular imperative. But by the time I got the Saab restarted and headed out of the lot, I knew I had to go after him—even if it seemed slightly insane.

I could see the station wagon one block down Granite Street, waiting for the light to change at the intersection of Main. I hung back for a moment when it did change, then followed him across the village.

Granite Street soon became County Road 53, twisting and turning on its way into the countryside. Trying to keep some highway between us, I lost sight of the station wagon and worried that it might have slipped down one of the would-be suburban lanes at the edge of town. But I didn't turn to investigate. I leaned on the gas pedal instead. The Saab did a four-wheel-drift in front of Krepp's Korner, a drinking establishment, and I almost hit a pickup truck backing out of the lot. Rounding the corner, I caught sight of the dark-green car again.

I followed it down Route 53 for ten miles, a gloomy, craggy, unpopulated valley, and watched it turn left off the paved highway onto a dirt road. I drove past, made a U-turn, then followed at a prudent distance.

A light veil of dust hung over the road. It meandered lazily through the woods. No dwellings were visible, or even driveways. Eventually, it wended along the sun-facing side of a large hill, not quite a full-fledged mountain. Ahead, the road swelled with that rich, amber evening light that is so emblematic of summer's end in New England. I slowed the Saab to a crawl.

To my left, a broad, downward-sloping meadow came into view. It was overgrown with shrubs, abrupt clumps of sumac and saplings. To my right, removed from the road by 200 feet of weedy yard, was an old stone house, an eccentric structure, two stories of closely fitted fieldstones with an odd, Dutch-looking stepped facade capped with red brick. On one side of the house stood an enormous elm tree. Leaves grew at its uppermost branches and were rusted yellow with blight. Some of the ancient lower limbs had broken off and lay scattered on the ground like great bleached bones. At that hour, the house threw a long, liquid shadow across the weed-grown side yard, all the way to the darker margin of the woods, where the shadows converged like the water of a stream entering a mysterious lake.

Behind the house, a series of interconnected pastures bounded by stone walls and hedgerows rose haphazardly to a high wooded ridge. These pastures too were overgrown, but the expanses of waist-high weeds, so far away, looked as plush as velvet in that special light. Between the house and this series of lofty fields stood an old barn. The bare wood was weathered to the color and texture of dark-brown fur, as was the post-and-beam skeleton of a smaller, semi-attached structure, possibly an old henhouse. There was no sign of any livestock on the property though, and the barn evoked nothing so much as stark abandonment and loss. The sagging roof seemed to mimic the act of a human sigh, as if the very buildings had lost all hope. Parked between the barn and the house on a scruffy dirt driveway, and standing inert in a haze of settling golden dust, was the green station wagon. Nobody was around.

The last thing I was about to do was stop, pound on the front door, and ask the person inside if he just happened to be a rock and roll star who died in London in 1971. I drove past the place, uncertain where the road might take me, my brain reeling with the shocking implications of a discovery I could hardly accept. It was difficult enough just getting a grip on myself. Here were the facts of Byron's death (I thought out loud): he died of heart failure alone in his hotel suite; no autopsy was performed; there was no funeral ceremony (according to the terms of his will) and his casket had remained closed up to its interment. Over the past decade there had been half a dozen reports, all dismissed as crackpot, of Byron Jaynes being sighted in such far-flung locales as Venice, Chicago, Tangiers, Mexico City, Los Angeles, and in the Catskills around his old mansion in Tamberlane, where his spirit continued to reign as a kind of latter-day Headless Horseman. These "sightings" of Byron were a neat reverse of the "Paul is dead!" rumor that ran wild back in the early seventies—the one where Paul McCartney was supposed to have secretly died and been replaced by a "ringer," and no amount of denials or even public appearances by the ex-Beatle could squelch the ridiculous story.

But Byron's death was no rumor, no prank, no joke. His well-known self-destructiveness was part of his huge appeal. His career was an ongoing flirtation with death. Death and Eros walked hand-in-hand through so many of his lyrics—especially the tracks that were assembled from the London tapes after the tragedy and released as the posthumous album *Sleeper*. Byron's *danse macabre* seemed both calculated and sincere, and in the end it was brutally ironic that his death was attributed to natural causes—though nobody believed it. Everyone, from his most naïve fan to the musicians who played with him, assumed that he had really OD-ed, and we in the rock press thought that the British physician who had signed the death certificate wrote "heart failure" just to be polite.

The dirt road curved into the west and soon I was driving straight into the sun. It flashed through the overhanging foliage in disturbing, strobe-like bursts as the words to one of Byron's songs kept running through my head. It was "Jesse's Song," the lullaby he wrote for his son on the *Sleeper* album:

> *Let the sun rise*
> *Close your eyes*
> *You and I will sleep away*
> *The terrifying light of day*

I tried to envision that sad young man, still supernaturally beautiful, in the weeks between his wife's appalling crime and his own final end, but rearing up to take its place was the image of that figure limping in the supermarket. And I had to wonder what possible alteration of character, of circumstance, of fate and aspiration, might have led Byron Jaynes from the world's center stage, through a false death's shadow, to the obscurity of this New England backwater.

---

Then, what on earth was *I* doing in Cardiff?

It happened that my wife Allison's parents owned property here, on an obscure remnant of the last Ice Age called Ampersand Pond, and it coincided that Allie's parents had made plans to spend the whole summer of their fortieth anniversary in Europe instead of at the cottage, while I needed a place to retreat and write a book and a screenplay.

At the age of 35, after fourteen years at the magazine, I was facing that time of life when one sees the specter of his own mortality and begins to question what he's got to show for it all. In short, it was make-or-break time. I had a reputation as a journeyman rock writer, critic, and editor, but Allie and I wanted to have a baby, and we were not going to be able to do that on my $27,000-a-year salary and continue to live in New York City. Besides, a magazine is like any other big business: as long as you're on someone else's payroll, you have to dance to your employer's tune, and I was getting tired of this particular boogaloo.

Over the years, I'd gotten to know quite a few people in publishing and in the film industry, so in January of 1981 I started systematically to pitch them with projects. By March I found a publisher willing to advance me $15,000 on a proposed musical history of the sixties. There was a catch, of course. The standard arrangement in a deal like this is that you get half the money up-front, on signing, and the rest when you turn in the finished product. In real terms, then, the advance meant $7500. Allie earned $14,000 as an assistant art director for *Danse* magazine, but the night we sat down at the kitchen table to figure it all out, we saw that her salary plus my half-advance wouldn't begin to cover our city expenses.

Then the cottage in New Hampshire became vacant. But going up there meant Allie would have to quit *her* job. And we would need a dependable car. . . . The whole thing was starting to seem impossible. I had finally decided to keep my job, stay in the city, and try to write the book on the side when, one evening in May, I got a call from Alex Rothchild, a young producer at United Artists. He was excited about a movie idea I had presented him months earlier, and made me an offer. Here was the deal: I was to get $5000 for a "treatment," that is, a narrative outline of the story. If they liked the treatment, they'd pay me $26,000 to write the first draft of the full screenplay. And if they liked the screenplay, they'd buy it outright for $100,000. As Senator Dirkson used to say: ". . . a billion here, a billion there, sooner or later you're talking about *real* money. . . ."

A little quick arithmetic showed that I could now count on a minimum of $12,500 for living expenses (book advance plus five grand from Alex), with a decent chance of boosting it to $38,000, and an outside shot at the Big Nut!

The average mind levitates at the thought of so much hypothetical profit, but I didn't stay airborne for long. We were looking at a hard $12,500 for the year ahead, Allie reminded me, not counting the price of a decent used car. And I was looking straight into a shitload of work.

Later that week I broke the news to Wenner at the office. To many people in the music industry, he is regarded as the equivalent of Vlad the Impaler, but Jann and I have always understood each other. We must have, to stick together all those years. He was determined, though, to refer to my departure as "a sabbatical," and I didn't have the heart to correct him on that score. When my last paycheck arrived two weeks later, there was a second check in the envelope. It was for $1000 and the note attached said, "Dear Rick, Please accept this small bonus for countless services rendered. With the best wishes for good luck. [Signed] Jann. P.S. This ought to keep you in yogurt and Perrier."

---

The dirt road eventually led to the tiny hamlet of Haverfield, and by the time I got back to the cottage, silver scales of moonlight glittered on the pond. Allie was sitting in a wicker chair on the screened-in porch we used for a bedroom during the dog days of summer. The yellow glow of a hurricane lamp lighted half her face and she twirled an empty wine glass by its stem. I could tell by the way she said "hi" that she was in a troubled mood.

"I'm home," I said awkwardly, after she'd already said "hi."

"I know you're home."

Luke, our golden retriever, came over to me, sat down, and served up his paw.

"When I want your paw, I'll ask for it, dummy."

"Where have you been?"

I was afraid to tell her the truth. What was I going to say? That I thought I saw a supposedly dead rock star down in the village market and tailed his car out into the hills? Besides, I asked myself sarcastically, what if I just happened to be wrong? Byron is almost certainly planted six feet under that modest headstone in Knightsbridge. Allie's worried enough as it is—she'll think I've reached a new height of creative procrastination.

You see, I hadn't written a damn thing in weeks. In fact, I had studiously avoided working all summer, preferring instead to putter in the garden, cast for trout in Ampersand Pond, swim, ramble around the countryside, or just malinger in the sun. Allie knew I was goofing off but didn't say anything. Nights, I watched ball games from Montreal or Boston, the players fading in and out on the ancient black-and-white TV set like polar explorers lost in a blizzard. Come the fall, I kept telling myself, I'd put my nose to the grindstone. Now fall was practically here, approaching with the cold inevitability of a prison door closing. I was beginning to doubt if I was really up to the challenge of a book and a screenplay, and I think Allie was starting to panic for both of us.

"Well," she said, "where were you?"

"I . . . went to the store for a few things."

"A few things?" She could plainly see that all I had in hand was the box of Liver-Snaps. Meanwhile, the dog was making a perfect pest of himself.

"Luke, I don't *want* your goddam paw just now—"

"Don't yell at him!"

"Good doggie."

"Really, Rick . . ." she said. I could see her trying to compose the rest of the sentence, stumble mentally on the words, and give up. Finally, in a calmer tone of voice she said, "You spent two hours in the market and that's all you managed to buy? What on earth is happening to you?"

"Nothing's happening to me," I told her with all the conviction of a man falling off a cliff. "Everything's fine."

Later that night, in bed, I whispered what I thought she desperately needed to hear.

"I'll hunker down and get to work tomorrow. I promise."

But even as we made love, the eerie image of that figure in the dull-green work clothes swam desperately across my sightless field of vision like someone drowning at the bottom of the ocean.

---

When I *am* working, I like to get cracking early in the morning. In fact, the earlier the better, because by midafternoon my brain is as sluggish as the AMTRAK local that crawls through Cardiff on its way to St. Johnsbury. Allie is accustomed to my habits, and so the next day when I did sit down at the typewriter from eight until noon, my stock rose sharply in her nervous estimation.

"Good boy," she said, and I wasn't sure whether she was talking to me or the dog.

I worked on a chapter of the music book. It dealt with the great New York City bands of the mid-sixties—The Blues Project, The Lovin' Spoonful, The Fugs, The Velvet Underground, The Young Rascals—and it led inescapably to Byron Jaynes's band, The Romantics. And once I began thinking of him, and the man in the Top Shopper, and that house out in the hills, I began to wonder what I was going to do about it. I knew I would have to do something. My production for the day effectively ended at less than a page.

Allie's parents had a large map of the area on the living room wall. It was made of four U.S. Geological Survey maps spliced together and framed. Allie's dad had all the good trout streams, hiking trails, and picnic spots marked in red crayon. While Allie made lunch, I studied the map and found the dirt road I'd been on the day before. The house and barn were indicated as tiny black squares. It was called Content Farm Road.

After lunch, Allie set up her easel on the back lawn overlooking the pond (she loved to work in the heat of the afternoon) while I drove to Cardiff, supposedly to use their one-room library, but actually to visit the town clerk's office. The clerk was a tiny white-haired lady with ruddy apple cheeks and she seemed delighted to have a visitor. Fifteen minutes later she handed me a Xerox copy of the deed to the property I'd come to inquire about, a parcel on Content Farm Road. (Deeds, being matters of public record, are available to anyone who desires a copy.) At the lower right-hand corner of the second page was the owner's name: Joseph Doaks. At the lower left was the signature of one Luther Hawes. The deed was dated May 24, 1971. My palms began to sweat. I asked for the phone book. No Joseph Doaks was listed. On a crazy impulse I searched the J's, but, naturally, Byron Jaynes was not listed among them.

"Who is this Luther Hawes, ma'am?"

"Lawyer," she said brightly.

"Is he here in Cardiff?"

"Ayuh. Right on Main."

I looked him up in the phone book and called his office for an appointment. The secretary said I could come in anytime after two.

"We were in high school together, Luther and I," the clerk said. "Luther is a Yale man."

---

"What can I do for you, Mr., uh—"

"Jones," I said. "Bert Jones." When I made the appointment, I'd given the secretary a phony name. If Joe Doaks was indeed Byron Jaynes, there was a chance he'd recognize my real name. I didn't want to throw him into a panic and have him vanish on me. As for the alias, Bert Jones used to be the Baltimore Colts quarterback—it was the first name that popped into my head.

Everything in the office belonged to another era, especially Hawes himself, a slight, shrunken figure with skin the color of yellowing ivory. His face was not furrowed, exactly, but etched with fine, spidery lines, like the cracks on an ancient piano key. The green satin draperies which hung from the high windows of his inner sanctum were brown at the edges with age. On his massive and not particularly tidy desk, behind which he looked so small, was a brass lamp with the most beautiful green opalescent glass shade. It was the only source of light in the room, the shades being drawn. Behind Hawes, a wall of leather-bound legal volumes rose on shelves that reached the ceiling. An old Regulator clock ticked loudly on the wall in its oak cabinet. Hawes leaned back in his leather swivel chair. The chair creaked. He folded his hands across his gray vest.

"What can I do for you?" he asked.

"I . . . I have an interest in one of your clients," I began nervously.

"Who?"

"Joseph Doaks."

He looked blankly at me for a moment, then reached forward and punched a button on his phone. My heart flew into my throat. For a moment I was afraid he was calling Doaks directly.

"Frances, look and see if we have a file on Joseph Doaks, D-O-A-K-S," he said, glancing at me to corroborate the spelling. I nodded. "Thank you, Frances," he added and dropped the receiver back into its cradle perfunctorily.

"What kind of an interest, Mr. Jones?"

"You don't know if he's a client of yours or not?"

"Well, now, we have a great many clients. Sometimes I do a job of work for someone, never see the fellow again. Others I see more regular. We'll know in a minute."

The door opened and Frances, the secretary, came in with a folder. Hawes thanked her again and she left. He leafed through the contents of the folder making little grunting noises of satisfaction, as if his memory were being refreshed. It was not a thick folder. Finally, he closed it and looked back up at me with a tight, lawyerly smile on his lips.

"What kind of an interest, Mr. Jones?" he asked again.

"Then he is a client of yours."

"That appears to be the case." He cleared his throat. "Mr. Jones, if you'll just answer my simple question—"

"I realize this is a somewhat irregular."

Hawes leaned forward, fingertips pressed together like miniature bellows.

"Mr. Jones, it seems to me that whatever information you're seeking about my client is likely to be of a privileged nature."

"I only have a few questions," I told him. "If any of them involve privileged information, then you can say so. But let me ask them."

He leaned back again in his leather chair and closed his eyes for a moment, indicating, I believed, that these terms were agreeable.

"Is he a fairly young man, about my age?"

"Seems to me he was a young man. Yes. Are you a professional snoop, Mr. Jones?"

"No," I said, though this wasn't strictly the truth. As a journalist I had often functioned in just that way. In any case, I brushed off his remark. "Does he walk with a limp?" I asked.

Hawes made a sour face and glanced at various points around the dimly lit chamber as if he was straining his memory or losing patience with me, or both.

"Seems to me he might have done. Now, look here, Mr. Jones—"

"Just one more question, sir. Can you put me in touch with him?"

"Put you in touch? Hell's bells, son. Call him yourself."

"His telephone's not listed."

"Oh. . . ?"

"I thought you might have it."

Hawes rubbed his jaw.

"I'm sorry, but I can't do that," he said. "If the number's unlisted then I have to assume he doesn't want to be disturbed."

I felt a crimp in my stomach and it made a gurgling sound. The idea of having to go to his house, bang on the door, and confront him in person seemed dreadful and ridiculous.

"But if you leave *your* name and number, I'll see what I can do," Hawes added, and my pulse quickened once more. I took out a pen and waited for him to give me a scrap of paper, but the old man said, disdainfully, "You can leave it with Frances."

"Sure. Thank you very much."

I stood up.

"I'd like to be able to tell Mr. Doaks what it is you want to talk to him about."

"It's . . . it concerns a mutual acquaintance."

"Yes. . . ? And the name of this acquaintance?"

"It's someone who has passed away," I said gravely, lowering my eyes to the floor, as if it would be in poor taste for him to inquire further. Fortunately, he fell for it.

"I'll see what I can do," he said. We shook hands and I left.

Driving back to the cottage, another of Byron's lyrics ignited in my mind, where his songs are stacked in my memory like cord-wood. It was from his first album, *Rising Son*, recorded in 1966, months before he became a national figure.

> *Bury me in an unmarked grave*
> *Far from the reach of posterity's game*
> *The burning hand of eternity's flame*
> *History has no consolations*
> *When I'm gone let nobody know my name*

Like so many of his songs, it was eerily and deceptively prophetic. If I was correct (and I was not at all sure that I wanted to be), if that man who dwelt on a lonely hillside in northern New Hampshire *was* Byron Jaynes, then his wish had failed him doubly.

For in whatever form obliteration had found him, he had somehow failed to find death, while his name soared into the transit of legend.

———————

For three days nothing came of my meeting with Luther Hawes. One of those afternoons I even made a dry run out to Content Farm Road, a rehearsal for that agonizing moment when I would have to knock on that door and satisfy my curiosity once and for all. I drove past the stone house, so desolate in its dry pool of midday light, no one around and not a leaf stirring in the heat.

Then, the evening of the third day I stood on the porch watching Allie swim. Our nearest neighbor was a quarter mile down the shore so it was our happy custom to go without bathing suits. Allie was doing a strong breaststroke, her small buns so pale against the dark water. I hadn't done a lick of work since my meeting with Hawes. Oh, I made a charade of sitting at my desk for a few hours each day, the cigarettes piling up in the Granite State souvenir ashtray, while I thought only of Byron and *what if. . .* ? I never realized what exquisite instruments of torture those two words could be. Allie now stood in the shallows next to our dock, soaping her fine athletic body. *What if . . . I let you down*, I thought. She dove in to rinse the soap off. I was about to fix myself a drink when the phone rang.

"Hello?" I said.

"Jones?"

"Yes," I said. Blood pounded in my ears.

"Doaks," he said without elaboration.

"I, uh, spoke to your attorney."

"I know you did. What do you want?"

It was a poor connection and somewhere in the background I heard two voices, the shrill intonations of a woman arguing with a child. Furthermore, in the little he had said so far, Doaks sounded like he had some weird multi-regional accent, not quite Yankee, not quite southern drawl.

"What is this about, Jones?" he demanded.

"I . . . I wanted to talk to you about . . . about a mutual acquaintance."

"That's what I heard. Only I don't see how we would have any mutual acquaintance."

"He passed away."

"I don't consort with the dead."

"His name is Byron Jaynes."

I was shaking so badly I could barely keep the phone pressed to the side of my head. There was no reply from the other end of the line, though I could hear the two others continuing their angry exchange. It seemed to have something to do with laundry.

"I don't know anyone by that name," the caller finally said, "And I don't know any Bert Jones, either."

"My name's not really Bert Jones. And you're not Joe Doaks."

There was a click followed by a loud dial tone.

Allie strode out of the water, golden beads of water glistening on her. She bent down to pick up a towel off the pebbles and shuddered as she pressed it to her face. The same shudder ran through me. I staggered into the kitchen, poured myself a jelly-glass full of vodka, and downed it in a few gulps.

---

"Are you all right?" Allie asked as she slid a platter of cold chicken onto the kitchen table. "Rick. . . ?"

"Huh. . . ?" I said, snapping out of what must have seemed like a daze. "Yeah, I'm okay."

It *was* Byron. I *knew* that voice. Who was he trying to fool with that accent? Or am I losing my grip? Is this how you crack under stress? But I know I didn't dream up that man in the supermarket.

"Maybe we ought to take a few days off," Allie suggested, "go down to the city and see a few people, charge our batteries."

"Huh. . . ?" I said, fading out again. "No, babe. I've got to stick around."

"It would do you some good to get away, I'm sure—"

"It would do me good to get up some momentum on these projects. I can't go anywhere now."

"All right," Allie said coolly.

Should I tell her? Sure. And what would that accomplish? Scare her probably. She'd fear for my fundamental sanity, that's all. I'm beginning to worry about it myself. Scared, admit it. Jesus Christ, I'm afraid it's really him. I'll handle it, I'll *handle* it. . . .

We finished supper in silence. It came back up on me anyway, and I ran the shower to conceal the noise of my heaving. A short while later I was sitting out on the dock restlessly watching the sun go down. Allie called from the porch to tell me there was an Expos game on the tube. And she is no baseball fan.

I couldn't tell you the final score of that game, or even what team they played. And when we went to bed, I lay for hours in that darkness so full of balsam, the scent of living water, and Allie's familiar sweet musk, not knowing just when I crossed the shadowed boundary into a turbulant sleep that disintegrated with the ring of the telephone. I threw the covers off and lurched into the living room. The air was cold and my skin was damp with sweat.

"Yes. . . ?"

"Jones. . . ?"

"Yes."

"But you're not any Jones, are you?"

"No."

"Who are you then?"

"I'm Rick Sears."

I could hear him breathing at his end of the line.

"You know where I live? Of course you do."

"I do."

"Then you better come see me tomorrow."

He hung up, just like that.

I stood there for a long time, then crept back out to the porch, shivering. Allie was a dark mound under the blankets. There was a great icy ring around the moon and a terrible stillness lay heavily on that blue, moonlit world beyond the screen.

"Who was that?" Allie asked groggily.

"No one," I said.

"No one? It had to be somebody," she mumbled.

"Wrong number," I told her gently. "Go back to sleep."

---

It turned hot the next day, a final blast of summer, and out in the hills an oppressive sun kept everything down but the dust. I'd put in four hours at the desk that morning—four hours of staring into the keys, crumpling paper, and idly reading lists of aviation disasters and sports records in the *World Almanac*—so when I left the cottage that afternoon to "take a drive and clear my head," Allie didn't hassle the issue.

I parked in the dusty driveway of Joe Doaks's farmhouse and

crossed the weed-choked lawn to his front door. The rhythmic mur-
mur of crickets in the hot grass was a more persuasive quiet than
simple silence. From the front steps you could see past the scrubby
meadow across the dirt road to the faraway Vermont peaks, vague
and mauve colored in the afternoon haze. My jeans clung moistly to
my legs where I had sweated against the vinyl car seat. I knocked
on the wooden part of the dilapidated screen door, waited, and when
no one answered, I knocked again.

"Sears. . . ?"

I wheeled around.

He stood below on the lawn, wearing the same, or similar, green
garb as before, and wiping black grease off his hands with a rag. The
grease had gotten under his fingernails and into the furrows of his
knuckles. His eyes looked bloodshot and there were dark bags under
them. Altogether, he looked older than he had in the supermarket,
and in the daylight you could see more gray in his hair.

"Byron . . ." I gasped.

He winced at the name as if the sound was capable of inflicting
physical injury. His eyes turned to the ground for a moment, then
back up at me with a gaze of the most abject helplessness. He stuck
the rag in a back pocket.

"Do you like to walk, Sears?"

"Yes."

"Good. Let's walk."

Without announcing any particular destination, he began limping
around the rear of the house and I followed. I had no idea what to
say next. We walked up the dirt driveway past the parked station
wagon and then the barn. An old barbed-wire fence ran behind the
barn and he held the single rusted strand while I ducked underneath. Each step we took through the weeds roused a spray of leaping grasshoppers. Though he limped, he seemed to climb uphill
effortlessly, while halfway through the second pasture I was gasping
for breath.

"You smoke, Sears?"

"Yes."

"You shouldn't."

"I know."

We continued upward. He began pointing at flowers along the
way.

"Ragweed," he said.

We climbed higher.

"Yarrow."

He stooped to inspect it. I tried to catch my wind. He straightened up and continued forward.

"See those red leaves down there?"

"Yes," I said.

"Wild strawberries. In June these hills are covered with them. Tiny little things. You have to work hard to get a handful. You see the movie?"

"What. . . ?"

"*Wild Strawberries.*"

"Yes."

"Me too," he said. "A long time ago." I noticed that he had dropped the weird accent from the phone calls.

We traversed the last pasture to the tree-covered hilltop. It was quite steep there, and gray, lichen-covered rocks protruded from the weeds and the earth. He sat down abruptly on one of these outcroppings and I joined him on it. He sidled away, though, as if there were something unwholesome about my presence. Down below, the house and barn looked like playthings. I could feel the beginning of a heat rash on my thighs.

"On a clear day, you can see forever," he sang in the husky voice I recognized at once. He seemed to find his joke wildly amusing. In spite of the heat, I was shivering. "But it's not a clear day, is it, Sears?" he said, no longer laughing.

"No," I agreed.

"Sometimes you can see St. Johnsbury from here. On a super-clear day you can see the white church steeples. They look like sails against all that rolling green." He pointed to another flowering weed below the rock outcrop. "Goldenrod," he said. "I suppose I could offer you money."

"Wait a min—"

"You think I have loads of money? Like Scrooge McDuck, right? I have money, but not loads of it. I can live, but nothing like what you probably think. You want money?"

"I just want to know where you've been, Byron. What you're doing here—"

"Nowhere. Nothing. How much? Five thousand?"

"I'm not a blackmailer—"

"So I give you five thousand. Great! A few months later, who rolls back up the driveway in his sensible Swedish car? You need *more* money? Okay. Sure. Here's another five grand to keep your mouth shut. Uncle Scrooge McDuck. Joe Moneybags Doaks."

He stopped suddenly.

"Oh," he cried despairingly, "what am I going to do with you?"

"Byron—"

"Joe to you, pal." He glowered at me with a child's sullen face. It was hard to tell whether his behavior was artiface or genuine. A decade earlier the put-on had been his stock-in-trade, at least with the press.

"Do you remember me?" I asked him.

His eyebrows scrunched together and he searched my face for a long time.

"I don't know," he said. "Maybe."

"Anyway, I'm not a blackmailer."

"Says you."

"Believe me, I'm not."

"Hey, everybody wants money. Even saints need money. You guys kill me, you parasites!"

And then I knew that he recognized me. *Parasites* had been his code word for members of the press.

I paused to try and find the right words. "I don't know what I want, Byron. I just know that you're here, you're alive, and it's incredible. I don't want your money. I don't even work for the magazine anymore."

He continued to glower at me.

"That was you following me around in the supermarket the other day."

"Yes."

"You almost set your face on fire."

I nodded. "I had to find out for sure," I explained.

"Goody for you. Now you know." He stood up. "I don't feel so great. I have this bug."

"You have the flu?"

"I have this bug. A worm. It's inside me."

With this bizarre declaration he climbed off the rock and began striding downhill. I followed him, but even in his loping, uneven step I couldn't keep up. He reached the barbed-wire fence behind the barn several minutes ahead of me, but waited there until I made it all the way down. He held up the wire for me again, crossed the dusty yard to the back of his house, and climbed the first step of a short wooden stairway.

"You come back tomorrow when I'm feeling better," he said, and added ominously, "I'm not through with you yet." He looked sharply around himself for a moment, like a man who has forgotten where he is, exactly.

"Do you *want* me to come back tomorrow?"

"That's what I said, right?"

"Yes."

"You have to, right?"

"I don't know."

"Of course you do. You'll come back."

"Okay. I'll come back."

"I have this . . . thing. Hey, do you live alone?"

"No. I'm married."

"Married," Byron repeated, looking through me. "I was once."

"I know."

"She was a very beautiful child. Talk about bugs. . . ."

I had the disquieting feeling that he was speaking in a private language, the kind you might hear from prisoners kept in solitary confinement, in dungeons, for years on end.

"Hey, don't tell anybody. Not a soul. Not even your wife."

"I won't."

"Promise."

"I promise."

"You want money?"

"No!"

"Look, if that's what it takes—"

"I said 'I promise.' You can trust me."

He glanced over my head, way up at the hill we had just climbed down. He ran the tip of his tongue over his lips and swallowed hard.

"Simon used to say that to me all the time. Those exact words. He's dead, you know."

"I know."

"He's *really* dead."

He looked back at me and limped slowly into the house, leaving me in the dusty lagoon between the house and the barn. I could still see him, though, on the other side of the screen door, an agitated shadow.

"Come back tomorrow."

# CHAPTER 2

RS: Do you resent the critics who try to mine the songs for juicy clues about your personal life, your head?

BJ: How can I stop them. Hey, I don't encourage them. Incidentally, are you talking about yourself?

RS: Maybe a little.

BJ: So you think you know me because you know the songs, huh? Well, you don't.

—The *Rolling Stone* Interview with Byron Jaynes, 1968

It was sultry and overcast the following day and Allie had her easel set up on the porch. She was painting her hundredth-odd rendition of Ampersand Pond. Her canvases reminded me of Winslow Homer and Edward Hopper—Homer's subject matter, Hopper's style. Her compositions always convey a solitary, yearning feeling; it's always the end of a season in one of Allie's paintings. Twenty feet away, in the living room, I agonized at the typewriter, utterly unable to concentrate on the task ostensibly at hand, sunk deeply in worry and, yes, amazement.

What was he going to do about *me*, Byron had asked. What was I going to do about *him?* The question spawned more potential problems, puzzles, and points of confusion than the mind could process, and I fairly reeled in my chair. Then Allie's voice asserted itself through that whirl of thought, and I turned abruptly to discover her standing behind me.

"What?" I said, my throat parched.

"I said, 'Would you like some lunch?' I'm going to make myself a ham sandwich. I'll make one for you."

"No thanks," I tried to sound pleasant.

"You have to eat."

"I don't have to eat. I get fat if I eat."

"You get fat because you skip lunch and then you eat a whole bag of pretzels before dinner."

"Okay, make me a sandwich," I said, trying anything to avoid an argument, but she just stood there behind the chair.

"It's me, isn't it?" she said.

"Pardon? What's you?"

"You can't work with me around here, can you?"

"Sure I can."

She leaned over and turned the roller on my typewriter. The page curled out of the machine. It was absolutely clean and white.

"It's not you," I insisted.

"What is it then?"

"It's me," I told her. "I've been, I don't know, out of it lately."

She nodded her head as if she understood and marched to the kitchen. But she stopped in the doorway and turned back around.

"I think it's me," she said, and went in to make the sandwiches. "I think you need to be alone to get over this 'block' you seem to be having."

Afterward, I returned to my desk for a while, made a great show of exasperation, and announced that I was taking off for a few hours to cruise the hills and think.

"See you later," Allie said distantly from the porch without missing a brushstroke.

---

A damp wind rattled the leaves in Byron's blighted elm tree. He came to the door this time when I knocked, stepped outside, and quickly shut the door behind him as if to foreclose any designs I might have had about invading the interior. He was wearing a different outfit, a faded brown jumpsuit with a Molsen's beer insignia on the breast pocket. His mood, however, seemed much brighter than the day before and he greeted me with that rare, shy and appealing smile you see in the photos from the old days.

"Have a seat," he said, and pointed to the front steps. I sat there while Byron paced back and forth on the grass in front of me, his hands shoved into the slash pockets of his jumpsuit, his brow furrowed as though he was working out some abiding and intractable problem. "So, how've you been?" he eventually asked.

"Okay," I replied uncertainly. "Fine."

He nodded but I sensed that my answer failed to satisfy him.

"When did I last see you?" he asked.

"Yesterday," I ventured cautiously.

He cackled and shook his head.

"You must think I'm. . . ." He drew tiny circles in the air next to his temple with a forefinger.

"No—!"

"I'm a bit weird, maybe. I admit it. How could you do what I did and not be? Right? I buffaloed the whole world. I mean, I was good. There was *some* talent there, I think." His voice fell to a hoarse whisper. "I don't know how much of it was me, or . . . what." His eyes darted energetically for a few moments, then he looked back at me and resumed a normal tone of voice. "Where did I meet you before? I feel like I know you from somewhere."

"Your house. Tamberlane."

"When?"

"In 1968."

"Sweet Jesus. That was you?"

"Yes."

"*Rolling Stone?*"

"That's right. I thought you knew that—"

"You were a kid."

"I was young. We both were."

"No, but you were a kid."

"The whole world was back then."

"I kept wondering why they sent this kid. You had those gold wire-rim glasses. You looked like some English schoolboy. Where are your glasses?"

"Contacts," I said, and pointed to my eyes.

"Oh. . . . You were a bright kid, though. That was one of the only intelligent interviews I ever did."

"You answered some of the questions, for a change."

"Yeah, I was a real pain-in-the-neck, huh? You guys caused me a lot of grief. A *lot* of grief." His eyes glazed over again. An instant later, he came out of it. "Hey, but you—you know, I felt sorry for you. I was afraid you'd get fired if you didn't come back with something. It was like you were somebody's kid brother. And you had that denim jacket with a fur collar and fur cuffs and roses embroidered on the pockets, right?"

"That's right."

"You know something funny? That jacket killed me. I coveted that jacket of yours. It was great. I remember it clearly."

"I didn't know you liked it so much. I would have given it to you."

"Are you crazy? I could have had fifty of them made overnight. But, no, it wouldn't have been the same. Yours had . . . character. People were always trying to make clothes for me. You know how Tamberlane was: there must have been a thousand chicks with sewing machines up in those hills. Remember that wall around my property with the stone gateposts?"

"Yes."

"I used to drive out of there and those gates would be festooned with garments, silk, spangles, all this day-glo stuff, like a Christmas tree. Godalmighty! I felt terrible about it, all those poor souls slaving away to make me things I'd never wear. Anyway, I remember that great jacket of yours. Do you still have it?"

"No. I wore it to a Zappa concert at the Cow Palace years ago and somebody swiped it off the back of my seat."

"Too bad."

"I'm not such a flashy dresser anymore."

"Hey, who is, right?" Byron said, and did a kind of awkward arabesque in his baggy beer suit. A peal of thunder resounded off in the distance. We both turned our heads toward the west. Dark, muscular clouds were scudding above the far hills. A crooked bolt of lightning reached toward the earth. Byron's face seemed to grow as dark as the horizon. "So that was you," he said quietly.

"Yes."

"They send you here, those parasites?"

"No," I said emphatically. "I told you yesterday, I don't work for the magazine anymore."

"You expect me to believe that?"

"It's the truth."

He rested one foot on the step I was sitting on and, in a menacing tone of voice, leaning in on me, said, "Well, what *are* you doing in New Hampshire, then?"

I tried to explain my situation to him as briefly as possible so I wouldn't bore him. He seemed preoccupied, however, only half-listening.

"You *could* write it, though, if you wanted, right? For them or somebody else."

"Write it? Write what?"

"You know what I mean."

"Byron, that's not why—"

"Don't give me that. If you wanted to, you could. You know it, and so do I. Hey, we've both been around the block a few times by now."

I began to realize that refuting him was not the way to assuage his paranoia.

"I wish you'd trust me," I finally said.

"Oh, get off it," he retorted bitterly. "I don't trust anybody."

The storm was drawing closer. I counted beats between the strokes of lightning and thunder.

"So, what am I going to do about you?" Byron asked. "I could pay you double what they'd offer you. Triple. No, that wouldn't work. They wouldn't make you an offer in the first place unless you let the cat out of the bag. Right?"

"I have no intention—"

"Shut up! You know I could clear out of here in a matter of hours. *Ppphhht.* You think I'm kidding? It's been done before. Go ahead and tell the world. Bring them all back here. They'll think you're out of your skull."

"I have no intention of telling the world."

"Then maybe you're even a bigger fool than I think."

"You've got no right—"

"I've got every right—!"

I sprang to my feet. At that very instant, a stroke of lightning flashed literally over our heads, so close that the surrounding static charge made my skin crawl. It struck a pine tree at the edge of the woods and the upper half of the tree disintegrated.

"Sweet Jesus. . . !"

For those of you who have never seen lightning in action, believe me, the destructive force is an awesome sight to behold. The tree didn't just catch on fire or topple over—it blew up. For a few seconds the air was filled with smoke and splinters. I hit the weeds, flat on my belly, as if we were under an artillery attack. The next thing I knew, Byron and I were both scrambling for the door. I got inside first and rushed to a window. The hail started at once, mothball-size stones, while thunder boomed continuously, one terrible peal rolling into the next. Finally, the hail turned to rain and warping sheets of water coated the windowpanes. My heart wouldn't quit pounding and I felt giddy. Byron had a strange, cracked smile on his face.

"Smell that?" he said.

"Yes." It was an unusual odor, like scorched turpentine.

"I better do something about that dead tree next to the house," he said. Suddenly we were both laughing. "You're not going to believe this, but your hair stood right on end out there."

"I felt it before it struck."

"I saw that hair of yours stand up and I thought, this is *really* the end. Jesus, this is too much excitement for one day."

We were in what ordinarily might have been described as a living room, or front parlor, except that it was not quite like any living room I'd ever been in before. The opposite wall was one solid set of bookshelves, with volumes crammed into every cranny. But the strangest thing was on the floor. The far half of it was painted deep blue, and upon it were arrayed model sailing ships of every conceivable type: frigates, yawls, barques, schooners, ketches, whalers, men-o-war, brigantines. A few were running with full sail, others rested peacefully with lines cleated and spars bare. In the dimness of the room, with the storm raging outside, it was like a seagull's view of a safe harbor in the last century. I must have been gaping at the bizarre, yet enchanting, display.

"It's a hobby," Byron said nervously.

"A hobby. . . ?" I echoed him. Byron seemed to shrink visibly, and in the storm's violent and uneven light his face went taut with emotion, whether rage or shame or grief, I couldn't tell.

"It's just something I do," he mumbled.

"It's . . . I didn't mean to—"

"I know it's weird."

"It's amazing."

He studied me for a moment. Apparently, he decided that my remark was a compliment, for his physical deflation seemed to reverse itself and he stood up straight again.

"It's a secret vice," he said confidingly, with that shy smile of his, and I thought, with a pang of sorrow, how long and empty his years here must have been. Thunder kept rumbling outside. "Would you like some tea?"

"Tea. . . ?"

"Yes. It's a hot beverage. I'll put some water on and you can decide when it's boiling." He limped through an arched doorway into an adjoining kitchen.

The portion of the floor that I was standing on was covered by an old beige, rose, and mint-green oriental rug, about six feet by eight. The only other real furniture in the room was a parson's table and a simple wooden chair that went with it. The table was covered with newspaper, various tools, pieces of wood, dowels, and little jars of paint. It was his miniature shipyard, and a new vessel was under construction on the slips. It wasn't a plastic model, either, but a painstakingly handcrafted wooden original.

Oddly enough, there wasn't a piece of stereo equipment or a single record album or a tape anywhere to be seen, and no guitar. There was, however, a small foot-operated parlor organ set against the wall next to the table. Altogether, the room had the quality of an attic, the carefully arranged ships like tokens in a child's secret ritual. Byron, in his solitude, seemed like a spider in that attic, endlessly spinning a troubled web, the pattern of which no one would ever discern, except in the instant between its discovery and its destruction.

"It'll be ready in a minute," he said, returning with another chair. "Have a seat."

"Thank you," I said. An eternity of silence followed.

"Do you live here alone?" I finally asked.

"Hey, you're getting kind of personal now, aren't you?"

"I just assumed . . . I heard voices on the phone the other night."

"I don't have a phone."

"Oh?" I said. "Well, you must have called from somewhere."

"I called from the laundromat in Haverfield."

"Oh."

That answered one large, nagging question. No wonder they were arguing about laundry. Byron, meanwhile, had a leg crossed over the other and was jiggling his foot rapidly. His shoes, I noticed, were bargain-basement workingman's oxfords.

"So, what do you hear on the radio these days, Rick?" he asked. There was something ominous about the tone of his question, a feeling that in some strange way he was testing me, as though I were a plaything in the paws of a cunning animal.

"It's a dull era," I told him. "There's some new stuff I like."

"Music for androids," he sneered.

"I notice you don't have a stereo."

"You guys think you don't miss a trick, huh? It so happens I have a radio in the car." He uncrossed his legs and slumped down in his seat. "I shouldn't knock them. It's a whole new generation, Rick. I bet some of those kids don't even remember the Kennedy assassination. Vietnam is like the Franco-Prussian War to them."

He got up suddenly and went into the kitchen, returning shortly with two steaming mugs of tea.

"I hear you on the radio," I told him.

"That's not me," he said. "It's an imposter."

"They were playing 'Rebellion in a Minor Key' just the other day. It's still a great song."

"I don't remember it."

"You expect me to believe that?"

"Hey, you expect me to encourage you?" he retorted.

He put his tea down on the table, sighed, and began rubbing his face. When he stopped, he gazed over my head, out the window, with a faraway look in his eyes.

"I knew sooner or later someone like you would come along," he said quietly. "I dreaded it, and I wondered what I'd do when it finally happened. Now, here you are. And what am I doing? Having a nice warm cup of tea. How civilized. Did you read those biographies they wrote about me? It hurt me to read that garbage. How could they publish stuff like that?"

"It happens every day, Byron."

"Oh, yeah? Well, wait until it happens to you. I bet you wouldn't have such a world-weary attitude about it. I don't think there was a truthful sentence in any of those books."

He puffed out his cheeks. The only sound in the room was the nattering of raindrops against the window.

"Do you want to know what it was like? What really happened?" he eventually said.

"I'd be lying if I said I wasn't curious," I admitted.

"Still the old news-hound?"

"No. I've told you three times, I am not a reporter anymore."

"But you could write it, right?"

"I don't know."

"Sure you could. You know that. Hey, who's kidding who?"

"I'm not kidding anyone."

"Neither am I."

He looked directly into my eyes, his gaze so penetrating that I longed for something to hide behind. It took a great effort not to look away.

"You've stumbled right into the mummy's tomb, my boy," Byron said. "How do you like that?"

"It frightens me."

"It should. Some things in life should frighten you. You know why?"

I shrugged my shoulders. "Why?"

"Because they're scary," he said.

I was tempted to ask him if he enjoyed making me feel foolish, but I refrained.

The thunder boomed more distantly now and the rain had stopped beating on the windows. Byron got up, limped across the room, and threw the front doors open. Sunlight poured into the gloomy chamber along with the tantalizing smell of wet grass.

"Storm's over," he announced matter-of-factly and walked outside.

I followed him.

He was inspecting the dying elm on the side of the house. Meanwhile, I silently rehearsed a speech to assure him that his secret was safe with me, that I was ready to butt out of his life with no conditions, and desist from intruding again, if that's what he wanted. But Byron spoke first.

"Here's the deal, Rick," he said dryly. "I'll tell you what happened. How I ended up here. The whole thing. You can take notes, tape it, whatever. And you can publish it if . . . if I die, or if I . . . if I . . . I'm not sure how to put it."

"If you come out of hiding?" I suggested.

"Is that what I've been doing?" His eyebrows arched and a look of the utmost bewilderment clouded his face. At first I wasn't sure whether he was putting me on again or not. But his eyes did not seem to search mine so much as his own interior, as if an idea he had always privately cherished about himself had been revealed to him from a new angle, in a different light, and suddenly defied his understanding of it.

"I don't mean to put words into your mouth," I said.

"No, you're the writer. Hiding?"

"It just came to mind."

Byron grunted.

"And remember," he said. "You mustn't tell *anyone* what you're doing here. Not your wife, not your kids—"

"I don't have any kids."

"No? Hey, you better get on the stick before it's too late."

"We're planning to. That's one of the reasons—"

Before I could finish my sentence, Byron had turned away and was limping hurriedly back to the front door. I caught up with him at the stoop, but he wouldn't turn around to face me.

"Come back at two o'clock tomorrow," he said. "I have to stop now."

He crossed the threshold and pulled the screen door shut behind him. It slapped against the inner jamb emptily.

"Okay," I said. "Tomorrow."

In those early days of our association he was subject to violent swings of mood and emotion. It wasn't until after we began our work together that I realized he hadn't had a single personal conversation with another human being in more than ten years.

---

Allie was curled up on the sofa facing the woodstove, her legs bundled in an afghan and a book propped open in the crook of her arm. Luke had been snoozing on the braided rug. He lifted his head and wagged his tail listlessly when I came in, as though whiffing the odor of iminent conflict.

"It's gotten damn chilly," I observed, "hasn't it?"

Allie grunted noncommittally. I ducked into the kitchen, slapped two slices of rye around some Swiss cheese, popped a beer, and returned to the living room.

"Fire feels good," I said.

Allie finally closed her book.

"Where were you?" she asked.

"I drove down to Hanover to use the Dartmouth library."

"Why didn't you tell me you'd be gone all afternoon and half the evening?"

"I didn't decide to go there until I was already on the road."

"You could have phoned from the library."

"I, uh . . . it was thoughtless of me."

"You're goddam straight it was," she said, throwing off the afghan and storming into the kitchen. I remained behind, sandwich and beer in hand, a liar and a fool. She returned shortly, though, with a drink of her own, a tumbler of red wine, and took up a defiant stance near my desk. Luke was on his feet too, as though all the excitement portended some special treat for him.

"I think we should go back to the city," Allie announced resolutely, as though she had thought out every painful detail of our situation. "We've had a lovely summer. Now, let's go home, get back into a productive frame of mind, and—"

"I can work here."

She winced at this statement, reached behind her, and picked a thin sheaf of papers off the desk. Her hand was shaking badly.

"Rick," she said, struggling to control her voice, "we have been here 102 days. I figured it out today. You have written 27 pages. That works out to less than a third of a page a day."

"I told you I was going to buckle down this fall, and I meant it. I know I goofed off all summer."

"I think you need to be back in the city to—"

"Why don't you let me worry about what I need," I replied angrily, my own self-control slipping away. "You seem to forget that *this* is our home for the time being. We don't have an apartment in the city anymore."

"We could get another one."

"Not without an enormous hassle. And not at the point when I'm primed and set to go to work. You want me to drop everything and go down and screw around for a week, a month, God knows how long? And where do we stay in the meantime—?"

"Friends."

"Right. Sure."

"Carol's got a *huge* loft."

"You think I could work there with those dancers bouncing off the walls? Forget it."

"How about here with *me* bouncing off the walls?" Allie said and stalked off onto the porch, slamming the door behind her.

Luke by this time, was bounding all over the place himself, throwing his paws against my legs and carrying on. Still used to the life-rhythms of the city, he required a nightly walk. It wouldn't do just to let him out. You had to accompany him.

"Come on, handsome."

Later, I cautiously entered the sleeping porch, took off my clothes, and climbed into bed. The sheets were icy on my side. Allie still had her clothes on. She tried to shrug my hand off her shoulder.

"Don't be mad at me, babe. I can't go back to New York now, that's all."

"Well, if you can't do that, then maybe you should be here by yourself for a while," Allie said. A chilly gust of wind rattled the pages of a paperback on the night table. "I think I'll call Carol tomorrow."

"Okay," I said. "You do what you have to do."

"And so will you," she said.

"And so will I."

# CHAPTER 3

RS: Are you inspired by the times we're living in, or bummed out by
    them?

BJ: Everybody always thinks that they're living in the last days of civ-
    ilization. We'll probably look back on all this and think it was very
    quaint.

—The *Rolling Stone* Interview with Byron Jaynes, 1968

I s it rolling, Rick?"

Byron flashed a grin at me, then flicked the switch on the microphone of the cassette recorder. The switch activated the drive motor,
or stopped it, at the speaker's will. I'd bought the expensive machine
over in St. Johnsbury earlier that afternoon for more than $200. I
owned another portable tape recorder, but it was inconveniently
packed away at my parents' house on Long Island, with the rest
of our mothballed effects. Byron flicked the switch to "on" again
and the tape rolled.

"*Have you guessed you yourself would not continue? Have you
dreaded these earth-beetles? Have you feared the future would be
nothing to you. . . ?*"

The tape stopped.

"What was that?"

"A poem," he said.

"One of yours?"

"Lord, no. Someone else. Would you prefer 'testing–one–two–
three'?"

I shrugged my shoulders. We played it back. The recording level
was fine. Byron had been sitting Indian-style on the rug in his parlor. Now he stretched out.

"Whenever you have a question, don't hesitate to ask," he said. "You know. For clarification."

I was impressed at how quickly and how completely he had assumed control.

"All right," I said.

He looked at me blankly for a moment. Though it was a crisp, fall-like day, and even cooler inside the stone house, a damp mustache of perspiration beaded his upper lip, and a half-moon of sweat spread darkly under the sleeve of his T-shirt. He let out a deep breath. There was a click inside the recording unit and the tape began to move behind its tiny window.

## The Life of Byron Jaynes—Tape 1

It was all glitter and glamor, champagne and caviar, starry nights and fleeting days, late risings for the revolution, dreams, castles, furs, jewels, servants, poetry, the adoration of the multitudes, sunburst afternoons on the shimmering lawns, power struggles in the upper stories, Lear-Jet frolics above the fruited plain, days of lust and nights of magic, rainbows in the eyes of virgins, a million laughs in a million limousines, cucumber sandwiches at the Sherry, piña coladas at the Polo Lounge, Romilar at the Ritz, tight pants and narrow escapes, fun fun fun till daddy took the T-bird away, roses and lollipops, lollipops and roses, and Christmas every morning. How am I doing?

*You're doing fine, Byron.*

Great. Where do you want me to start?

*Start at the beginning.*

How about the end?

*Start wherever you like.*

That's easy for you to say. The end is really the middle, anyway. You tell me how it ends.

*You were in London.*

London? That's right. I remember it was the week after Thanksgiving because they don't celebrate it over there and I missed it. They found the bodies late in the afternoon, Catherine and Jesse. There was no hope. I was informed right away. I remember how logical it seemed. It was like watching *Hamlet:* you know from the start that everyone's going to end up dead, but you still follow the whole story to its conclusion, right? It tears you apart, but you knew it was coming. I knew it was coming for more than a year. Maybe not that way, exactly. Maybe not so soon, but eventually. I guess, in my own mind, I anticipated a disaster of a . . . more accidental nature. That's why I took the baby away from her. Then, when the inevitable happened in London, somehow I was hardly surprised at all. We were all doomed.

I sent Catherine back to her people. On a plane. In a box. I didn't want to have anything to do with the . . . arrangements. Let them do it. Indulge her one last time.

I took Jesse back to Scotland, to where we were so happy for a time, and put him to rest there, on a hill overlooking Loch Orrin. I went there with every intention of joining him. I couldn't see the point of remaining . . . anywhere. Then, the night after the funeral, I lay awake in the hotel and had this . . . conversation with him. It's hard to explain. I heard a voice. In reality he could barely say a few words. . . . Anyway, it was a child's voice, but older than Jesse had actually been. Maybe ten, eleven. What Jesse might have sounded like now, as a matter of fact. Or maybe what I sounded like when I was a boy. We had a debate. He said I was giving in to exactly what she would have wanted: another grand gesture.

Catherine was so fond of grand gestures. Isn't that what rock and roll is all about? A series of them, each one more extravagant than the one before? The magician stands at center stage yanking bunnies out of a hat. Pretty soon bunnies aren't good enough. How about an elephant? Hey, great! What else can you show me? I can turn myself inside out, make myself vanish in a puff of smoke. Would you like to see that? You bet. Okay, here she goes. Poof. . . ! Only where's the magician? He's gone. How can we bring him back? We can't. Oh. . . . Well, what do we do now? Get another magician.

Jesse's death demanded something other than another stage routine. I decided that night that the only way to dignify his death was to keep on living. But how?

I remained in Scotland a few more days. The reporters had already found out where I was. It was like trying to be by yourself in a glass cage. I thought if I didn't die, I'd go crazy. Then it came to me! I could go on living without being Byron Jaynes. It was that simple. From that moment on, I was like a machine. All the parts functioned smoothly.

It took more than a month for me to take care of everything. Some of the details were very complex, very sensitive. On January 12th, Byron was legally dead. It was a magic trick in a way, I suppose. But it was not a grand gesture. The magician just turned himself into a rabbit, and the rabbit got away.

———————

Byron switched the machine off and rested the microphone on his stomach. Sunlight filtered through the leaves outside and flickered like sea light over the model ships on the floor, imparting the illusion of motion.

"Am I telling it okay?" he asked.

"You're doing fine," I told him. "Would you like to stop for the day?"

"No. I'd like to go on."

"Okay."

"That *is* what happened, right?" he asked, and for a moment I wasn't sure if he even *understood* the sequence of events that ended in the death of his wife and son, or if other, long-suppressed details were painfully jogging his memory.

"Isn't it?" I asked carefully, sensing his insecurity.

"I guess. I don't know anymore," he said. "It all seems unreal. Not just the end. Everything." He paused and stared into the rug. The room seemed filled with his breathing. " *'Snail, snail, glister me forward,'* " he chanted, " *'Bird, soft-sigh me home, Worm, be with me. This is my hard time.'* "

He looked up as if expecting a comment from me, but I didn't know what to make of the odd little quatrain. I assumed the lines were his.

"Roethke," he said, as though he had read my mind. *"The Lost Son."*

"Oh?" I said, and then to cover my ignorance: "I was a rotten student."

"Heaven has no entrance exam, my boy," Byron said with a surprising surge of energy. "But Beal College did. You know something? I actually did well on my boards. It was the only thing I ever studied for."

## The Life of Byron Jaynes—Tape 1 (Cont.)

Ah, Beal! It was one of the more bohemian schools of its day. The land originally belonged to the painter Frederick Hinton Beal, and when he died, in 1912, they made it into a college. The administration building was his mansion. I'm sure you've seen pictures of it: a fantastic, turreted monstrosity on a hilltop overlooking the Hudson River on the Dutchess County side. They didn't even have a name for the architectural style, it was so weird. I think they ended up calling it Byzantium Revival. Beal was a pretty strange guy. I loved his paintings, though. In fact, I eventually owned one.

I arrived in 1963, fresh from the Westchester suburbs, in a seersucker suit and oxblood brogans, the very soul of the Brooks Brothers' Young Man's Department. Beatniks and folkies were the trendsetters back then and I guess I wanted to cut a different figure. If I'd gotten into Princeton, I probably would have grown a goatee and worn the same wormy sweatshirt all semester. Or if I'd gone to the University of Hawaii, I would have stepped off the plane wearing snowshoes. Some kids are like that, right?

The week I hit the campus, "I Want to Hold Your Hand" was number one on the charts. Nine out of the top ten singles in America were by British groups. Meanwhile, the older students were still caught up in the folk music scene, which was very much a part of the Civil Rights movement. The purpose of the music was to help spread the message: social justice. A lot of Bealies rode the Freedom buses. Now, I'm not saying it was right or wrong, but by the fall of '63 the whole we-shall-overcome scene was getting tired. Then, the Kennedy assassination turned the world upside-down.

I'm talking about JFK, not Bobby. It was like all the starry-eyed idealists in America had to fold up their tents overnight. There they were, all neat and clean in their humble proletarian workshirts and jeans with SNCC buttons pinned on, and it was like somebody poured a bucket of ice-cold blood over their heads and ruined everything. How could you listen to Pete Seeger yodel about lonesome hobos after that?

I was in an Intro to Acting class when his assassination was announced. We were watching these two dorks do a scene from *Death of a Salesman* when this girl came down the aisle, handed the prof a note, and just walked out again, as if it was a message from his wife to pick up a pound of pork chops on the way home. The prof just stood there scratching his head and sort of chuckling.

"I don't know if this is a joke, or what," he said, "but this note says that President Kennedy just got shot in Dallas."

The two guys on stage interrupted their lousy acting for a moment and crept down to the apron. Some titters broke out. People made faces at each other. No one had the slightest idea what to do next. Eventually, one by one, and without a word, we all drifted out of the theater until the room was empty, knowing our lives would never be the same again.

Many of us left the campus prematurely that night for the Thanksgiving break that was due to start the following Tuesday. When we came back, you had the sense of returning to a transformed world.

Dylan was always one step ahead of it all, and if it hadn't been for him, a lot of us would have remained lost. I don't think people realized how important he was. He was the bridge. A lot of people crossed that national chasm of the spirit over his skinny back. With one mass movement falling apart, he demonstrated the value of being true to yourself. At the same time he was also breaking a trail straight to the Beatles. He hadn't quite gone electric yet, but he was recording that personal, visionary stuff that was paving the way, and it made a tremendous impression. The folkies hated it almost as much as they hated rock and roll. But it was like trying to command a tidal wave to stop.

Anyway, when I came back to Beal after that summer for my sophomore year, you could hardly recognize the place. Everybody had let their hair grow out over the summer, mimicking the Beatles and the Stones, and you could smell marijuana all over the campus. The jukebox in the student union was playing "Time Is on My Side" instead of "Michael Row the Boat Ashore." Physically, Beal was a beautiful spot, full of wooded glades opening to a view of the Hudson, with mock-ruins of classical temples all over the place that Frederick Beal had constructed to save himself the trouble of shlepping to Europe. It gave the campus this flavor of an Arcadian fantasy that couldn't have been more perfect for the times. It was in the fall of that year that I met Charles Rego Duncan.

He called himself Rego. He was a transfer student from Montclair State College in New Jersey, where he had to go for two years because he had gotten such miserable scores on his SATs that he couldn't get into a decent school. After his sophomore year, when he proved that he wasn't a mental defective, they finally let him into Beal.

He was a suburban kid, like me, and also about my size, but with a great physique. He could do over a hundred push-ups in a row. He had the same brand of wire-rim glasses you used to wear—his eyes were so bad he couldn't even recognize you when you walked into his room in the morning. The Selective Service classified him as legally blind. He had the most wonderful smile in the world. It was like standing in front of a fireplace after coming in out of the sleet, and it made him extremely popular with the ladies. Of course, you had to be a basketcase not to make out at Beal. The ratio of girls to guys was about three to one.

The way we met was somewhat complicated. During my freshman year, I had gotten involved in the theater department. They had one of these hip, young Svengali-type profs that kids tend to cluster around. Dick Henderson was the kind of guy students always described as "brilliant"—since young people can't always discern talent from egomania—and being part of his clique was a big status symbol. I got suckered in, I admit it.

Anyway, in the fall of my second year, Henderson came up with this "brilliant" project. It was a stage adaptation—his own—of the novel *Wieland* by Charles Brockden Brown, possibly the most obscure work in all of American literature—which, I'm sure, is why he was so wild about it. I don't think half the English faculty ever heard of it. It was published in 1798 and it was this gothic mish-mash about a mysterious traveling ventriloquist named Carwin who imposes himself on the Wieland family and drives the old man insane so he butchers his wife and children. Sounds groovy, huh?

The theater department was in the same building as the department of music, and Rego was a music student. He had his eye on this particular girl and he followed her into the *Wieland* auditions. He read for a part and ended up getting cast in a small role as a servant—all this just to get into some girl's pants. That was old Rego. I was cast as a servant too.

Well, the whole thing was a disaster. Even the girl Rego was chasing turned out to be queer. The play was boring and bombastic and everybody was sorry they tried out for it. Henderson started hitting the bottle, and people weren't so sure about his "brilliance" anymore, and the kid who played Carwin took a walk and had to be replaced. It was terrible, but Rego and I had a great time. We used to goof on it backstage by doing this Edgar Bergan and Charlie McCarthy routine. It was the only thing that cheered up the troops.

Then, one night, a bunch of us in the cast went over to Rego's room after rehearsal to smoke pot and dump on Henderson. We smoked a few bowls, and after a while Rego got his guitar out and started playing. He was a piano student, officially, but the guitar was his true love, and sweet Jesus could he play, even back then. He had a Fender Telecaster and an old beat-up amp. Meanwhile, I borrowed a guitar from another guy on the floor (I lived way over across the campus in the Kitteridge dorm) and soon that joint was rocking. I was never a terrific guitar player, but I knew enough to play "Under the Boardwalk" and "Heartbreak Hotel" and the rest of the stuff we grew up with.

We rocked out until four o'clock in the morning. You could tell what a naturally gifted musician Rego was. He could play a song he wasn't really familiar with after hearing you do it once—and he'd stick in better changes than the ones you played. He could sing harmony with total ease, just following the melody as if his voice were a natural extension of yours.

Eventually, everybody else drifted back to their own dorms, but Rego and I had dropped a couple of black beauties and we were wired. I couldn't play anymore because the pads of my fingers were sore from this guy's cheap guitar, so we speed-rapped about music. Rego was full of ideas and theories.

"There's a revolution going on in the studios and the hi-fi stores," he said. "It's gone way past the point where they're just trying to accurately reproduce a performance. The LP is going to be the art form of our generation."

"It's the song that sells it, though," I'd argue back, although I didn't disagree. "You can pour on all the reverb and strings you want, but you still need a good song at the bottom of it."

"Not just good songs," Rego said, *"original* ones. It's coming up with them that's the problem."

That morning I went back to my dorm, terrifically excited and speeding my brains out, and I wrote three songs. One of them was "Rebecca's Window." I brought the songs to the *Wieland* rehearsal the next evening and gave them to Rego. One of his great qualities was the way he respected something you created. Most people would jam the stuff into their pocket and forget you ever gave it to them. Rego would actually sit down and read it, right then and there.

About fifteen minutes later we were on stage running through one of the scenes we had to stand around being servants in when Rego leaned over and whispered, "We shouldn't be doing this. We should be playing rock and roll."

When they finished the scene I asked him what he thought about the songs.

"Do you have tunes for them?" he asked.

"Sort of."

"Well, after we're done with this foolishness, you come back and play them for me."

"Hey, you think they're okay?"

"One of them's great. The other two are just real good."

I was thrilled to pieces.

So that night we went back to his dorm again, only the two of us this time, and I played the melodies for him.

"We should definitely play rock and roll," he said. "Do you have any more of these things?"

I told him, no, those were the first songs I had ever written, and he just sat there with his jaw hanging down. Frankly, I thought they were pretty good myself, for a first effort, but nothing more than that. The next couple of hours Rego and I tried out some harmonies, changed a few chords around, and polished them up. We couldn't keep going for long because we were burned out from speeding and staying up all night. But we agreed to get together again the following evening.

That was a Saturday, meaning no *Wieland* rehearsals, thank God— and when I showed up at Rego's room two other guys were already there: Gary Knowles and Bobby Schumann, both fellow music students of Rego's, Gary a bass player and Bobby a drummer. Gary was from the suburbs outside of Detroit, where his dad was a G.M. exec. Bobby was the only one of us who wasn't a suburban kid. He grew up on the west side of Manhattan. I had no idea what was happening, however, and before I could ask, Rego was saying, "Let's go."

I followed them across the campus, in one of those cold October rains, to the music department and we ended up in a small recital hall. A whole bunch of equipment was set up there, amps, a couple of mikes, and some drums.

"Why didn't you tell me you were in a band?" I asked Rego. Bobby was adjusting his traps. Nobody was talking. It was spooky.

"I wasn't until tonight," Rego said.

"Oh."

"Neither were you," he added with one of those fireplace grins of his. All at once it occurred to me what was going on. I felt like a kid who takes clarinet lessons and is suddenly being forced to play for company.

"Uh, I don't think—"

"Try this on for size," Rego said, and put an electric guitar around my neck. It was a Fender Strat. I didn't know it at the time, but Rego had bought it for me in a hockshop in Rhinebeck that day. The only guitar I owned was an old Epiphone F-hole jazz model, not exactly a rock and roll axe. Anyway, there I am with a Stratocaster hanging around my neck.

"Let's start with 'Rebecca's Window,' " Rego said to the other guys. Gary adjusted a mike in front of me. I was getting really upset. I was about to make an ass out of myself in front of people I didn't know, and I felt that Rego had invaded my privacy by bandying my songs around, songs that were essentially personal poems.

"Uh, listen—" I started to protest again, but Bobby slammed into a downbeat, the other two joined in, and I was stunned. They were playing it as if they knew it. In fact, they did know it, because Rego had spent most of the afternoon running through it with them. And what was more incredible, it sounded good.

"Come on," Rego tried to encourage me. He was stroking his Telecaster and doing all these Chuck Berry shuffles. Bobby was laughing and slamming away at his drums. Gary, always so earnest and restrained, closed his eyes and rolled his head around as he laid down the bass line.

"Come on, play!" Rego yelled.

"I don't know how."

"Of course you do. It's no different from your acoustic."

But I just stood there like an idiot.

"We're going to play this over and over again until you're ready," he said.

"Jesus. . . ." I was disgusted, as much at myself for acting like a prima donna as I was at them. But I was terribly inhibited. Finally,

I gave the Strat a strum or two. It sounded wonderful, so loud and powerful. Rego drifted over and adjusted a couple of knobs. "Have you got an extra flatpick?" I asked him.

"Thattaboy!"

I started playing the chords, the rhythm part they called it then. Rego started playing riffs and figures around it.

"You're doing good," he said. "Now sing it."

I opened my mouth at the mike and this tremendous squawk of feedback squealed out of an amp behind me.

"Don't point your pickups at the mike," Rego said.

"Cheap equipment," Gary muttered.

I started again and sang the whole first verse.

"That was horrible," Rego said. "Do it again."

So I did it again.

"You're holding back!" he shouted.

"Hey, I'm new at this, you know."

"Shut up and sing!"

And then I let it out, figuring I couldn't make a bigger ass out of myself than I already had.

"That's much better! Keep going!"

I sang the next two verses, and then on the chorus Rego came in with a high harmony that just fused the whole thing together. It sounded so good it was like hearing somebody else's song on the radio for the first time, a song you'd want to turn up the volume on to hear better.

When we were done, Rego came over and made the sign of the cross over me with the neck of his guitar and mumbled a few words in Latin.

"Congratulations," he said. "You are now an overnight sensation."

The other guys snorted and made some rude sounds. I have to admit it felt great shouting into a microphone and making all that lovely noise, but I had an awful lot of doubts about actually playing in a band. The rest of the night was strangely businesslike, though we didn't have any agreement, tacit or otherwise, about what we were rehearsing for. We ran through "Rebecca's Window" several more times, altering the phrasing, trying different tempos. And the amazing thing was, the song sounded better each time. Then we did "Apollo at Ground Zero," the one that goes "On wings the horseman's chariot. . . ." I was always sorry we didn't include that one on the first album. When we had that down, we did the last of the three songs, "Let Patience Have Her Perfect Work," which I did lift from the New Testament, it's true, but which was a love song and had nothing whatsoever to do with religion, or Zen states, or anything remotely related, in spite of what you geniuses in the press wrote a couple of years later.

Around midnight, the security guard came by on his rounds and ejected us from the premises. Rego took care of him too, the next day. He paid the guy 25 bucks for a duplicate key to the building, and we didn't hear another peep out of him. Anyway, that's how the Romantics got their start. Byron Jaynes, as a persona, had hardly been conceived.

Those other writers—the ones who wrote those trashy biographies, who characterized Rego as a creature of my will, some kind of Igor to my Frankenstein—didn't understand our relationship at all, at least in the beginning. I miss him a lot. If it wasn't for him, I might have ended up like . . . like anybody else. I have to stop now.

---

Byron switched off the machine and lay down the microphone as if it were an explosive device that could go off at the slightest touch. Though it was still light outside, the sun no longer splashed through the windows on his miniature harbor. I was aware, suddenly, of being chilly. Byron stood up with a grunt, stepped to the door with the shuffling gait of someone in a trance, and left me alone inside. I unplugged the microphone and put it back in its storage compartment, then followed him out the door.

By the time I strode through the weeds around the house, he was a green speck a few hundred yards away in the first of those steep pastures beyond the barn. It took some moments of observation to realize he was literally charging uphill. He didn't stop until he reached one of the rocky outcroppings in the loftiest pasture, and then he sat down.

I had no heart to follow him up there, and likewise assumed he had no further desire for my company that day. So I shouted good-bye as best I could and returned to the Saab in his driveway.

I had met Rego Duncan just once and spoke to him only briefly then. It was at the Mariposa Festival in Toronto in 1972, when he was working as one of Joni Mitchell's backup musicians—he never lacked for gainful employment from the day Byron dumped the Romantics and struck out on his own. And on that sunny summer afternoon in the park beside Lake Ontario, Rego remembered Byron in only the most admiring and affectionate terms. There was about him none of the cultivated neuroticism you find in almost all rock musicians. He was friendly, even voluble, and when we touched on the painful particulars of Byron's last days—or what we both knew of them from hearsay—the damp tracks on his cheeks were real and deeply felt.

I liked him at once, and it was a blow to learn two years later that, as a member of Glen Campbell's backup band, he was run over by a drunk in the driveway of the Flamingo Hotel in Las Vegas, and killed instantly.

———

On the way back home, I picked up a bottle of the Rumanian pinot noir Allie likes and a couple of strip steaks. In my family we were always bribed with food, so I thought I would try that ploy with Allie. But after I arrived, she remained aloof, distant, and took herself for a long swim while I blundered around the kitchen fixing dinner.

"Water must be getting pretty brisk," I remarked when at last she came back inside, toweling her short hair. I handed her a glass of wine and noticed that she was working hard to avoid my eyes. "You've become a heckuva dedicated swimmer," I added, awkwardly.

"I called Carol today," Allie said and finally looked at me.

"Oh? How is she?"

"She says I can stay at her place."

"Well, what are friends for?"

"To count on. Where were you this afternoon?"

"Out in the hills."

"What's out in those hills?"

"Nothing special," I said. "Space, quiet. So you've made up your mind to leave?"

"No, I've created an option for myself in case I do."

"An option. Sounds so practical, so coldly calculating."

"Oh, for Godsake, Rick, we're driving each other nuts in this place." She knocked back her wine, refilled her glass, and slouched sullenly against the door jamb.

"How do I know if it's me or just the cottage you're really leaving?" I asked.

"Does it have to be one or the other? Can't I just take a break from a situation?"

"Isn't that what a marriage is? A situation?"

"No, a marriage is . . . oh, I don't know anymore," she gave up angrily. "But it's more than that. It's got to be more."

# CHAPTER 4

RS: Has success spoiled you?

BJ: If you're implying that success is the same as failure, then the answer is no.

RS: Doesn't any kind of great success carry in it the seeds of its own destruction?

BJ: I don't subscribe to that brand of metaphysics.

—The *Rolling Stone* Interview with Byron Jaynes, 1968

The next day, an air of false normality pervaded the cottage like the odor of a dead rat rotting in the laths. Skipping breakfast, I retreated to my desk, where I enjoyed a tacit immunity from conversation. But this gambit was only another exercise in futility. While Allie painted on the porch, I squirmed in my seat like a kid condemned to study hall, and the three and a half pages I ground out had about as much value as the phrase "I shall be a good boy" scribbled 100 times in a composition book. By early afternoon, I had deliberately worked myself into a half-crazed state and announced that I was taking off for a few hours.

"I'll come with you," Allie said.

"It'd be better if I was alone," I told her.

"Okay, fine. Be alone," she said in an acidic voice. She held open the screen door for me and I stumbled out to the Saab, the whole performance a sickening mummery. And for what? For Byron's sake. Yes, for Byron's sake, forgetting for the moment, my own.

---

When I arrived at his house, worried and distracted, it took me a while to notice a strange development. Then it hit me: he had cleared all the model ships out of his front parlor. Not a single one remained.

"Where are they?" I pointed to the empty, blue-painted floor.

"They're gone," he said.

"Gone where?"

"On a long voyage. To a strange land."

"Why?"

"You ask too many questions. Here, give me that." He took the cassette unit out of my hands, sat down on the rug, and set it up, obviously impatient to begin.

"I better put on a new tape," I said.

He glanced at me menacingly.

"You haven't been playing this for anyone, have you?" he asked.

"No!" I told him, my patience stretched to its limit. He must have sensed my indignation.

"What's the matter with you today?" he asked, but I didn't answer the question.

"Look, if it'll improve your peace of mind," I said coldly, "we can leave the tapes here."

He glared at me.

"Nothing can improve my peace of mind. When you understand that, you'll begin to understand me. Let's get on with the job. Where was I?"

"College."

"Oh, sweet Jesus! Beal!" He closed his eyes and expelled a deep sigh as a tremor of emotion shook him. He seemed grateful to return to the past, as though it was a real place offering literal sanctuary. I was grateful myself.

"You left off in the fall of '64," I reminded him. "That first night with the band."

"Anything you want to know about it in particular?" he asked rather fliply. Part of him was still resisting the journey backward.

"Whatever you'd like to tell me," I said.

"Sure."

He switched on the machine.


### The Life of Byron Jaynes—Tape 2

Do you realize just how long ago that was? It was the year Johnson ran against Goldwater for president. An entirely different world. Everyone was for Johnson, if you can feature that. He was still the big Civil Rights hero. Vietnam was nothing yet—a little jungle skirmish in some far-off corner of the globe nobody ever heard of. It wouldn't be a big deal until the Tonkin Gulf incident, the following summer. No, Johnson was still quite popular, even on the campuses. Goldwater, on the other hand, was considered a menace to civilization. I was always interested in politics, but I was never political, if you know what I mean. The only reason I mention it is because election night was the first time I ever performed in front of an audience as a musician. Besides, I was too young to even vote that year. You still had to be 21.

By the last week of October, Rego and I were no longer required at the *Wieland* rehearsals, for the excellent reason that Dick Henderson threw us out of the cast for screwing around. Frankly, I don't know what took him so long. I was worried about how it might affect me academically, because I was in one of his courses and I was officially a theater major. But I was really caught up in the whole band thing, all of a sudden. We hadn't formally discussed *being* a band, but it was obvious that's where we were headed, and we were all very excited over how well it was all meshing. We'd meet every night and play until early in the morning. During the days, Rego coached me to improve my guitar playing and taught me some of the rudiments of the musical vocabulary so I'd know what the hell everybody was talking about. The two of us ignored our regular classes.

After about two weeks we worked up a list of twenty tunes. Many of them were numbers we copped from those old Folkways albums, stuff like "I Ain't Gonna Be Bad No More," by Fred McDowell, and "Hellhound on My Trail," which was Robert Johnson's, if I recall correctly. We did a whole bunch of Elmore James: "Dust My Broom," "Rollin' and Tumblin'," and "Shake Your Money Maker." A few years down the road, four middle-class white kids doing this kind of material would be commonplace, a cliché in fact. But back then it was still unusual. Most white suburban bands were doing "Love Potion Number Nine" and surfing songs.

We called ourselves the Romantics because the name appealed to our sophomoric sense of irony. I don't even remember who came up with it, exactly. I think it just evolved as a joke, because a lot of our tunes were anything but romantic. It was loud, screaming, dancing music. It wasn't that hard to play, either—eight-bar, twelve-bar blues. All you had to do was keep changing the keys around so they sounded somewhat different. We added a few tunes off the radio: "Little Red Rooster," the version Sam Cooke did; "Let the Good Times Roll." We did Jerry Lee Lewis's "Whole Lotta Shakin'," and "Little Sister," which Elvis recorded back in the stone age. For laughs we did a Joey Dee number called "What Kind of Love Is This." And we had those three original songs of mine, which sounded absolutely incongruous in the context of our, uh, early repertoire. Oh, yeah, there was also a ditty Rego and I co-authored called "Amy the Snake Charmer," about Beal's reigning nymphomaniac.

On election night there was a big party planned in this great, glass-roofed, octagonal building that used to be Frederick Beal's winter garden, but which the college had converted into a ballroom for special functions. Everybody was expecting Johnson to wipe up the floor with Goldwater so the bash was supposed to celebrate the rescue of mankind. The Romantics ended up as the entertainment.

We got the job for the simple reason that we agreed to play for free. We told ourselves it was a dress rehearsal in front of a friendly audience. But I was scared to death, totally convinced that I was going to make a jerk out of myself. To make matters worse, Rego came up with the idea that we should put on our most conservative outfits, button-down shirts and blazers, rep ties, and loafers. Bands had to have matching outfits back then, you understand, but humble work clothes just didn't make it. We didn't want to go out there looking like a bunch of dippy folksingers, so we went completely in the other direction and dressed up like four Andover boys on their way to a mixer. I hadn't worn a tie in months.

There were at least 500 people packed into the ballroom, students and faculty. They had TVs set up everywhere with the election returns coming in, and they had the Beatles playing on the PA system. We filed out in our cute outfits, and you could tell from the expressions on their faces that they didn't know what to make of us. Most of them weren't even paying attention. A few wise-acres yelled up remarks, guys we knew with their girls.

We could hardly hear ourselves tune up over the Beatles playing "Can't Buy Me Love." My legs felt like I had multiple sclerosis. I could barely stand up, I was so nervous. Next thing I knew, Bobby was whacking his drums, Rego came in on the downbeat, and I was screaming "Dust My Broom." I never saw so many heads turn in one second flat in my life. They looked absolutely bewildered.

Somewhere during our first song, they cut the canned music. We finished "Dust My Broom." There were a few stray noises, whistles, shouts, some clapping here and there, but mostly this big pregnant stupor. You could hear the anchormen on TV.

"They love us," I said to Rego, sarcastically. I wanted to melt through the floorboards.

"Just keep going," he said and started twanging out the intro to "Whole Lotta Shakin'." This time a few brave souls ventured out to dance in front of the bandstand, just girls at first, then regular couples. You could see other people start to whisper things to each other and nod their heads. I was beginning to think we might pull it off after all.

Halfway through that first set, Chet Huntley made it official on TV: Johnson beat Goldwater by a landslide. After that, everybody got shitfaced, including us. It turned out to be some wild party. By midnight, guys were dragging their girlfriends to the corners. You could smell pot burning all over the place. I was drinking vodka, with my shirt stripped off and my tie tied around my head. I was totally into screaming and singing, though my voice was about shot by then. It would be a while before I learned how to take care of it. People were still dancing at 2 A.M. Rego was playing blistering solos. Our debut was an unqualified success. Three different girls tried to entice me back to their dorms.

My life changed considerably in the weeks that followed. One day I was a simple, one-celled organism drifting aimlessly in a drop of pondwater. And the next I was sprouting arms and legs, and poking my snout up onto dry land. Or to put it another way, one day I was a nineteen-year-old drama student with no serious aspirations, and the day after, for all intents and purposes, I was embarked on a career as a professional musician.

But there wasn't much time for reflection. We played our first paid gig Friday after the election at a bar down in Rhinebeck. We made $100—$25 each. The bar scene was very fertile for bands just starting out. A band would usually draw a crowd, even if they weren't that good, and it was no sweat off the owner's back because he could pay you straight from the door.

Jo-Jo's, this place in Rhinebeck, had a mixed crowd of college kids and rustic dolts. Kids from Connecticut and Massachusetts also went there because New York's drinking age was a lot lower, eighteen.

Rego had gotten us the gig, as he would get us all our gigs until Simon came along. We played Jo-Jo's the two weekends before Thanksgiving.

When we weren't playing, we were rehearsing, and when we weren't rehearsing, I was writing songs. Once I discovered I had this facility, and got some reinforcement for doing it, the stuff flooded out. Writing songs for me was like discovering I had hands. I was learning a great deal, and very quickly, but some of the songs I wrote in that period are still my favorites because they were the simplest: "Snakes and Dogs," "The Stranger Will Depart," "Janey," "Hysterical Girls," "Behold the Fugitive," "Then She Laughed," "Time Will Tell."

By the beginning of December we were playing four nights a week. We'd do a Wednesday night in Peekskill, Thursday in Albany, Friday in Kingston, Saturday back in Rhinebeck. Some kids from Amherst saw us at Jo-Jo's and booked us for a frat party at their school. We played whatever we could get, and Rego worked his butt off getting us jobs. It helped that we were starting to do quite a bit of original material. I certainly didn't feel like the leader of the band, even if I was the lead singer and wrote a lot of songs. I just felt that that happened to be my contribution, and we all deferred to Rego when it came to making important decisions. One thing everybody agreed on, though, was that we needed better outfits. I felt like I was in a straitjacket. I wanted something loose and air-conditioned.

The solution turned out to be one of the few good things that ever came out of that abortion *Wieland*. We had the key to Ruddman Hall, the performing arts building, right? So one night in December Rego and I paid a visit to the basement where the theater department stored all their old props and furniture and costumes, and we appropriated the costumes that the characters had worn in the play. They were these great-looking, white, blousey, dueling shirts. They looked especially great after you worked up a little sweat on a bandstand. And they were air-conditioned!

Meanwhile, my career as a college student was going straight down the tubes. I was occasionally sleeping in Kitteredge Hall, but it was like maintaining a room in some weird resort for young people. I stopped making any pretenses about keeping up with my work. We all did, except Gary, who was a senior and somewhat compulsive about getting his degree. After Christmas, we got our marks for the fall semester. My grade-point average worked out to 0.80—two Fs, two Ds, and a C. They put me on academic probation.

I had a couple of weeks away from the other guys during Christmas to think about what was happening, and each day away from school, the more unreal the events of that fall seemed. Finally, I decided that it had been a lark, that I had better get the old marks back up and not take the band so seriously. I even wrote out a speech, explaining my decision to the others.

Well, I never got a chance to use it, and the new leaf I intended to turn over just withered on the vine. When I returned to Beal after New Year's, we were busier than ever, and making damn good money. We were averaging $250, $300 a week, each. The first thing we did was plow it back into the band, upgrade our equipment. We got bigger amps, column speakers, and a Farfisa organ for Rego, and we bought a secondhand Dodge van to schlep it all around.

We played up and down the Hudson Valley, from Albany to Nyack, as if the river were a string and we were the yo-yo. We developed followings at the clubs we played. Girls started coming around regularly, hanging out. You'd go to the bathroom on a break— one of those wormy back rooms that the management always gave you to change in—and Bobby would be banging some girl against the sink, his pants dangling around his ankles and the girl's creamy legs stuck out akimbo with her shoes still on.

Sometimes we stayed in motels. It was fun. We played this one joint, for example, called The Warehouse, in Albany, an enormous cinderblock box that some sharpie turned into a rock club near the state university campus. They'd get huge crowds. We'd invite a 150 different girls back to our motel after the show and pick out the best-looking baker's dozen and send the rest of them home. You'd wake up in the morning with one girl's bush in your face and another girl's boob in your ear, and everybody's clothes strewn around and bras hanging off the rabbit ears on the TV, and bottles all over the place. We'd straggle back to Beal like it was some Trappist retreat and gratefully lock ourselves in our rooms.

It was near the end of March when there began to be open talk about taking the next big step. I tried to ignore it or change the subject whenever it cropped up because I was still hanging onto the illusion that sooner or later I'd get serious and finish college. The big step they were talking about was moving the band down to the city. I managed to evade the whole question until Easter time, and then everything changed.

I have known two truly scary individuals in my life, and my father was one of them. There was really nothing in the world I wanted so badly as his approval, and I doubt that there was anything in the world I failed so miserably to obtain.

He was district attorney of Westchester County at the time. When you broke the law in Westchester, you had to answer to my dad, Morris Greenwald. He was first elected to that office in 1958 as a sort of Javits-style moderate liberal Republican. He was suave and gregarious, and he worked constantly. I remember that campaign. I was in the seventh grade and I helped out stuffing envelopes and calling voters telling them to go to the polls and vote. Most kids idolize their fathers, of course, but most kids aren't surrounded by four-foot-high posters of their dad while they're growing up. So as I got further into my teens and found out he had feet of clay, it came as quite a shock. It was around the same time that my father's liberal social conscience started to deteriorate.

Republican politics were very byzantine in New York state back then. The machinery of the party and the state government itself was controlled by the so-called Rockefeller wing. They maintained an uneasy alliance with the liberals like Senator Javits and John Lindsay, who was an ambitious Manhattan congressman. Then there was another group of upstate conservatives, basically Goldwaterites. Finally, there was the old joker in the deck, Nixon, who moved to New York City and a Wall Street law practice after he got drubbed in the California governor's race in '62. All these forces were operating when I was a sophomore at Beal in the spring of 1965.

My father was an ambitious man too. I think he was gauging the scene with a very shrewd eye in those crucial years. He had been a delegate to the National Convention in '64 and watched Rockefeller get hooted off the rostrum at the Cow Palace, and I think he decided right then and there which way to go.

He'd gotten to know Nixon socially. They weren't close friends, but my father was a real country clubber and he knew a couple of the partners in Nixon's law firm who lived up around where he did, Bedford–Mount Kisco. So he fell in with that group, and politically it turned out to be a very canny move because they were the future. In the meantime, he sat tight, prosecuting suburban burglars. He was elected on Rocky's shirttails three times, but he didn't have to hassle with the state party apparatus because my father had next to no patronage power in his particular office. In his secret heart, though, he was metamorphosing into a Nixon law-and-order stooge. Anyway, I came home for that long Easter weekend to see my mom and dad.

We lived on a ten-acre spread on Radnor Road in Bedford. It had its own little pond and you couldn't see any neighbors from our house. It looked like the type of house where Katharine Hepburn lived in *The Philadelphia Story*, one of those big, white, rambling, clapboard country-manor jobs, and at that time of year it looked its loveliest. All the flowering trees were blossoming, the forsythia, the dogwoods. The grass was all greened up. Tulips and daffodils were sprouting in the flower beds. My parents were having it out, in their own way, for the last time.

I never understood my mother at all. I mean, I can tell you precisely what she looked like, the color of her hair, her nail polish, what kind of clothes she wore, her jewelry, her perfume, the tone of her voice, favorite foods, songs, books, movies, all those things. But when I actually try to picture her face, it's like a photograph of someone taken at a very slow shutter speed, a blur. Or sometimes I associate her with a fine musical instrument, like a harpsichord, which you could never really understand without delving under the burnished cover to the heart of the machine, where all its strings and plectrums are.

In the case of the harpsichord, I think the cover was nailed shut. And the blurred photograph stands for her alcoholism.

I got home around five that Friday afternoon. Mom was in the sun room, a glassed-in den full of potted palms and ferns and begonias. She was wearing her gardening clothes, khaki slacks and one of dad's old shirts. You could hear a Rodgers and Hammerstein record playing in the living room. There was a pitcher of Rob Roys on the glass table.

"My own dearest darling!" she cried when I stepped down into the sun room. She had a very exaggerated way of greeting you, like you just returned from an Antarctic expedition instead of a couple of months at college. She threw her arms around me and held on so tight that I sensed something was wrong.

"How are you, mom?" I said, afraid to really find out.

She squeezed me again and then abruptly pushed herself away.

"I'm taking care of all my darlings," she said, and returned to a clump of begonias she was repotting on newspaper spread over the flagstones. I was her only child, so she meant her plants. You could tell in the few steps she took that she wasn't all that steady on her feet. Gertrude Lawrence was singing "Whistle a Happy Tune" in the background, the music of mom's generation.

"My God, Peter, look at you," she said, calling me by my real name, my only name then, and the funny thing was, she wasn't even looking at me when she said that. "When was the last time you had a haircut?"

"Everybody's growing their hair long."

"Well, you better not let your father see you like that. He'll positively flip. And that outfit!"

I was wearing one of the *Wieland* shirts. You know how kids are with some favorite article of clothing. They wear it all the time.

"You look like Byron at Missolonghi!" she said.

"Actually, it's Carwin at Philadelphia."

"Who. . . ?" She obviously wasn't a big *Wieland* fan. Who could blame her. "Wouldn't it be lovely to go out for dinner tonight?"

"Sure," I said.

"Then take my car to the village, darling, and get your hair trimmed—"

"I'm not getting my hair cut, mom."

"—and put on your gray flannel slacks and your blazer—"

"I'll change my clothes, but forget about the hair."

"It'll be your funeral, darling."

I sat down on one of the white wicker chairs and watched her work on the begonias for a while.

"We could go to Sans Soucci tonight," she said after a long silence. "You could have frogs' legs." It was a family joke. The first time they took me to Sans Soucci I was ten or so, and I ordered frogs' legs because I thought it would shock them. The joke was on me, though, because my father made me eat them.

"That would be real nice, mom."

"Why don't you call and make a reservation for seven o'clock?"

"Okay."

"I'm going to take a long, hot bath. The keys are in the car."

"Fine," I said. "Is Arlene off?"

"Yes. She's in the city."

Arlene was our maid. This was back in the days when domestics got paid less than slave-wages. I'd brought her some presents. She had so few things.

Mom dusted off her hands, picked up the cocktail pitcher, kissed me on the cheek, and headed inside the main part of the house.

"I'm so glad you're home, darling," she said.

"Me too," I told her.

When she was upstairs, I made myself a drink, a scotch and soda, and called up the restaurant. Then I went upstairs to shower and change.

About an hour later, my father still hadn't come home. It wasn't all that unusual. He frequently worked late or had staff meetings. I wasn't even sure he knew I was coming home for the weekend. My mother would forget to tell him things like that. Anyway, I went upstairs to her room to see how she was coming along because she could take forever. I knocked on the door but there was no answer, so I coughed to announce my presence in case she was running around naked, and then I went in. She was in bed, under the covers. The pitcher was on the dresser, practically empty. I sat on the edge of the bed and ran my fingertips along her hairline. She stirred and opened her eyes halfway.

"You look so beautiful," she said. "My little Lord Byron."

"It's quarter to seven."

She rolled over slightly toward me. A billow of perfume and scotch wafted up.

"You two go ahead," she said groggily. "I'm so tired."

I was about to tell her there wasn't any two of us, that dad still wasn't home, but I realized I'd just be stating the obvious.

"We can show up late," I said. "They'll hold the table for us."

"Of course they will," mom said. She was falling asleep again. I kissed her and left the room.

Downstairs, I made myself another drink and put a Fats Waller record on the hi-fi. When it was over, the house seemed oppressively quiet. All you could hear were the spring peepers out in the pond. I went into the kitchen and tried to call up Becky Bucholz, the Rebecca of "Rebecca's Window," who was my girlfriend for about a year and a half when we were in high school. We were friends, but it was hard to keep the old flame burning with her out at Antioch and me at Beal. Anyway, her mother answered and said Becky was digging up ancient bones in the Yucatan on a school trip. I called up another friend of mine, Stuart Goldberg. He had mononucleosis and could barely speak into the phone, let alone go out for a drink. Finally, I decided to drive over to the club to see if my father was there.

The Twin Hills Golf and Tennis Club was a bastion of old-fashioned colonialism. I think we were about the first Jewish family they ever let in. They had to because my father was the county D.A. and could have taken them to court and spoiled all their upper-crust fun.

I remember the slight undercurrent of anti-Semitism. You'd be in the locker room putting on your tennis togs and pick up the word "yid." But for the most part, they realized that Jews could replace divots and eat with a knife and fork and do the fox trot like anybody else. Then again, you didn't see too many black families around Twin Hills. In fact, you didn't see any, just old black men, and they either carried golf bags or trays. So you can see where my father's liberal social conscience ended with his self-interest. He was a golf nut.

When I came in that night, the bar was empty. The cocktail crowd had already moved into the dining room. It was a herd thing. Smitty, the black bartender, was polishing up the glasses.

"Well, hello, young man!"

"Hiya, Smitty. Have you seen my father, by any chance?"

"No, I ain't seen the judge tonight." That's what he called my father.

"I'll have a scotch and soda," I said.

"You old enough for the hard stuff?"

"For Godsake, I'm nineteen, Smitty. Here, look." I whipped out my driver's license. He made me the drink and put a couple of cherries on a napkin for me. It was an old routine from when I was a kid. I used to get one in my Shirley Temple and then keep asking for more.

I smiled and was trying to make some conversation when Frank Havermayer stalked into the room. He was a cardiologist who lived down Radnor Road from us, and also one of my father's regular golfing partners.

"Is it a boy or a girl?" Frank said jovially when he saw it was me. The older generation thought this was a hilarious remark back in those early longhair days.

"Want to go into the cloakroom and examine me?" I dished it right back at him.

"Hey, I'm only joshing, Pete. But what is it with you young people? I just don't understand it."

"I don't either, Frank."

"Hmmp. Can I buy you a drink?"

"You bet."

He sat down on the stool next to me and drew a little circle over
the bar to indicate a round.

"You're a college man now."

"Sure am." I told him where I went, but the subject made me
nervous because I was on probation and everything. Luckily, Frank
started telling me about his days at Cornell in the thirties, the football games, dancing to Fred Astaire records, the "broads" he went
out with. Actually, I enjoyed listening to him. I was sorry Beal wasn't
more like that. We bought each other another round or two.

"So what are you majoring in, Pete?"

I made a big deal of looking around the bar—it was still empty—
and then leaned over and whispered in his ear.

"Rock and roll," I said.

"They teach that there, where you go?"

I nodded conspiratorially.

"Well, what the hell are you going to do with that?"

"I'm going to be an overnight sensation."

"Does your dad know?"

"Nope." I put my index finger across my lips. "Sssshh. This is
confidential, Frank."

"He'll love that. Rock and roll. Jeeesh. You're going to have to
buckle down, Peter. Rock and roll, or whatever you call it, is not
something to build a life on."

"How much money did you make a week when you were in college?"

"Money. . . ? I didn't have to work. We were, uh, comfortable."

"Hey, I made $350 last week. How do you like that?"

"Doing what?"

"Playing rock and roll."

Frank seemed baffled.

"How much do you figure you make now, Frank?" I asked him.

"That's between me and my accountant, sonny boy," he said and
swirled the ice around in his glass.

"Well, whatever you make, I'm going to be earning twice that, three times that, a year from now. How do you like that?"

He looked up at me sharply.

"I think you're a very arrogant young man," he said and glugged down the rest of his drink. He got off his stool and hiked up his pants.

"Uh, Frank, I didn't mean to—"

"I know. You have a whole lifetime to get rid of that chip on your shoulder."

"Just do me a favor," I said. "Don't mention this conversation—"

"Don't worry about it," he reassured me. "Incidentally, I hope Morris knows the links are opening tomorrow. Take care, Peter."

I watched him leave the room, really sorry I'd brought up the whole stupid money issue. Obviously, I was trying to impress him on terms that I thought would mean more to him than rock and roll, but boy, did it backfire. Anyway, after he was gone, there was nobody to talk to except Smitty, who was a nice guy, but who, I'm sad to say, was the quintessential Uncle Tom country club Negro, an unfortunate product of our special brand of Westchester colonialism. He agreed with everything you said. If you said the place sure was crowded, he'd agree, even if you were the only two people there. So I made some more small talk, signed the tab, said good night, and went home.

Every Saturday morning during the warm half of the year my father played golf. In the afternoons he liked to putter around the grounds of the house. We had a professional gardening service that mowed the lawns and did all the weeding. What my dad liked to do was the masonry work. He had built a big flagstone terrace with different levels and a whole bunch of stone walls around the various plantings.

I came down at one in the afternoon, hungover. Arlene was in the kitchen. We clowned around together for a while until the Alka-Seltzer started to work, and I gave her the presents I'd brought, a robe and a small pin shaped like a butterfly. The fog was finally clearing from my brain. I asked Arlene where mom was.

She lifted her eyes to the ceiling ruefully.

"She's still upstairs?"

"Yup," she said and shook her head.

"Well, God, she went to bed around seven o'clock last night."

"She ain't been right, Petey."

I knew what that meant. In our private parlance that meant mother was really into the sauce lately. I figured as much from the hour I arrived. Arlene slid a plate of eggs in front of me on the counter.

"It 'cause of *him*," she said vehemently and jerked her head at the window. "He been so mean." You could see my father out there, way down by the pond. She always referred to my father simply as "*him*" when things weren't "right" with my mother. Arlene had worked for my mother's family from the time mom was a teenager, and she was very protective of her. Dad and Arlene had an adversary relationship, but over the years it had become ritualized, so the jabs and put-downs they were always exchanging lost a lot of their cutting edge. He probably didn't care, anyway. To him, Arlene was simply another fixture in the house, more or less a warm-blooded appliance.

My appetite was gone. I put down the knife and fork and stepped outside. It was a gorgeous day, temperature in the high sixties, birds singing. I walked slowly down to the pond. My father was mixing sand and cement in a wheelbarrow with a hoe. He was wearing an old LeCoste tennis shirt splattered with gray cement splotches. You could see the muscles in his arms bulge as he mixed the mortar. My father was half a foot taller than me. I had pretty much stopped growing by then.

"Hi," I said.

"Well, look who's here!" he said merrily. My father's specialty within the bosom of his family was sarcasm, sarcasm without a true particle of humor, meant to injure deviously, like a sucker-punch. I could play that game too. I was his son.

So when he said that, I pretended to look behind me as if he must have been talking to someone else, and then I said, "Oh, you must mean me."

"You're the one, pal."

"I was looking for you down at the club last night."

"I know. Frank Havermeyer said he ran into you."

"Oh. . . ?" I said. I was afraid to open up that can of worms, so I just said, "He wanted me to remind you about the links."

"We went a round this morning. Took him over the coals, as usual. My God, that man is a terrible golfer. I don't even know why I play with him."

"Because you like to beat him."

My father ignored the remark. "Come," he said. "Give me a hand with this." He wanted me to hold one end of a string while he checked it with a spirit level. When it was correct, he told me to tie it off on a wooden stake. Today's project, apparently, was a small retaining wall under a raised bed of ornamental trees. A magnolia was bursting into bloom and it smelled delicious. My father began globbing mortar on the last layer of stones, set a line of new ones on it, and tamped them into place with the handle of his trowel.

"I got a very interesting document in the mail last week, Peter. Can you guess what it was?"

Since it was a rhetorical question, I just waited for him to tell me. But he was in one of his more playful moods, meaning he was extremely ticked off.

"Let me give you a hint. It was from your school."

"I was going to talk to you about that."

"Really? When were you planning to bring it up? In June? After you flunk all your courses?"

He chucked his trowel into the wet cement, where it stuck point first, like a knife. Next thing I knew, he was hovering over me, jabbing his index finger into my chest. I was backpeddling and bumped up against the little hill where the magnolia tree was planted.

"I have to find this out in a letter! You lied to me about your marks this fall—"

"I didn't lie about them. You didn't ask."

"That's not a lie?"

"No, it's an omission. You could even call it a lack of interest on your part."

He suddenly cuffed me one to the head. It wasn't a particularly hard blow. It was just meant to shut up my sassy mouth. Meanwhile, though, he was really livid, doing this thing with his jaw, grinding his molars. It was a good thing the voters never saw him like that. They would have thought he had hydrophobia.

"First you take up some cockamamie course of study—drama, for Godsake! Then you flunk all your cockamamie drama courses. You're beautiful."

"I didn't flunk them all."

"Do I exaggerate? Well, pardon me. But when I went to Columbia, Ds were not acceptable either. This is all beside the point, because now they inform me that you're flunking *all* your classes this semester, and you're going to be out on your tush unless some miracle occurs."

"I'm—"

"Shut up. I'm not finished. This is how it's going to be from now on: every mark you get below a B, you're going to reimburse me proportionately in dollars. I'm not going to shell out three grand a year so you can putz around like you're on vacation. You're going to work, pal. And this arrangement will be retroactive to last semester, so you better start making plans to earn next fall's tuition this summer, because I will not be footing the bill. Do you read me?"

"I don't think I'll be going back in the fall."

"Oh, really? This gets more and more interesting as merrily we roll along. What did you have in mind instead? The Marines?"

"I'm going to play in a band."

"What was that?"

"I am going to play in a rock and roll band."

"This is really too much. You're going to be the next Elvis Presley, I suppose."

"Why not?"

"You are simply beyond belief."

"I've been playing in a band since October."

"So you aim to go bigtime now?"

"Maybe."

Instead of hauling off and swatting me again, my father seemed to deflate like a pontoon raft someone punctured with a screwdriver. One moment he was erect, hanging over me, and the next he just sagged, went over and got his trowel and began laying stones again, silently. Eventually, I got up and went over to where he was working.

"It's not the end of the world, dad."

He looked up at me slowly from where he was stooped over his stones.

"You don't see what a disappointment you are to me?" he said.

"Hey, give me a chance. I'm only nineteen years old."

He turned away once more, retreating to somewhere inside himself where he was safe from the innumerable disappointments of his family.

I started walking back to the house. Halfway up the lawn, I heard him hollering at me.

"I don't approve of this idea at all, Peter."

I stopped.

"Do you hear me?"

"I read you, loud and clear."

"You think you can count on me for handouts while you wait for lightning to strike? Huh, Elvis?"

"I don't think I can count on you for anything."

"Do me one favor, pal. Get yourself a stage name."

"Afraid I'll embarrass you?"

"Isn't that the whole idea?"

"Your egotism is really out of this world, you know that?"

"Don't be in the house when I'm done here, pal."

"That, you can count on," I said.

Obviously, there was plenty of egotism to go around both ways, but mine could at least be explained as youthful arrogance, as Frank Havermeyer put it. My father's arrogance was more complete. It had a full-blown purity to it that was uncorrupted by innocence or idealism or even failure. It's too bad, though, that neither of us could ever forgo the satisfaction of having the last word.

I went into the house, put some clothes into a knapsack, and called a taxi. Then I went into mom's room to say good-bye. The shades were drawn and she was just a lump under the covers. I turned on the light next to her bed and sat on the edge. She asked me to turn it off. She looked pretty terrible, all puffy with bags under her eyes.

"I have to go, mom."

"Go. . . ? Where?"

"To the city. I promised someone I'd visit them."

"A friend from school?"

"That's right."

"But you just came home."

"I know, mom, but I made these plans."

"Why didn't you tell me yesterday?"

"It slipped my mind. I'm sorry. You know, all the excitement of being home and everything."

"When are you coming back?"

"Well, actually, I think we'll head directly back up to school from there."

"They don't give you much vacation, do they, darling?"

"No, they really put your nose to the old wheel."

"We didn't have time to talk or anything."

"There'll be time, mom. Next time."

"Do you need any money?"

"No."

"Hand me my purse—"

"It's okay, mom. I've got plenty of money."

"Have you seen your father?"

"Yes."

"He was very anxious to see you."

"I know."

"Did the two of you have a nice reunion?"

"The years go by and he's still the same old dad."

"He worries about you."

"I know he does. And I worry about you."

"Oh, don't worry about me. Good gracious. If you want to worry about someone, worry about Betty Stern. They . . . you know, a woman's operation."

"I'm sorry to hear that."

"It was devastating. Oh, but Peter, don't send her a card or anything. It's not the sort of thing—"

"I won't, mom. Don't worry."

I heard the taxi then, honking its horn in the driveway.

"Is that your friend?"

"That's right, mom. I've got to go."

"Have a wonderful time, darling."

I hugged her, but I could hear Arlene downstairs already hassling the driver.

"Ain't nobody here called no taxi," she was telling the guy. I hurried down there. The poor driver was trying to check with his dispatcher over the radio while Arlene berated him.

"It's okay," I told her. "I called it."

"You. . . ? Where you goin', chile?"

"To the city. Bye-bye, sweetie." I gave her a squeeze and a kiss and climbed into the cab. Arlene was shaking. She knew everything was going wrong, everything was falling apart between the two of them. She saw me and the old man going at it, but she knew that was only a tiny part of the larger picture, and there she was, left in the middle of it. What a lousy position to be in. The cab pulled around the circular driveway. I waved good-bye to Arlene. It was the last time we would all be together in the house I grew up in.

I don't remember much about the train ride except that all I did was run through that stupid argument my father and I had over and over and over. When the train pulled into Grand Central, I called Bobby Schumann, our drummer, who was the only person I knew in the whole city.

"I may have to flop at your place," I told him.

"Oh yeah? For how long?"

"I don't know. I got thrown out of the house."

"What for?"

"For being a disappointment to my father."

"Don't sweat it. Our whole family was a disappointment to mine. Only, *he* moved out."

"Yeah, well. . . ."

So I took a cab up to his place and we spent the rest of the afternoon browsing around the Museum of Natural History, looking at the dinosaurs and the stuffed gorillas and the shrunken heads. On our way out, you could see all the trees in Central Park bursting into bloom, and kids playing around that statue of Theodore Roosevelt, and I made up my mind to leave Beal and move to the city with the other guys. I had no choice, anymore.

That night we went to a party downtown, some NYU kids that Bobby knew from high school. That was when I got cubed. . . .

———————

The machine stopped. The cassette had run out of tape. It was dark outside and the only light in the front room seeped cheerlessly in from a bulb in the kitchen. The bald spot on Byron's head glistened damply. He ruminatively nibbled his lower lip.

"You got *cubed*?" I asked

"Yeah."

"What do you mean?"

"You don't remember the terminology, Sears?" he asked. I shook my head. "Remember when they used to put LSD in sugar cubes? Well, that's where the term comes from. The verb *to be cubed:* to be given LSD without your knowledge or permission. It was an extremely unpleasant experience."

"What happened?"

"We went to this party. There was a big bowl of punch. It was full of rum so it never occurred to me that there was anything else in it. Acid was still relatively rare then, at least on the East Coast.

I'd never had any before. Anyway, I had a classic bummer. Did you ever freak out on acid?"

"No. I never did."

"You were lucky. Did you trip much?"

"Oh, yeah."

"You know, I envy that. I could never handle it. The problem with LSD is that when it goes wrong, you're not just the victim, you're the witness too. I never touched it again. You look surprised."

"I am. When I think of those years, especially your records, a lot of it's bound up with the drug memories. I guess we thought you were driving that bus."

"Nope. Wasn't me. I was hardly even a passenger."

"Somebody on the magazine once referred to you as 'The Crown Prince of Psychedelia.' "

"Yeah? Well, I guess that proves how bottomless the public's appetite for malarky is. Crown Prince of Psychedelia," he chuckled. "What horseshit!"

"*Childe Byron* was an extremely trippy album."

"It was all effects."

"But the imagery, the lyrics—"

"It was the language of a nightmare, not drugs."

"Wasn't it one and the same to you?"

"It was just words and music."

Byron got up and limped over to the window, leaning against the sash.

"There's a ring around the moon," he said.

"What does it mean?"

He turned slowly to me.

"It means there's a ring around the moon."

---

"I've made up my mind," Allie said when I returned to the cottage. She was sitting in the rocker next to the woodstove, wrapped in a blanket. Two suitcases stood tellingly in the center of the braided rug. "There's a train out of St. Johnsbury at eight-thirty in the morning, and a bus—"

"I'll drive you down, Allie."

It would be pointless to replay the recriminations that flared spo-
radically that night, for the themes were the same, but it was well
after midnight when sleep overtook us and a bitter autumn sun that
woke us up a few short hours later. After a stop at the bank in Cardiff, we crossed the Connecticut River at Woodsville, followed
Interstate 91 clear down to New York, and made it to Broome Street
by the middle of the afternoon. The daytime din and filth were a
revelation to me after more than three months in the country. The
sidewalks were crawling with art fops. Allie and I had trouble looking at each other. I handed her an envelope.

"Here's some money, babe."

It was $1500, roughly half of what we had left in the bank.

"Write, huh?" Allie said quietly, eyes scouring the sidewalk.

"I'm going to work hard. I swear, Allie."

"No," she said. "I mean write *me*."

"I'll call."

"Want to come upstairs for a little while?"

"Sure," I said, and a painful hour of forced pleasantries with Carol
Bostwick went by, Allie and I attempting to put a bright face on it
all. *Oh yeah, country life is fantastic. Rick's just going back to wrap
up these writing projects of his, and then, well. . . .*

When she walked me back down to the car, there were tears in
our eyes.

"We'll survive this," I said, and all she could do was try to smile
and nod her head gamely. "You'll see."

And so I left her standing out there on the sidewalk, looking so
small and hurt amid all that filth and tumult of Soho. I got right back
on the F.D.R. Drive and headed north. It was almost midnight
when I staggered back into the cottage. Luke had taken a crap right
in the middle of the braided rug.

# CHAPTER 5

RS: Is it really lonely at the top?
BJ: Does a bear really shit in the woods?

—The *Rolling Stone* Interview with Byron Jaynes, 1968

Ⅰt was raining when I drove out to Byron's house the day following my return from New York, a steady, dreary, punishing rain that carved gullies in the dirt roads and left the woods reeking with the wet rot of dead things. The leaves were beginning to turn color in the maples, and purple asters, those harbingers of the coming cold, flowered somberly in the overgrown pastures.

I let myself into the house and began setting up the tape recorder in the front parlor. When I happened to look up, Byron was slouched darkly against the arched doorway that led to the kitchen.

"You think you can walk right into someone's house without knocking or anything?" he said.

"It's pouring buckets out there. You must have known it was me."

"Where were you yesterday?"

"I have a regular life to lead, for your information," I told him bluntly.

"No, you don't," he replied. "You left that in the real world when you came here."

"Oh, get off it, Byron. What am I supposed to do? Call the laundromat in Haverfield and leave a message."

"No."

"Then what am I supposed to do?"

He didn't answer. Instead, he shuffled out from behind the doorjamb with his hands thrust into his pants pockets. He was wearing a fine, tailored tweed jacket over his janitorial trousers and shirt, with a bright-yellow scarf draped loosely around his neck. I realized, with some satisfaction, that for the first time I had called one of his bluffs.

"I just didn't know who was barging in here, that's all," he muttered.

"Why don't you get yourself a phone, Byron?"

"No!" he cried, as if the idea was abhorrent.

"Why the hell not?"

"People might call."

"People? What people?"

"I don't know," he barked back at me. "It could get around."

"What could 'get around'? That Joe Doaks has a phone? Who would care?"

He grunted noncommittally. I could tell he was anxious to drop the subject.

"Hey, let's set up in the kitchen today, huh?" he said. "It's warmer in there. We can sit by the stove, like a couple of oldtimers. I'll even make you a hot beverage, you lucky, lucky boy."

By that time I could have used a stiff drink, but it was evident that Byron was off liquor and didn't keep any around the house.

"Fine," I said.

It was the first time he had allowed me into another part of his house since we'd struck our bargain. The kitchen was austere, like the front parlor, but there was a table and chairs and a warming woodstove, and the room seemed generally better suited to ordinary living. The only decoration on the walls was an insurance company calender from 1972. The sheaf for December of that year was stapled to a color print depicting three bear cubs frisking in a pine forest. He must have noticed I was staring at it.

"Absurd, huh?" he said sheepishly.

"Do you know what year it is, Byron?" I asked.

He recoiled at the question. "Hey, come on," he scoffed at me.

"No, really."

"It's 1981, right?"

"That's right."

"See, I'm not a total whacko yet. I keep up on things. Ask me who's president. Go on, ask me."

"Who's president?"

"Rutherford B. Hayes. Hey, gotcha. Well, it might as well be. Sit down."

The heat from the woodstove was reassuring. I put a new cassette in the Sony while Byron gazed at the calender.

"I really ought to take that thing down," he said. "It's goddam morbid. Where were we?"

"New York," I reminded him. "After you freaked out on acid."

"Boy, I guess I did. Well, here we go: the further adventures of that Crown Prince of Psychedelia, that Knight Errant of Aquariana, that Halley's Comet of Electric Minstrelsy—"

## *The Life of Byron Jaynes—Tape 3*

After that Easter, we all went back to Beal for the last month and a half of the semester. There were a lot of reasons. We had a whole bunch of dates still lined up to play upstate, and it was an opportunity to get some cash together for the move. Gary wanted to collect his B.A. Also, I was having a little trouble with the aftereffects of taking that acid.

*Were you having flashbacks?*

I was having—I don't know what you call it, but it was none too pleasant. I'd be doing something perfectly innocuous, standing on the grass or taking a shower, and the most unsettling warpy feeling would come over me, and I'd start to panic. For a while I was afraid I'd damaged my brain. I'll tell you one thing: it didn't make me all that hot to try acid again, and there was plenty around as the year wore on. The other guys were taking quite a bit of it, especially Bobby. He would trip for days on end sometimes. I think it eventually affected his personality, to tell you the truth. He was much less obnoxious before that.

On the other hand, I was writing better songs than ever, really cranking them out: "Swallow the Earth (With Rage)," "Cold River," "She Sends Me," "Peaceable Kingdom," "Love It to Pieces," "Sarah Knows"—a lot of songs that would end up on *Rising Son* in '66, and a lot more that other people recorded. By that time, late in the spring of 1965, most of the tunes in our live act were originals by me, which helped distinguish us from other bar bands who were playing warmed-over radio hits. You were beginning to get a feeling about who was going somewhere and who would be left behind.

In May, as predicted, I flunked out of school. So did Rego. We got drunk on champagne and celebrated. Two weeks after that, we found a brownstone on Grove Street in Greenwich Village for $400 a month, and all of us moved in.

Those stock stories about how the Romantics struggled, rehearsing in flooded, roachy basements, living on stale rolls—none of them was true. I think Simon's publicity girl had an overactive imagination. Compared to many of the bands who eventually made it, we were living comfortably from the start. We always made the rent and had a few dollars in our pockets.

It's true that the first few months we had trouble getting jobs in the city clubs. But we still had the van and plenty of connections upstate. We could easily shoot up to New Paltz or Albany to play a gig or two. Meanwhile, we argued about finding a manager. Rego still thought he could handle it himself. At that point, until we could find a reputable pro, I didn't feel like turning over fifteen, twenty percent of our earnings to some fast-talking schlemiel in a shiney suit. We debated all through the summer and half the fall. Then, in November, just when we were beginning to get discouraged, Rego got us a job in an East Side bar named Zelda's.

It was named after F. Scott Fitzgerald's loony wife. There was this whole nostalgia-for-the-twenties scene going on that was the uptown equivalent of being hip. Zelda's was on Second Avenue between 78th and 79th, around the corner from Harlow's, where Dylan had been holding court. It was a big room for an East Side bar, and one of the few that had live bands. The guy who owned it, Frank Lemanczyk, was this roly-poly young operator, about thirty, who dressed in double-breasted suits and drove a restored Pierce-Arrow, and was living out his Roaring Twenties fantasy to the hilt.

We played two Wednesdays and a Friday that month, then twice a week through December, and by the new year—1966—we were the house band, meaning we played Thursday through Saturday every week. Frank wanted to make us over in his image, but we went along with him as little as possible. For example, he wanted us to wear the same kind of 1920s gangster togs he wore, so we let him dress us up in pinstriped suits and Panama hats, and he had some photos of us taken grouped around his Pierce-Arrow, Rego holding his guitar and me with a shotgun and all of us smoking gigantic cigars. He even tried to rename us Elliot Ness and the Untouchables, but we talked him out of that one. As for the costumes, I think we wore them on the bandstand once. They were so hot you practically died of heat stroke up there.

But we had a lot of fun in those months, more real good times, probably, than we would ever have together again. Frank paid the band $1000 a week in straight salary, which was actually somewhat less than we earned barnstorming upstate, though we didn't have anymore out-of-pocket expenses like gas and motels. It was plenty to live on and there were fringe benefits.

Frank thought he was Jay Gatsby, right? We'd finish playing at three in the morning, then we'd all pile into that beautiful old car and take off into the night, hitting all the after-hours joints in Manhattan from Slugg's in the East Village to Small's Paradise in Harlem. There were girls, there was champagne and pot, and there was plenty of acid for those who wanted it, meaning everybody but me, and Frank always picked up the tab. He was very, very good to us, and unlike a lot of other people, all he really wanted was to have a good time.

In March of that year we got our first newspaper notices and I became Byron Jaynes. It was Thursday night, and I was sitting at the bar between sets when this reporter from the *Herald-Tribune* came up to me. He was fairly young himself, about Frank's age, with longish hair, but dressed in a really well-cut tan suit so nobody would mistake him for what was becoming known as "a hippie." He bought me a drink—which was unnecessary because we drank for free— and complimented me on the band. He had his reporter's pad on the bar and asked me my name.

I was about to tell him Peter Greenwald when I remembered what my father said when we had that fight on the lawn almost a year earlier: "Better get yourself a stage name, pal." The strange thing was, I didn't feel that I was obeying my father, but rather defying him, in an odd, inverse way—denying his name.

I told the guy my name was Byron.

"Byron what?" he asked.

*Byron what?* I thought. *Lord Byron?* I couldn't tell him that. There was a poster of Jayne Mansfield on the wall behind the waitress station, one of those lurid, campy, Warhol-type posters where they blow up a black-and-white newspaper halftone and color in the lips a smudgy red so that poor old Jayne looked as awful as possible.

"Jayne," I told him. The jukebox was blasting, though, and he couldn't hear me well.

"J - A - N - E - S?" He asked?

"No, with a Y."

He nodded. "J - A - Y - N - E - S?"

"That's right." Actually, I liked it better with the S stuck on the end. He asked who wrote our material and I told him I did. Then he asked where we were from and I made up this cockamamie story that we were four lads from Cleveland who met in cosmetology school where we were studying to become hairdressers. He took it all down on his pad. I had a pretty good buzz on from drinking scotches all night, and for some reason I didn't take it seriously until the reporter excused himself and left, and then I thought, *Jesus, what if that gets into the paper!* But by that time it was too late. I was afraid to mention to the other guys what had happened. The next day, the shit hit the fan.

Gary was a voracious reader, as well as an early riser, and every morning he went over to the newsstand on Sheridan Square and picked up all three morning papers. Then he would go over to the Bagel-Nosh and spend a couple of hours poring over them. He was very well informed. I sometimes went with him.

That morning, though, I was hungover and stayed upstairs with the covers pulled over my head until three in the afternoon. We were supposed to rehearse two new tunes that day. Rego was like a Prussian drillmaster as far as rehearsing went, and I kept waiting for him to come in and yank the covers off. But he never did, and I began to get curious. So I dragged myself into the shower, took three aspirins and a valium, and finally went downstairs.

The house was a pigsty, like the worst kind of fraternity you could imagine. Gary and I were relatively neat but Bobby and Rego were a couple of slobs, and we could never agree about hiring a maid because we didn't think it was fair to pay the same amount to clean up *their* mess, so the place was always disgusting. Anyway, I went to the kitchen to get some coffee. There were Chinese food cartons and pizza boxes with moldy crusts all over the place, and whoever was the last one to use the coffee managed to drip water into the jar making the crystals solidify into a rocky lump. I could hear Rego strumming his acoustic in the living room, so I went storming in there with this jar of coagulated Nescafé in my hand, and started yelling, ". . . is it so goddam difficult to put the cap back on the goddam coffee jar. . . !"

The three of them were in there together, and I could tell by the way they looked at me that something was up, and I had a creepy feeling I knew what it was.

"Good afternoon, Byron," Rego said cheerily. My stomach was growling so loud we could all hear it. He began plucking an Elizabethan galliard on his guitar. Bobby started drumming to it, obnoxiously, and Rego shot him a glance. Gary just rubbed his chin while I stood there with the stupid coffee jar in my hand. "Have a seat," Rego said, pointing to this director's chair we had with the back missing. "We have a surprise. Our first rave review. Want to hear it?"

"Certainly," I said, full of the kind of dread only guilt and a hangover can produce. Bobby was still drumming, in a frantic, idiotic way, and Rego barked at him to knock it off. Meanwhile, Gary took a newspaper clipping out of his shirt pocket, unfolded it, and cleared his throat.

" 'Life is full of wry surprises,' " he said, " 'and among them this week is our discovery that some of the most arresting folk-rock—' "

"That's what we play, you see," Rego explained professorially with his fingertips pressed together, "folk-rock." He nodded at Gary to go on.

" '. . . some of the most arresting folk-rock in all of Rotten Gotham may be found in an uptown watering hole called Zelda's, where account executives and other predator species of those posh latitudes vie for the favors of mini-skirted and Sassooned secretaries amid an ambience suggestive of the St. Valentine's Day massacre—' this guy's a regular mannerist with the quill," Gary paused to remark.

"A what?" Bobby asked.

"Go on," Rego said.

"Ahem. 'The surprise in all this is the music of Byron Jaynes and his band, the Romantics. . . .' "

I really started to feel sick.

" 'Mr. Jaynes is writing some of the most powerful and original material, either uptown or down, that this ear has encountered in an otherwise dreary season, songs informed with a convincing lyricism that is a breath of fresh air after three years of secondhand Beatlism. Looking for all the world like his poet namesake, the youthful, dark-haired Mr. Jaynes sings in an appealing, husky baritone of a nightmare world redeemed by beauty—' "

"I think the guy's a fag," Bobby said.

" 'His songs are peopled with grotesques, outlaws, criminals, desperate youths on the run, unattainable golden girls, and a vengeful God. The lead singer's presence is shy, seductive, almost reserved, then intermittently explosive as his melodies shift between the harmonic refrains of familiar folk idioms and the driving beat of blues-patterned rock, and he is supported ably by his sidemen—' "

"Sidemen! Shit."

"Oh, there's more," Rego said.

" '. . . in this undertaking—' "

"What are we, sidemen or undertakers?"

"Shut up, Bobby."

" 'But to compare this new talent's work to that of other troubadours—Donavan, Dylan, Paxton, or Ochs—would be a misleading disservice. This is a voice of its own with something original to say. The borrowings may be obvious, but Byron Jaynes synthesizes them so adroitly that the thefts are far outweighed by the uses to which they are put, and we hope to be able to find them on vinyl soon. Byron Jaynes and his band hail from Cleveland, where they met at a trade school. They are on display at Zelda's Thursdays through Saturdays, weekly. We cannot believe that they will remain indentured there for long.' "

Gary looked up, folded the clipping fastidiously, and put it back in his pocket. Nobody said anything for the longest time. They just stared into the wooden floor. Outside, you could hear the afternoon sounds of the city, horns, people clomping down the sidewalk, kids.

"What's all this 'we' shit?" Bobby finally said. " 'We' think this, 'we' think that?"

"It's the editorial 'we,' " Gary explained somberly. He would know something like that. He did crossword puzzles.

"Sounds affected if you ask me," Bobby said.

Rego pointedly ignored him. "So, what do you think?" he asked me.

"I talked to the guy for maybe all of five minutes," I said, as if that explained it.

"Where did you get this *Byron* thing?"

"The name? I made it up."

"You make up Cleveland, too?" Bobby said. "Jesus, Cleveland."

"Yeah, I made it up, Bobby."

"Well, it stinks."

Nobody said anything for at least a minute. Finally, Gary shifted around in his chair and said, "I'm afraid we're going to have to live with it."

"Maybe we could write a letter to the paper," Bobby said. "Get a retraction."

"No, the damage is done," Gary said.

"Are you going to be this Byron character from now on? Is that the idea?" Bobby asked. "And we get to be the Romantics?"

"Look, I didn't tell this guy I was fronting the band. What does it matter if I'm Peter Greenwald or Byron Jaynes or Fidel Castro?"

"I guess it doesn't matter at all. Not one bit," Rego said bitterly. "Let's just forget it and work on those tunes."

Needless to say, they were all so worked up about the distortions in the review that they overlooked the fact that it was a rave. I had completely overlooked it myself.

We customarily showed up for work around ten o'clock and started playing around eleven or so. That night, I went off by myself and had dinner at this Greek place on Bleecker. I was really depressed. It bothered me that some stranger could just grab hold of your ego and flog it around in public like that. I was still worrying about the whole thing when my cab pulled up in front of Zelda's. There was a line of people stretching halfway down the block waiting to get in. You don't realize how powerful the New York papers are until something like that happens. The city has a population of over seven million, right? Let's say, conservatively, that out of seven million, maybe ten thousand of them actually read that review of us over their morning coffee. And then, let's say that maybe two percent of those who read the review were inspired enough to check us out that night. Well, you add them to the normal neighborhood crowd who came to see us on a Friday night, and all of a sudden you have a mob scene on your hands.

Luckily, nobody on the sidewalk recognized me. The review hadn't included any pictures of us, and I was all swaddled up in this wool cape I bought in a secondhand store. Anyway, I went right up to the door where Tom Morrisey, Frank's regular bouncer, was taking cover charges. Only, I noticed that the cover charge was suddenly up from two bucks to five bucks a head. The next thing that caught my eye was a big poster in the window—one of those painted jobs they make for those perpetual going-out-of-business-sales on Times Square—except this one said in big red letters: BYRON JAYNES AND THE ROMANTICS. Next to it was a big blow-up of the *Herald-Tribune* review.

Well, I was just nauseated. Tom helped me slip through the door—he said "congratulations," which made me feel even worse—and I went looking for Frank at once. The tables were all filled and the area around the bar was three deep, with people hollering for drinks, and they were still letting people in. Frank was at the waitress station down at the far end showing a new girl how they worked the check system.

"Hey! Hey! Byron! Don't you love it?" he cried and grabbed me by the shoulders and kissed me right on top of the head. It was embarrassing, but he meant well.

"I've got to talk to you, Frank."

"Sherry," he said to the new girl, "just start schlepping drinks, and if you don't understand it, ask Melanie, okay?" She trundled off with her checkpad, scratching her head. Frank rubbed his hands briskly. "Kid," he said to me, "we are doing some business here. But where did you get this Byron Jaynes? Don't get me wrong, I like it. Byron Jaynes! It's very musical sounding, it's—"

"You've got to take that sign out of the window, Frank."

"Are you crazy?"

"The other guys are madder than hell."

"Well, fuck them."

"I don't want to fuck them."

"Pete, Pete, you've got to make hay while the sun shines. Don't be a schmuck—"

"Can't you just tear off the part that says Byron Jaynes and leave up the Romantics?"

One of the other waitresses barged in between us and started hollering out drink orders to the bartender, who was going batshit behind the bar by himself with the rush. Frank craned his head around her and seized my shoulder.

"You think you can control something like this, Pete? You can't. You're riding the bull now and you just have to hang on. Hang onto that bull. I've got to give Jimmy a hand."

He meant the bartender. I would have torn down the sign myself except there was a solid wall of people between it and me. So I gave up and headed for the dressing room, this grimy hole in back of the bandstand. The others were already in there, meaning that they had already seen the sign in the window. And they let me know it too. Bobby was lying on the scungy sofa with a bottle of Heineken balanced on his stomach. Rego was tuning our guitars to Gary's bass. They didn't even say hello or acknowledge my presence.

"The sign was Frank's idea," I told them right out.

They continued to ignore me.

"You guys are acting like such babies, I can't believe it."

"We're happy for you, Petey," Bobby said with a big, phony, smirky smile.

"Would it make you feel better if I played shitty tonight, so nobody'll get the wrong idea? Huh? I'll play shitty tonight—"

"Nobody plays shitty, tonight or ever!" Rego said fiercely.

"Hey, I always give it 100 percent," Bobby said.

Rego handed me my guitar. "Here you go, Byron."

"Hey, you don't have to call me that."

"Yes I do," he said. "It's Byron from now on."

I ached to correct him on that point, but I couldn't see prolonging the whole goddam stupid argument either. In a way, I guess I knew it was true. Anyway, we headed out to the bandstand.

I never saw the place so jam-packed. The space between the bar and the door was one huge milling clot. People who were standing crowded right up against the ones seated at tables. Two girls were perched on top of the cigarette machine. It was hotter than hell up on the bandstand, and you could see people fanning themselves with menus.

Our usual procedure was to climb aboard, plug in, and start playing. Half the time they didn't even cut off the jukebox until we were well into our first number. But that night it was already off. When we climbed up, the huge crowd hushed. For a few very eerie moments, all you could hear was Gary tapping his fingertips on the mikes to see if they were live. I was nervous for the first time, really, since we played Jo-Jo's Drop Inn in Rhinebeck. Then Rego came over and whispered in my ear, "I'm sorry we've been acting like such assholes."

"Hey, I understand," I told him.

"Let's focus that energy where it belongs," he cocked his head toward the crowd. "At them."

"Okay, Rego."

We began with "Behold the Fugitive," which struck just the right tone for me, considering the events of that day. I wanted to scream my brains out. The next forty-five minutes went by in a flash. When we climbed off the bandstand, I was soaked with sweat.

Back in the dressing room between sets, you could see that the other guys' moods had improved too. But we weren't alone in there for long. First Frank barged in with a case of champagne. All sorts of people came pressing in behind him. One was a *Village Voice* reporter who had strayed uptown on account of the *Trib* review to see if we were for real or not, and he must have decided we were, because he wanted to interview me. After that initiation the night before, I played it very cagey and close-mouthed. I told him to judge us by the performance and to make sure he referred to us simply as the Romantics and leave Byron Jaynes out of it.

"Aren't you the leader?" he asked.

"This is a band, not a political party," I told him. "If you're interested in leaders, go talk to Lyndon Johnson." He even wrote that down on his pad. The press can really exasperate you. It took a long time before I learned how to handle them.

Anyway, after he buzzed off, I was backed into the corner by a dapper young guy about thirty. He had a determined gleam in his eye and was very well dressed.

"Hi, Dave Dickstein," he said and kind of scrunched his hand up between us to shake. We were crammed very close together in that teeny room. He was drenched in some wicked aftershave, Moonlight at Laguna Beach or something.

"What paper are you with, Dave?" I asked.

"I'm not with the press," he said. "Atlantic Records. Can I be upfront with you, Bryon?"

"Hey, if you were any more up-front, I'd have trouble swallowing you," I joked around. He giggled hysterically, like I was Bob Hope.

"No, really, can I?" he asked.

"Sure."

"Are you signed with anybody?"

"Uh,uh," I shook my head.

"How long have you boys been playing together?"

"Ten years," I said.

"That long?"

"Yeah. Hey, did you happen to see that story about us in the *Trib*?" He nodded. "Well, that stuff about us coming from Cleveland—hey, get your elbow out of my face!" I hollered at some twit next to me, not Dickstein. "Anyway, we're not really from Cleveland."

"It doesn't matter—"

"You know the press. They believe anything."

You could tell he didn't want to discuss the vagaries of journalism just then.

"Right," he said. "Well, Byron, the reason I ask if you've signed is because I'd like it very much if you'd come down to our studios next week, see what you sound like on tape, talk for a while—"

"What do you want? To sign us or something?"

"You."

"Me?"

"Say, Monday morning—"

"I'll have to speak to our manager about that."

"Uh-huh," Dickstein said. That made him nervous all of a sudden. "Your manager. Who's your manager?"

"He was here a little while ago. Excuse me a minute, Dave. . . ."

I squeezed out of that corner and found Frank and asked him to please clear all the civilians out of the room. It took some yelling and shoving, but eventually we got them all out of there, including Frank himself, and managed to lock the door. We could breathe again.

"Some record company guy just cornered me," I told the others. That woke them up. Bobby went over to where Rego was sitting on a pile of Schlitz cartons and passed him the joint he was smoking.

"What did you tell him?" Bobby asked.

"Nothing. Not a damn thing."

"Well, what'd *he* say?"

"He wanted to know if we were signed."

"Wow! Show me the dotted line!" Bobby said.

"That's exactly the kind of attitude that's going to get us in trouble!" Gary told him angrily.

"We need a manager, Rego," I said and Gary agreed.

Rego shifted around anxiously on the cartons, resisting the idea physically, though he couldn't argue the point any longer.

"So, where do we find this manager?" Bobby asked.

"I don't know," I said, "but in the meantime, if any of us get buttonholed by anyone from a record company, tell him the same thing I just told this guy."

"Which was what, exactly?"

"Tell him we have to talk to our manager."

"There's no business like show business," Rego said.

The following night, Saturday, was as much of a mob scene, if not worse. A piece appeared in the *Times* that morning, shorter than the *Trib*'s review, and more restrained, though also very favorable. Like the other piece, it harped rather stupidly on the Lord Byron thing—but I had only myself to blame for that. Also, this time Rego was singled out for his playing and the other guys were at least mentioned by name, so it didn't look like I was ego-tripping at their expense. They actually allowed themselves to get somewhat excited over it—even Gary, who was about as emotional as an Ampeg speaker.

Anyway, going up on the bandstand that night felt like being under a microscope. I knew that quite a few record industry people were out there because Frank told me they had called up to reserve tables. You could even see a few celebrities around the room: Truman Capote, the writer, was at a table near the front with Jackie Kennedy's sister. I thought I saw Warhol, too. It was scary. Just before we started, one of the waitresses reached up and handed me a note. I jammed it into my pocket without reading it. We played the set, then ran like hell to the back room so we could lock the door and get a little breather. It wasn't until we were safely in there that I read the note. It said: "*Please be my guests tomorrow evening at La Goulue, 112 East 53rd Street, at 7:30 p.m.*" It was signed "*Simon Lewisohn.*"

I handed the note to Rego. He studied it for a long time, chewing on his lip.

"Let me see that," Bobby said and snatched it away. "Well, how do you like that? Simon Fuckin' Lewishohn. Anybody actually see him?"

"I don't even know what he looks like."

By this time Gary was reading over Bobby's shoulder.

"He's heavy-duty management," Bobby said. "He handles Reuban Shays, Seabird, the Midnight Creepers."

"Then we should accept, right?"

"Maybe we ought to play it cool," Bobby said. "You know, work up his appetite—"

"No," Gary said. "You don't jerk-off someone like Simon Lewisohn."

"Then let's go see what he has to say, huh?"

"I guess it can't hurt to listen," Rego said.

Soon, we were back out on the bandstand. Bobby banged into the downbeat of "Time Will Tell" while Rego stroked the intro. I grabbed hold of my mike.

"We'll be there tomorrow, Simon," I said to the audience, "wherever you are."

There were quite a few well-dressed middle-aged men in the crowd, and it looked like they all started gnashing their teeth at the same time. . . .

---

A frightening, pathetic, puling cry came from beyond the kitchen door. It sounded like a wild animal in terrible distress. Byron punched off the Sony, shot out of his seat, and limped hurriedly to the door, fumbling with the knob. Outside, on the top stair, was what appeared to be an unusually large, long-legged rodent.

"Sweet Jesus, where have you been?"

A cold draft blew into the room, rattling the leaf of the defunct calender on the wall. The rain dripped noisily off the eaves into cold puddles below. The miserable animal just stood there crying in a hoarse, shrill, cracked voice. Byron bent down and scooped it up, clutching it close to his chest. It was shivering violently.

"I'll be back," he said, adding, "stay where you are," as though I might rummage through all the cabinets in his absence. It annoyed me, slightly. He clambered unevenly up and then down the stairs, and returned with the animal swaddled in towels, rubbing it vigorously.

"Poor guy," he said. "I've missed you something awful."

When at last he set it down on the floor beside the stove, the animal could be identified as a black cat. It stood, for several moments, stiff and dazed, as though it had barely survived electrocution. Byron warmed some milk in a saucepan at the stove and emptied a can of cat food into a bowl. He set both the pan and the bowl on the floor. The dazed cat, shaking water out of its paws, wobbled over to the food and began eating greedily with tiny, audible grunts.

"Thataboy," Byron said, smoothing its fur with his hand. "They say that black cats have a lot of Siamese blood in them," he told me.

"Oh? How's that?"

"You know: traits."

"Which traits?"

"You know: Siamese ones."

"What's his name?" I asked, abandoning the previous line of inquiry.

"Whitey," Byron said.

I couldn't help laughing, thinking this was another one of Byron's jokes, but he cut a sharp, disapproving glance at me. His anger, if that's what it was lasted only a moment.

"He showed up at the beginning of the summer," Byron explained. "I don't know where he came from. We're great friends, though. Don't you run off and leave me like that again!" he warned it sternly. The cat continued eating. "See? You can tell them something a million times and they still won't listen. You like cats?"

"I have a dog."

"Oh. . . . Catherine hated cats. She was a lot like one, as a matter of fact. You could tell her something a million times. . . ."

Byron stared into the floor, then stood up, grimacing with pain. I gathered that his bad leg hurt him especially on rainy days.

"Whitey. . . ." I chuckled quietly to myself.

"Well, what do you think I should have called him? Death?" Byron lashed out at me. Again, his anger was short-lived. "Hey, I'm basically an optimist, right?"

"I really don't know, Byron."

"Well, I am. Wait until you get to know me better. You'll see."

He returned to his chair and carefully eased himself into it, bracing it with his now-powerful upper body and carefully extending his bad leg.

"Where were we?" he asked.

The cat, Whitey, backed off from its food, stretched, and sat down beside the stove. Soon it was washing itself, pink tongue against black fur.

"Simon," I said, and put a fresh cassette into the recorder.

Byron leaned forward, banked the embers in the woodstove, and pushed a new log in.

"Memory lane leads to a haunted house," he mumbled. "Sure, I'll tell you about Simon."

## The Life of Byron Jaynes—Tape 4

We showed up at the restaurant the next evening, a Sunday, at the appointed hour, and the captain immediately hassled us about our clothes. I had on one of my dueling blouses, Gary had on a billowy shirt with bright red polka-dots, Bobby had on a T-shirt under a double-breasted gangster jacket, and Rego was wearing a turtle-neck. All of us had jeans on and, naturally, no ties. They kept a supply of all the proper accessories in the coat-check room and we were outfitted appropriately with somebody's shiny, twenty-year-old lost tie or sportcoat. My shirt didn't even have the kind of collar you could tie a tie around properly, so I just tied it around my throat. I'm sure we looked more ridiculous than when we first walked in. We didn't learn until later that Simon *owned* the goddam restaurant.

We created quite a sensation as we traversed the dining room in our natty outfits. People dropped their forks. You could hear indignant muttering. Simon was seated at a horseshoe-shaped banquette with an ethereal-looking woman about half his age. He greeted us without getting up. We reached in, one at a time, and shook his hand, and also the woman's, whom he introduced as his wife, Claire. Then he invited us to sit down. I slid onto the polished leather seat next to his wife, with Bobby next to me. Rego and Gary slid into Simon's side.

He was 51 years old when we first met. Even just sitting down, you could tell he was a large man, physically. Everything about him was a couple of degrees out of proportion to the world around him. He was six-four and probably weighed about 260, though the only really noticeable fat on him was this pouch under his chin that made his whole neck seem puffy. His hair was a tangle of tight, steel-gray ringlets, though later he would grow it quite long, even wear it in pigtails. He had these slitty eyes that were never quite fully open, as if he was always squinting into direct sunlight. At the time, he wore that great, bushy gray Slavic mustache. His hands were enormous.

He was one of those men from my father's generation who took great care in the way they dressed and their personal grooming, but who didn't like looking too fastidious and rumpled themselves up as a finishing touch. For instance, that night Simon had on a black velvet sportcoat with a pink oxford button-down shirt and a swirly, brightly colored tie—a psychedelic tie, though the word was barely coined then. All of his clothes were obviously expensive and clean, but they looked like he drop-kicked them around the room for an hour or so before putting them on, the way you might break in a new baseball mitt before using it in a game. It gave him the look of a businessman who had just come from a scuffle, and who would as soon clamp a full nelson on you as shake your hand.

You would have expected from his sheer size and looks that he would have had a gruff, booming voice. But, oddly enough, his voice was as high as Jimmy Carter's—though the accent was pure New Yawk—and he spoke so softly that you sometimes had to make an effort to catch what he was saying. He talked that way to everyone: me, his wife, his chauffeur, his staff, promoters, the Gemini people. It was an effective display of his power. Jerry Zuckerman could be screaming bloody murder, tearing his hair out, ranting and raving, and Simon would just chirp back at him like a big, overgrown chickadee, and he'd get his way too, because it was the words that counted, not the velocity of the wind used to propel them.

Let's take you and me for example, Rick. We're sitting at this table, right? And I want to get the message across that if you do such-and-such a thing, I will destroy you. Now, if I screamed it at you, you'd be so concerned about the sheer volume hurting your eardrums that the actual message might not get through. But if, on the other hand, I sit here calmly and say, "Rick, if you do such-and-such a thing, I'm going to pull your brains out through your nose," then you're probably going to get the message, right?

Not that he was violent. He just understood the true nature of personal power. Besides, most of the people he dealt with were mental midgets compared to him. Simon had a terrific advantage over them that had nothing to do with his physical size: he simply knew what he was doing.

Claire was 26 then, Simon's third wife. The second wife and their two kids, grade-schoolers, lived in Los Angeles. He married his first wife in 1942, before the Army Air Corps shipped him to England, but it was annulled in '45. Anyway, Claire was a former model, a deerlike creature, all legs and eyes, the kind of woman who, if she walked into a crowded room, everybody would stop what they were doing and look at her, the women as well as the men, because her beauty was so compelling. She had long, black hair, but that night she had it up in an elaborately braided bun, the type ballet dancers wear to expose their beautiful faces to maximum view.

"You boys look downright spiffy," Simon remarked as we settled into our seats. You could tell he was getting a big kick out of the way they made us dress up—he even turned around and straightened Rego's tie. A waiter materialized with two bottles of Tattinger and filled our champagne glasses. I was incredibly nervous and glugged down my first glass in three swallows.

"Okay, first the good news," Simon began earnestly, and I had to lean real close, practically pressing against his wife, to hear him. "You guys are going to make it. How do you like that?"

"I like it," Rego said.

Simon smiled. We all did.

"What's the bad news?" Bobby asked.

"You're going to make it," Simon said again.

"I don't get it." Bobby said.

"You can put out a couple of records. You can sign bad contracts. You can hire accountants and lawyers. And you can get fucked. You'll have your pictures in the magazines. You'll be famous for eleven months. And then you'll be back in Cleveland. Busted."

"He thinks we're from Cleveland too," Bobby said, as in *get a load of this doofus*.

"We're not from Cleveland," I said.

"Where are you from?"

We told him.

"Well, that's nice. Nothing wrong with Cleveland, though. One kid who's doing real well for himself comes from a hick town way up in northern Minnesota, but that's neither here nor there. . . ."

We all knew who he was talking about.

"The important question," Simon continued, "is whether you want to go about this thing right, or make all the mistakes that can possibly be made and lose everything you thought you'd earned."

"We're doing all right so far," Bobby said.

"You haven't done anything yet."

"We're talking to you, aren't we?"

"That's right. And this is your first chance to make a serious mistake. For instance, here's something you probably don't know: this boy here—" Simon gestured at me with a papal thrust of his hand "—this boy, Byron, is the whole band."

That straightened everybody up, especially me. Rego blinked as if a bomb had gone off two inches from his nose. Bobby's jaw dropped. Even Gary went pale.

"That's right," Simon said. "This boy is the whole act. You—" Simon dipped his head at Rego "—you're a good guitar player."

"Thanks a million."

"I could count on both hands and all my toes the guitar players I know in this town who are as good as you are, or better, who don't have a pot to piss in, and never will. You—" Simon nodded at Bobby "—what's your name?"

Bobby told him.

"Bobby," Simon continued, evenly and softly, "drummers at your level of accomplishment are a dime a dozen. And a lot of them are better looking too—"

"Do we have to listen to this?"

"I stink too, huh?" Gary said, in an unusual show of emotion.

"You're a mediocre bass player. Better than you I've seen at a college sock hop."

"Let's go," Bobby said. But nobody moved.

"You want flattery or you want help?" Simon asked. "You want bullshit, it's all over town. They'll pile it so deep you'll think you landed in a Denver feedlot. Now, you can go shopping for a manager. Maybe you'll find one who will tell you the same thing I just did. Maybe you'll find one who won't. He'll be wrong. And sooner or later he'll discover that this kid is the whole act and you three guys will be out on your tushes. Or you can come along on this kid's ride, and take my advice, and make yourselves a tidy sum of money, you know, have a few nice things—"

"Nice things," Bobby said. "Sheesh. . . ."

Two waiters arrived in unison and began sliding plates in front of us.

"I hope you don't mind," Simon said, "but I ordered for us in advance. Saves a lot of aggravation. This is a salmon mousse. I think you'll find it very tasty. The green stuff is a dill sauce."

Rego and the others looked down at their plates as if they were being served humble pie with shit sauce. My appetite wasn't all that great either.

"I'm wondering," Rego looked up at me. "Have you two met privately, you know, before tonight?"

That really hurt, though I could see why he would think such a thing.

"No," I said.

"I thought it was only fair that you all heard what I had to say at the same time," Simon told them.

"Well, you've got a right to your opinions," Rego said. "It's his opinion."

"He saw us play once, for Godsake," Bobby said. "Maybe we were off or something."

"I saw you twice," Simon said.

"Oh," Bobby said.

"So, what's your pitch, Mr. Lewisohn," Rego asked bluntly.

"You sign a personal management contract with me, and I will make you rich and famous." Simon began digging into his appetizer.

"That's it, huh?" Bobby said.

"You want more?"

"I want to know how come, if we're so lousy, you're doing us such a big favor."

"You're ordinary, not lousy. This kid is not ordinary. He's got something special. Incidentally, Byron, you are a lousy guitar player."

"Thanks loads," I said, actually grateful for that.

"Yeah, but how come you don't just sign him and boot us?" Bobby persisted logically.

"You want to play with these guys?" Simon asked me.

"Of course I do! They're the only guys I've ever played with. Look, we're a unit, as far as I'm concerned."

Simon made another papal sweep of the hand to show how I had proved his point. Then, for the first time, Claire weighed in. Her throaty voice had a surprising southern accent.

"You're going to do very well for yourselves, and you're going to be glad that Simon told you the truth right from 'go.' " she said.

"That sounds very decent and all," Bobby said, "but how do we know you won't get rid of us later, when it happens to be more convenient?"

"I can't stand this discussion we're having—" I said.

"We have to talk about it," Gary shot back at me.

"None of these are *my* ideas—"

"Mr. Lewisohn was your idea."

"My idea? We all agreed to come here. Besides, we haven't signed a damn thing."

"That's why we're having this discussion," Gary said wearily.

"Okay then, let's talk."

"We were doing just that," Bobby said, "so shut up, *Byron*, okay?"

"Why don't you try the mousse, fellas," Simon suggested. We all took a forkful at the same time, automatically obeying him. It was like God telling you to be a good boy and eat your mousse.

"Let's leave it this way," Simon said. "Nobody here is inadequate. Whatever decisions are made about the ongoing configuration of the band, personnel changes, who comes, who goes, that'll be up to the group as a whole."

"You wouldn't try to influence it a teensy-weensy bit?" Bobby asked.

"You're all young," Simon said. "Who knows, maybe you'll work hard and get better."

On that note, the waiters reappeared and refilled our champagne glasses. They removed the appetizer plates and brought on the main course, a veal thing stuffed with truffles and asparagus under these little pastry puffs. Simon was a rapid eater, and while he attacked his food, Claire asked us questions about our backgrounds, and commented about what she saw us do at Zelda's, mannerisms she noticed, licks she liked. She was not only quite knowledgeable and perceptive, but she had a way of putting things that was positive.

". . . I love that progression in the song about the animals—" she meant "Peaceable Kingdom" "—at the end where you lift it through all those minors and resolve on the D major . . ." she told Rego.

". . . I just love it when you're down on the floor with that microphone like you were lyin' on a shady riverbank somewhere with the girl you loved . . ." she told me, referring to this shtick I did on "Then She Laughed."

". . . wherever did you get that wonderful suit-jacket?" she asked Bobby.

"Barney's Boys' Town," he said.

"My daddy used to wear suits like that," she said, ignoring his sarcastic crack. "We're from Charleston. He was a tobacco broker."

And so on. She poured on the charm. Between the veal and the dessert, Rego and Simon sparred over the question of Simon's commission, his cut of our earnings, and Simon said 25 percent of everything.

"That's kind of high, isn't it?" Rego said.

"No, it's my standard commission."

"Seems high to me."

"It's not negotiable, son."

The session wound down with Simon saying he'd like to hear our decision by Wednesday, and finally degenerated to small talk, mainly Simon holding forth on the subject of food. That was when we found out that he owned the restaurant. This final disclosure seemed to demoralize the other guys more than any previous shock of the whole, long evening.

They put up a brave front, but I knew they were depressed. And though I felt for their predicament, I was tired of having to buck them up at my own expense. We decided to stop off at the White Horse Tavern, back down in the Village. Nobody said a word in the cab the entire way. It was drizzling out, and the city was one long multicolored neon smear.

Though it was Sunday, the bar was crowded with Village types: old bohos with white beards and Greek fisherman caps, slutty-looking blondes in leotard tops, burnt-out NYU professors on beer drunks, young painters smelling of turpentine and their girls with raincoats and B.O., spades with goatees speaking French—every regular denizen.

I started knocking down double brandies, and after all that champagne I got drunk quickly.

"I'm gon' sign with him," I told the others.

"I thought we were going to shop around," Rego said.

"I don't trust the sonofabitch," Bobby said.

"Then don' sign. I'm gon' sign."

"You're fuckin' hopeless," Bobby said.

"You shut your goddam mouth. I'm sick of your goddam belly-achin'. All I get from the three of you is whining and backtalk, an' I've had it up to here. I'm gon' call him tomorrow morning and tell him to get that contrac' ready. What you do is your business. You wanna come 'long, fine. But I'm through bein' everybody's goddam whipping boy, or crutch, or whatever the hell I am."

They were having a hard time dealing with this display of anger. Nobody said anything.

"You make up your own minds an' lemme know," I told them, and lurched over to the bar for a refill. There was an attractive brunette there chatting with this middle-aged alcoholic poet who lived in the neighborhood. I horned right in on him. Around midnight, I saw Rego and the others skulk out the door. The girl took me back to her place on Mercer Street and gave me a dose of the clap.

In the morning, I went directly to the Manhattan Probate Court and legally changed my name from Peter Greenwald to Byron Jaynes. Around noon, I returned to our house on Grove Street and called Simon Lewisohn's secretary, making an appointment. The four of us took a cab up to his office. It was a posh brownstone on 64th Street between Park and Madison. By four o'clock that day, an act to be known as Byron Jaynes and the Romantics was signed to a two-year personal management contract with Simon Lewisohn. For all our squabbling and fears, we didn't even think to engage a lawyer to so much as read it over.

Speaking of lawyers, that same Monday, almost exactly a year to the day since I walked out of the home I grew up in, my parents were quietly granted a divorce. My mother moved to an apartment on Sutton Place. My father got hitched to one of his deputy prosecutors, an ambitious Wellesley bimbo (class of '62) and Yale Law go-getter named Sheila Prentice, whom dad had been schtupping on the sly since the week after he hired her. The house on Radnor Road had a realtor's sign planted on the lawn and the property was snapped up by another golfing ninny of the medical persuasion.

---

Byron switched off the machine. He leaned back in his chair and his chin slumped down to his chest. "You think this is getting anywhere?" he asked after a long and disturbing silence.

"I think so. Yes."

"It's me I've been talking about, right?"

"Yes. It's you."

"Incredible," he said quietly and shook his head. Then he did something which startled me because it was my first glimpse through a crack in the edifice thrown up by the outer Byron to protect the bewildered creature deep within. He began to cry, not boisterously, but with a silent, stolid letting of tears. I didn't even know that he was weeping until I saw the first tear fall on his yellow scarf. He kept it up for a short time, then sighed and it was over.

"You'd better run along now," he said.

"I could stick around, if you—"

"No!" he said angrily. "I have things to do. Go on."

I gathered the equipment together and got up. The black cat, awakened by the scuff of my chair against the plank floor, opened its yellow eyes warily and then yawned with a shocking display of pink mouth and white fangs.

"I'll come by tomorrow, at the usual time," I assured him from the door.

"I'd like that," he said.

"Well . . . good-night."

The cat curled up again, burying its head in its own dark fur. Byron turned his head away from me, deliberately, I felt, as though he didn't want to see me standing there when he looked back. I left him alone.

I was, perhaps, a quarter of a mile down the dirt road in the Saab when a feeling of irresistible curiosity seized me, and then it was my turn to do a rather strange thing. I pulled the car over to the side of the road, got out, closed the door carefully, and began creeping up through the rain and darkness to the house. Only the feel of gravel under the soles of my topsiders informed me that I was still on the road, so completely did the moon-obliterating storm obscure it. A lamp went on in the front parlor of the distant house. I stole forward.

My hair was soaked and water began seeping under the collar of my wool shirt and down my neck. I was about to return to the car in shame when music suddenly welled from the house. I could not recognize exactly what sort of music it was until I reached the lawn, and then I could make out the chords of a broken-winded organ. A window cast a yellow trapezoid of light on the weeds. I crept closer, staying in the shadows, and peered inside.

He sat with his back toward me, his body shifting to the left and right as he pumped the foot pedals, the organ's ragged bellows producing chords with a quality as pure as heartbreak. Then he lifted his head, and in a voice as plaintive as the instrument, he began to sing these words of an old Negro spiritual:

> *Oh, I can't . . . stay away*
> *I can't . . . stay away*
> *I can't . . . stay away*
> *I wish I had died in Egypt land*
>
> *Children grumbled on the way*
> *Wish I had died in Egypt land*

*Children stumbled in the clay*
*Wish I had died in Egypt land*

*Oh, I can't . . . stay away*
*I can't . . . stay away*
*I can't . . . stay away*
*I wish I had died in Egypt land*

# CHAPTER 6

RS: If you could start all over again, what would you do differently?

BJ: I think I would have tried to remain more aware of the fact that we pass this way but once.

—The *Rolling Stone* Interview with Byron Jaynes, 1968

I could hear the chain saw's stuttering whine long before I got to the house. Byron was in the side yard, wielding the noisy machine against the trunk of his dying elm tree. A length of rope was looped through the crotch of the tree, about forty feet up, and the two ends dangled to the ground. When he saw me pull up, he put the chain saw down and limped through the weeds to the driveway. It was a brilliantly clear day, the sky spanking clean, as though the rainstorm had passed across it like a gigantic vacuum cleaner, sweeping away every imperfection. The temperature was in the sixties, cool and invigorating.

"I hope you ate your Wheaties today, my boy," he said cheerfully. "Come, give me a hand with this."

One could easily size up the task he had in mind, and I balked somewhat shy of the job site.

"Come on," he said, "it's not going to fall on your head."

"Do you know what you're doing?"

"Uh, yes and no. I know what I *want* to do. We're going to take this tree down. Now, as to the means I've selected, I don't know if we're dealing in established technique. But I've given it a lot of thought and I believe our chances of success are right up there in the high percentiles."

"So the idea is to get the tree down without letting it fall on the house."

"You're really quick on your feet today, Sears."

"I don't know, Byron. It's an awful big tree. How did you get that rope up there?"

"With a ladder."

"Oh. Before you started cutting."

"That's right. Then again, if you were making a Laurel and Hardy movie, you'd do it the other way around. But this seemed more, I don't know, scientific."

"So we each grab one end of the rope and pull?"

"Don't tell me you've done this before?"

"I've never done this before. What if it falls in our direction?"

"Okay now. We're finally getting to the tricky part. I figure we have, oh, three to seven seconds, roughly, to get out of the way. Once she really starts going, just drop your end of the rope and run like hell."

I rolled my eyes.

"Sears, some guys can run half the length of a football field in five seconds."

"Why not call a professional?"

"It's too late for that, Rick. I've taken matters into my own hands. She's all set up to go. Come on."

We approached the tree. Byron handed me one of the lines.

"Hey, you're doing fine," he said. "Now, let's sort of walk these ropes back, and don't take up any slack until I say so."

We walked the lines across the yard, fanning out slightly.

"Okay," Byron said. "Now, you'll want to peel off to the left, and I'll scram this way, to the right. Got it?"

"Yes."

"Ready?"

"Yes."

"Okay. Take up your slack."

I did.

"You got it nice and tight?"

"Yeah."

"Okay, hit it!"

I pulled with all my might. There was a sharp crack. I dropped the rope and ran like hell toward the road, then realized that nothing had happened. Byron was lying on his back in the weeds. My end of the rope had jerked more than halfway through the crotch of the tree, dangling far above the ground.

"That was real punk," Byron said. "What'd you let go for?"

"I thought she was coming down."

"Well, don't just stand there. Get your rope."

I crept cautiously up to the tree, but the end of the rope was clearly way beyond my reach. I glanced back at Byron, who was sitting down.

"This is another fine mess you've gotten me into," he said.

I scratched my head.

He got up, limped over to the side of the house, and lifted an aluminum extension ladder out of the weeds. He jammed it into the ground forcefully, leaned it against the trunk, climbed up to the top rung, grabbed the rope, and brought it down to me. Then he kicked the ladder out of the way.

"Let's try a little teamwork this time, huh?" he said.

We walked the lines back out.

"Once again, with feeling. Take up your slack. Ready?"

"Yo!"

"Okay, hit it!"

I slung the rope over my shoulder, dug my heels into the ground, and really put my weight into it. There were several sharp cracks, then an ominous groan. Suddenly, the rope went limp.

"Run, you dummy!"

I was in a kind of thrall. There was something hypnotic about the arc of all that descending wood. It was like being in a dream where you can't scream, only in this case I couldn't get my feet moving.

"Run, goddammit, Sears!"

Suddenly, I was sprinting toward the road. I felt a powerful whoosh of air as the tree came down behind me, and then a crash that sent tremors through the sod. I lunged forward and did a shoulder roll. Silence followed, then I heard Byron hooting victoriously on the other side.

"We did it! Goddammit, we did it, Sears! Yahoo!"

He limped around the fallen giant and helped me to my feet.

"You did a hell of job, my boy," he said, helping to dust off my wool shirt, "and for being such a good worker, I have a special surprise for you."

"What's that?"

"It wouldn't be a surprise if I told you, now would it. Go get the equipment."

---

Byron's surprise turned out to be "a picnic." That is, he made four peanut butter and jelly sandwiches, packed them with a quart of orange juice and a bag of Oreos, and took me on a hellish trek into his woods. We bushwhacked through the brambles for half an hour, then arrived at a pine-covered ledge overlooking a brook. As usual, it had taken an effort to keep pace with him.

Byron took out the sandwiches and carefully unwrapped the tinfoil. I noticed that he ate his sandwich like a kid, first nibbling the crust all the way around. He also pried open his Oreos and licked off the white creme.

"This is fun, isn't it?"

"Oh, yes," I agreed. "Quite a lark."

"You didn't like your sandwich?"

"I adore PB and J."

"Did you know there's more protein in peanut butter than an equal amount of baloney?"

"I didn't know that."

"Well, there is. And it's better for you."

Byron crept over to the edge of the overhang on his hands and knees and signaled for me to join him.

"See those shadows down there?" he pointed to a dark pool, perhaps ten feet below us. The water was a deep russet color from tannin, and fallen leaves bobbled on the lazy current. Deep below the surface I could make out two shadowy, undulating forms. "Trout," Byron said. "They've been lurking down in that same hole all summer. Adam and Eve."

"Do you fish?" I inquired.

He glanced at me, scowling. "No," he said. "Do you?"

"I took it up recently. Our place is on a pond."

"Well, don't you sneak back here and catch these two. This is a preserve, pal." He broke off a piece of Oreo and chucked it into the pool. One of the dark shapes rose liquidly to the surface, inspected the morsel and let it float away. "Catherine was a fanatic about it. She thought she was Ernest Hemingway or something."

"I didn't know she was a writer."

"She wasn't."

"Oh."

"She just thought she was Ernest Hemingway."

Byron crept back from the edge and picked up the tape recorder. "You got batteries in here?"

"Yup."

"Then let's proceed."

## The Life of Byron Jaynes—Tape 5

I was telling you about Simon, right?

*You signed with him.*

Yes, I signed with him, and then everything changed overnight. For starters, we never played Zelda's again. I felt bad about shafting Frank Lemanczyk like that, but we didn't have any contract or written agreement with him and Simon had other plans for us which he put into effect immediately. First, he intended to showcase us and get a bunch of labels bidding competitively to jack the price up.

We opened for John Lee Hooker on two dates in the middle of April at the Café Au Go-Go downtown. A week later we played the fieldhouse at Stonybrook, the big state college out on Long Island, opening for the Butterfield Blues Band, who were opening for Simon and Garfunkel. It was the biggest audience we ever played for, several thousand kids. They had no idea who we were, but we ended up playing two encores, which really pissed off the other acts. They told us we were "behaving unprofessionally." It's true that the last thing a headliner wants is for the warm-up act to steal his thunder. I guess it shows how much we knew at that point: less than we thought. Anyway, we didn't make that mistake again.

Back in the city, in May, we opened for Tim Hardin at the Vanguard. Simon arranged for half the audience to be A and R men from all the majors. After the Saturday night show, he threw a party for us at the Dom, this grundgy old Polish union hall over in the East Village where Warhol had been staging his Exploding Plastic Inevitable show, and it seemed like every freak in the city showed up. I got drunk and started spouting the most preposterous malarky to every newshound who steered me into a corner—heaping on the old pseudo-philosophy of life, talking in Zen riddles. They took down every syllable.

I left the place with this towering Swedish girl, a real hulking brute of a blonde bombshell, who took me home to her apartment off Astor Place. I had bruises over my kidneys for weeks after that.

The next morning I woke up hideously hungover. My valkyrie woke up even more out of sorts than me, and through the open door to the bathroom I observed her shooting up between her toes.

"You sick too?" she asked.

"Horribly," I said.

She held up the needle like it was a lollypop.

"No thanks," I said.

She laid out a neat little line on a hand mirror and came over to the bed.

"You try," she said.

I blew the line up my nose. I regret to tell you that it was heavenly. The cab trip home was a magic carpet ride. What a mistake.

We got our record contract, all right, and in short order. Jerry Zuckerman signed us to Gemini. Atlantic, Columbia, and MCA had pursued us hotly, but as Simon used to say, "Money talks and bullshit walks." They paid us a quarter million in advances, which was just about unheard of at that time. Simon set up a publishing company for my songs, Believable Music, Inc. Other groups were starting to cover my stuff. The Cyrkle did "She Sends Me." The Creepers cut "Cold River." We went into the studio at the beginning of June and spent a month completing *Rising Son*, with Ed Teasdale producing. Two things occurred during that frenetic month: I was replaced as an instrumentalist; and the U.S. Army called me in for an audition.

My replacement as guitarist for those *Rising Son* sessions was Steven Spagnola, one of the most curious individuals I have ever met. I guess you know the story of how he entered the University of Chicago at fifteen as a math whiz, and how he learned his chops personally from Elvin Bishop, and surpassed him as a pure technician within a year.

Spag was still eighteen the day Simon brought him over to the Gemini studio, a lost, wan-looking child with hair down below his shoulders and harlequin pants and elf boots. Your first impulse was to take him down to the vet's office for distemper shots. He'd been doing studio work for about a year already, a lot of it without credits because he'd been too young to join the union. We had heard of him. People talked about him because he was so good, and so eccentric. The problem was the way Simon brought him around. He just marched in with his great big arm draped around Spag's narrow shoulders and said, "I'd like you all to meet a new Romantic."

Well, Rego came prowling out from behind his isolation screen and eyed the kid like a mountain lion circling a chipmunk.

"What does he play?" Rego asked, but you could see the kid was carrying a guitar case.

"You play, what? Nine instruments, Steven?"

"Mostly guitar," Spag said and smiled meekly.

"This is a personnel change!" Bobby cried, "A goddam personnel change!"

"No, Bobby," Simon said quietly, "this is an addition, not a change."

"We don't need him."

"That's what you think," Simon said. "Steven, why don't you plug in over there."

The kid took out his guitar, an unbelievably beat-up old Gibson that looked like somebody took a Rototiller to it, and plugged the jack into Rego's amp. Then, without so much as a word, he played five minutes of the most stupifying guitar I ever heard in my life. When he was finished, all Bobby could say was "Who's paying him?"

"You boys are. He's on salary."

Of course, that hit Rego where it hurt, in the old pocketbook. "We don't need him," he said dryly.

"I'll pay his salary, for Godsake," I said.

"He doesn't even know the tunes."

"Hey, you're overdubbing most of my guitar anyway. Give him a try."

"He's got a photographic memory," Simon said matter-of-factly. I don't think Simon knew how preposterous that sounded until Gary laughed sardonically. "He hears something once and *zappo*, it's engraved on his brain," Simon explained. "Isn't that right, Steven? He's a genius."

"Are you a genius, kid?" Bobby asked him.

"I don't know," Spag said.

"Take my word for it," Simon said. "If I say you're a genius, then you have it on good authority."

"What's going on down there?" Ed Teasdale asked over the mike, from the booth.

"Nothing," Simon told him.

"That's what I thought. Three hundred and fifty dollars an hour, Mr. Lewisohn. Let's hop to, eh gentlemen?" Ed said, a Gemini man all the way. On the other hand, the only times I ever saw Simon act even the tiniest bit insecure was in the recording studio, where he wasn't able totally to control or dominate the situation.

"I'm going now, Steven. You play nice for these boys, okay?"

"Thank you, Mr. Lewisohn."

And that was how poor, amazing, doomed Spag came into our midst. It was less like having another musician around than acquiring an exquisite musical instrument that happened to live and breathe. From that first day, even with all the crap the other guys heaped on him, he fit himself effortlessly into our music, did whatever we asked, and then added little touches that *were* marks of a true genius—like the slide riff on "The Stranger Will Depart," the fiddle on "Light Years from Home," and that beautiful mandolin solo on "Let Patience Have Her Perfect Work."

The trouble was, beyond being able to express himself musically, the kid was practically a mute. After three weeks with us in the studio, the only vocabulary he seemed to possess was "yes," "no," and "I don't know."

At the end of that first day, for example, I asked him how much Simon had arranged to pay him.

"I don't know," he said.

"Didn't you discuss it with him?"

"Yes."

"Well, come on, how much?"

"Hundred and fifty."

"A day?"

"I don't know."

"You know. Tell me."

"A week."

"A hundred and fifty a week! You agreed to that?"

"I don't know."

You see what I mean? He was exasperating. I raised it to $400 right then and there. All he said was "okay." Not that I wanted him to drop down and kiss my feet. He was just totally uninterested in material things. For instance, he was a decent-looking kid, but you

never met someone so unconcerned about his appearance. You had
to remind him to take a bath. Eventually, I made Simon's secretary
take down his clothing sizes and buy him stuff from time to time.
He never took anything to the cleaners. He lived alone in the most
depressing studio apartment on West 4th Street until the day he
died, and when they collected his things, they found uncashed checks
amounting to over $80,000 in his drawers.

Obviously we wouldn't have kept him around if he hadn't been
such a superlative musician. Without him, *Rising Son* would have
been a better-than-average debut album, musically, and maybe I'm
even being conceited to say that, but certainly not exceptional. Spag
did for our sound what Ray Manzarek did for the Doors the following year. He sold Morrison's songs as much as Morrison did. Poor
Spag. When I think of him, I think of a streetlight burning on a
dead-end road. It illuminates a foresaken little patch of the world
for a while, then flickers out, and nobody notices. It makes me so
sad just to think about it. Shit.

*What about the army?*

Huh. . . ? Oh, you mean my physical? I received my notice to
report at the end of June. It was one of those things you don't think
about, for some stupid reason, and then *blammo!* it whacks you over
the head. I should have known better.

The war was getting completely out of control and dropping out
of college was like a one-way ticket to Vietnam. Rego was already 4-
F because of his eyes. Bobby and Gary hadn't been called yet. Anyway, I got this damn telegram and I freaked out. I took a cab up to
Simon's office, barged right in, and dropped the telegram on his
desk.

"What am I going to do? I said. I was shaking.

"I've got a doctor," Simon said calmly.

"W-what does he do, this doctor?"

"He writes a letter stating that you're a homosexual."

"Aw, Simon."

"It's the easiest way, son."

"I don't like having a thing like that on paper. It could come back
and haunt you."

"When you've got a Viet Cong bullet between your eyes, you
don't get a chance to be haunted," he said. "Go see this guy."

So I paid a series of calls on Henry Klein, M.D., a psychiatrist.

Anyway, the week of my physical rolled around and I just couldn't do it Simon's way. There were plenty of booklets out telling you how to beat the draft physical, and actually, I had a pretty good head start after spending a whole month in the studio. We'd been speeding during the sessions, and I was drinking whiskey to take the edge off the speed. Then I'd come home and snort some smack to get a few hours sleep. The last week, I went full bore for the drugs. I started popping smack with a needle. I had slipped beyond the point where it was under my control. I began to need it.

I stayed up for 72 hours straight before the physical. I had sugar under my fingernails for the urine test. My blood must have been composed of equal parts of alcohol, methadrine, and smack. I was a longhaired babbling idiot with tracks on my arm and I flunked the physical with flying colors. I never handed in Klein's letter.

The limo was waiting for me on Whitehall Street when I was done and they poured me inside. Dr. Klein was in the back seat with Claire. He gave me an injection of some sort. I slept fitfully as the big car headed up to the Catskills. I remember the Tappan Zee Bridge, the sun glinting off the river, the city shining like Oz so far away between the green bluffs. It was like viewing the world through six inches of lime Jell-o. I remember the smell of Claire's perfume, the hills around Tamberlane, the large, clean room, the smell of grass and pine trees.

I was sicker than a dog for a week, like one of those tropical deliriums from the World War II movies combined with the blind staggers. There was a nurse, a blue-haired lady, who was a Yankee fan. About all I remember from those first two days up there was the continuous sound of Phil Rizzuto's voice: "Holy Cow!" I was so weak I couldn't even hold onto a magazine. The withdrawal was terrible, and I had just a little bitty habit. Then, one bright summer morning, it was over. I woke up feeling like a human being again. The nurse, Gladys, helped me practice walking around the room. Right before the Yankee game came on, she let me go downstairs.

There was a whirl of activity going on down there. It looked like moving day or something. Crates were being carted into the house. A crew was setting up a striped tent outside. Caterers were busy in the kitchen, wrangling with hams, turkeys, and haunches of beef. Claire was there, in a sarong and a bikini top, directing all this activity like Leonard Bernstein conducting the Philharmonic.

"Why, Byron! You are a sight for sore eyes! Come here and let me look at you." She spun me around the way you might inspect a younger brother to see if he's grown over the summer. "You look very much intact."

"I feel a lot better. Is Simon here?"

"Simon is in his gym. I'm afraid you might find him a trifle cross this morning, but remember, he has your best interests in mind."

"What's going on here?"

"We're having a party tonight."

"Oh."

"In your honor."

"Oh. . . ! Holy Cow!" Phil Rizzuto had subverted my brain. "Why?" I asked.

"Why?" she echoed me. "You are a silly boy."

"How did you know I'd even be fit?"

"Because Henry said you would be, and he is a very good doctor. Now, run along to Simon."

I had to ask a maid for directions. The house was quite large, about twice as big as our place on Radnor Road, kind of a bastardized French château style. The living room was about sixty feet long with a wall of french doors leading out to a broad terrace. There was a large fieldstone fireplace on the other side, with swirly art-nouveau andirons. You could see they had knocked down several walls and modernized the place. A great floating wing of a staircase soared upward and you could see a stained-glass window shimmering with red and blue light. Factotums came and went from every direction, carrying vacuum cleaners, flowers, chafing dishes, cartons of liquor. I was absolutely astonished that they were doing all this for me.

Simon's gym was in the farthest wing of the house. When I came in, he was bench-pressing about 250 pounds on a barbell, wearing cut-off jeans and a green Jets jersey with the number 12 on it. A reel-to-reel tape deck was playing across the room. It was a band I never heard before and they were singing one of my songs, "Janey." Simon rested the barbell in the stanchion.

"Hi," I said warily.

"Feeling better?"

"Lots. Thanks."

"That's good. That's very good. Shall we go for a stroll, you and I? Are you up to it?"

"I'd like a stroll. Who's the band?"

"They call themselves the Soul Survivors. S-O-U-L. Get it? I'm thinking of signing them. What's your opinion?"

"I don't know whether you should sign them or not."

"Don't you like the way they sound?"

"It's okay. How'd they get the song?"

"I gave it to them. It hits, you get a royalty, they get a royalty. Nice little business. Shall we?"

Simon held the door for me and I walked outside for the first time in a week. It was hot out. A swimming pool was set in a stone patio at a level below the formal terrace. Beyond the pool was an upward-sloping back lawn, acres and acres, like a beginners' ski hill in its summer greenery, with groves of trees that culminated in woods at the top. Someone was mowing it with a tractor. Off to the right, the tent crew workers were pounding in stakes with wooden mallets. Beyond them, others were setting up a stage out of folding portable risers.

"Are we supposed to play tonight?" I asked, nervously jumping to conclusions.

"No, you're not supposed to. You can if you want. There'll be no shortage of egos, I assure you."

We crossed the lawn, then Simon led me up a cool, graveled path through the piney woods. It led to a plain wooden building painted the same dark green as the pines. You could smell horses. Inside, a couple of bare bulbs were burning up in the rafters, but it still seemed awfully dim. The horses huffed and shuffled in their stalls.

"Richmond. . . ?" Simon called.

A thick-set, middle-aged black man came out of a back room. He wore glasses that were taped together at the bridge. I couldn't help feeling that I knew him from somewhere.

"Did Mrs. Lewisohn come up today?" Simon asked him.

"No. Not today."

"Well, then, better turn them out. She's got her hands full now. Oh, come over here and say hello to a new act. Byron Jaynes, Richmond Petty."

"Nice to meet you, young man," he said coolly.

I was stupified. We exchanged pleasantries about the weather and the country air. Richmond went over to a stall and clipped a lead shank to a big gray horse's halter and took him out the rear door to the pasture.

"*That* was Richmond Petty?" I asked Simon.

"The one and only," Simon said.

"What happened to him?"

Simon looked at me for a moment before he answered.

"He's got strung out on smack, Byron," he said, and strolled out the rear door. Richmond came back and turned out two more horses. They cantered across the pasture and joined their buddy at the far end where he was grazing in the sunshine.

"I know you're pissed off at me," I said.

Simon hung his arms over the white fence and stared at the beautiful green fields.

"I'm concerned," he said. "You'll be going on the road soon. There'll be temptations. I'm concerned about those temptations."

"I had to beat the army."

"You could have done it my way."

"I didn't want to do that. I told you—"

"So now there's a document on file somewhere that says you're a whacko and a heroin addict. That's not as bad as pretending to be a swish for a couple of hours?"

"I don't know."

"Because with the heroin you weren't pretending. See? It wasn't make-believe. That's what concerns me. You think there's pressure now? You don't even have an album on the racks yet. A habit's one thing. I mean, God forbid, it's bad enough. What happens if you get caught holding? Or making a buy? Huh?"

"I know it would be bad news."

"Bad news?" Simon laughed. "It could very easily be the end. Ask Richmond about the four years he did at Lewisburg. Ask him what happened to his career. I'm a good personal manager, but I'm not Merlin the Magician. After he got out of the joint in '64, I couldn't sell him to a sickle-cell benefit. You can't count the ways it's possible to fall on your ass in this business, Byron. Jerry Lee Lewis could have been bigger than Elvis. He had more natural talent and he was a better showman. This is what comes from a lack of self-restraint. Look at Elvis. He hasn't made a decent record in ten years. He makes hula movies, for Godsake. The guy's a clown. Grossman tells me that his boy is gobbling down this LSD shit like it was M & Ms. What a waste! You see, Byron, the hell of it is that you can make all the right moves, respect yourself and your talent, and still wind up on your ass."

"Sounds hopeless."

"No, it's not hopeless. It's goddamned tough, son. You don't have to go out of your way to fuck it up, and there's only so much I can do to protect you. Let's leave it at this: I'm available anytime. You have a problem? You come to me and we'll find some intelligent way to solve it. You're on the road? I'm a phone call and a plane ride away."

He felt his pockets, then went over to the stable door.

"Hey, Richmond, you got a dime?"

"A dime, Mr. Lewisohn?"

"That's right."

Simon returned a moment later and pressed the coin into my hand.

"You hang onto this," he said.

"Okay."

He tousled my hair.

"Stick around and chat with Richmond," he said, then walked back through the stable, leaving me hanging on the fence. The prospect of chatting with Richmond Petty about what it was like to be a total washout did not fill me with joy. What do you say to a guy who goes from being "Soul Brother Supreme" to a goddam stableboy. I was going to try and sneak away around the building when he emerged from the gloom and joined me at the fence.

"They're beautiful horses," I said. "What are their names?"

"John, Paul. The sorrel is Ringo."

"What happened to George?"

"He was a bad horse. Kicked old Simon good one time, so he got rid of him. I hear you been dancing with the devil."

"Who from?"

"Who do you think?"

"You have a lecture for me, right?"

"Yeah, I got a lecture for you. A real short one. Look at me, young son."

I did.

"You lookin' at a dead man that's still alive," he said. He started chuckling in a low, throaty way, and soon he was squealing with laughter. "Good luck, boy." He backed into the stable, laughing and hooting all the way. I could hear him halfway down the gravel path.

About eight-thirty that evening I watched from my bedroom window upstairs as a steady procession of cars began plying up Simon's long driveway: black Cadillac limos, a whole fleet of Rollses, flashy sports cars, Alphas, Jensens, Astin-Martins, a yellow Lotus, a cherry-red Stingray, and many more turned up the country lane onto Simon's property and parked under the maple trees on his polo-field-sized front lawn. The characters who emerged from these sumptuous machines looked like extras from a movie lot where films set in a dozen different periods and locales were being shot at the same time. They had on denims, brocades, silks, caftans, frogged military tunics, embroidered jerkins, gauzy gowns, jodhpurs, cossack hats, buckskin jackets, Flash Gordon leathers, leopard-skin capes, and they hurried up to the house in excited clusters. From the rear of the house, all muffled and warpy from the distance, you could hear electric guitars tuning up, speakers crackling, and a drummer thwacking his equipment. A squawk of feedback made me shut the window.

I knocked back a tumbler of Bromo-Seltzer and looked at myself in the mirror, trying to discover a consistent impression to give these important strangers. I was even thinner than the year before. When I sucked in my cheeks I looked like a malaria victim. I had on white pants and a white shirt with a black velvet vest. I remember looking at my image in the mirror and being amazed that I was still so young. Then I went downstairs.

They were swarming out on the terrace and the lawn like colorful moths. Waiters in red jackets swooped around balancing trays of champagne glasses and canapés. The sky above the hilltop glowed pink and the warm air was full of fireflies. The band had begun playing. I recognized the song from the radio: "*. . . I love that dirty water . . .*"

Claire looked beautiful in a silvery gown. She had Clive Davis on one suntanned arm and Jerry Zuckerman on the other.

"This is my Next Big Thing," Zuckerman told Davis, and I shook Clive's hand.

"I hear you've made a very nice album," he said.

"Nice!" Zuckerman said. "We're shipping gold on a debut album and he says 'nice.' Eat your heart out."

Just then I spotted Rego down by the tent where the caterers had set up the bar and buffet. I excused myself and jogged down from the terrace.

"Boy, am I glad to see you," I said.

"You look like a cadaver."

"Hey, I beat the army."

"I guess it was worth it then, huh?"

"Hey, you'll never believe who Simon's got working as his stable-boy here," I said.

"Who?"

"Guess."

Rego made a face. "Nikita Khrushschev."

"No, really."

"God, I don't know. Why don't you just tell me."

"Richmond Petty."

"I thought he was dead."

I suddenly felt one of those warpy twangs in my spine that I always associated with my acid experience. For a couple of seconds I felt disoriented and I started to panic.

"Are you okay?"

"I need a drink."

I tripped over to the bar and ordered a double scotch and glugged it down. Boy, I was really shaking! Rego had seen me get like this before, but I don't think he knew what to make of it. Anyway, after a minute or so the liquor began to take effect and I felt better.

"Are the others here?" I asked.

"Yes. Simon sent a limo."

"That's good." In fact, I could see Bobby now over by the bandstand. He was talking to Butterfield's drummer. "Is Spag here too?" I asked.

"We couldn't get hold of him."

"Did you try, Rego?"

"He doesn't have a phone. I'm telling you, that kid is—I don't know—he needs a caretaker or something."

"You could have stopped by his apartment—"

"Look, isn't that Donovan over there?"

I looked where Rego was pointing and sure enough, there was Donovan himself, standing about fifty feet away talking to Larry Hardesty, the bass player from Seabird. Donovan had two girls with him, one on each side. They were both wearing the same kind of white linen outfits as Donovan, and they were identical twins.

"I wonder what he's doing here?" Rego said.

"Him? It's us I wonder about."

Rego glanced back at me with one of those warm smiles from the old days. I realized it had been months since I'd seen it.

"Hey, I've got an idea," I said. "You want to go for a ride across the Hudson River?"

For a second I didn't think he understood. Then he said, "Oh, no."

"Come on. Walk around the old campus. It'll be great. Nobody'll be around this time of year."

"You're getting sentimental in your old age."

"It'd be fun."

"Maybe some other time."

"We could reminisce about our origins."

"Some other time . . . Byron," he said.

At that point, I gave up trying to coax him into a side-trip to Beal. But I was still in a nostalgic mood.

"Hey, did you ever think in your wildest dreams that we'd come this far?" I asked him.

He looked wistful suddenly, gazing out at the lawn and all the pretty young people fluttering around. "I thought we were getting damn good. I knew you were good. I didn't need Simon to tell me that. But we can still flop, you along with the rest of us. That's why we better enjoy this party while it's here."

"Aw, we're not going to flop."

"Everybody does, sooner or later."

"Not everybody—"

"Everybody. They either fall on their face right from the start, or they sell out and pervert whatever they started out doing. Either way, it's the same thing."

"I had no idea you were such a fatalist."

"I'm a realist, that's all."

"Remember two years ago? How we stayed up all night long talking about the future of rock and roll?"

"Yes."

"You weren't so fatalistic back then."

"I was different then. So were you, Pete."

He looked back at me with this sort of cracked expression on his face, and for the first time I saw how unhappy he really was. But we didn't get a chance to talk about it anymore because Simon and Claire suddenly materialized.

"May we borrow him for a while?" she asked Rego. You could tell he knew he was being snubbed. It was always me they made a big deal out of.

"Sure," he said politely. "We were just reminiscing."

"I'll see you later," I told him.

Simon and Claire then proceeded to haul me around and introduce me to everyone in sight—to Ahmet Ertegun, the president of Atlantic Records, and his wife; to John Sebastian and Joe Butler of the Spoonful; Lonnie Dart of the Scoundrels; John and Michelle Phillips; Peter Asher of Peter and Gordon; Paul Stookey; Danny Kalb, the lead guitarist of the Blues Project, who I'd already met when we opened for them at the Café Au Go-Go in April; Sandy Lockhart, the English chanteuse who had once been a girlfriend of Mick Jagger's; to Richard Goldstein, the *Voice* rock critic; Paul Morrisey, Warhol's house movie director; Lou Adler, the producer and impressario; John Cale of the Velvet Underground; to beautiful, tiny Christy White of Seabird; Marva Faith ("Sister Soul"); Gerry Goffin, who wrote about half the songs you used to hear on the radio, along with his wife, Carole King, who hadn't started her career as a performer yet; to Billy Joe Dean, who peaked in '65 with "Swampfire" and who would be dead inside of a year after running a hose from the exhaust pipe into the cockpit of his gold T-bird; to Scott Muni, one of the most powerful disc jockeys in the country; to Eddie Holland of the Holland-Dozier-Holland songwriting team; Mitch Wiley, the Midnight Creepers' crazy drummer, who went beserk in the Electric Circus that fall and wounded three people with a .22-caliber pistol; to Alexis Mayday, originator of "The Shout"; to Smokey Robinson; to Snuff Garret, another producer; to Phil Ochs, already pretty swollen from all the booze; to Huey Rush, Walter Leslie, and Tom Riddle of The Ghosts; to Jac Holzman of Elektra, the up-and-coming label; to Riley Parker, the legendary studio guitarist; to Neil Sedaka, Ike and Tina Turner, Sam Lay, Eddie Montgomery, Junior Ransom, Teddy Livingston, Duane Crocker, Rusty Means, Ray Kramer, Randy Orloff, Michael Azakian, Donna Withers, Steve Katz, Al Kooper—every musician or singer with bands on the way up that year—and to Donovan, who told me he had listened to a tape of "Peaceable Kingdom" and wanted to cover it on his next album. I was in a daze.

Besides all these performers and creative types, there were dozens of corporate bigwigs—from Gemini, our label; some of Clive Davis's Columbia people; Don Kirshner, the rock show producer;

Albert Grossman, who lived a few mountains away over in Bears-
ville; several club owners from the city; a whole clutch of freelance
writers; and an untold number of girlfriends, wives, and party girls.

Not everyone was pleasant. There was that sense of rivalry among
so many young musicians that made for instant friction. Or maybe
egomania is more like it. Junior Ransom looked at my hand like it
was unclean. Quite a few of the others had no idea who I was, and
they didn't hide it too well, either. I guess it was just another party
to them. All in all, it was embarrassing to be hauled around like that
and I was relieved when the grand tour ended up at the bar. Simon,
meanwhile, had been buttonholed by Don Kirshner back at the
swimming pool, and Claire left my side when some crisis in the
kitchen erupted, and suddenly I was alone, with no one paying the
slightest bit of attention to me, which was fine.

I convinced the bartender to let me have a whole bottle of Johnny
Walker and then I slipped past the party's outer perimeter, up the
swooping lawn to the top of the hill, just shy of where the woods
began, and settled down in the cool grass with my back up against
a birch tree.

Seabird was onstage now and Christy White was striking defiant
poses and joking around with the crowd while Randy Orloff and
Michael Azakian finished tuning up. Somebody tried to pass her a
joint from down below, and when she bent over to take it, one of
her breasts flopped out of the loose camisole she was wearing. I
could see it from way up on the hill. She even hammed it up for a
while, pretending not to notice, then "discovering" the mishap and
modestly tucking it back into place. You could tell, even back then,
that she was a good actress, and the crowd ate it up.

But they had a very tight, clean act musically, as professional as
anyone, and when she was through with her shenanigans, Orloff
started strumming his guitar, Rusty Means fired a machine-gun burst
on his drums, and Christy started belting out "Lost in the City."

From where I sat, the music echoed off the house so that the band
sounded like they were playing through a giant reverb. "Lost in the
City" was not a particularly danceable tune, and one party girl down
in front of the bandstand was trying to entice someone into doing
the Watusi with her without any success, so she took her top off,
imitating Christy—or trying to—and got one of the silver-haired
corporation boys out there, twisting and frooging. I saw somebody
get pushed into the swimming pool. Above the house, a light plane

beat steadily into the horns of a crescent moon and I wondered if the pilot could see this big party going on from up there.

I was pouring myself another drink when something rustled the bushes behind me. Claire had mentioned a bear rooting through the garbage, and I jumped to my feet expecting a face-to-face confrontation right out of the *Field and Stream* this-happened-to-me department. But it was only a girl, and she was equally startled to find me crouching in her path brandishing a whiskey bottle. For a moment we just stared at each other, and then she said, "Did you get a good look?"

"No."

"I bet."

I couldn't help it, but I started laughing. She was still crouched over waiting to be assaulted.

"You look like you could use a drink."

"No, thank you."

"It would calm you down."

"I'm perfectly calm," she said and finally straightened up.

She was a very pretty girl. But Catherine always looked different, from one moment to the next, and even though I could describe her features, it was always hard to gather a final, dependable impression of her, because every time she shifted her head an inch, or the light or her expression changed, she became a different person. I'll say this much for her: you never saw a moodier goddam person in your life.

She was about five-two, with long auburn hair. That night she was wearing a plain white T-shirt with Franz Liszt's picture on it, and a black skirt with red ballet slippers. I noticed immediately that we were both dressed in black and white. It made a strong impression on me, the way coincidences sometimes do. Anyway, you could see her nipples very clearly through the T-shirt, on each side of Franz Liszt's head, and it was funny, in a way, because it made him look like he was wearing headphones.

She wore her hair parted to one side, with a little girl's blue plastic barrette holding it in place. She had a black ribbon tied around her neck with a small cameo pinned on it. She was altogether the weirdest combination of a grown woman and a child that you ever saw, and it just fascinated the hell out of me. I invited her to sit down and get acquainted. To my surprise, she did.

"Terrific view from up here, huh?" I remarked.

"Do you always lurk in the bushes at a party?"

"No. How about yourself?"

She ignored the retort. "Are you a musician?"

"Are you?"

"Do you always answer questions with another question?"

"No."

She was starting to thaw out a bit and even grudged up a smile. I noticed she had a small white scar above one side of her upper lip, but you could only see it when she smiled and the skin stretched. I was becoming more fascinated by her each minute.

"So, are you a musician, or what?" she asked again.

"No. I'm Simon's valet."

"His valet!"

"That's right. I brush off his clothes in the morning, drive into town and fetch the paper, polish his loafers, you know, the usual valet routine."

"Really?" I could tell she was straining herself to sound thrilled. "You almost look like a musician." That was supposed to buck me up.

"I do play a little guitar. Just mess around on it."

"You ought to practice more. God. A guy in your . . . situation could really take advantage of it. Look at who's here tonight. You could meet people. It's all who you know."

"Simon doesn't like his employees fraternizing," I said.

"He didn't invite you to his party?"

"Of course not. I work for him."

"Well, that's creepy. It's Victorian, if you ask me."

I think she was starting to feel sorry for me. I told her that's why I was taking in the scene from a distance, and she started rattling off the names of all the stars who were down on the lawn. I kept saying "No kidding? No kidding?" But what she really wanted to know about was this Byron Jaynes character they were throwing the party for.

"I heard that Simon keeps him up here practically under lock and key," she said.

"For what reason?"

"Because he's so paranoid someone might steal him. That's what I heard."

"He's not under lock and key," I told her. "He's just closely watched."

"Oh? What does he look like?"

"He's sixteen. A black kid."

"A Negro?"

"That's right. And he's blind."

"A blind Negro?"

"Yes, a blind sixteen-year-old Negro."

"God," she said. "He didn't used to be Little Stevie Wonder, did he?"

"I don't think so. His real name was Roosevelt Johnson. What's yours?"

"Catherine Ordway."

"Catherine. Cathy?"

"Uh, Catherine will be fine."

"Sounds so formal."

"Well, I'm a formal sort of girl, sometimes. What's your name, incidentally?"

"Arthur Schopenhauer."

"How did you ever get this job of yours, Arthur?"

"There was an opening. I applied for it. And how do you occupy yourself, Catherine?"

She sighed. "I was going to the University of Colorado, but I sqwooshed up my car at the beginning of the year."

"Were you hurt?"

"It rearranged my face somewhat, if you must know."

"I'm sorry to hear that. I think you've got a very pretty face."

"I bet you say that to all the girls."

"What year were you in?"

"Junior."

"I dropped out when I was a junior."

"Where?"

"Beal."

"Big druggie school."

"Rah rah."

For a while we just watched the people down on the lawn. The party was really beginning to rock. Christy White was smoking.

"How did you happen to get invited here," I asked Catherine after neither of us had spoken for a long time.

"I came with Walter Leslie. Do you know who he is?"

"The bass player for the Ghosts."

"That's right," she said. Actually, Walter Leslie was this enormous hulking moron who liked to throw televisions out of hotel windows.

"Is he your boyfriend?" I inquired.

She giggled. "I met him last night at a party."

"Sounds like you go to a lot of parties."

"You have to go somewhere at night. I don't just stay home and watch TV, you know."

"Not with Walter around," I said.

That put her back in a good mood for a few moments. For Catherine, that was a long time.

"Walter's all right," she said.

"I take it you live in the city."

"Yes."

"Where?"

"Wouldn't you like to know."

"I would."

"You're very cheeky for a valet."

"I'm just curious. Tell me where you live."

Catherine smiled again. "My parents have an apartment on 72nd Street. They're hardly ever there, so I use it."

"Do they travel a lot?"

"They have other houses."

"Oh."

"I'm a rich bitch."

"Sounds like fun."

"It has its virtues."

"Hey, it's got to be better than being a poor bitch."

"I imagine it is."

Just then Seabird started playing "The Nantucket Waltz," off their recent *Storm Warnings* album. Catherine stood up and tried to pick grass cuttings off her skirt.

"I have to go," she said.

"Hey, stick around for a while." I stood up too.

"No, I have to."

"How about a dance before you go. You must know how to do the waltz, right." I put my arm around her waist before she could think up any more excuses. We started swaying to the music, trying to pick up the three-quarter time, then waltzing slightly, feeling out each other's range of movement. A pedal steel guitar quivered over Christy's fiddle. I can't tell you how much Catherine excited me.

"You're very polished for a valet."

"Cheeky *and* polished too. You'll make me blush. I want to see you again."

"I'm afraid that would be impossible."

"Are you a snob?"

"Oh, yes. The worst kind."

Then we were whirling across the grass, the trees spinning and the sky wheeling like one of those time-lapse photographs, a pinwheel of diamonds. Catherine closed her eyes. "You're a good dancer," she said. When the song ended, I gathered her in both of my arms, leaned her way back, and kissed her right on the mouth. At first she tried to push me away, but then I felt her stop resisting and kiss me back. When we straightened up again, both of us were breathless. There was a kind of eerie hush from down the hill, where the party was, and then I realized practically everyone down there was looking up at us. The next thing I knew, they were all clapping. Even Seabird, onstage, was clapping.

"Now you're really going to get canned," Catherine said angrily and obviously embarrassed.

"Aw, Simon will understand. Come on, let's go down there."

"I thought you weren't allowed—"

"Hey, you only live once."

I put my hand around her waist and started guiding her down the hill. She tried to pry my hand off, but I held on tight. The applause continued until we were down in the party again.

"Very nice, Byron," Jerry Zuckerman said. "See why they call 'em the Romantics?"

Catherine stopped dead in her tracks and finally peeled my fingers off her waist. Boy, did she turn red! She had one of those milky complexions that turns pure scarlet when they blush.

"You bastard," she said under her breath, trying to maintain a smile. "You're Byron Jaynes!"

Before I could say anything, she reared back and let me have it, right in the puss, a long, looping shot right out of left field. The people who were immediately around us laughed, thinking, no doubt, that this was just another part of some act we had worked up. But let me tell you, she really clobbered me. Knocked me right off my feet. Next thing I knew, Bobby was helping me up. I could see Catherine storm up the terrace and disappear into the house. Walter was not far behind, with his buckskins flapping in the breeze.

"Who was that chick?" Bobby asked.

"That was the girl of my dreams," I said. It's odd the way you get an idea in your head. I was definitely obsessed, possessed, with the *idea* of her from that moment on. I hurried down to the house. Inside, Donovan was holding forth in the living room, playing and singing for an audience of about thirty people, incense smoldering on the coffee table and the twins on either side of him, motionless with adoration. By the time I made it outside to the front portico, a green Austin-Healy was pulling out of the long driveway. Catherine was behind the wheel, with Walter beside her in his groovy duds. There was nothing left to do but go back to the party.

I managed to stay fairly sober the rest of that night and was up early the next morning, before the Lewisohns or any of their other house guests were stirring. The first floor was a mess and a platoon of maids was breaking out the vacuum cleaners. Two men were out on the lawn with plastic bags, picking up debris. I went straight to Simon's gym/office and consulted the Manhattan telephone directory. There was a Kenneth Ordway listed at 9 East 72nd Street. I found a set of car keys in the top drawer of the desk. They were on a plastic tab marked "T-bird."

Simon kept three cars at the Tamberlane house, not including the limo. There was a station wagon for errands, Claire's Morgan four-plus-four, and a white '56 Thunderbird that was Simon's personal toy. I took the T-bird. I made it down to the city by eleven and put it in a parking garage around the corner from the Plaza Hotel. Then, after picking up a few necessaries, I walked back to 59th Street, along the park where the horse-drawn carriage drivers park their rigs, and I hired one. The driver thought it was a tad irregular taking some hippie on a lone joyride to 72nd Street, but I kept on pulling out ten-dollar bills until he saw things my way. When we got there, I asked him to wait in front of the awning. I went around to the service entrance off the alley and took the back elevator to the fifth floor. Nobody answered when I rang the bell. Frustrated, I leaned on it.

"All right. All right, already!" It was Catherine's voice. "Who is it?"

"Delibery man," I said in this Spanish accent.

"Delivery. . . ?"

"Jes. Flowers, señorita."

"Flowers. . . ?"

There was some incoherent muttering. A chain came off the door. I held the paper-covered bouquet in front of my face. The door opened. She tried to grab the flowers, but I held onto them tight.

"Let go, will you?"

"Geeme teep first."

"What! Why, you greedy little—"

"Geeme teep!"

"Oh . . . go to hell!"

She tried to slam the door on me, but I wedged my sneaker in the door. I lowered the bouquet.

"Remember me?" I asked.

Her face went beet red again.

"You!" she said. "You asshole!"

She tried to smoosh the door closed, but my foot was still in the way. Eventually she gave up and I forced my way in. It was a kind of pantry room. She had on a Japanese kimono.

"Is Walter here?"

"Of course."

"Hmmm. Don't you even want to open your flowers?"

She just stood there. I opened the stapled-up end and removed the paper for her.

"Lovely," she said sneeringly, took them from me, and chucked them on a nearby counter. Then she folded her arms.

"Most people send red roses, right?" I started explaining. "I bet you didn't know this, but in the Middle Ages, sending red roses to someone was an invitation to war. When you were stuck on someone, however, you sent white roses."

"These are yellow."

"Yeah. I couldn't find any white ones. Anyway, it's just folklore."

"How interesting."

"I'm stuck on you, Catherine."

She shifted her weight to the other foot and kept glaring at me.

"Sorry about last night," I said. "Hey, bet you'll never guess what's waiting outside."

"Ringling Brothers, Barnum and Baily Circus."

"Close. That's a damn good guess. Have you had lunch yet?" Stupid question, I realized. In fact it was obvious she hadn't gotten around to breakfast. But this smirky smile was beginning to bloom on her face. She was thawing out again. "You just woke up, right?" I ventured.

She nodded.

"Go get dressed. I'll find some way to amuse myself in the meantime."

"You know, you're a nervy bastard."

"No, I'm real shy once you get to know me. Go get dressed."

Catherine looked at me the way you might regard some hopeless retard. She shrugged her shoulders and showed me through a swinging door that led through the kitchen and then the rest of the apartment. We ended up in the living room.

"It'll take me half an hour," she said, as if that might persuade me to forget it.

"Fine," I said, taking a seat on the sofa.

"What about Walter?" she asked.

"What about him?"

"Is he invited too?"

"I should say not."

"Shall I tell him?"

"Certainly. He might worry otherwise."

"Okay."

She vanished down a long hallway. A few minutes later, who should wander into the living room in his Fruit-of-the-Looms but Walter. "Hi," I said.

"What's happening, man?"

"Nothing much."

"No, really, man. What the fuck are you doing here?"

"Hey, Walter, relax, man. Catherine and I, we go back to high school. We were in the chess club together. Wasn't that something, though, running into her last night at that party? It's such a small world."

"What the fuck's a chess club?"

"It's this club where you play chess. It was purely platonic, don't worry. Besides, I'm queer now, anyway."

"You're queer!"

"Yeah, I turned queer a few years ago. Don't worry about a thing."

"I hate fucking queers."

"Hey, me too, Walter. That's why I was so glad to run into Catherine. When you're queer, all you do is run into other queers, seems like."

Walter glanced around the room like he was looking for a TV set to heave out the window, but he ended up just scratching himself and yawning and turned back up the hall muttering ". . . fucking queers . . ." under his breath.

It was a large and expensively decorated apartment, but you could tell that her parents hadn't been around in quite a while. A new stereo system was set up on the carpet underneath a baby grand piano, haphazardly wired together, too. There were albums scattered all over the place, a lot of them unopened yet, and with stickers on them that said "promotional copy." A coffee table was piled high with Village Voices and magazines and overflowing ashtrays. There were empty glasses and beer cans on side tables. Plates with scraps of food were deployed at various places, and there was a big, smarmy red ketchup stain on the arm of the sofa. Her folks were going to love this, I thought. The Beatles' *Revolver* album was on the turntable. I switched it on and lay down on the carpet with my head between the speakers. I was listening to "Got to Get You into My Life" when Catherine emerged from her boudoir. She had on a lacy white sundress and a broad-brimmed straw hat in her hand. The way she looked just knocked you out, she was such a little dish.

"You look smashing," I said.

"Are you going to plotz around on the carpet all day, or what?"

"No, I'm going to take you out for lunch."

"Then take me."

"Yes, ma'am."

I turned off the stereo.

In the elevator, she said, "Did you tell Walter you were a queer?"

"Yes."

"Are you?"

"Wouldn't you like to know."

"Well, are you?"

"I'm crazy about you."

"Unnnnhhhh. . . !"

When she saw the horse and carriage, her eyes lit up noticeably, though she tried to act casual about it. I had a bottle of Moët stashed in the back, and I popped the cork as we crossed Fifth Avenue to the entrance of Central Park.

It was the type of broiling day the Spoonful sang about in "Summer in the City," but the park looked lovely—like one of those paintings by George Inness, hazy and fuzzy green, with kids dressed in bright splotches of color playing around the conservatory pond.

"Still mad?" I asked.

"I don't know why I'm letting you take me out."

"I'm sweeping you off your feet. You can't resist, right?"

"Hardly."

"You're bored with Walter."

"Walter's all right."

"Hey, you know there's this rumor going around that *he's* queer."

"Walter is *not* queer. He may be dumb, but he's not queer."

"You never know. Maybe it's a transition period."

"Shut up about Walter, already."

In a short while we pulled up to the Tavern-on-the-Green. I gave the hack the rest of the champagne and asked him to stick around.

After a couple of cocktails, Catherine finally began to lighten up. I asked about her family and everything. Her paternal grandfather founded the Central Hudson and Champlain Railway. Her mother's father was a confectionery tycoon whose company produced those chalky wafers that come about fifty to the roll that we always got when we were kids. They also made those licorice rolls that taste like naugahyde. Anyway, all her father and mother did was travel and collect art. They had houses in New York, Palm Beach, and Cooperstown, and an apartment in Paris.

When she was fourteen, Catherine said, her parents shipped her off to a series of schools in France and Switzerland. She was asked to leave each one in succession for flouting the rules. The last straw fell at l'École Ste-Bernadette where she got caught trying to seduce the laundress's son, a sturdy mountain lad named Josef. There was a flurry of transatlantic phone calls, and within hours the mother superior had Catherine at the TWA boarding gate in Zurich. Her parents, Kenneth and Miggs (Margaret), enrolled her in the public high school in Cooperstown, where they could keep an eye on her. It was supposed to be a punishment, right? Ha! Catherine had the time of her life. She was the Daisy Buchanan of Lake Glimmerglass, with an Austin-Healy Sprite, an allowance larger than most of her classmates' parents' yearly income, and a gatehouse on the estate that she set up as her own personal party shack.

Finally, it was off to Boulder, simply because she heard the trout fishing and skiing were good there. She was an outdoor nut, of all things. She knew how to hunt and handle guns. It just intrigued me to no end. Anyway, in the fall of her junior year she wracked up her car and broke several bones in her face. All that winter there had been small operations. Now, at the beginning of the summer, she was reconstructed and ready to resume having a good time.

We drank quite a bit that afternoon: cocktails, champagne. On the way back, in the carriage, her head lolled sleepily against my shoulder. It had grown overcast and gotten muggier. We pulled up across 72nd Street from her awning.

"Would you like to come upstairs?" she asked drowsily.

"Is Walter still there?"

"I don't know."

I paid the carriage driver and let him go. We took the elevator back up to the fifth floor. In the apartment, Catherine called out Walter's name but there as no answer. "Guess he's gone," she said.

"What if he's lurking in a closet?"

"Walter doesn't lurk in closets."

"I heard that he does."

"Shut up."

She took my hand and led me down the hall to her bedroom. There was a large canopied bed and innumerable "art" projects strewn around on the floor—watercolors of leaping trout, not too bad either, and collages with pictures snipped from magazines waiting to be glued, and piles of clothing absolutely everywhere.

Catherine reached back dreamily and slid the straps of her sundress off. She shimmied a bit and the dress fell off her. The mature body underneath was somehow surprising.

"Aren't you going to get undressed?" she asked.

"What if Walter comes back?"

"He doesn't have a key."

"Oh."

"Once he's gone. Pphhtt. That's it."

"I see."

She reached down and unbuttoned my jeans, then started foraging around inside.

"I want some," she said.

"Some what?"

"You know."

"Do you always get what you want?"

"Always."

"Then I guess there's no point fighting."

"No point," she agreed.

I kicked off my jeans and pulled my shirt over my head.

"You're hard. You must want some too," she said.

She slipped out of her panties. I was shaking, though it was quite warm and sticky. We hadn't even turned on the air conditioner. She stepped forward and her hips pressed warmly against mine. She smelled like apples, so young and sweet. My arms closed around her. We fell onto the bed.

We made love with the kind of repetitive ravenous energy that only the young have. It got dim and gray outside. Through the window, you could see lightning crackle over Central Park. Then the storm ended and a rose-colored wafer of sun came out above the rooftops on Central Park West.

"Will you drive me to the airport?" she asked.

"Sure. Where are you going?"

"Europe."

"Europe, huh? When?"

"Tonight."

"You're going to Europe tonight?"

"Yes, I guess I forgot to tell you."

"I guess you did. God, Europe!"

She giggled and placed her hand on my cock.

"I want some more."

"Cut that out! Europe!"

"You want to come too?"

"I can't just take off like that."

"Why not?"

"I've got commitments. We're going out on tour in a couple of weeks."

"Come over for a week. We'll go to the south of France. You could get a tan. You need one."

"No I don't."

"You're so pale. We could make love in French."

"I don't even have a passport, Catherine."

"Oh. . . ."

We lay there quietly for a while. She stopped trying to play with my weenie.

"When's this plane of yours taking off, anyway?" I asked.

She grabbed a folder from her night table. It was a Lufthansa ticket. Her plane was at ten-fifteen.

"What do you have to go to France for anyway?"

"I feel like it."

"Do you always do what you feel like—no, don't answer that. Of course you do."

She giggled some more and started kissing my neck, clowning around, making these big slushy, slurpy, suckling noises.

"Quit sucking my neck."

"Can I suck your cock?"

"I don't know."

"I really want to."

Needless to say, it's hard to stop a woman so determined, and it was a while before we could get back to our discussion.

"Are you going to be a big star when I come back?"

"Maybe. When are you coming back?"

"The fall. Maybe."

My heart sank. "You're going to be gone all summer?"

"Aren't you going to be on tour?"

"Yes. . . ."

"So, there."

"You could come along on part of the tour with us."

"I don't want to spend the summer hanging around a bunch of smelly hotel rooms." She nuzzled under my chin and started playing with the hairs on my chest. "You better be a star when I come back. I won't see you if you're a flop."

"As long as you like me for myself."

"You have to be a big success. If you're a big success, I'll be your personal number one groupie."

"Oh, yeah? What if you meet Mick Jagger on the Riviera?"

"Then you'll have to fight for me."

"Would you fight for me?"

"Not if you're a flop."

"What if I turn out to be a flash in the pan?"

"I've never even heard you play, you know."

"Well, we're pretty damn good. You'll see."

"I hope so, Flash."

"Flash. . . ?"

"That's your new name."

"What about Walter?"

"You want to know the truth?"

"Certainly."

"I was trying to throw him out when you rang the doorbell."

She laughed, kissed me on the stomach, and climbed off the bed.
"We better hustle it up," she said. "I've got a zillion things to do
before we can get out of here."

We showered. She ran around the apartment trying to make some
effort to clean it up, but you could see that it was totally beyond
her. I pictured her parents coming back and finding all that crusty,
moldy smarm in the living room. Anyway, she changed into jeans
and a dark-green leotard top, crammed a few more items in her
carry-on bag, and gave up even packing.

"I guess I can buy stuff over there," she said resignedly.

The only thing she showed any real concern about was her flyrod.
She was taking her fishing tackle to France, for Godsake. She was
so strange. Finally, we left the place in the mess it was in, took a
cab to the parking garage on 58th Street, and picked up the T-bird
for the trip out to Kennedy. At the boarding gate, I attempted to be
serious.

"I like you, Catherine. I want to see you again."

"You're a sweet boy."

"I'm not just a sweet boy. You'll see."

I tried to kiss her but she giggled and evaded me.

"Don't be like that," I said.

"I'm a heap of trouble, Byron. I could end up driving you batshit."

"I can take care of myself."

"Do," she said.

The boarding attendant announced that it was time to get on the
plane.

"I'll send you the record when it comes out. Where should I send
it?"

"American Express, Monte Carlo."

I grabbed her and kissed her, like I did on the lawn the night
before after we waltzed. It seemed like ages ago. Then she was running across the tarmac with her shoulder bag and flyrod.

Now, at that particular time, the summer of '66, right before *Rising Son* was released, I wasn't really living anywhere. Most of my
clothes were up in Tamberlane. Rego and Gary had moved out of
Grove Street, which was now Bobby's personal pigsty. So the night
I saw Catherine off, I crashed at the Sherry Netherland, and late
the next morning, dreading it, I took a taxi over to Sutton Place.

In hardly more than a year my mother had changed from a middle-aged suburban housewife into a hopeless old lady. She'd lost everything she cared about, and all she cared about was the life she'd constructed around my father in Westchester. She could have stayed up in Bedford if she'd wanted to, so the move to New York was basically an act of surrender. Even Arlene was gone, shipped down to South Carolina to live out her last years with relatives she didn't know anymore. My mother lived in a dream world now, and it was a dream of death. You could smell it in the upholstery.

"My dearest darling!"

I hadn't seen her in a couple of months, even though we both lived in the same city. I called her a lot on the phone, but . . . well, why make excuses. I should have stopped by more often. Anyway, I gave her the presents I brought—Sarah Vaughn sings George Gershwin, Mel Tormé sings Rodgers and Hart, stuff I knew she liked—but she did a weird thing. Instead of looking at them, or maybe even playing one, she immediately put them in the cabinet and shut the door.

The apartment was neat as a pin, and the furniture was from our Bedford house, but it looked totally out of place. In fact, it made me angry to see it there, like having your house robbed and walking into some strange place where the robbers stashed all the things you loved.

"You really did catch me on the run, darling. I'm meeting Jeanie Leiber for lunch. You look wonderful. Would you like something? A glass of milk?"

"Milk? No."

"A Coke?"

"Sure. I'd love a Coke."

She got me one and then I followed her back to her bedroom where she put on her jewelry and brushed her hair. You never saw someone do such a simple thing, brushing their hair, with such total resignation. The room smelled like Joy de Patou and mothballs.

"How sweet of you to drop by."

We returned to the living room. My mother sat down stiffly on one end of this right-angled sectional sofa, and I sat down on the other side.

"It's so nice to see you."

"It's nice to see you too, mom."

"You should come by more often."

"I will. I'll come by more often."

"That would be nice."

I drank my Coke.

"The record will be out real soon," I told her. She knew we'd been in the studio and playing clubs and concerts recently, but she'd never seen me perform. My father had fucked her head so completely that I think she stayed away out of duty to him. He would have disapproved.

"I hope you'll bring me one," she said, "as soon as they come off the . . . whatever they come off of."

"They press them."

"Off the presses."

I put my Coke down on the coffee table. I could picture her getting the record and stashing it immediately as far back in the record cabinet as she could. It made me mad, but not at her.

"I don't like the idea of you living here alone," I blurted out suddenly. "If you want to move back home, I'll take care of it."

"I can't move back home, Peter," she said ruefully. "They've sold the house."

"I'll buy it back. I can do it."

"Don't be silly, darling."

"Okay, I'll buy you another house up there. Don't you miss your friends, the garden?"

"Peter, darling, my friends are in the city practically every day. They arrive in droves. I love the city. When we lived in the country I could hardly wait to come here. There are the theaters, the restaurants, the museums—"

"Oh, horseshit!"

"Peter!"

"I know why you're here."

"Will you excuse me for a minute, darling?"

She got up and went to the bathroom, not entirely steady on her feet. It was painful to watch her navigate around the furniture. I heard water running. When she returned, I excused myself and went in there too. It didn't take me long to find what I was looking for. There was a bottle of Dewer's White Label in the cabinet under the sink, right behind the Ajax and the Sani-Flush. At first I thought of pouring it down the drain, but I figured what's the use. Then I did something myself that was a little spooky. I was feeling so unsettled that I glugged down a drink right out of the bottle and put it back in the cabinet. Then I flushed the toilet. When I came back out, mom was standing in the foyer with her purse and umbrella.

"I really must leave now," she said. "Jeanie gets furious if you're not there right on the dot."

"I'll drop you in a cab. Where are you meeting her?"

"Lutèce."

We walked down to the elevator together.

"Look, mom, they're sending us on tour. I'll be gone most of the summer—"

"Where?"

"All over the place. Across the country."

"That's wonderful, darling. Will you call? You can call collect."

"Of course I'll call. Will you think about my offer?"

For the first time, I got the feeling that something was getting through to her. She turned to me and in a quiet, cracked voice she said, "I couldn't go back to Bedford, darling. I just couldn't." Then the elevator door opened.

In the cab, mom said, "Have you heard from your father?"

"No."

"He's your father."

"He knows how to operate a telephone."

"He's a very stubborn man, your father."

Just then we pulled up in front of the restaurant.

"Oh! We're here already," mom said. She leaned over and hugged me. "Don't hold a grudge," she whispered in my ear. "He's your father."

I didn't say it, but I think you need a grudge sometimes to keep your heart from breaking. It would have helped *her*.

"Have a lovely time on your trip, Peter."

"Good-bye, mom."

She kissed me once more and climbed out of the cab. I watched her lose her footing slightly when her heel caught in the rubber mat under the awning, but the doorman caught her. She turned and waved good-bye. I told the driver to take me to the parking garage where I left the T-bird. I wanted to get out of the city so bad I could hardly stand it. Tamberlane was so idyllic in comparison, like one of those pastoral paintings by Thomas Cole. All my needs were taken care of. Too many of them, maybe. It was a week after Catherine left that the incident with Claire occurred.

I remember it was a Monday, my last free day before the tour. We were scheduled to have four days of rehearsal and then open a show at the Stockbridge Bowl Friday night. The Byrds were head-lining. Anyway, Simon was down in the city. It was after lunch, a hot, hazy afternoon when the whole world seems asleep except the crickets. Heat squiggles rose off the lawn. I was downstairs at the piano working on "Restless Girl," the song to Catherine, when Claire seemed to materialize out of thin air. Actually, I could smell her perfume before I saw her. I looked up and she was leaning over the lid with her chin propped up in her hand. I was not a terrific piano player. I'd begun picking it up lately. Mostly I just knew some chords.

"Hi," I said.

"Am I interrupting you?" She was grinning, as if she knew the answer.

"No," I said.

"Let's go for a ride."

I didn't answer, still trying to hang onto my concentration.

"You're working your fingers to the bone, Byron. I won't take no for an answer."

"I'm hardly working my fingers to the bone."

"Is that a new song?"

"Yes."

"Just think," she said dreamily. "I was present at the creation." At the same time, she deviously reached down and pulled the lid of the keyboard shut. "Watch your fingers," she said, about a half a second before she almost decapitated them.

"You really don't want me to finish this, do you?"

"I told you, I won't take no for an answer."

"I'm not being a good guest, huh?"

"You are atrociously diligent."

On the way to the stables, we stopped in the kitchen. Claire pulled a bottle of white wine from the fridge and put it in a little canvas bag wrapped up in a wet dishtowel.

"What's that for?" I asked. The heat, the stillness, was making me nervous.

"We call this a refreshment," she said.

Soon I was standing to the side while Richmond and Claire sad-dled two horses. I hadn't seen him since that afternoon before the party. He was never around the house itself, and to tell you the truth, I didn't actively seek his company, since it was pretty obvious he hated my guts. Now, as he tightened the cinches, he kept shooting these glances back my way. He really gave me the goddam willies.

Claire put the bottle in a saddlebag. We mounted up and headed out on the labyrinth of trails that were blazed through Simon's property. At one point the trail ran alongside a neighbor's apple orchard, so we turned off and galloped up and down the orderly rows of trees. Claire was an excellent rider and even something of a show-off. For example, there was a stack of beehives at the rear of the orchard and she jumped them. I didn't think it was a very good idea, but she took it perfectly.

It was too hot in the orchard, though, so we headed back into the cooler woods, got off, and walked the animals for a while. Eventually we came to a pond, a couple of acres in size. At one end there was a rocky hump rising abruptly against the water with a few small pine trees growing out of it.

"Have you seen our ruin?" Claire asked.

"Ruin. . . ?" I said, apprehensively. Richmond came to mind, among other things.

"We have our own personal ruin," Claire explained. "It's nothing romantic like a castle or an abbey, but it's authentic. See that old rocky thing? That was the wall of the millrace. It thrilled me to pieces when we discovered it. Back home we live more or less cheek by jowl with our dead, you know."

We led the horses down to the water's edge and they began to drink.

"They'll be all right, Byron. Come with me."

She took my hand and led me up over the moss-covered foundation. You could see a keystone arch under the cap of moss and sod, and water trickling underneath it. We climbed a little higher up the piney hump and sat down on the grass. Claire handed me the wine bottle and a corkscrew.

"You're going to be a big star in a few months, Byron."

"You know, the way everybody's been harping on that lately, it's beginning to get on my nerves. It's not fair, saying that all the time. Besides, I don't even know if they know what it means."

"It means that everyone's going to want a piece of you."

"Sometimes I think everybody's just trying to scare me."

"Do you scare easy?"

"Sometimes."

"We're trying to prepare you."

I took a hit off the wine bottle and passed it to Claire. She took a couple of deep swallows.

"Are we in heaven?" she asked.

"Only the Catskills."

"Try to be a bit more romantic, Byron. Did you have a good time at your party?"

"I had a wonderful time. It was very kind of you to have it for me."

"Who was that girl you were dancing with?"

"Just a girl."

"Is she your girl?"

"I don't know."

"You ought to have a girl, Byron. How come you don't have one?"

"Too busy, I guess."

"Nobody's that busy. Simon is the busiest human being I've ever seen."

"Simon's Simon."

"Are you going to see her again?"

"I hope so."

"Are you in love with her?"

"Only a woman would ask a question like that. It's so full of assumptions."

"Maybe you don't know what love is, Byron."

"Hey, I know what love is. Sometimes I think you've got the mind of a teenager."

"And sometimes you sound like my granddaddy. Such an old grouch. I don't think Charleston ever gets this hot. I'm going for a swim. You can roast your grouchy self to a cinder, for all I care."

Before I knew it, she was up on her feet taking her clothes off. Man, it scared me to death. I didn't know what the hell to do—run away, turn around and not look, go take a stroll in the woods until she was finished. What I did was . . . nothing. I lay there trying to be casual, watching her strip. And the whole time, she had this big smile on her face. Boy, I was really shaking! Finally, she was standing right in front of me, completely naked. She had these white half-moons on her breasts from where she wore her bikini around the pool, and a pale triangle around her hips. It accentuated the very places I was trying not to look at.

Then she turned around and dove off the millrace with hardly a splash. I sucked down about half the bottle of wine while she stroked her way out to the center of the pond.

"Are you going to sit up there and fry?" she said.

"I thought you didn't care."

"You could injure yourself, Byron. I'm concerned about your well-being."

"I'm fine. Don't worry about me."

"Stop being a silly boy and come in here."

"Forget it."

"You are despicable!"

She breaststroked around for a while, then did a surface dive. You could see her pale white backside down under the surface. But when she came up for air, she started flailing at the water, making these choking sounds and saying, "Help!" I was sure she was clowning around, but she kept it up. Then, she was bobbling way down under water, coming back up again, and really screaming her head off. Now I was still pretty sure she was faking it, but part of me was starting to wonder if maybe she might be in trouble, and I thought how they're always telling you never to swim without a lifeguard because even good swimmers can get a cramp and drown, and suddenly I was pulling my boots off and my jeans and shirt and I dove in. When I got to her, she was actually under water, with all these air bubbles coming out of her mouth, and I literally had to haul her up to the surface. I dragged her over to the edge of the pond and got her up into this mucky, weedy stuff and flopped her out on it. She lay still for a few seconds. I was afraid she was unconscious, and I was about to turn her over on her stomach and start pumping her lungs when she opened her eyes, fluttered the lids, and said, "My hero. . . !"

"I knew you were faking."

"You did not, chump."

"I should have let you drown."

"Is there no end to your gallantry, Byron?"

I got up from the weedy muck where I was kneeling. She reached up, grabbed the band of my underpants, and pulled them down all in a second. The pants caught around my ankles and I went toppling backward into the muck. Claire started grabbing handfuls of the oozy black stuff and flinging it at me. She was hooting and hollering and having a grand time, and it really pissed me off, so I started flinging it back at her, big gloppy globs of it, and in a minute both of us looked like we were made up for a minstrel show. The stuff really stunk too.

There was nothing to do but dive back in the pond and wash it off. My underpants were ruined, so I flung them off into the trees. I was washing the crud out of my hair when Claire swam over and started clowning around and wrestling with me. She felt so sleek, I couldn't help getting . . . excited. And, I guess, that's where I started losing my head. She swam back to the millrace and climbed the old stones to the grass on top. I stayed in the water, watching her stretch out in the sun. You could feel the icy springs coming up from underground. Eventually I climbed out too and sat down on the grass beside her, getting more and more bent out of shape, hoping she might start something so I wouldn't have to blame myself for it, and she did. She started rubbing my back and kissing it, and I knew I was lost.

We made love there, in the woods, on top of their old ruin, and when it was over I looked down at her. Her hair lay in tangly strands across her face, and she didn't look so smug and certain anymore.

"How do you suppose he'd feel if he knew about this?" I asked. It was unnecessary to even say his name.

"He's very secure" was all she said.

"How about you?"

"You are so young, Byron. And so beautiful."

"Will you tell him, then?"

"Of course not."

"See that you don't."

She reached up and touched my cheek. "Don't be angry, Byron. It's unbecoming."

"Just tell me one thing: are you in love with me?"

"I thought only women asked questions like that."

---

It was twilight and the woods were full of ominous, unclear shapes. The temperature had dropped. I was shivering and anxious to get back, but the cold didn't seem to faze Byron in the least.

"What's your wife's name?" he asked.

"Allison."

"That's a nice name. Is she a good wife?"

"I think she'd have trouble relating to that label: wife."

"I'm asking you, not her. Is she a good wife?"

"She's a good woman."

"Can't you answer a simple question?"

"It's not a simple question."

"Oh, Sears, Sears. . . ."

"It's not."

"You ever screw around on her?"

"I don't know."

"Come on. Did you or didn't you?"

"Yeah. Once or twice."

"She find out?"

"She found out once."

"First time or second time?"

"I don't know, Byron."

"You know. Now tell me!"

"Second time."

"How'd she find out?"

"I told her."

"She ever screw around on you?"

"No."

"You sure about that?"

"If she did, she didn't tell me."

"That's the difference between men and women," Byron said. "We're stupid. We expect to be forgiven. Give me a hand up, huh?"

I helped him to his feet. His leg had stiffened up on him.

"Hey, you and me, we understand each other, right?"

"No. Not entirely," I said.

"Well, maybe we can work it out."

# CHAPTER 7

RS: Is rock and roll a valid revolutionary act?
BJ: No, it's just an act.

—The *Rolling Stone* Interview with Byron Jaynes, 1968

I called Allie half a dozen times between eight o'clock that night and one in the morning, but all I got was an answering machine saying that Carol Bostwick was out and so on and so forth. When I started calling again at nine the next day, the line was busy for two straight hours. Then, around eleven, I called and got a ring. The machine answered. Needless to say, I did absolutely no work between calls, so I left the cottage in disgust before noon and headed out to Byron's.

Because I was somewhat earlier than usual, he made me wait in his front parlor while he puttered around in the kitchen. For all my preoccupations, I could tell that he was in another strange mood himself. To begin with, pinned to the chest of his Molsen's beer jumpsuit was one of the shooting star/rainbow logo pins designed for his disastrous 1969 tour. He was humming the melody of one of his own songs, "Lay Waste Jerusalem," while he fed his cat, Whitey. I was able to keep my eyes on him through the arched doorway from his wall of bookshelves while I pretended to peruse the titles. It was what he did after feeding the cat, though, that was really bizarre: he took a slice of whole-wheat bread from a plastic bag and sprayed it lightly with canned insecticide. Without so much as a pause, he folded the bread in half and ate it in three bites, chasing it with a glass of milk. I turned away, aghast, and went to the window. Byron limped in a minute later.

"Let's climb the hill today," he said, taking the recording equipment away from me.

"Whatever you say."

"Hey, someone's on the rag today."

"I brought my dog," I said, unable to deal with any question of my own mood. "I didn't know if you'd mind or not."

"Where is he?"

I pointed out the window to the Saab. Luke had his paws pressed against the window. Byron glanced excitedly back at me and hurried out to it. I followed. He threw the door open and Luke leaped out.

"My kingdom and all my chattels are yours!" He cried. Luke danced circles around him in the weeds, an idiot canine hornpipe of glee. Byron found a stick and tossed it for him.

"Better not start that," I warned him. "You'll never see the end of that stick."

Luke returned and deposited the stick at Byron's feet. Byron squatted down and rubbed his ears. "Daddy says no more sticks, pal." Then he lifted up one of Luke's floppy ears and made like he was whispering into it.

"What was that all about?" I tried to play along.

"A secret," Byron said. "Between him and me. I'll give you a hint, though. It was about something long and hard with bark."

"You promised him a blow-job later on?"

Byron looked up sharply, "That's really sick," he said bitterly, and I could tell he meant it. "Come on, let's get this show on the road."

He started marching off toward the first pasture. I caught up with him at the barbed-wire fence. He was holding it up for me.

"I saw what you did back at the house, Byron."

He winced. "What'd you see?" he said stiffly.

"That stuff you sprayed on the bread."

He lowered the wire and began shifting his weight from leg to leg, his eyes searching the ground, as if he might locate some explanation in the brown-turning weeds.

"That bug I told you about. . . ?"

"Yes?"

"That worm."

"Uh-huh?"

He looked back at me fearfully.

"It's getting out of hand," he said.

"What is it doing?"

"It's gotten very active," he whispered, as if he were in danger of being overheard. "Sometimes I'm afraid it's going to explode me."

I nodded my head and grunted as if I understood the symptoms he was describing.

"Have you seen anybody about it?" I asked. "A doctor?"

He shook his head emphatically. "No!"

"Well, how do you know it's there?"

"I can feel it, Rick. A person can tell these things."

We both stared into the weeds for a while.

"How long have you had it?" I asked him finally.

"A long time. Since right after I came here. It comes and goes. It has these, I don't know, dormant periods. Every now and then I try to starve it out, but I always weaken before it does. Have you ever heard of anything like this before?"

"Byron, if you've got worms, I'm certain that you could get rid of them by going to a doctor. They've got medication. Hell, Luke gets worms and the vet gives him pills."

"Maybe you could lay a few of them on me."

"They're dog pills, Byron."

"Well, there's nothing wrong with him."

I didn't know what to say.

"Can't hurt, right?" he persisted.

"I really don't know."

"Just bring me a few. I'll try them and if they make me sick, we'll see about something else."

"A doctor, Byron," I reminded him forcefully.

"Yeah, okay, goddammit. A doctor."

I didn't like the idea of giving him Luke's medication at all, but Christ, I figured it had to be less harmful than letting him continue to treat himself with bug spray. God knows how long he'd been doing it. I was afraid to find out. In the meantime, Byron held up the wire for me.

"We're getting to be like old friends, actually," he said. "I'll probably miss it when it's gone."

"Your worm?"

"Yeah. We've been through an awful lot together. And he hasn't killed me yet. He'd probably die if I did. Sometimes I think it works both ways, you know?"

At that point, I opted out of the discussion, fairly sure that the whole thing was in his head, and not wanting to reinforce his belief in it.

Luke was having a grand time pronking up and down in the rag-weed and asters. From the top of the highest pasture you could see whisps of smoke rising amid the sea-like expanse of red and ochre foliage. Chain saws whined far away as other natives made ready for the winter. Byron reclined on the shelf of rotted granite and checked the cassette.

"It's a fresh one," I told him.

"You're always prepared, aren't you? Like a Boy Scout."

When he saw I wasn't willing to engage in anymore badinage, he drew a deep breath and said, "Fall comes fast around here. It's like the other shoe dropping. *Wham!* Then, it's the long, long night."

## The Life of Byron Jaynes—Tape 6

We opened for the Byrds our first night out at the Stockbridge Bowl. The Byrds were real big. They had a hot single on the charts, "Eight Miles High," but it got stymied in the number 12 position when radio stations caved into pressure and stopped playing it on the grounds that it promoted drug use. In fact, it was about riding in an airplane, but what did the station managers know?

Meanwhile, "Rebecca's Window" had also entered the *Billboard* and *Cashbox* charts. It was released as a single with "Then She Laughed" the week before the tour started, and it was getting tremendous airplay. I don't know whose palms Simon had to grease to arrange that—

*It was an outstanding song, Byron.*

Yeah. Maybe. I don't know. Anyway, we even heard it on the radio in the limo, on our way to the amphitheater. Talk about feeding the ego. I couldn't wait to get up there and rock out. We were all raring to go that first night of the tour.

Now, you know how everybody's got this idea about the camaraderie of the road, the fraternal fellowship of musicians, all that backstage brotherhood bullshit? Well, in fact, it's extremely competitive. We had discovered that months before. Also, you hardly ever play on the same bill with one other band night after night. You've got all these bands criss-crossing the country, and their itineraries are all different, right? So one night you open for the Byrds, the next night you open for the Mamas and the Papas, the night after that some other band opens for you, depending on your comparative status, meaning current record sales. It's like one huge jigsaw puzzle that the managers and promoters and labels try to piece together.

When we hooked up with the Byrds at Stockbridge, they had been on the road, oh, for months and months, and they showed it too. They were wearing their nerve endings like hair shirts, squabbling among themselves. You needed something like a corporate flow-chart to figure out who was still on speaking terms with who. Was Crosby pissed off at Hillman? Was McGuinn on the outs with Crosby? And why was Michael Clarke banging his head against the wall in the green room?

"God, I hope we don't get like that," Rego said as we ran up to the stage that night.

In fact, we got worse. And fast too.

After the show, Gemini threw a party for us at the Gray Fox Inn in Stockbridge, one of those 200-year-old Yankee landmarks where people like Frank and Elsie Havermeyer go for the weekend to watch the leaves change. It was a big bash. Simon couldn't be there, but Jerry Zuckerman was. The Byrds were invited, of course. Gemini flew in a Lear-Jet full of press for the night. It was a first-class launching.

McGuinn and Hillman came by around one in the morning. They were older than us. I had a lot of respect for them. Unfortunately, Bobby got to them first. I knew he was tripping—he was *always* tripping then—but he was also in the process of getting drunk, not an attractive combination. He starts running this number on them as soon as they set foot inside the party. First he tells them how great they are, and then he tells them how lousy they played that night. You could see that McGuinn and Hillman were sorry they stopped by. What happened next I'm not sure, because I was across the room, but evidently they were trying to leave and Bobby was more or less blocking their way, running his mouth and acting like a complete asshole, until one of the Byrds' roadies, who had accompanied them, shoved Bobby out of their way.

So Bobby got two of our roadies and followed them out to the parking lot where there was a scuffle. Bobby comes lurching back into the party with blood running from his nose. He wants all of us and the rest of the road crew to drive up to the Holiday Inn in

Lenox, where the Byrds are staying, and have some kind of gang war. Can you imagine?

"You're ridiculous," I told him. "Nobody's going anywhere," and I told Billy Keough, our road manager who Simon got us for the tour, to take Bobby up to his room and lock him inside.

Well, about a half an hour later the Stockbridge police burst into the inn. Someone's up on the roof throwing beer bottles at cars driving down Main Street, they say. It took them another half hour to get Bobby down from there. They charged him with reckless endangerment, drunk and disorderly conduct, and resisting arrest.

Jerry Zuckerman went nuts. Simon, meanwhile, was in no mood for pranks. The reason he couldn't be with us that night was because Marva Faith OD-ed in her home out in Great Neck and Simon was waiting around the goddam hospital in Manhasset to find out whether she was going to live or die. Bobby spent the rest of the night in jail.

It ended up costing several thousand dollars to get Bobby's charges knocked down to plain disorderly conduct and then charter a special plane to deliver him to Portland, Maine, the next night, where we were opening for Sonny and Cher, of all people.

The message came up from New York to the effect that any more shenanigans on Bobby's part would cost him his job.

"My job?" Bobby echoed him snidely over the phone. "This isn't a job. You can't fire me."

"That's what you think," Simon said. You could hear it across the room. Then, apparently, Simon read him a portion of both our management and recording contracts which stated, in rather legalistic language, that they could all be fired at any time. The provision was in the fine print, and we had signed the management contract without a lawyer's advice, remember. And it was in the Gemini contract because that agreement was drawn up with the aid of Simon's lawyer. So all that diplomatic talk about no personnel changes without our unanimous consent had no real legal basis in fact. And when Rego realized that this was the case, he started a long, slow burn— not that he approved of Bobby's behavior—but he saw how Simon had pulled a fast one. Gary said he wasn't the least bit surprised. Naturally, everybody's bad feelings ended up getting dumped on me.

Two nights later we were playing the Veterans Auditorium in Boston, on a bill with Mitch Ryder and the Detroit Wheels. This time Spag got caught in the middle. He had come on the tour with us because we couldn't reproduce the *Rising Son* arrangements in concert without him, and it was important, on a promotional tour of this kind, to play your stuff the way it sounds on the record.

Anyway, we were supposed to open the show at nine o'clock, and by nine-thirty Spag still hadn't shown up backstage at the arena. I sent Keough back to the Copley Plaza, but he wasn't there either. The promoter, a sebaceous radio station owner, one Herschel Resnick by name, was growing more upset by the minute. Soon he was threatening us with courts and attorneys unless we went onstage.

"Your glands are showing," Rego told him.

"You want to stick around in this business more than a week, don't be such a wise guy," Resnick said, waving a fistful of signet rings in Rego's face. You could hear them stomping their feet and yelling out in the auditorium like *Riot in Cellblock B.*

"You know, I wanted to go into radio," Rego kept it up, "but my glands couldn't take it."

"Fuck you, twerp."

"Don't you love these guys with their fast-track patter?"

"You'll love it even more in court," Resnick said, and swaggered out in his ill-fitting gabardines.

"Fuck it, let's go on without him," Rego said.

I said no.

Finally, at ten after ten, Spag finally appeared, looking frightened and bedraggled.

"You crazy little shit!" Bobby practically jumped down his throat. "Where have you been?"

I stepped between the two of them.

"Not now!" I said.

Keough handed Spag his guitar and fiddle and steered him out toward the stage. He played beautifully that night, a tremendous, powerful solo on "Cold River" that just blew the dust off the rafters. I dreaded to think what we'd have sounded like without him.

We had a fast load-out after that show and a charter to catch for Buffalo, where we were playing Kleinhans Music Hall the next night. I managed to get Spag alone way off behind the loading dock while the others were still backstage meeting girls and the roadies were moving the equipment into a truck. After considerable coaxing, I got him to tell me what the hell made him so late.

It developed that he had rented a car that afternoon in order to drive to Providence and see his parents. On the way back, outside of Walpole, the car had broken down, and in his childish terror Spag had taken it to a service station to have it fixed. A rented car, right? He was in the goddam shop until eight-thirty that night. What could you say in the face of such foolishness? On top of all that, his parents hadn't even been home. I told him to forget the whole thing. I told him to never again make an unscheduled side-trip without checking with Keough first. He said what he always said: "Okay."

Then, in the plane later on, Rego came down the aisle and slid in the seat next to me. It was dark. You could hear the others snoring.

"After this tour, if he makes it through the tour without getting fucking lost or something, I want him out of the band," Rego said.

Worcester was going by down below, like a mass of phosphorescent plankton in the sea.

"Maybe he can just play in the studio," I said.

"No, Byron, he can't *just* play in the studio, and you know it," Rego said, trying to keep his voice down. "If he plays on the albums, he'll have to come on tour too. It'll be the same goddam thing all over again. And don't think Simon's not going to hear about this escapade."

"You don't have to tell Simon. What are you? A goddam tattle-tale?"

"Where were you when Simon shit all over Bobby?"

"Bobby deserved it and you know it. He did a stupid thing."

"What do you call what Spag did?"

"It's not the same. Spag's a—"

"Look, either he's a basketcase or he's just as responsible for his actions as the rest of us. And either way, I don't care to gig with him anymore, okay?"

"Okay, Rego," I said.

He got up and left me alone. The jet hummed dreamily into the west.

In Buffalo, a girl who looked like the offspring of Betty Boop and Dracula offered to immortalize our cranks by making plaster casts of them, and since it seemed to be about the most important thing in the world to her, we obliged. In Detroit, Bobby and Rego picked up two tasty morsels and decided to take them on a Trans-Love plane ride to our next stop, Cincinnati. At 30,000 feet they made the slightly alarming discovery that the two girls were fourteen and fifteen respectively, and ditched them in the VIP lounge with air-fare home as soon as we landed. In Louisville, we headlined for the first time, on a bill with the Critters. "Rebecca's Window" was num-

ber 24 on the *Billboard* chart with a bullet. In Memphis, Spag
astonished us by appearing in the hotel coffeeshop for breakfast with
a girl on his arm. True, she was a slutty-looking peroxide blonde on
the shady side of thirty. But it was still a hopeful sign. And then,
leaving Atlanta, Spag pulled another corker: he bought an English
sheepdog puppy which proceeded to have diarrhea up and down
the carpeted aisle of our chartered plane. Keough delivered it forth-
with to the ASPCA in Jacksonville, our next stop. When I asked
Spag whatever possessed him to buy the dog, all he could say was
"I don't know. . . ." The more I was around him, the more bizarre
I realized he was. But as long as he was with us, he deserved to be
treated like a human being. After the sheepdog incident the roadies
nicknamed Spag "Woofer" and Bobby didn't miss an opportunity to
flog poor Spag over the head with it until I cornered him behind a
stack of amps backstage at the Lake Charles Civic Center and told
him I didn't want to hear it one more time.

"Fuck you. We've got something called the first amendment in
this country," Bobby said.

"You want to blow this gig for yourself totally, don't you?"

"Haven't I already?"

"Who told you that?"

"Don't play games with me, Pete—"

"You're playing games with yourself, asshole, and you're going to
lose if you keep it up."

"You knew about those contracts, didn't you."

"No, I didn't."

"You think you're such hot shit? I'll tell you one thing: you're a
lousy liar," he said and walked away, as if he had anything to gain
by scoring debating points. To tell you the truth, I could understand
why he thought I was lying about the contracts and all. You couldn't
be angry at him anymore. He had such a dim sense of his own best
interests that you could only feel sorry for him.

The roadies, though, were another matter. They lived in their
own world of crazy hours, low pay, hard labor and little glory. I told
Keough to warn them about riding Spag. But, in Little Rock, one of
them hadn't gotten the message. He said "woof woof" to Spag as we
were leaving the auditorium after the five o'clock sound check and
I fired the kid on the spot.

By the time we got to Kansas City, "Rebecca's Window" was
number 6 on the charts. *Rising Son* was breaking out on the album

charts. We were full-time headliners now.

Before the show that night we went to a steakhouse down by the riverfront that Keough recommended. A car full of teenage girls followed us there. The management was not delighted to have us—a bunch of long-haired freaks—but we greased the maître d's palm and, *voilà!* a table magically became available.

There was a real cowboys and Indians mentality brewing in the country at that time, and crossing that dining room to our table, there was no doubt about who was who. We ordered a round of drinks, and another. A reporter and a photographer from the Kansas City *Sentinal* were with us. The reporter was a young guy, only a few years out of school himself, and fairly hip, though he wore a suit and tie for his job and all, and he was asking me a lot of questions about the war. This guy's own feelings were pretty obvious, judging by his questions—"Was the bombing of civilians in Hanoi a new low for U.S. foreign policy?"—and I think he just wanted me to supply him with some juicy quotes.

". . . I'm confident that with the kind of spirit we've got in this country now, we can reach much greater depths . . ." I told him.

Meanwhile, the teenage girls who followed us from the hotel were causing a ruckus in the entrance of the restaurant. One of them slipped through the maître d's line of defense and was approaching the table, gliding eerily toward us with this glazed, psychotic look on her face, obviously whacked out of her skull on something. I was getting the feeling that soon we'd be back at the hotel ordering a bucket of chicken. The girl was hovering right beside me.

"If you'll let me make love to you, I'll give anything," she said.

I tried to ignore her, but then I saw Gary, who was sitting across from me, put his hand up like he was shading his eyes and say "oh, no," and start chuckling. The photographer started firing his flash-bulbs off. When I looked back over my shoulder at the girl, she had her shirt pulled off and her pink-tipped breasts exposed, right there in the middle of the restaurant.

"Don't I have a nice body?" she said.

By this time Keough was behind her, trying to get her to put her shirt back on. She wasn't actively resisting, but she wasn't being much help either.

"It would mean so much to me. . . ."

Finally, he managed to hustle her out with the help of a couple of waiters. I knew that there was no way we could stick around and have a normal meal. Everybody in the room had stopped what they

were doing to watch this outrage. I stood up and was about to rec-
ommend a diplomatic withdrawal when a guy from one of the nearby
tables sauntered over. He was about six-three, a gaunt-faced, sin-
ewy, middle-aged plainsman in a sky-blue suit and white shirt with
a string tie. He had the huge, red-knuckled hands of a rancher, and
his thumbs were hooked into his belt on either side of a silver
longhorn steer buckle.

"You boys are a disgrace," he said in an even tone of voice, "and
I want you to get out of my sight right this minute."

"We were just leaving," I tried to assure him, not being in the
mood to pick up any gauntlets.

"See that you do, queerbait," he said.

The next moment, a fist went flying past me and caught the
plainsman right in the solar plexus. He hit the floor and literally
started squealing like a pig—which is the sound human beings make
when they have the wind knocked out of them. After that, all hell
broke loose, as they say in the heartland. Tables flipped over. Plates
and glasses crashed everywhere. Women screamed. Fists flew
through the air and all you could hear were these sickening thuds
and groans when they connected. I was grappling with some fat
bozo who kept slapping me in the face with the flat of his hand, and
I could see a woman banging Gary over the head with the heel of
her shoe. Finally, all these blue sleeves reached in, pulling everybody apart.

They took us—the band, that is, plus Billy—down to the precinct
station and booked us under all these cockamamie charges: assault,
criminal mischief, you name it. The promoter of the show had to
post a $10,000 bond to get us the hell out of there. There was a
stopover at the hospital emergency room. Gary had to get a dozen
stitches in his scalp and a skull x-ray. Rego had a cracked rib. It was
a miracle that we played that show at all. A band called the Blues
Magoos opened for us, and they had already been onstage for two
hours when we showed up at eleven fifteen. Their claim to fame was
that they wore electric suits that lit up. The audience was throwing
tangerines at them when we arrived. Then, it turned out, we could
only play until midnight because the city had a new ordinance pro-
hibiting concerts from going past that hour. We would have played
past the curfew, but they turned on the houselights and cut the
juice to our equipment, which was especially stupid because it just
made the kids angry. They started ripping up chairs. The police had
to clear them out. It was a disaster.

Simon was at the airport at eleven o'clock the next morning, having flown straight from New York. He was especially reserved as he herded us into the conference room off the VIP lounge. He had a copy of the Kansas City paper under his arm. We'd already seen it, and I don't need to tell you what was on the front page.

"The only bad publicity is no publicity," Bobby said, trying to shed some cheer over the meeting. Simon ignored him, but his face radiated pure disgust.

"I only have one thing to tell you boys," he said quietly. "The only public places I expect any of you to be seen for the remainder of this tour is onstage, or in the restaurant of whatever hotel you're booked into, or in the airport. That's all. You can get on the plane now."

We glanced at each other, then got up to leave. Simon took my sleeve.

"May I have a word with you?"

The others marched out, casting these sullen, suspicious glances over their shoulders. Even Spag gave me the hairy eyeball. Keough held the door for them and followed. Simon leaned back on the rear legs of his chair, rubbing his face. He hadn't slept at all that night.

"You shouldn't blame them," I said, and tried to explain about the stoned teenager and how the whole thing happened, but Simon waved his fingers.

"Byron, there's an evil climate in this country. You're a bright kid. You know what you stand for—everything that these conservative bastards are against. For Chrissake, stay out of their watering holes. Look, I'll give it to you straight: the criminal charges, that's all bullshit. But this cowboy Rego popped, a Lyle Peebles, has already filed a civil suit as of this morning—"

"He's got a case! He started it!"

"Yeah, well, if I may borrow a locution from his attorney, he's got a string of witnesses as long as your arm who'll say whatever's convenient. It'll be a long, drawn-out suit, and it's going to cost money. We can't have any more incidents—"

"That's really justice, boy. . . ."

"It's how things are. Believe me, there's no advantage for you to get a reputation as a problem booking. It's strictly business with these guys. We make it as easy as possible for them to help us make a lot of money. And they get a nice piece of the action. Now, I've got this fellow Resnick from Boston on my ass—"

"Wait a minute, right there. That was your boy, Spagnola."

"Steven is a genius."

"He's a retard, Simon. You don't know what he did up in Boston?"

"No."

So Rego hadn't tattled after all. I felt hypocritical doing it, but I filled in Simon about Spag's foolish excursion. It seemed only fair. While I told him, we watched the others cross the tarmac to the waiting plane.

"He's younger than the rest of you," was the only thing Simon had to say about it.

"Not that much," I said. "And I don't think he's going to improve with age."

Simon grunted noncommittally, got up, and stuck the newspaper under his arm.

"They're all on probation," he said, looking down at me. "When the tour is over, we'll decide what happens. You need stable people around you, Byron, people you can depend on to do their jobs and not cause a lot of unnecessary aggravation. You'll see I'm right." He reached down and patted my cheek a couple of times, a little roughly, I thought. "Incidentally, Claire sends her love."

Now, I don't know if it was my guilty conscience or what, but something about the way he said that really gave me the creeps. Somehow, I was sure he knew.

"Give her my regards," I said, without looking him in the eye.

"I'll be sure to. We'll see you in L.A., then."

And that was the end of the meeting. We said good-bye and went to our separate planes.

From that morning on, I was socially blackballed from my own band. The others never found out exactly what had transpired between me and Simon, or about their being on probation. They never asked. I think they assumed the worst, though. That they were goners.

Oddly enough, all this distrust and hostility didn't subvert our performances. It added a dimension to them. With rock and roll, you're always dealing in overblown adolescent emotions, right? Only in our band it was real, and it came out onstage. And I think the audiences could pick up on it. There was incredible tension in the halls where we played. It scared me. I'd come off stage wringing wet and drink three or four scotches before I could even talk to anybody. Each night, I felt like I was farther out there, closer to the edge, and I began to wonder if I was going to make it through the rest of the tour. Then, all of a sudden, we were on the West Coast.

When we got to San Francisco, "Rebecca's Window" was the number 1 single in the country. The radio and TV stations came after me for interviews. I spent an hour with a guy from the *Chronicle*. Nobody was interested in your favorite food or color anymore. It was all politics and religion. You'd make some remark about the weather and people would say, "What'd he mean by that? Good weather for what? For walking on water?" Sometimes I felt like the whole country was losing its marbles.

We did one San Francisco show at the Fillmore Auditorium on a bill with Lothar and the Hand People and a local band that RCA was putting a lot of their money and hopes behind called the Jefferson Airplane. I was backstage afterward, trying to decompress, when three hippies were shown into my dressing room, two blond girls and a somewhat pudgy guy with round glasses and an owlish face. All of them were dressed up in expensive psychedelic garb, satins and silks. The man complimented me on the show and we talked for a while. The scotch was starting to calm me down. He invited me to a party at his place down in Portola. Under any other circumstances I probably wouldn't have gone, but since the Kansas City debacle I hadn't seen anything except the insides of hotels, airplanes, and concert halls. I was aching to get away from it all, if only for a few hours. Besides, a number of Bill Graham's people at the Fillmore seemed to know this guy, so I figured he was all right. What ended up happening had a lot to do, I think, with why I never wanted to live in California.

We got into a midnight-blue Rolls-Royce that looked like one of those celestial maps from the *Golden Book of Astronomy*. Stars and constellations were painted all over it. The guy—Oliver was his name—drove while I sat in the back between the two girls. They had enough drugs in that car to start a mobile college of pharmacology. Tabs of acid, joints, hash—they offered me whatever I wanted, but I politely declined and had some cognac from the built-in bar instead. The girls were quite attractive and playful, though not much for conversation, so I mostly chatted with Oliver. We drove down the Pacific Coast Highway for about a half hour, turned off it, and then up what proved to be a long dirt driveway that snaked between walls of glossy rhododendron bushes and finally ended in a beautiful redwood forest.

There were dozens of cars parked under the mammoth, widely spaced trees, many expensive models—Porsches, Jaguars, and Mercedes, as well as junky-looking jalopies, and an old school bus covered with multicolored swirls like the paintings done by schizophrenics in your old college psychology textbook. Further in, you could see dozens of people milling around under the Japanese lanterns that were strung between the trees, some dancing, some just grooving to the music, others standing around talking—though how they managed it was beyond me because the band that was playing sounded like bombers in the Great Tokyo Air Raid, they were so loud. Strobes flashed like shellbursts in a war zone. To an easterner like me, the whole place was everything we'd been hearing about the West Coast scene. Tripsville, U.S.A. Freak City.

We had barely gotten out of the car when people started coming up to me, clustering, mouthing my name, trying to touch me. They didn't mean any harm by it, but I was disappointed when I realized I wouldn't be able to just roam around the party freely. It was also a somewhat alarming demonstration of how fast and completely the fame machine starts chewing up your life as a normal human being. But as things turned out, Oliver had never intended to let me simply mingle and enjoy myself.

"There is someone who especially wants to meet you," he said loudly over the music. "Come with me." I was a bit hesitant but I told myself it was all right, Keough knew I was down here, it was safe—in other words, fighting off my usual paranoid tendencies.

Straight ahead through the redwood grove, and all lit up, was a fairytale castle of a house built farther against a canyon wall, made of honey-colored wood, with turrets, spires, and domes reminiscent of the Russian churches they built in Alaska in the 1800s. To get to it, you had to climb a twisting log stairway hewn out of the earth. All the way up, spacey-looking party-goers recognized me, saying "Hello, Byron" or just plain "Byron" as we passed them.

Inside the main foyer of the house was a large medieval-looking room with a gaping fireplace at one end and a huge woven mandala hanging over it. The other walls were hung with psychedelic tapestries. Some kind of lavish feast was in progress. Over fifty people were seated around a big semicircle of tables that groaned with haunches of meat, platters of fruit, and bottles of wine. A hush fell over the festivities as we entered.

"This way," Oliver said pleasantly, and steered me toward an elaborate wooden staircase with blue lights built into the risers and signs of the zodiac carved on the treads.

The stairway led to one of the towers, six-sided, six-windowed room with a ceiling of up-gathered, pleated blue silk that made it appear like the inside of an Arabian tent. The room was lit with candles and incense filled the air. A round bed occupied the center of the room, and on the bed was an enchantingly beautiful girl in a red robe with pink azalea blossoms woven in her shiny black hair. Six other young women surrounded her attentively on cushions. They were passing a long-stemmed hash pipe among themselves. The girl on the bed was telling some sort of fable about the moon and a "grand wizeer." She told it with hand gestures that seemed choreographed and her voice had a sing-song quality to it that gave you the feeling she'd told the story many times before. Except for passing the pipe, her attendants paid rapt attention. Oliver cleared his throat.

"Adrianna," he interrupted her gently.

The girl stopped and lifted her head while the most radiant smile came upon her face.

"Did you bring him?" she asked.

I realized then that she was blind.

"Oh, please, everybody, excuse us, would you?" she said.

Boy, did they clear out of there fast! Oliver was the last one to leave. He took my hand, squeezed it damply, and said, "Thank you for coming. It means so much to her." Frankly, I didn't relish being left alone with her like that, but I didn't want to hurt anyone's feelings either, so I stayed.

"Come over and sit by me," Adrianna said when they were gone. She patted the velvet bedspread. I went over and sat down, telling myself it was like being a famous baseball player visiting one of the kids in the hospital. She lightly ran her fingertips over my face, my hair, and even inside my shirt. It gave me the shivers. "Don't be afraid," she said.

"I'm not," I said. "It's chilly."

"Oh, it really is you!"

"It's me, all right," I said.

"I absolutely love your album. The Beatles are my favorites, of course. They were just here." As a matter of fact, they had played San Francisco the week before, but I had a feeling that wasn't what she meant. "You know, they have only four more years."

"Four more years of what?"

"Of being Beatles."

"Oh . . . ?" I said, but she didn't elaborate.

"Dylan is my biggest single hero," she declared. "I helped him write some of his songs."

Here we go, I thought.

"You don't believe me?" Adrianna said.

"I'm trying to."

"We communicate secretly. I helped him write his new album."

"Well, I hope he appreciates it," I said, not meaning to be snide.

"I doubt it. He's so full of himself. Worse than you. Besides, I didn't do it for the credit. I did it because I love him. Just like I helped you."

"You helped me write my songs?" I echoed her. She smiled. "Which ones?"

" 'Time Will Tell,' 'Peaceable Kingdom,' 'Phantom Cargo.' "

Now, that made my stomach squinch up, because I had only written "Phantom Cargo" a few days earlier in the plane between Spokane and Portland. And I hadn't performed it at the Fillmore that night, either. To tell you the truth, she was beginning to give me the willies. I was afraid to even ask how she accomplished these neat tricks.

"Did you like the show tonight?" I asked instead, trying to change the subject.

"I didn't go," she said.

"You didn't—"

"I never leave this place."

"You never leave this room?"

"No, silly. I leave the room. I go outside. I just don't stray into the world beyond."

"Why not?"

"I don't have to. I have everything I need here. You're here."

I was more painfully aware of that fact with each passing moment.

"Oliver brings me everything I want," Adrianna continued and then made a pouty face. "Everything but the moon."

"You wouldn't want the moon. In the first place, it's too big. It would take up half the state of California."

"It is not! The moon is *this* big." She spread her arms to show me. "They don't know. Nobody's been up there. The moon is made of gold brocade and it fits right into this room." It then occurred to me that she may never have seen the moon, and it made me sad.

"Do you mind if I ask, how long have you been. . . ?"

"Blind? All my life," she said without a trace of self-pity. "But I can sense things. I can tell things. Don't be sad."

My stomach tightened another notch.

"Adrianna, are you a witch?" I asked.

"A witch?" she said, giggling. "I was born Adrianna Selkirk in Palo Alto. My dad is vice-president for consumer credit of the Wells Fargo Bank and my mom is a housewife. I went to high school like anybody else, and I had a dog named Deedie. I am certainly not a witch."

"But you can . . . tell things."

"I have my talent, and you have yours. Are you afraid of your talent?"

"You tell me."

"There's a lot I can tell you, Byron. Would you like to make love to me? Don't be afraid."

"Can't you just tell my fortune."

"I am *not* a fortune teller, either! Oooh! I can't believe you said that. God. . . !"

She carried on angrily for a minute, but then her hand stole back into my shirt again.

"Make love to me, Byron."

"Wouldn't Oliver object?" I said, trying desperately to be polite.

"He's devoted to my happiness. Didn't he bring you here?" She slipped the robe off her shoulders. "See now nice my body is?" It was very nice indeed. "Touch me, Byron," she said breathily. Though I can't deny I felt my blood rise, the whole thing was altogether too flipped-out for me. I wanted to leave. The guitars were shrieking down in the canyon.

"I, uh, have to go, Adrianna," I said, getting up off the bed.

"Poor, poor Byron," she said and shook her head. At first I thought she was making fun of me, but then I realized she was crying.

"We've got to catch this plane for L.A. first thing in the morning," I tried to explain. "I probably shouldn't have even come here—"

"I can tell things," she said, quietly weeping. "I can tell things, but I can't change them."

"Sure. Nobody can," I said and started edging toward the door.

She suddenly sat bolt upright and said, "Don't you see? We all have to die!"

Boy, that froze me up solid.

"Pardon me," I said.

"Go!" she screamed. "Go catch your stupid plane!"

"Hey, it's not going to crash or anything, is it?"

"No, it's not going to crash. Did I say it was going to crash?"

"No."

"You make me so mad!" she groped around the bed, found a brass box, and flung it at me. It bounced off the door and a chunk of hash the size of a golf ball fell out.

"I can't change it! I can't change it!" Adrianna shouted.

I felt behind me for the doorknob.

"Next time we play here, you'll have to come see us," I told her, wincing at my ill-chosen words. But I was so anxious to get out of there I could barely think straight. "Anyway, it's been a pleasure meeting you. Well, good-bye. . . ."

I tiptoed out and closed the heavy door behind me. Oliver was waiting for me on the first floor. The merrymakers had been eating and drinking and watching a juggler. When I appeared on the stairs, all eyes turned to me. The juggler stopped. Oliver smiled and began clapping his hands. Soon, the others joined in with loud applause and cheers, some lifting their goblets to toast me. Finally, Oliver took me damply by the elbow and tried to lead me over to the table, but I steered him aside.

"I have to go back to the city right away," I told him.

"But we prepared a feast for you."

"Hey, I appreciate it. I really do. Only we have an early flight in the morning."

"They'll be disappointed," he said and bit his lip. Then, he looked back at me excitedly. "Did you sow a seed in Adrianna?"

"Did I what?"

"Did you have intercourse with her? Don't be embarrassed."

"Did you want me to?"

"Oh, yes."

"Oliver, I have to get going—"

"But did you?"

"Yeah, sure."

"Oh, I'm so happy!"

I was ready to hot-wire somebody's car to get out of there. But when he was satisfied that I had had sex with his girlfriend, or wife, or whatever she was, he cheerfully led me back down the log stairway to his Rolls. The party was still going strong out in the red-woods. We were halfway down the stairs when a cherubic teenage hippie came up to Oliver and told him, "The Angels are here."

"Make them welcome."

Angels, I thought. What next? The beast of Sodom? But then I heard the motorcycles whining down below and saw a dozen mounted thugs roll in on their choppers. I managed to lead Oliver around the outskirts of the party to the car. He got behind the wheel but he didn't start up the engine.

"Why don't you take it," he said, "and leave it at your hotel."

"You trust me with this car?"

"Certainly. Would you like to take some acid back for your friends?"

"I don't think so, Ollie. They have plenty, thanks."

"This is special stuff. Each one has a little star on it, see? That's how you can tell it's ours. The pink star is 500 mics, the blue one's 1000, and the purple is a four-way. Purple's the royal buzz—"

"Okay, great," I said to shut him up and took the envelope and chucked it in the back. Oliver got out and handed me the keys through the window. "How do I get back to the city?" I asked.

"It's simple," he said. "Just take a right at the end of the drive-way, keep going until you reach the Pacific Ocean, and take another right. It's the 'right' way, get it?" he chortled.

I pretended to laugh at his lame joke. Meanwhile, he reached inside, grabbed my left hand off the wheel, and kissed it. I was nauseated.

"We'll always remember you for this," he said.

"I won't forget it either, Ollie. Bye."

I started up the engine. The scene in the redwoods was starting to look like a panel out of Hieronymus Bosch. I let out the brake and headed down the shrub-lined driveway, a little bit surprised that I was being allowed to leave in one piece. It was five-thirty in the morning before I made it back to the Fairmont Hotel in San Francisco. Keough was already up, going over his ever-present checklist. We had breakfast together in the hotel coffeeshop. I was never so happy to be surrounded by Formica, Muzak, and hum-drum people in my life. I told him what it had been like down in Portola. Keough had been on the road with various bands for a cou-ple of years by then, and he'd been in a few strange scenes himself.

"Gets a little weirder every year," he chuckled, trying to be phil-osophical.

"I could handle that," I told him. "What bothers me is that they think *we're* the leaders."

Anyway, I had an uneasy feeling about that plane trip, so instead of flying to L.A., I made Keough drive with me all the way down. It took damn near eight hours. That flight never did crash. I guess she really got to me, though, Adrianna.

*That was Oliver Sankey, wasn't it?*

Yes, indeedy. That was Sankey, all right. He was taking too much of his own acid, I think.

*He was a legend out there. Supplied the whole Bay Area for years. Tomorrow's Children, he called that tribe of his. Practically everybody who ever played San Francisco ended up being taken to his place at one time or another. His wife was the greatest starfucker of the era.*

Yeah? Well, she didn't get me. Whatever became of them?

*Sankey was stabbed to death in Vacaville Prison, 1972.*

Jesus! What about Adrianna?

*I don't know.*

Well, so much for Tomorrow's Children. God, stabbed to death. . . .

*Getting back to the '66 tour—*

Huh . . . ? Oh, the tour? It was supposed to end in L.A., but when they'd made up the itinerary back in June, nobody had planned on us having a song at the top of the charts when we got there. In other words, it was a record company's dream. So instead of letting us go home, Simon booked us into more than a dozen colleges on our way back east—the big schools, the huge universities of the Midwest. Altogether, it was worth a great deal of money. You just had to grit your teeth and do it. The other guys were furious.

"Fuck you, I've got tickets to Maui!" Bobby exploded when he heard the news.

"I'm afraid you'll have to cancel them," Simon told him, "or learn how to play the ukulele."

Needless to say, this colloquy did not improve the ambient fellowship of Byron Jaynes and the Romantics. Physically, it was all we could do to drag our butts through another two weeks of one-nighters. But they were good performances, and good audiences, people who knew what I was trying to say and listened. And our sales showed it. When I finally got off the last plane at Kennedy Airport, *Rising Son* was the number 1 album in America, "Rebecca's Window" was still the top single, and "Observe the Fugitive," which was released as our next single just after we split from L.A., was number 19 with a bullet on the *Billboard* charts. We were the hottest band in America.

I slept for eighteen hours straight at the Sherry and called my mother the next day around noon to see if I could take her out to lunch. She wasn't home. Finally, I got up some momentum and walked a few blocks over to Simon's office. It was a gorgeous October day, but already the city was getting to me.

"How does it feel to be a star?" Simon asked, leaning back in his big padded execu-chair from behind his cluttered desk.

"I feel like the golden calf," I said wearily. "Or is it the golden goose?" I didn't mean to be sassy. I was still burned out from the road.

Simon cleared his throat. "Jerry's got studio time reserved for you starting October 11th."

"That's next week, the eleventh."

"That's right."

"I don't want to go right back into the studio."

Simon peered at me over the rims of his half-glasses. "I know you've got the material."

"The other guys aren't even in town."

"Yes. Well, I could make some calls," Simon said. "Line up some top-flight people for you. It doesn't have to be anything formal. No finished tracks. Just lay down whatever you feel like: a work tape."

"For that I need top-flight people?"

"Gemini's paying for it anyway."

"Hey, you know what I want, Simon? A car."

"What for?"

"To go away."

"You just came back from 'away.' "

"No, I came back from a tour."

"That's not 'away'?"

"No."

"I see."

"It's really nowhere."

Simon smiled patiently. "A studio," he said. "A studio is really somewhere."

"Why are you pushing so hard?"

"Jerry is looking forward to a spring release, and I agree with him. It's not wise to wait a full year. Besides, you're not such a national monument yet that you can afford to sit on your hands."

"Get him to move the sessions up to November and I'll do it," I said, thinking the others would probably be back by then and we could hash it out in the open, instead of pretending they didn't exist anymore and sneaking into the studio without them. Simon seemed relieved, though, that I gave in at all.

"Let's go get some lunch," he said, and led me from his inner sanctum to the outer office where his assistants and Marcia the secretary were slaving away in a morass of paperwork, tour schedules, and grungy coffee cups. The phones rang continuously. "California Dreamin' " was playing on the radio.

"Who's smoking pot in here again?" Simon asked the crew. They ignored him. You got the feeling he said that twelve times a day.

"Lou Adler called," Marcia said.

"Where is he?"

"L.A."

"I'll call him after lunch. Get Gordon on the horn and have him meet us at Sun Luck at one."

"Okay. That guy from the Vishnu Rangers—"

"The Vishnu Rangers!" Simon cried with obvious delight. "You'll love these guys. They play gourds. I'm going to sign them, all right. Into the state hospital. You've got to hear this tape to believe it, Byron."

"—and Ron Delsener wants to know if the Academy of Music is all right for Reuban on Halloween."

"Tell him affirmative. You don't smell pot? It's against the law, pot."

Marcia handed me one of those pink telephone memos. It was dated September 30, the previous Friday, and it had Catherine's name and number on it. I picked up the nearest phone. I was about to hang up on the fifth ring when she picked it up.

"Hi," I said. "It's me, Byron."

"Flash!" she said, all excited. "I was in this beer hall in Düsseldorf and they played your record!"

"What on earth were you doing in Düsseldorf?"

"Don't ask. I'll never make that mistake again. But then I heard it in Milan and Paris and Monte Carlo. They were playing it all over Europe. It really is happening for you."

"Something is," I reluctantly agreed.

"Oh, Byron, I want to see you."

"It would be nice to see you too," I said.

Simon snatched the phone away from me and cupped one huge hand over the mouthpiece. "We've got an interview with *Look* after lunch, and the *Billboard* people are coming in to give you your gold record."

"Can't they mail it—?"

"They have to take your picture for the magazine." He handed the phone back to me.

"Hello, Catherine?"

"What's going on there?"

"I'm at my manager's office."

"Oh, Simon," she said crabbily.

"How about later today? Four?"

"Fine. Are you still crazy about me?"

"Sure," I said, probably unconvincingly. The truth was I remembered the *feeling* of being crazy about her a lot clearer than I remembered the girl herself. But I was certainly anxious to see her, if only to find out what I'd gotten so worked up over back in June.

Anyway, I hung up and we went over to Sun Luck for a Chinese lunch. Simon's lawyer, Gordon Davis, met us there and tried to explain how much money I had all of a sudden and what they were doing with it. Gordon was only a few years older than me, and I couldn't help thinking how he was the very image, in his tweeds and tie, of what my father wanted his son to grow up and be.

Back in the office afterward, the *Look* magazine reporter vainly inquired into my origins, and I stuck to the fiction that I was an orphan raised by wolves in the wilds of New Jersey. Pam Schneider, Simon's long-suffering publicity girl, sat there grinding her teeth.

"There's a story going around that you're the son of Westchester County D.A. Morris Greenwald."

"Really? Where'd you hear that?"

"I've done a little legwork myself—"

"This interviews's over, bud."

"Byron!" Pam said.

"The guy's a peeping Tom!"

Pam was exasperated with me. The *Look* reporter was too embarrassed to even get up and leave. He just sat there staring at his notepad. I didn't want him to get in trouble with his boss.

"Hey, why don't you ask me about the war or something, okay?" I finally said.

When that was over with, the *Billboard* guys came in to give me my gold record and shoot some pictures. After they left, Simon sat down and signed a blank check, which he handed to me. I hadn't even been back in the city long enough to get personal checks.

"Go buy yourself a car," Simon said.

"Hey, thanks."

"You don't have to thank me. It's your money. You earned it. Only do me a favor: stick around until Friday. Jerry's throwing a party for you at the Rainbow Room—"

"Oh God, Simon. Can't you get him to postpone it? I'm so tired of being around mobs of people I could cry."

"Son, do me a favor and be there. You don't have to stay long."

"I wish someone would ask me, once in a while, if I even wanted a party. They never ask."

"You don't shit where you eat, old boy. Just tell me you'll be there."

"Okay."

"I hope you find yourself a very nice car. Now scram."

I walked the ten blocks or so from Simon's office to Catherine's place. Halfway up, at 68th and Park, three coeds from Hunter College recognized me and asked for my autograph. Then, at 71st, a bigger and younger mob of teenage girls latched onto me outside one of those private day schools. It was just my luck to be traveling on foot through the heart of the Upper East Side when school let out. A bunch of them trailed me up to 72nd. I jogged across Park and at Madison I broke into a flat-out sprint until I made it to Catherine's building. Through the little diamond-shaped window of the elevator, I could see them swarming in the lobby.

Catherine had a beautiful tan. I remembered instantly one of the reasons I was attracted so strongly to her back in June: she was so damn pretty.

"Byron! What's the matter?"

"There's a mob after me?"

She looked skeptical, to say the least.

"I'm not kidding. I'll show you."

"Don't you want to come in for a while."

"No. I want to buy a car. Come with me."

I had this inspiration. I took her down the service elevator. Once outside, we skulked up the alley to 72nd Street, crossed to the other side, and took cover behind a parked car. The doorman was still fighting with that mob of teenagers.

"My God! Look at Filipe!" Catherine gasped. Poor Filipe, the doorman, was brandishing the long-handled dustpan that he used to keep the entrance tidy. In his green and gold uniform, he looked like some absurd latter-day hussar beating away a mob of peasant rabble. Next, an N.Y.P.D. cruiser pulled up in front of the building with a screech and the girls scattered. I grabbed Catherine's hand and hurried up to the corner at Fifth, where we got in a cab. I told the driver to take us through the park. I could see him stealing glances back at me through the rear-view mirror. He was young, a hippie type.

"You folks get high?" he asked.

"We sure do," Catherine said.

He smiled and lit a joint, took a toke, and passed it back. "I know you," he said.

"No you don't," I said.

"Yes I do."

"You don't."

"I bought your album, man."

"I don't have any album—"

"Hey, isn't he Byron Jaynes?"

"He certainly is," Catherine said, beaming.

"Whose side are you on, anyway?"

"Yours," Catherine said and threw her arms around me. "I'm so proud of you, Flash," she whispered in my ear.

"Hey, Dan—" I could read the driver's name, Dan Sternweiss, on his hack license posted on the dash "—I want to buy a car. Do you know any dealerships in Manhattan?"

"Well, Byron," he answered like we were old buddies, "what kind of car are you looking for?"

"Gee, I don't know, Dan. Something fun to drive."

"What price range did you have in mind?"

"Money is no object."

"Buy a Rolls, Byron."

"You think I should?"

"Oh, absolutely."

"You think that's the car for me, huh?"

"That's the car for you, Byron."

"Then take me to the nearest dealer."

There was a showroom at 49th and Park. We said good-bye to old Dan. I gave him a C-note and told him to keep the change. It blew his mind. That kind of thing is pretty juvenile, I admit, but it's an incredible thrill when you first have that much dough and can throw it around like Monopoly money.

The boys in the showroom couldn't believe it when I said I'd take the white Silver Shadow in the window. I sat down and filled in the check. They said they'd prep the car, and if the check cleared I could drive it away tomorrow. I told them to call the bank and see if the check was good immediately because I wanted to leave with the car today.

They said that would be impossible.

I said in that case I could easily take myself to the nearest Mercedes dealer.

They called the bank.

We drove out of there in the Rolls at a quarter to five. Soon we were on the Saw Mill River Parkway heading into Westchester.

It was twilight when we got to the house on Radnor Road. The new owners had repainted the shutters blue. I liked them a lot better green.

"So this is where you grew up?" Catherine said.

"Do you like it?"

"It's very nice. So . . . normal."

"Not like you, with your fairytale castles, huh?"

"No," she agreed, smiling. "Would you like to see one of my favorites?"

"Sure," I said, not knowing that meant driving 250 miles north, to the Adirondacks.

The "cottage," as Catherine called it, was a hulking log mansion outside the mountain village of Big Slide. It was built by Catherine's grandfather, the confectioner, and represented a turn-of-the-century gentleman's exalted ideas about Roughing It.

The main room was huge. The walls were studded to capacity

with the heads of quadrupeds, whole herds of disembodied deer, moose, and elk. Stuffed trout leaped among them. A pike with a fantastic, needle-toothed mouth gaped over the mantelpiece. The furniture was draped with dustcovers. Nobody had been up there in a couple of years.

I took Catherine's hand and she led me upstairs. Our oil lamp cast spooky shadows on the wall and a stuffed bear on the second floor landing looked so real I almost messed my pants. Catherine took me around and showed me all the rooms. A lot of the furniture was that rustic style made out of sticks. The furnishings alone must have been worth a small fortune. Her grandfather's bed was a massive four-poster of birch logs. Each post was surmounted by a rack of antlers.

"Your grandad was a horny bastard, huh?" I cracked, and she sneered at me. "Sorry," I said.

We had picked up some steaks and things at the store back in Big Slide, but the kitchen wasn't really in order—the gas for the stove hadn't been delivered in years, for instance—so we grilled them in the big main fireplace, impaling them on the bronze antler andirons and eating them with our hands, naked, on the bearskin rug before the fire. Catherine looked so wild in the flickering light, the red juices running down her chin. Wild and beautiful. And what a rutting we enjoyed afterward, beneath the sightless gaze of all those slaughtered beasts.

"I think I love you," I told her.

"Keep on thinking," she said.

In the morning Catherine broke out the shotguns and we marched all over hell looking for partridge. She seemed to know what she was doing, but by midafternoon we hadn't had any luck.

"We need a bird dog," she said. "Byron, will you buy us a bird dog?"

"I'll be your bird dog," I said. She groaned.

We stayed up at Big Slide another day. Then Catherine got bored and restless. She could only take country seclusion for short stretches. A constant whirl of other people was essential to her well-being. On the way back to the city, we stopped at her parents' place in Cooperstown. It was even grander than the log palace at Big Slide, a wonderful Italianate villa on Nine Mile Point, a peninsula of about 700 acres jutting into Otsego Lake, just up the shore from James Fenimore Cooper's estate. Kenneth and Miggs were "in residence" then for the fall foliage show.

They were more elderly than I expected (72 and 60 at that time), and they behaved in their daughter's presence like two people trapped in a cage with a dangerous carnivore. They didn't seem to know what to make of me, with my long hair and odd clothes, but they were faultlessly polite. We had dinner in a big, cold room the size of a hotel lobby, and the chow (creamed chicken and peas) was surprisingly horrible. I tried to chat with the old man about art, which he collected. They had a Caravaggio and a small Rembrandt right there in the house in Cooperstown. Can you imagine?

The next day I dragged her down to the Baseball Hall of Fame—which she'd never been to even though she lived in the same town—and that's where I asked her to marry me, right in front of Babe Ruth's locker on the third floor. For a minute she didn't even acknowledge the question. She just gazed into the display case at all of the Babe's old things.

"What I can't figure out is how they ever caught the ball with those flat little mitts," she said quietly. "They look like gardening gloves."

"Hey," I turned her around by the elbow, "do you want to get married, or what?"

"I want to be immortal, like Babe Ruth."

"You can't."

"Okay, then I'll marry you."

And that's how we settled it. Anyway, as soon as we landed back in New York, I called up Simon to break the wonderful news. He sounded cold and downcast over the phone.

"You better come over right away, Byron," he said quietly.

"Aren't you even going to congratulate me?"

"Just come down."

"Look, if it's about Zuckerman's party—"

"It's not about Zuckerman's party."

"Well, what is it?"

"Don't argue, son. Do what I say."

So I hopped into a cab and went over to his office immediately. Simon looked quite perturbed, but the words came out of his mouth without hesitation.

"I have some bad news for you," he said. "Your mother is dead."

Byron shut off the tape recorder. The sun had set into a cloudbank above the far horizon, leaving us in an oppressive and premature twilight. The distant chain saws were quiet now, and the crickets were either dead or underground for the duration.

"Raw out here," he remarked. "Come on down below. There's something I want to show you."

We got up and started down the hill. It felt good to be moving again. By the time we reached the barn, I'd made a difficult decision. The problem was telling Byron. In the meantime, he took a key ring from his pocket and opened a massive padlock on his barn door. He slid the weighty thing open on its rusted rollers, reached inside, and threw a light switch. The fluorescent tubes balked and flickered, then revealed the most incongruous sight. There, lined up in even rows, were two dozen motorcycles.

I stepped inside cautiously. Some of the bikes were old-fashioned rigs with bicycle seats and odd, elongated tanks. There were the classic Harley hogs of the fifties, flatheads, shovelheads with jeweled mudflaps. There were the muscular British bikes, stolid Germans, and a few Japanese. The near corner of the barn was set up, evidently, as a repair shop with workbenches, tool chests, and a small, pneumatic lift. One bike was under repair on the lift, reduced to the bare bones of its tubular frame, the tank off and engine pulled.

"And you thought the boats were weird," Byron said.

He limped slowly up the first row, touching the chrome and leather lovingly, his brow furrowed in concentration.

"Indian Power Plus," he began reciting the name of each machine as if he were intoning a roll call of the honored dead. "Brough Superior SS100, BSA Gold Star, Ariel Square Four, 'Squariel,' they called it, Norton Dominator, powerful, finicky bike. Ah, here we go. This is the one."

He stopped in front of an absolute brute of a two-wheeled speed machine, the tank painted black and a fantastic snarl of exhaust pipes curving back from the V-shaped engine. Its styling had a distinct and disturbing insectile quality, both powerful and poisonous.

"This is the one that almost killed me in Tamberlane," Byron said. "Vincent Black Shadow. It would do 150 in nine seconds out of the box. Have you ever been in a wreck, Rick?"

"No."

"It's quite something. You're used to seeing the scenery come at you from the front, over the handlebars, right? It's an orderly

sequence of images. A wipe-out changes all that. Suddenly everything is shifting deplorably. Trees start rushing at you from the most
unorthodox angles, from the side, from behind you. And the strangest thing is how absorbing the experience becomes. You realize in a
fraction of a second that you no longer have the slightest control
over events. It does wonders for your concentration. I'll always
remember the sight of those trees coming at me. . . . This is the
actual bike, too, right here."

"You did a nice job of putting it back together. Do you mind if I
ask how you managed to get it up here?"

"No. You can ask."

"How?"

"People do things for money."

"I see."

"No, you probably don't see at all."

"You paid someone to acquire it for you," I ventured, not wanting
to be made a fool of again.

"That's right," he agreed. "And you know something else?"

"What?"

"You pay people a little more money, and they don't ask any
questions. Still, it wasn't easy." He limped on down the row. "This
is my baby. Triumph 500 banger. I rode it across the country and
back in the summer of '62. God, that was almost twenty years ago.
Can you believe it? My old man was so pissed off. I split the last
day of school with a sleeping bag on the bitch bar and an old beat-
up bicycle pannier full of camping stuff over the seat. It was the
first time I was really away from home, by myself, and it was wonderful. I had $150 saved up from caddying down at the club. It cost
about fifteen bucks in gas to get across the whole country. Boy,
those days sure are gone. I had the time of my life.

"When I got home, the old man sold it right out from under me.
He didn't approve of sixteen-year-old boys running off on their bikes
like that. Anyway, this isn't the same bike I actually made the trip
on, but it's just like it."

Byron limped up to the lift, switched on a work light, and began
fiddling with the rear sprocket assembly. A chill ran through me. It
was even colder in the barn than it was outside.

"I think I'm going to have to go away for a while, Byron," I said.

He glanced back at me, a stricken look of disbelief on his face.

"Where are you going?" he asked timidly.

"The city, I guess."

"You guess?"

"The city."

"Why do you say you guess, though?"

"Just an expression."

"I mean, if you're going to the city, then you're going to the city. There shouldn't have to be any guessing about it. You should *know* where you're going."

"It was only a turn of phrase."

"Words are important. You're a writer, you ought to know that."

"I have to go away for a while, that's all."

"Sure. It's a free country. Go away. I'll see you around."

"Byron, I—"

"Go on. Get out of here. Scram. Beat it. Buzz off."

My heart sank. I took a deep breath.

"Will you just shut up and get out!" he said.

I dawdled over to the open door and picked at the dark, punky wood, trying to find the words to explain.

"I've had some problems at home," I finally said.

"Problems? What kind of problems?"

"Well, it's nothing, really—"

"Do you have problems or not? First you don't know whether you're coming or going. Now you don't know if you have problems or not. If I gave you a mirror, do you suppose you could find your asshole?"

"You're my problem, Byron."

"Me? I'm interfering with your domestic arrangements? Ho! That's rich—"

"You're taking over my goddam life. That's what you're doing!"

"Well, pardon me! Here you've been listening to me and my problems day after day after day. You're right. It's time for a little quid pro quo. You want to tape it? Come on, set up the tape recorder. We'll get the whole thing down—"

"You don't give a fuck about me and my problems, Byron."

"Hey, look, I'm deeply concerned. Come on. Roll the tape. Spill your guts out."

"This is pointless."

"Then get the hell out of here. Nobody's stopping you."

"Okay," I said. And though I couldn't bear the thought of leaving him this way, he had left me no choice. "Whatever you say." As I turned to leave, I heard the clank of some tools falling to the floor, and I was afraid to look back.

"Sears, you're the most wishy-washy sonofabitch I ever met in my life, you know that? You've got the backbone of a snail!"

His words cut at the center of me with almost physical power and it took a tremendous effort not to lash back. "Luke!" I cried.

"Don't ever come back here, Sears! You're persona non grata, you snail!"

"How much backbone does it take to hide from the whole world for ten years?" I muttered into the dust.

"What'd you say?"

I heard the quick dull footfalls come up on me. He caught me right behind the knees and I went down. My chin struck the ground and a fierce pain filled my head like electricity. My ears resounded with his shouts. "Get up, you sonofabitch!" And somehow I did, whereupon he grabbed two handfuls of my jacket, swung me around against the outside wall of the barn (banging the back of my head this time), and pushed his forearm up against my throat.

"What makes you think you're free to just walk out on me like that?" he shouted.

My brain was swimming. I was laughing and crying at the same time.

"You kicked me out," I gasped. "Remember? Or is your memory failing you too?"

He pushed against my throat even harder. He'd become amazingly strong.

"I don't know why I ever let you into my life, you worm."

"So *I'm* the worm now?"

"And don't think I can't squash you."

"Let go of me right now, Byron! Luke!"

My dog stood idiotically five feet away, happily watching someone trying to choke me.

"See, it's not a game, Sears," Byron said, his teeth clenched, his eyes blazing. I could barely breathe. I groped for his face but he just banged my head against the wall.

"Worm! Worm!"

My lungs burned. Everything looked red. With all my remaining strength I hoisted my right knee sharply into his groin. His eyes rolled into his head and he fell away. I gasped for air. Byron was on all fours, on the ground.

I stumbled across the barnyard to the driveway and clawed at the door handle of the Saab.

"Luke!"

He was sprinting up and down the lawn.

I fumbled with the keys. The car cranked and cranked but wouldn't start. I fluttered the gas peddle desperately. In the rear-view mirror I could see Byron stagger to his feet, a menacing silhouette in the twilight against the brighter, unreal fluorescent glow that filled the mouth of the barn.

"Luke, goddam you to hell!" I screamed again, and in vain. He dipped his forebody close to the ground in that familiar feint of dog-play. Byron was stalking down the driveway toward me. The engine finally fired up. I threw the gearshift into first and patched out in the dirt. Byron's malevolent image vanished behind twin spumes of dust.

A quarter mile down the road, I slammed on the brakes. Luke had been chasing the car. Byron's place remained in view, glowering darkly on the hillside like the ghost house of your childhood dreams. I got out of the car.

"Here, boy! Here, Luke!" I held out my hand, slightly cupped, as if I were hiding a treat in it, and he fell for it as he had a hundred times before. I grabbed his collar, got hold of the rest of him, and virtually flung him by main force into the passenger seat.

They were playing Byron Jaynes on the radio station out of St. Johnsbury. With my hands still trembling, I reached for the knob, switched it off, and drove away from that place as fast as I could.

# Spring

# C H A P T E R   8

*Pharaoh, old Egypt's king*
*Put up his pyramid*
*Thinking it was just the thing*
*To keep his memory whole and his mummy hid*
*But a sneak thief came rummaging*
*And burglarized the coffin's lid*

—"Time Will Tell"

New York was haunted for me that winter and the ghost was 300 miles away in the hills of New Hampshire. My predicament was already desperate, but I couldn't go anywhere in the city without thinking of Byron, and looking back on that unhappy time, it seemed like all I did was wander the streets of Manhattan, obsessed with him like some combination of a lovesick teenager and a worried parent. It was bad enough feeling that what we had undertaken together, the tapes, was unfinished business, or worse, a failure. But back in the city I couldn't fool myself any longer. I realized what the tapes had stood for all along: my personal effort to rescue Byron Jaynes from a condition that was neither life nor death but only a tortured, lonely vigil at that gray margin where the two overlapped.

Just as disturbing was what this suggested about my own egotism, the self-serving way I cherished my assumptions. Who was I to say that Byron Jaynes or Peter Greenwald or Joe Doaks didn't have the right to live alone in the hills of New Hampshire? Who was I to decide that he was miserable, or even so, that it was possible for him to live any other way? And who was I to presume I could rescue him? Who was I . . . ? That was becoming a good question by itself. I would shamble along snowy Houston Street, or 8th Street, or Bleecker asking myself the same questions, over and over, my face buried in a wool muffler, hands thrust into the pockets of my down jacket, looking past the people hurrying homeward on the side-walks, noticing nothing and no one, just turning over the same old crap in my head, at looser ends than at any time I could remember since adolescence.

And the worst part of all was knowing he was still up there, being the only one in the world who knew that Byron Jaynes still lived. In the meantime, would you believe that his records, his image, his whole goddammed legend were enjoying a revival among a new generation of kids? I don't know how aware of it he was in the polar fastness of New Hampshire, but the radio stations in New York City were playing his old hits right along with the B-52s and The Clash. In the Village bars I would see punkers dressed in Byron Jaynes T-shirts. The old biographies about him were back in print, being displayed on the checkout counter at Dalton Books, and were climbing the paperback bestseller list. *Rolling Stone* ran a piece about how he had become a cult figure once again on the campuses. To say he would have loved it is probably somewhat wide of the mark, but I think he would have appreciated the irony.

But knowing he still lived was a burden that sometimes left me breathless with torment, and there were a few occasions in the weeks following my return when I ached to tell Allie, if only to relieve some of the pain—another facet of that selfish egotism I came to despise in myself. Foolish or not, selfish or not, I did not share the secret with her. I still believed in keeping my promises. In fact, it was one of the few enduring principles that still made any sense to me.

Once I was back in the city, I began to understand why he had turned on me in the end. Not that I meant to excuse his attack, but I realized how hard I must have been pushing him, how frightened he must have become as the days went by and he could no longer avoid the stark choices which our association raised about his future. It was probably the first time in ten years that he had any sense of a future. And at the end, I wonder if he really knew what was worse: the sudden idea of a future, or the return to limbo which my leaving posed. The terror of his loneliness must have been overwhelming. Finally, there was my conviction, brightened one day by hope, shaded the next day by dread, that the two of us were not finished with each other. The pavements of New York City were like egg-shells for me that winter.

Allie and I were in deep trouble no matter how you looked at it.

Talk about assumptions! When I thought about how naïve I had been eight months earlier to suppose that all my little financial arrangements would work out so neatly—I just wanted to bang my head against a wall. First of all, we were broke. The $7500 installment of my advance from Dover House, for the rock music history, was gone. I had altogether 38 measily manuscript pages to show, and though I tried every ploy short of crawling across my editor's floor on hands and knees, I could not get them to relinquish the other half of the $15,000 total. My editor, Betty Kalish, said she wished she could help, but company policy called for a strict reading of the contract. They'd been burned too many times to make exceptions, and it didn't escape me that I was the very picture of what company policy was devised to protect them against.

Meanwhile, I'd collected and spent that $2500 from Alex Rothchild on the basis of a five-page letter outlining a movie idea, and I might have gotten the other $2500 if I had delivered the full thirty-page "treatment." But the truth was I hadn't done a damn thing on the project since the previous April. Of the two projects, the movie treatment offered a better chance at some ready income, but our living situation was so chaotic that I didn't even have a place to set up my typewriter.

On top of this, the rental situation for apartments in New York had just gone through the roof that year and every halfway decent building in town was being turned into condos. Our old place on 11th Street, a four-story walk-up, had been a bargain at $425. Now you couldn't find a comparable place for under $800. So, with no money, and nowhere to go, Allie and I were at the mercy of our friends, and, believe me, there is no surer way of poisoning friendships.

All of these tribulations might have been bad enough if our marriage hadn't been coming apart. But when I came back to the city in November, broke, frightened, and demoralized, I had to place myself at Allie's mercy as much as at Carol Bostwick's—the dancer friend who took Allie in when she fled from Cardiff—and that first week at Carol's loft the vibes were so confusing that I felt like a wayfarer stranded in a foreign country. I knew she was furious at me, but my sudden reappearance was greeted with the most peculiar show of indifference. Our problems went undiscussed. Then again, I couldn't tell her what had really happened in New Hampshire.

We slept on a mattress on the floor under the huge industrial windows of Carol's loft. Most nights, I'd wake up at two in the morning, always two, damp with terror, and search the sooty panes of that great window for a few simple answers. And every morning around six, when gray-yellow light filled the enormous room, I'd sink back into an exhausted, febrile sleep until the day's first convoy of trucks outside jerked me roughly awake an hour later.

Then, one particularly dismal, rainy dawn in the heart of the Christmas season, I woke up not to the coughing and clanking of diesel engines, but to the drone of Allie sobbing into her pillow. I reached over and touched her shoulder. She raised herself slightly, and looking straight at me with wet, red-rimmed eyes, asked, "Rick, what are we going to do? What are we going to *do?*"

Carol wanted us to leave. She wasn't being nasty about it, and who could blame her. We'd been there a month. But I guess Allie's question, her use of the word *we*, was enough reassurance that she was still on my side to unclog some blocked circuitry in my brain.

"I'll find us a place today," I said.

"With what?"

"I'll go see dad."

My father and I were not great buddies, but for years we'd maintained a kind of truce based on the mutual right to disagree. You could say that the generation gap never really closed in our family. My childhood cronies had all ended their flings with music, drugs, or some other weird way of living, and now, in the eighties, as they entered early mid-life, they were all back in some mainstream occupation, making bundles of money and pumping out armloads of grandchildren—but not Ricky Sears. No sir. My father had never been altogether thrilled with my career as a rock journalist. He considered the music odious as far back as Bill Haley and the Comets. He nearly had a coronary when I dropped out of Boston University in '67. And though I quickly carved a niche for myself in the music scene, I never did earn much real money. In fact, a desire to do something he might approve of—to make some decent money, to write books and movies, not just magazine pieces—had a lot to do with my decision to quit *Rolling Stone* the previous spring. And when it all came apart that fall, I was ashamed even to inform him that I was back in the city, let alone ask him for help. But now I no longer had the luxury to indulge in feeling ashamed.

I called him that morning and met him at his office down on Broad Street a couple of hours later. We went to a restaurant popular with his crowd of brokers and bankers. The walls were paneled in dark wood and decorated with sporting prints. My poor old dad was beginning to look somewhat worn out. At first, just being with him roused up such a welter of emotion that my old childhood stammer returned. But aside from this, the lunch did not go badly at all. I was able to level with him, up to a point, without becoming pathetic or ridiculous. I didn't tell him about Byron, of course (whom he might have only remembered as a footnote to an abysmal decade), but I told him that there had been problems, that things had come up, that I simply needed money, and he was considerate enough not to cross-examine me for details. After lunch we went back to his office, and at two-thirty I walked out with a check for $5000.

Before the day was over I found a sublet on Astor Place. It was Stu Miller's, my old colleague from the magazine. The catch was we could only stay there for two months, since Stu would only be out in L.A. that long. So, while it was better than Carol's floor, it was not like having a home. Christmas came and went, a drearier version of that problematical holiday than I've ever known. In January, Allie got a job helping to design publicity material for the American Ballet Theater. It was only twenty hours a week, but it helped. Then, the week before Stu was to return, I found another sublet, a four-room place in a brownstone, uptown in Turtle Bay. It belonged to an elderly travel writer who was going to spend the next eight months in Japan. He was looking for a "responsible couple" who wouldn't rip off his valuables or destroy the furniture. Aside from Luke, whom we conveniently omitted mentioning, we fit the bill, and on March 3rd Allie and I moved in.

I was finally breaking out of the morbid daze that had gripped me all winter. The very air was redolent of renewal in those nautical breezes off the nearby East River. The travel writer had a spare bedroom set up as an office, and for the first time in many months I actually started focusing on work again. Somehow I mustered the courage to call Alex Rothchild in California and apologize for not coming across with the goods all year. But he was flush with the success of *Laughing Cowboy*, and when he came to New York a week later on routine business, I spent an hour with him at the Helmsly talking about my proposed screenplay, and the meeting managed to fire up some enthusiasm for the project again in both of us. In short, my life was returning to a pitch of gainful normality when Byron called.

It was late on a Wednesday night in early April. I was in the living room watching the Knicks play Boston on TV. Allie was in the next room, propped up in bed, reading. I could see her from the sofa. She picked up the phone on the night table.

"It's for you," she warbled sarcastically so as to imply the question: *Which one of your asshole friends would call at a quarter to midnight?* Though our circumstances had improved, there was still plenty of residual tension between us. The difference was that Allie was verbalizing her anger more, now that the worst was over. I guess that's how those things work. Anyway, I picked up the extension in the living room, assuming it was Stu. We bet on the games a lot together.

"Hello?"

"Don't hang up."

I didn't. But in the pregnant interval that followed I could hear the telltale crackle and hiss of a long-distance connection and my heart slid into my stomach.

"Rick. . . ?"

"I'm here."

"I have to apologize for my atrocious behavior."

"How did you find me?"

"Hey, you're a reporter. How hard is it to get a person's number when you really need it?"

"Where'd you get it?"

"I called up the old *Rolling Stone*."

"Did you tell them who you were?" I asked sullenly.

"You don't have to get all huffy about it, Rick. I'm trying to apologize."

"I'm sorry."

"So am I. I really am."

Allie turned out the light and pulled the blankets up over her ears. I was confident that the basketball game obscured the conversation.

"I got spooked," Byron said. "I didn't mean to hurt you."

"You didn't hurt me."

"Well, I didn't mean to do whatever I did. Will you accept my apology, at least?"

"Yes."

"I appreciate it," he said thoughtfully, and then in a more buoy-ant tone of voice added, "You've been a real pal, Rick, you know that? A pal and a comfort. Jeez, we could get all sloppy and senti-mental here. How was your winter?"

"It was all right."

"No, really."

"It was very difficult."

"How come?"

"You really want to hear this?"

"Sure."

"Okay. Because of you."

There was a pause you could have driven a Second Avenue bus through. Then, in a small, hurt voice, more surprised than maligned, Byron said, "How'd I do that?" And since he asked, I told him. I said that because of him I didn't get a damn thing done all fall, that we went broke and had to crash at our friends' apartments, and that my marriage almost fell apart—the whole stupid thing. "Is there some way I can make it up to you?" he said when I was through.

"You don't have to make anything up to—"

"No, I do. This is terrible."

"It's life, Byron. I went into this thing with my eyes open."

"Let me send you a little dough, at least."

"No way—"

"Hey, don't be a fool. What's your street address down there?"

"Don't send money, please."

"It's not ill-gotten. I'm not in the Mafia, you know."

"I don't care. I don't want it."

"Suit yourself," Byron finally dropped it. "So how's everything otherwise?"

"Okay, fine. Better."

"That's good to hear. Aren't you going to ask how I'm doing?"

"I'm sorry, Byron. That was rude of me. How have you been doing?"

"I have good days and bad days."

"What was today?"

"Medium bad."

"How come?"

"I don't know. I could use someone to talk to."

My insides tightened again. "How's your cat? Whitey?"

"My cat? A cat is not a person, my boy. You can't talk to your cat. Well, you can talk to them, I suppose, until you're blue in the face. But you can hardly have a conversation like this conversation we're having here. Anyway, Whitey's right here on my lap. You want to say hello?"

"You brought her down to the laundromat?"

"I'm not in the laundromat."

"Don't tell me you got a phone."

"Hey, I got a phone. You want my number."

"Sure."

"You got a pencil and paper handy?"

"No. Hang on a minute."

I went and got them off the desk in my study. Byron gave me the number.

"Hey, you know what would really be great?" he said.

"What?"

"To hear my own phone ring. That would really give me a thrill. How about hanging up and calling me back. I know it's dumb, but I'd really enjoy it. What do you say? Want to give me a ring?"

"Right now?"

"Certainly. You got anything better to do?"

By this time, as a matter of fact, the Knicks-Celtics game was over. They were showing the late news.

"Hey, you can reverse the charges, okay?" Byron said.

"Okay," I said.

"Well, I'm going to hang up now. You going to call me?"

"Yeah. I'm going to call you right back."

"Okay then. Bye."

"Bye."

We hung up. Trying to read the number I'd scrawled down, I pictured Byron sitting in the kitchen of his lonely house waiting expectantly for me to call him back, and the image made me want to cry. I dialed "O" and then his area code and number. The operator answered.

"Yes," I said. "Collect to Byron from Rick."

She put the call through. He let it ring four times before he answered, no doubt savoring each ring. "Collect to Byron from Rick," the operator told him. "Will you accept the charges?"

"Yeah," Byron said in a disguised, strangled voice.

"Go ahead," the operator said and hung up. There was an empty interval. Some static.

"Are you crazy?" Byron snarled at me.

"What's the matter now?"

"Collect to Byron! Sweet Jesus!"

"You told me to call collect."

"Collect to Joe! This is Joe Doaks's phone. There's no Byron here. Don't you ever call collect for any Byron here again. You understand?"

"Sorry," I said, feeling only slightly foolish, "but I think you're overreacting a little."

"Hey, one slip is all it takes," he said, calming down again. "I mean, a guy in my position can't be too careful."

"I understand."

"I didn't mean to yell at you."

"You were right. It was careless. I must be tired."

"It is kind of late, I guess."

"So, how'd you like hearing your phone ring?" I asked.

"Hey, I almost forgot in all the excitement. It was great. Terrific. Really, I enjoyed it tremendously."

"I'm glad."

For more moments than were comfortable, neither of us said anything.

"You ever think of coming back for a visit?" Byron finally asked.

"I'm really tied up down here," I told him. "I've got to get this movie treatment written."

"By when?"

"There's no definite deadline. As soon as I can get it done."

"Oh. Then what?"

"Then, if they like the treatment, they'll tell me to go ahead and write the actual screenplay. It's a multi-tiered type of arrangement."

"When do you think you'll know?"

"I told you. I haven't even submitted the finished treatment yet. I have to get that done first."

"You ought to try writing up here in the wilderness."

"I've tried, Byron."

"It's great, don't you think? The peace and quiet."

"I've got to be here in the city to do this. There are meetings with the producer, stuff like that. I can't take off."

"I see. How much are they paying you?"

"Uh—"

"Come on. You can tell me. Just between friends."

"Do you have any idea how bad your manners are sometimes?"

"What do you expect? I've got no one to practice on. It's only money, for Godsake."

"Well, frankly, it's none of your business."

"You don't have to get snooty about it. It's not like I'm trying to put the old touch on you, you know. I've got plenty of my own, thank you."

"How much?"

"I'm comfortable."

"No, give me an exact figure."

"It's privileged information, buddy boy."

"Come on," I pressed him. "Just between friends."

I could hear him chuckling at his end.

"See, that's why I like having you around, Rick. You practically force a guy to act like a normal human being. I don't mean to keep you up past your bedtime. If you're in the area, by some chance, drop in and say hello."

"I'll do that, Byron."

"Promise?"

"Yes."

"Or just call. You know, now that I've got a phone and all. Anyway, bye."

"Bye, Byron."

I stood there for a long time gazing blankly at the televised news, feeling the force of him, like an undertow, sweep into my life and threaten once again to pull my legs out from under me. And it was a sleepless night, Allie warm and sound asleep beside me, as I stared into the shifting squares of light on the ceiling.

Two days later I received an envelope in the mail inside of which was a certified check on the account of Joseph Doaks made out to me for the sum of $25,000. No letter or message accompanied it— just the check. Now, if I had been true to my highfalutin' principles, I would have ripped it up. But I didn't. I told myself it was a valuable "artifact" that ought to be preserved. I could take it out and enjoy looking at it, the way a connoisseur of fine books might fondle a rare first edition of *The Scarlet Letter*. This was, of course, the

worst sort of self-deceiving bullshit, and it didn't work. I kept the
check because I felt more secure knowing it was there, waiting,
tucked behind the flyleaf of my thesaurus, in case we got into trouble again. And in a few short weeks we did get into trouble because
Alex Rothchild rejected my treatment of a movie to be called *Love
in a Sad Season*, so there would be no assignment for me to write
the screenplay. Thus no more money, either.

We had $1400 left in the bank and a lot of bills to pay. I was on
the brink of crawling back to the magazine and asking, *begging*,
Wenner for my old job back. Allie was understandably much in favor
of my returning to a steady, salaried position, though I'm not sure
she realized just how much crawling and begging it might take.
Anyway, I was sitting idly in front of the typewriter one afternoon
late in April, fretting about the future and watching East Side
matrons walk their Yorkshire terriers up 44th Street, when Byron
called again.

"Hi there, stranger," he said. "How are you?"

"Fine," I told him. A lie.

"You get that check I sent?"

"Yes."

"You didn't cash it though."

"No. I told you I couldn't take it."

"Then why didn't you send it back?"

He had me there.

"Hey, the truth is you're not sure if you're going to cash it or not.
Isn't that the truth?"

"Yes," I admitted.

"How's your screenplay going?"

"Not so hot."

"That's what I gather. Why don't you just cash the check and
come up here for a few weeks and make a few tape recordings. It's
good pay for honest work."

"Why me, Byron," I groaned, knowing it was a stupid question.

"You're the one who stepped into the mummy's tomb, buster.
The mummy's curse comes with it."

"What if I decline the honor?"

"I don't believe that deep down you really want to. Deep down
you want to finish what you started, am I right?"

It didn't take me more than a few seconds of soul-searching to
realize that he was. "Yes," I reluctantly admitted.

"Then come back."

"Okay, Byron," I agreed wearily. "It might take me a while to tie up some loose ends. In any case, I'm going to have to do some fast talking down here."

"Rick. About your wife. I'm sorry this—"

"I know. I know."

"Anyway, I'll see you . . . when I see you."

"Right. Bye."

I hung up, hating myself for giving in. But it was like cursing the darkness. Besides, there was a chance that I could get out of this without sacrificing my marriage. First of all, I decided to go ahead and cash the check.

I deposited $20,000 in Allie's and my joint checking account and took the remainder in cash. Then I told Allie that I'd gotten a call from Alex Rothchild and that he wanted to fly me out to the coast to help work on the script of a rock movie being shot in Hollywood that was in trouble. I even called Rothchild himself, gave him a cock-and-bull story, and asked him to cover for me in case Allie called me out there. He agreed. Allie suspected nothing.

The next day I took a plane from LaGuardia to the sawed-off-mountain airport in Lebanon, New Hampshire, rented a Plymouth Horizon, and drove up through the lovely, budding countryside to Cardiff.

# CHAPTER 9

*Flame on, flame on*
*Restless girl*
*Forget about tomorrow*
*Tonight will bring you happiness*
*Another lover's fiery kiss*
*The future could mean emptiness*
*Why take a chance*
*There's no romance in sorrow*

—"Restless Girl"

I called Byron around noon that day from the booth outside the Top Shopper in Cardiff, our phone in the cottage having been disconnected months earlier. It was his suggestion to meet me in town, at Dottie's Lunch, and imagine what it was like to see him limp blithely into that indifferent lunch-hour crowd of a dozen-odd townspeople, some of whom must have at least heard his voice on the airwaves or seen his picture on the cover of a magazine at some time or other. It was even a little startling to see how, despite the surgery that had been done to disguise his nose, he looked so much like his old self from across the room. Over the winter he'd lost some weight and let his hair grow out so the thinning wasn't that apparent anymore. He looked very much like that photo on the cover of *Oedipus Forgiven*, even down to the sartorial details: blue jeans, a fine double-vented gray flannel jacket, cut in the sixties style with wide lapels and a nipped waist, and a long checked scarf thrown over his shoulder just like the old days. Considering his general level of paranoia, it struck me as surprisingly bold for him to appear in public like that, even if it was only Dottie's Lunch.

He stood in the front for a moment, searched the booths, and then strode energetically past the lunching shop clerks, farmers, and tradesmen to the booth where I sat in the rear, a broad smile on his face.

"Hello, old pal," he said.

"Hello, Byron."

He rolled his eyes, sank down into the booth, and pulled his collar up, muttering, "Sweet Jesus, it's Joe, for Godsake. Can't you get it straight?" Nobody was paying the slightest bit of attention to us, though, and I apprised him of that fact. After a while his mobile face, which always seemed to change expressions a few seconds in advance of his actual emotions, softened into a kid's smile of delight. "Hey, this is fun, though, isn't it? Meeting here for lunch."

A waitress promptly appeared and took our orders: burger and fries for me, poached eggs on toast and a vanilla shake for my companion. She looked about nineteen and if she recognized Byron, then she concealed it well enough to win an Oscar. As I began to calm down, it occurred to me that, in his own peculiar way, Byron was actually more composed, more relaxed, than I was. I don't think I ever saw him looking so buoyant.

"Did you cash the check?"

"Yes," I told him, wildly embarrassed. "It was a nice gesture."

"It wasn't a gesture."

"Yes, well, I did."

"Good. You earned it."

"You seem in excellent spirits," I said, anxious to change the subject."

"It's spring. Anything is possible in the springtime, right? Hey, you want to know something else?" He leaned forward and cupped his hand to one side of his mouth. "That problem I was having? That, uh, you know, bug that was giving me so much trouble. Well, I went to see a doctor about it. I'm okay, it turns out. He sent me to the hospital in Hanover, where Dartmouth is, and they did all these tests. You know what I had?"

"What?"

"A goddam little peptic ulcer. How do you like that?"

"I think it's great that you took care of it. *Is* it better now?"

"Oh yeah, lots. They put me on this diet all winter. I'm still sort of in the habit of it, but I could probably eat regular food now. The thing is, it's such a relief just knowing you have a normal disease that a million other people have, I can't tell you."

"How'd you like being in Hanover?"

"Hey, it was terrific. Walking around the old Dartmouth campus. Seeing all the kids."

"You walked around the campus?"

"Sure. Why not?"

"You weren't . . . nervous about it?"

"A little, maybe. But after being in the hospital, what the hell? No one recognized me there."

"How long were you in?"

"Three days. College is a great time in a person's life, don't you think?"

I agreed with him, but it was certainly ironic, two dropouts like us harking back to our college years with such fond nostalgia.

"Hey, you didn't bring your wife, did you?"

I shook my head. "She thinks I'm in Los Angeles."

Byron exhaled wearily. "Oh, Rick. I'm sorry I fuck up your life all the time. I'm sorry I make you lie. Lying is terrible, the worst thing one person can do to another."

"It's not a lie, really."

"Sure it is. You told her you were going to Los Angeles and you're here. It's a lie."

"Do you want me to call her and tell her I'm here?"

He looked down at his placemat, a propaganda sheet extolling the Granite State's scenic wonders.

"No," he finally said. "I guess you better not do that. Life's one long contradiction, isn't it?"

"It seems to me you're begging to be spotted."

"I've been coming into town for years," he scoffed at the idea.

"Not dressed like that," I said.

The waitress arrived with our food and Byron seemed relieved at the opportunity to change the subject.

"Great service, huh?" he said, and I could tell that he was not being facetious.

"They're right on top of things," I agreed.

"I hope you don't think this is pushy, but as long as your wife's not here, what do you say we crack a tape or two over at your place."

"Okay," I said.

"After all, you don't want to go back to the scene of the crime, do you?"

"The past's the past," I said.

"That's what you think."

It started raining while we were in the luncheonette, and it was coming down so hard by the time we got to the cottage that you couldn't even see the far shore of Ampersand Pond. The house was a disaster area. It hadn't been cleaned since I left so hastily in the fall. It smelled of mildew and mouse shit. It was interesting, though, to see Byron poke around the place, picking things up and examining them—a half-moon-shaped tree fungus, an antique blue medicine bottle, a small mammal's skull—as if he'd never held such charmed objects in his hands before.

"Who's the painter around here?"

"Allison."

"I thought so. She's good."

"I keep bugging her to take her slides around to a gallery, but she won't listen to me."

"You're right, she should. Hey, I'd buy one if I was still in the market. I used to buy a lot of paintings in the old days, when we had the big place in Tamberlane. We had a damn good start on a collection, for a couple of young kids, mostly American stuff, nineteenth century. We had that big Beal, *The Valley of the Genesee*, a small Thomas Cole, a Church, a Heade, a Kensett, a Ryder—boy, there was a weird guy—what else? Oh, yeah, a wonderful little Catlin watercolor of a Fox Indian chief. If we'd kept on going, we probably would have become a couple of art hotshots."

"I remember that Beal of yours. It was huge, took up half a wall."

"That's right. You know, I miss those paintings. It's a special privilege to own a work of art. A privilege and a responsibility. The money, the cars, all the rest of that crap, you never think about. But I miss the paintings. Your wife's work reminds me of Hopper."

"That's what I tell her."

"You're lucky to have such a talented wife. Catherine had some, but she let it slide. She let everything slide. It's chilly in here."

There was plenty of cordwood leftover from the fall. I built a fire in the woodstove while Byron excused himself and ran out to his car. He returned momentarily with something tucked inside his jacket.

"Ta-dum!"

It was the Sony. Seeing it again was like being reunited with a beloved but troublesome friend.

"You left it behind. I put new batteries in it and everything."

Soon we were seated comfortably before the warm fire, the rain beating steadily overhead.

## The Life of Byron Jaynes—Tape 7

Where'd we leave off? It's been a while.

*I know what you mean. Your mother, I think.*

What about her?

*She died.*

That's right. She did.

*You weren't really close, though, were you?*

No, we weren't. I wish . . . well, if wishes were fishes. I told you what she was like. Anyway, she was only 48. I couldn't stand the idea of sticking her in one of those ghastly metropolitan boneyards where all her relatives were planted, so I arranged a cremation. She wasn't a religious person. I doubt she ever set foot in a synagogue, except for a few of her friends' kids' bar mitzvahs. So I arranged for a simple service at Campbell's Funeral Home on 81st Street, made sure all her friends were duly informed, the Havermeyers, the Sterns, the Frankels, et cetera. Simon's publicity girl, Pam Schneider, helped me with a lot of the arrangements. We flew Arlene up from Carolina. Catherine was somewhat freaked out by the whole thing. You know, *Death!* She didn't want to deal with it. They had never met each other, mom and Catherine, so. . . .

*What about your dad?*

Funny you should mention old dad. He showed up at the service—

*Showed up? You didn't want him there?*

God, it was so complicated. I blamed him for pulling her life out from under her. But how could he not pay his respects to her after being her husband for 25 years? I was so mad at him I tried to pretend he didn't exist for those three days. But death's not a secret. He was notified. I say I tried to pretend he didn't exist. The truth is, I thought about him constantly, and I kept conjuring up these two different scenarios in case we met. One was a sort of sloppy, maudlin, sentimental scene with the two of us falling into each other's arms and begging forgiveness. In the other one I was shouting obscenities at him and trying to break his neck with a folding chair while their old friends held me back. But when we actually met at the ceremony, it didn't turn out like either of those two scenes.

We hadn't seen each other in almost two years. I doubt that he followed my career, or read the *Billboard* magazine charts, but I was quite sure he knew who I had become. And just knowing that he knew was like having something over him, something he couldn't deny the way I could deny his name. I certainly didn't feel like Morris Greenwald's schmuck kid anymore.

The ceremony was simple. Elsie Havermeyer read a Dylan Thomas poem. Betty Stern read one by Emily Dickinson, and broke down and couldn't finish. I read several stanzas from the end of Whitman's poem "When Lilacs Last in the Dooryard Bloom'd," the part that begins, *"Come lovely and soothing death / undulate round the world, serenely arriving, arriving / in the day, in the night, to all, to each / sooner or later delicate death."* Whitman was writing about the death of Lincoln, but it meant much more than that. *"Dark mother always gliding near with soft feet / have none chanted for thee a chant of fullest welcome? / Then I chant it for thee, I glorify thee above all / I bring thee a song. . . ."* It's more in the spirit of the Hebrew kaddish than the kaddish itself, in my opinion. *"Approach strong deliveress, / When it is so, when thou hast taken them I joyously sing the dead / lost in the loving floating ocean of thee / laved in the flood of thy bliss O death."*

My father entered the chapel just as I was reading, and stood in the rear with his hands crossed solemnly, looking into the carpet, the big phony. Then, afterward, when everyone was milling around and saying good-bye to each other, we found ourselves face to face.

"Thank you for coming" was all I could say to him. But they were just words. I was saying the same thing to everybody. That's what you say at a funeral, "Thank you for coming."

"How are you, Peter?" he said.

"I'm all right."

"You look well."

"I don't know what's worse. That you killed her or broke her heart."

"She was killing herself long before we divorced, Peter. I'm sorry to have to tell you this, since it's not the time or the place, but it's the truth."

"It's your truth. You were schtupping your bimbo a long time before the divorce too."

"Everybody's truth is only a version of the facts. That's why we have courts of law. In any case, you're not qualified to judge me."

"I'm your son. That's enough."

"Anybody can be a son."

"Just like anybody can be a husband, right? Or a father?"

"It was nice to see you again, Peter. Behave yourself."

And that was it. No tears. No fisticuffs. Just words. Words. I didn't see him again for many a year, as they say in the old folksongs.

*You went through a pretty sustained burst of creativity after that, though, the next two years.*

I wrote a lot of songs, if that's what you mean. After the funeral I was anxious to get busy, so I ended up doing what Simon suggested when we came back from the first tour: I went into the studio with a bunch of real pros: Cleanth Robison, Harvey Morrow, Preston Fergus, and Tommy Marks. And it was during those sessions that I discovered I could play without the Romantics.

*They took it pretty hard?*

They all took it differently. The way Bobby carried on in the trade papers, you'd think it came out of the clear, blue sky. Gary, I think, was relieved, if you want to know the truth. He wanted to play jazz, "real music," he called it. But Rego was hurt. He flew back from Mazatlán and found out I was in the studio without him and he freaked.

We happened to be staying at Simon's town house on 64th Street at the time because Catherine's parents were using the place on 72nd Street. Rego showed up after midnight one night, totally tanked, the only time I ever saw him out of control. A lot of hurtful things were said on both sides, things we didn't necessarily mean. Rego called me "a sellout," "a weak sister," "a chickenshit," "a pawn," and "probably a faggot." He took a swing at Simon, who was about ten inches taller and over a hundred pounds heavier, and he sprained his wrist falling down when he missed. Eventually he passed out on the sofa. The next day, Simon hosed him down with valium and we all got together in Simon's office. You could say that we bought Rego off, I suppose. But Simon really liked him, really cared about him, unlike the other guys. He even thought Rego was a good musician.

*Why didn't he just retain him, then, and form a new band around the two of you?*

He didn't want anybody cluttering up my future, and he was determined to separate me from the band totally, to get me all by myself.

*To have you all to himself, you mean.*

You make it sound so gothic. Look, let me put it this way: when there's a great deal of money at stake, say millions, you're suddenly forced to pay much closer attention to your own best interests. Simon was my manager. His job was knowing what my best interests were. He was a tough man, but he wasn't a venal one. He just couldn't let sentimentality affect these decisions. The upshot of it was that Simon offered Rego a separate management contract and, as you know, he never lacked work after that.

Anyway, those sessions with Cleanth and the others became *Childe Byron.* I knew we were going to have enough good tracks for an album after the first week in the studio. It was all in the can before Christmas. Jerry Zuckerman was ecstatic.

Catherine and I were married in Simon's living room in Tamberlane on New Year's Day. In April, *Childe Byron* was released and we found our house, our dream castle. You were there for the interview.

Man, you should have seen it when we first bought it. Martin McClanahan, the middle-weight champion, started building it in 1926, supposedly as a replica of this castle in Ireland where all his ancestors were from. He lost the championship in September of '29.

A month later the stock market went to hell. He never finished the place. When we got hold of it, it was just a stone shell where the high school kids came to drink Ripple and hump their girlfriends. We got the place, literally, for a song, and put about six more songs— half of *Childe Byron*—into fixing it up. The work went on that spring and summer, and in the meantime we crashed at Simon's house on the other side of Tamberlane. And that's when things began to get extremely weird.

When I remember that time, I always picture the three of us— Catherine, Claire, and myself—and the image in my mind is of a perpetual lawn party. Simon is never in the picture. In fact, he was in New York most of the time, and so the three of us were left to our own devices.

*Were you using?*

I started snorting, then popping. There was meth and coke too. Catherine had a whole routine: a little meth to open up the eyes, some smack to take the edge off, then coke to liven things up, and some more smack to mellow it all out.

*Why did you start again?*

Why do fools fall in love? I wish I knew, Rick. Tommy Marks had it during the *Childe Byron* sessions. You reach a certain peak of feeling, playing so intensely, and you don't want to let go of it. Drugs help you hang on.

*And you betrayed Simon. In his very house.*

Yes, I betrayed Simon. I already had, with Claire. Oh, it went far beyond that. Like one morning I woke up, feeling crampy and out of sorts. Catherine wasn't beside me in bed. I looked around for our stash and couldn't find it, so I went out into the hall to see if I could hear her downstairs, and I heard this feminine giggling coming from Simon and Claire's room. Now, I knew Simon was in the city, so I concluded that Catherine was in there, and I was right.

I knocked on the door.

"Come in."

The two of them were propped up together in bed, holding the blankets over themselves, as women do.

"Little pajama party?" I asked.

Catherine lowered her end of the blanket. "No pajamas," she said.

"Look, he's blushing," Claire said, her eyelids half shut, her long hair let out and wild around her shoulders. "Stop being a prude and come here," she shimmied over some and patted the space between her and Catherine.

"He *is* such a perfect prude sometimes," Catherine said. "It's sickening."

"No, he's just an old-fashioned gentleman," Claire contradicted what she started. "I like that in a man."

"You two look like you're doing fine without me," I said, trying not to sound ruffled.

"Did you hear that?"

"What are you suggesting, Byron Jaynes?"

"I bet he thinks we're a couple of—you know."

"Well, maybe we are."

With a knowing smile on her face, Claire slid down under the covers and I could see the lump she made under there burrow toward Catherine. I was curious to see how far they were going to carry this little conceit. Curious and—I hate to admit it—fascinated. Catherine's mouth tightened into a tiny circle of tension. She closed her eyes and moaned. The bump under the blankets moved forward and back over her hips. I just stood there on the carpet like a dummy, watching the whole thing. Then Catherine was gasping.

"Wait, Claire, no, I want him. I want Byron!"

Claire reemerged, looking so rapt and determined all of a sudden that it was scary. Catherine threw the covers off and drew her knees up.

"I want you, Byron," she moaned.

"She wants you," Claire said. "Go to her."

"Come to me."

"Let's all come to each other," Claire said.

Oh, Rick, how can you justify it? You can't. But we might have been able to live with it, if it hadn't been for the drugs.

Afterward, luxuriating there in Simon's bed, I felt the shakes coming on and leaned over to Catherine and whispered in her ear, "Where did you put the stuff?"

"It's right here, darling," she said out loud. She lifted a copy of the Italian *Vogue* off the night table and underneath it was the mirror we used for chopping and snorting our drugs and the cloisonné box that we kept them in. That's when I knew we were lost.

*Claire was using too?*

That's right.

*Catherine turned her onto it?*

That's right.

*Had she been doing it long enough to develop a habit?*

I wasn't sure, but I was too frightened to confront her. And she thought it was all a big game. A few days later I was tinkering at the piano downstairs. Catherine was in New York, at the dentist's. Claire appeared and reclined on a chaise across the room from me. I was playing "Time Will Tell" in a very slow tempo, like a ballad. She was wearing a loose-fitting caftan with nothing underneath, lounging there, staring at me. I tried pretending not to notice her. My whole life was getting to be an endless act of pretending not to notice what was going on around me. I sang the words quietly to myself.

"It's beautiful that way," she said. Outside, the sun came out from behind a cloud and the room swelled with light. "I believe I can have an orgasm just watching you."

I immediately started banging out "Snakes and Dogs" on the piano and screaming out the lyrics until I ran out of breath.

"Why can't you accept life's pleasures?" she asked in that melodic drawl of hers when I was done.

I pounded the keys with my fist.

"Because you have to pay a price for everything, Claire!" I said.

"You don't have to shout."

"What do you think Simon would do if he found out what's been going on up here all summer?"

"He would bark like a big old dog for an hour or so and then he'd be right back down in the city on Monday morning pushin' your little ole records," she said, really pouring on the gumbo-mouth. "Why, do you plan to inform him?"

"Do you suppose Catherine underestimates me the way you underestimate Simon?"

"She thinks the world of you, Byron. But she's used to having her own way, just like I am. Simon knew that when he married me, and you should have known that too. We're the beautiful wild birds you can't keep locked in the golden cage."

"But you still like to fly in and out of that cage. What if one day you flew off and when you came back the door was locked?"

"I have strong wings. I can fly far, far afield. This conversation is becoming awfully gloomy, Byron, and I'm not sure I wish to continue it, but there is one thing I want to impress upon you, and that is that nothing in this world is more futile, more unrewarding, than trying to gain happiness by denying others their pleasures—"

"I'm a junkie, Claire! I'm addicted to heroin and so is Catherine—"

"And so am I, Byron," she said breezily, as if she were disclosing her membership in some secret society that was a privilege to belong to.

"Oh, this is just great," I sank back onto the bench and hung my elbows off the piano.

"I don't like the word *junkie*. It's an ugly, unappetizing term."

"Well, whatever you want to call it, you've got a real problem. All three of us do."

"It's romantic, being the slave of a drug. I never quite understood it before."

"Wait and see how romantic it feels to clean yourself up," I told her, but I don't think she heard me. When I looked back up at the chaise, it was empty. Claire was outside dancing on the lawn.

Later that afternoon, Catherine came back from the city. I returned from walking in the woods and found the two of them out by the pool, basking in their bikinis. They were both wearing sunglasses. Catherine had on a pair of those ugly dime-store shades with rhinestones in the corners. She was smoking a cigarette out of a foot-long holder. She loved that kind of stuff. You could tell, though, that they were working a little too energetically to keep up the playful facade.

I sat down at the edge of Catherine's lounger.

They giggled.

I reached for Catherine's shades and carefully removed them. Her eyes looked terrible in the light.

"Hey—!"

"We've got to get clean," I told her.

Catherine crossed her arms and chewed on her lip nervously.

"I've got to get tan," Claire said. She unsnapped the hook between the two cups of her bikini top and rubbed suntan lotion on her dancer's chest.

"No, Claire, he's right," Catherine said.

"We'll go up to Big Slide and sweat it out there. You stay here," I said to Claire. "I've got some librium to help us through."

"I'm not an addict," Claire said, cavalierly.

"You are," Catherine corrected her. "Maybe not as bad as us, but you are."

"I was just pretending, to be part of the gang."

"You weren't pretending," Catherine said. "You'll find out when we're gone and there's no more stuff around. You're going to get sick, dearie."

Claire stopped rubbing the lotion in and looked pensive for a moment. Then she shrugged her shoulders and resumed oiling herself. "So be it," she said.

"It'll be like a bad case of the flu, probably," Catherine told her. "A very bad case."

"We've been bad, though, haven't we?" Claire said, like it was something we all should savor.

"Just stupid," I said.

"No, we've been wicked."

"Look at her," Catherine said. "She loves the idea."

"I do. I *do*," Claire exclaimed as if it were an eye-opening revelation. A hot breeze swept across the lawn and the terraces. "The world feels like it's on fire today," Claire said. She tossed her bikini top aside, got up from her chair abruptly, and dove into the pool.

A hundred yards up the sloping lawn, where the gravel path to the stables started at the edge of the woods, I could see the sun glint off of Richmond Petty's glasses.

*He was taking it all in?*

You bet he was.

Anyway, we left for Big Slide late that afternoon. What a place to kick, boy, the two of us lurching around that dark, dreary log mansion, holding our bellies, with those dead beasts looking down their big snouts at us. We came out of that forest after five days looking like we just got off the Bataan Death March.

We couldn't return to Simon's. It was too risky. The temptations were too great to become careless again. Our house still wasn't finished.

"Let's pick a place far away and go," Catherine said.

"You pick."

"Promise you'll go?"

"Yes."

"Okay. New Zealand."

"Why New Zealand?"

"Best trout fishing in the whole wide world."

"Ugh."

"You promised."

I went. We sat on the rim of a fjord under the Southern Cross with our feet stuck in sleeping bags, and I fell in love with her all over again. She was like a combination of Tuesday Weld and Teddy Roosevelt, and I was gone on her.

We returned to the States in the fall, healthy and relaxed and all set to devote our energies to becoming unhealthy and uptight. What better place than New York? Our castle in Tamberlane was now finished, but absolutely empty. So we stayed in the city under the pretext of buying stuff to fill it up, and we'd get invited here and invited there, and every night there'd be a party, or some scene to make. And before you knew it, all we were doing was waking up at five o'clock in the afternoon and getting ready for another night of parties.

Catherine adored it. She loved being the center of attention. She loved being made to feel special by the beautiful people.

Me? I was sliding. It was demoralizing for me. When I walked into a room, people didn't see a person, they saw an album cover. People never talked to you out of normal curiosity, to find out if you liked each other, if you could be friends. They wanted you to solve their life for them. Or they wanted to save you from some imaginary fate that was in their heads. After a while I wanted to hide in the closet, you know? But what did I do? Turned to an old standby: drugs. I thought if I could just stay away from smack, it would be all right. I used downs instead. Brilliant, huh?

Anyway, I managed to fritter away the fall and winter like this, tagging behind Catherine, dragging my puss from one soirée to the next, getting my picture in the papers. I didn't write so much as a verse the whole time we were in New York. Then, that spring, it caught up with me.

Gemini threw a party at the Plaza Hotel for Marva Faith's new album. I was supposed to meet Jerry Zuckerman in his suite upstairs beforehand. It was all set up. Simon was going to be there too. So I left Catherine down in the party and took the elevator up.

Jerry opened the door himself, in the final process of putting on his tux.

"Byron! Byron, my boy! Come in." Big smile gleaming out of that Acapulco tan, little pinch on the cheek. "Would you like a drink?" Sure. "Care for some pretzel nuggets. . . ?"

Simon was sitting motionlessly on the sofa. I hadn't seen him in the flesh for a couple of months, though we'd been in touch frequently by phone. His gray hair was down to his shoulders. He patted the place next to him on the sofa, which I took to mean that Zuckerman was about to give me the business, and that I should sit down and take it like a man. Jerry, meanwhile, stood before a mirror and deftly tied a real bowtie around his neck, getting it right the first time. I was impressed.

"I want you to know, Byron," he turned and gestured expansively, "that our studios are at your disposal."

"Thank you, Jerry," I said. "You're very kind."

"Anytime you're ready, we'll bump whoever, if necessary. You just say when."

"Okay," I said.

You could hear the ice clanking so loudly in our glasses it was like listening to the Beal College carillon.

"Simon tells me you've been writing some marvelous new material up in the country."

I glanced over at Simon. He knew damn well where I'd been and what I'd been doing.

"It's very inspiring there," I told Jerry.

"It must be. The fresh air! The birds singing in the morning. You look pale, Byron. And thin. Tell me, do you get enough exercise? Does he get any exercise up there, Simon?"

"I'm a night person, Jerry."

"Don't they feed you? All that good fresh country food? Eggs! Vegetables! Fruit! You're not on drugs, are you, Byron. I hate to be so blunt about it but . . . you look . . . unhealthy."

"Jerry. I abhor drugs. And I don't approve of people who take them. If I find that someone around me is taking drugs: phhhhht! That's it. I don't want them for a friend, or even an acquaintance. Drugs are the bane of this country's youth."

Simon patted me on the knee. It gave me the willies.

"You mean it?" Jerry said. "Does he mean that?"

"Absolutely."

"I didn't know you had such a highly developed sense of morality, Byron, and—God forbid you should misunderstand me—such a sense of patriotism. This asinine war isn't going to last forever, you know. One day it will be over, and America will still be here. A lot of you kids are making a big mistake—I say, 'you kids,' I don't necessarily mean you, Byron, personally, so don't misunderstand—but it's one thing to hate a stupid government and another thing to hate your country. You hate your country and sooner or later you end up hating yourself, you follow me? A year from now, Senator Kennedy is going to be in the White House and this Vietnam *mishigoss* is going to be behind us, you mark my words. I don't mean to go off on a tangent here, gentlemen, but this political situation aggravates me. But one thing I must tell you: I was so relieved when that horse's ass pulled himself out of the running the other night, I can't tell you."

He meant President Johnson. It was right around the time LBJ bowed out of the '68 campaign, after Gene McCarthy embarrassed him in the New Hampshire primary.

"I feel optimistic about this country, about its future," Jerry said. "I think the worst is behind us."

A dyspeptic look came over him and he went over to refresh his drink.

"So when do you think you might get back into the studio, Byron," Jerry pressed me, still trying to sound casual. "Roughly. I don't need dates."

"I don't know, Jerry. I haven't thought about it."

"With all this new material, I'd think a person would be bursting to roll up his sleeves and get it down—"

"There really isn't enough for a new album."

"Oh? Well . . . you could lay down as many tracks as you want for now. Then in a month or so you could finish it up."

"I just don't think what I have right now is very good."

"Simon says it's marvelous. Why don't you let us be the judge of whether it's good or not?"

"If I let you be the judge, I'd be doing "Strangers in the Night" and "To Sir with Love.""

Simon coughed.

"Show music is more my style," Jerry said with a thin smile. " 'Byron Jaynes Sings Rodgers and Hammerstein!' " The joke grudged up a sardonic cackle out of Simon, who otherwise had hardly changed his expression since I walked in there. He had his great stone face on. "What an idea!" Jerry said. He cleared his throat and swirled the ice cubes around in his scotch. "The thing is, it would be a good thing all the way around for you to have a fall release— good for you, good for Gemini, and good for your public. This is an election year, remember."

"So what?"

"The climate in this country is going to change with Bobby in the White House."

"What makes you so sure he's going to win?"

"Don't be a fool. If he gets nominated, he'll win. And he's going to get nominated."

"I still don't see how that affects me."

"If you don't release a record before then, you're going to be a voice from another age. It's as simple as that. You're going to be as relevent to what comes after Vietnam as Ricky Nelson was to civil rights. Look, Byron, in a way this is all beside the point. The last thing in the world I want to be is a pushy person, a nag, but let's be forthright: your last release was a year ago, almost exactly. Am I right, Simon—?"

Simon nodded his big gray head.

"—and so by rights you should have had a new album in the can now, ready for release."

"By whose rights?"

"Everyone's. Your fans. Us, Gemini. You. Even you, Mr. Byron Jaynes. If you think you're doing your career a favor, you're mistaken."

"Sometimes holding back is more important than putting out."

"Maybe. But you're taking a hell of a risk, because if that product is not really superior when you finally do put it out, forget it, it's the scrapheap for you, my boy. The public is not forgiving, and the youngsters out there who buy your records, those kids in their jeans and beads and wild hair, they'll drop you cold."

"They're not just a public, they're a movement." Did I believe this? Not really. But I thought it would shut him up.

"So what does that make you? Jesus Christ?" he jumped right on it.

"I don't pretend to be a leader," I said lamely, knowing that I was losing every round now.

"You kids!" Jerry poured it on. "Trying to have a discussion with you is like *Alice in Wonderland*! I say 'white,' you say 'black'!"

"I say 'good-bye,' you say 'hello.' "

"I feel sorry for some of these college professors. You . . . you reject elementary logic! Here two people sit with your best interests at heart and all you can give in return is sarcasm. It hurts my feelings, Byron."

He went over to the window to look at Central Park, ten stories below.

"I'm sorry, Jerry," I said.

"You act like I'm the enemy."

"I know you're not the enemy."

He turned sharply.

"Then do me a favor, will you? Get into the studio and make a record. Okay?"

"Okay."

"Enough said."

"Yes."

"Good," he said with a sigh. "There's a party going on. Simon, make sure that this . . . this Auchwitz victim gets some food in his stomach." It was ironic that he thought I was undernourished. At the time, actually, I had to struggle to keep my weight down. I was always on a diet.

We left the suite. Simon closed the door behind us. I muttered, "Thanks for sticking up for me. Whose side are you on, anyway?"

"He was right, Byron."

"Well, thanks a bunch—"

Suddenly he grabbed me by the shoulder of my jacket and dragged me to this door with a lighted EXIT sign over it and pushed me inside. It was a fire stairwell.

"Don't ever get smart with someone like Jerry Zuckerman again," he said, without raising his voice even a little. But he had me crowded into a corner, and he was breathing hard through his nostrils, so it was like being stuck in a stall with a big, angry horse. "It makes my life difficult," he said.

"And you know what makes my life difficult?" I answered him right back. "You making stuff up behind my back. 'Simon tells me you've been writing some marvelous material up in the country—' "

"Your life should be more difficult. What do you do with your time? Piss it away?"

"It's none of your business how I spend my time."

"That's what you think," he said, so coldly that I felt like all the blood was pumped out of my veins and replaced with some kind of icy sludge. "This girl you married—"

"You know her name."

"She's not good for you."

"You don't know her," I said desperately, trying to throw him off-balance, mentally, as if this were judo with words.

"Oh, I know her," he said right back, and all I could think of were the innumerable crimes the three of us had committed against Simon the previous summer. I felt sick to my stomach.

"It's not Catherine's fault," I finally said. "Don't blame her."

"Okay. I'll blame you."

"Fine."

"You're going back into the studio next week."

"I already said I would—"

"You didn't say when. Now I'm telling you. We're clearing that studio for Monday and you're going in there."

"What if I have nothing to lay down?"

"I don't care if you do bird calls. You're going into that studio," he said and stalked back out into the hall.

I waited in the stairwell until I heard the elevator and then I walked slowly back down to the mezzanine, found Catherine, and forced her to leave with me, even though she didn't want to go. She hated to leave a party.

The next day we were on a plane to Martinique. I fled. But not with completely cowardly intentions. It's true that I didn't show up at the studio that Monday, but why waste everybody's time doing bird calls? My idea was to go off somewhere, away from the distractions of New York, and write a bunch of songs so I could at least start recording an album.

But things didn't work out quite so neatly. I wrote one song, "Mystery School," in the VIP lounge at Kennedy Airport. Then, two nights after we got to Martinique, Catherine snuck out of our rented sugar shack on the beach into Fort-de-France and was promptly arrested while trying to make a buy. The whole thing was a set-up. She hadn't realized it because nobody made a fuss when we arrived on the island. But they were shrewd bastards. They knew exactly who we were, who I was, and Catherine walked right into their trap. It cost me $12,000 to get the charges dropped and get us off that island. The police chief wanted five grand. Then there was the magistrate, the French colonial flunkies. It was ridiculous. I was too depressed to argue about it, though, and the money meant nothing to me. But since she'd been busted for buying smack, I knew she was strung out again. Junkies have a special cunning. The fact that I was just as badly strung out on barbiturates hadn't really penetrated my little walnut brain at that point. Anyway, we were hustled off the island, and less than nine hours later, with a pit-stop in the city, we were back upstate in Tamberlane.

Instead of returning to a refuge, this home of ours—this Frankenstein castle on a mountaintop that we'd barely spent a month in, all told, since they had finished it—instead of coming back to a safe place, a haven, where you could at least get your head together, it was more like entering an abyss, a hot-spot of damnation. If it sounds like I'm describing a cheap horror movie it's because the next several days were exactly like one, down to the booming, crackling thunder and lightning storms that raked the Catskills that April week in 1968—the same week Martin Luther King was shot.

I had another plan! This was phase two of what proved to be an ongoing date with disaster. That pit-stop in New York I mentioned? Well, we'd copped on our way to Tamberlane, okay? Catherine was a sick girl when we got off that plane. I wasn't feeling too hot myself, since they'd confiscated my supply of Seconal. And while we were at it, I scored a couple of ounces of cocaine off the same ghoul down in Chelsea who sold us our narcotics.

So while Catherine wandered dreamily through the half-furnished rooms, like Ophelia in Elsinore, I snorked line after line of coke up my nose and pounded out one song after another at the piano. I felt possessed, a genius! Beethoven, Elvis, and all four Beatles rolled into one fantastically rich musical strudel! I wrote all the lyrics out in this maniacal teeny-little script, but since I had no facility for writing musical notation, there was no record of the tunes that went with them. But who needed that? I could keep them all in my head, right?

Try to picture the scene. It's about ten o'clock on a Saturday night. I haven't slept in over two days. I finish the last of twelve songs and then, armed with the lyrics, I gather up my beautiful spaced-out wife and climb behind the wheel of the Rolls for the two-mile drive over the river and through the woods to Simon's house. It's storming out, the rain coming down like a guillotine. I ring the front door bell. A black maid I've never seen before answers the door. Evidently not a fan of yours truly, she only stares blankly at me and my befeathered and bespangled mistress. It turns out that there is a late supper party in progress, but we manage to gain entry over the maid's fearful objections.

Six people are seated at a dining table set up before the french windows: Simon and Claire, Abel Stulz of Warner Brothers Records and his wife Nicky, and another middle-aged couple I don't recognize, a pair of Californians by the looks of them. It is an eerie goddam scene. All six of them turn their heads at once as we enter the room, the maid at our heels. Lightning crackles outside, momentarily whitening the faces of all present, heightening the look of ire on Simon's face in particular.

"It's all right, Minnie," Simon tells the maid. She withdraws. The lightning subsides. A cold draft causes the supper candles to flicker.

"It's Byron!" Nicky Stulz intones breathily, as if some combination of Buddy Holly and Jacob Marley had just materialized to sing a few songs and rattle his chains.

"Hello everybody," I say with the warmth of Captain Kangaroo greeting the six-year-olds.

"Hello, Byron," the others say in eerie unison—except Simon, whose expression keeps altering slightly from wrath to puzzlement to expectation. I introduce Catherine to all. She bows comically. Claire says they are about to have dessert and coffee and would we like to join them. Does she have to ask? Room is made at the table. A big pear tart is brought in and served. Java all around. Catherine takes a gold and enamel cigarette case out of her little silver-chain clutch purse and produces a nice fat joint, not that she especially relishes a smoke just now—most junkies can't stand pot—but rather to create an effect. She passes it to the gentleman at her right, an ICM agent from—where else?—California! Name of Lloyd Wolf.

One of those 45-year-olds who look 30. He lights it off the candle, has himself a toke or two, and passes it to Claire. Simon demurrs respectfully. Mrs. Wolf, a slightly over-the-hill starlet-type named Sandy, takes the sacrament as well. Stulz passes, but his wife Nicky takes a wee drag. As the thing goes round and round, Nicky inhales less timidly. Stulz and Simon share a wary glance. It's obvious they don't like what's going on, but to disapprove out loud would be too hopelessly unhip to imagine. A spooky silence has attended this whole ritual.

"You've been discussing business, right?" I say ebulliently to show that I understand why the conversation is suddenly so defunct.

"That's right," Simon says.

"Don't let us interrupt you."

"You already have," Simon replies, but to indicate that it's not such a big deal, he quickly adds, "Why don't we all retire to the living room for brandy."

"Brandy would be so nice," Nicky says. She's very stoned, you can tell.

"Scotch for me," her husband says.

"Wherever did you get that outfit?" Claire asks Catherine as we evacuate the table. Catherine is wearing this chiffon get-up decorated with sequins and feathers. "You look like a bird of paradise," Claire tells her. I notice Wolf copping a view of Catherine's cleavage as he rises out of his seat. It thrills me that he finds her desirable. We move over to the sofas and easy chairs—it's really just a different area of the same huge room. There is a fire blazing in the hearth. I'm feeling a slight sagging sensation right about now and excuse myself to go to the bathroom. When you've been on the kind of coke jag I'd been riding, you become very finely attuned to your body's little ups and downs, especially the downs. Actually, at this point I'm sagging sideways. Anyway, I retire to the lavatory and fire two fat lines into my brain. I return to the party feeling like the Joshua Light Show is going off in my head. Catherine has another joint going around the room, and it's still only the ladies and Lloyd Wolf who are indulging. There's drinks for all. Simon puts Reuban Shay's new record on the stereo, explaining that it's going to be released in two weeks. This is simply for my benefit, you see, because Reuban records for Warners so the Stulzes, at least, have already heard the tape.

"Put on one of Byron's," Nicky says.

"Byron doesn't record anymore," Simon tells her with a perfectly straight face.

The others look over at me, like Simon's kidding, right? Ribbing me. But have I got an ace up my sleeve? Oh boy!

"Just a second, everybody," I say. Out of the back pocket of my jeans I whip a sheaf of folded papers. "New songs!" I say triumphantly, as if, at long last, I have placed myself beyond opprobrium, beyond the niggling complaints of a mere manager. Bursting with confidence, I go to the piano and throw open the keyboard. Simon, looking skeptical but nonetheless interested, cuts off the tape recorder.

"This is such a privilege!" Sandy Wolf squeals, and I notice Catherine roll her eyes. It unnerves me because, theoretically, Catherine knows how hard I've been working and how fantastic the results are. I remind myself how hypercritical she is. I must be a saint to crank out so many terrific songs under these conditions!

I spread out the papers on the stand above the keyboard and raise my fingertips in anticipation when I suddenly realize, with a stab of fear, that I don't remember the tune, or even the chords that fit behind the lyrics.

"Slight problem," I mutter to myself and turn over the page. I scan a verse or two of the next ditty. I even play a few chords, as if it is an intro, covering up for myself, you understand. But I cannot for the life of me remember how it goes. The fear bumps up a notch. Okay, I tell myself, I'll fake it, and I start playing an ordinary blues progression in the key of E. I only play in two keys on the piano, anyway, E and C, major or minor, take your pick. In any case, the song sounds stupid this way. It sounds like I'm making it up as I go along. It even sounds like I'm making up the words, though they're right in front of me, because I can't fit them into the progression and I'm stammering and fumphering all over the place.

"I don't like that number anyway," I say, and crumple the lyrics into a ball.

"This is so exciting, I can't believe it!" I hear Wolf's wife whisper, and I wheel around on the bench.

"What can't you believe?" I ask her, snootily.

"How much fun it is to be here?" she replies, less sure of herself all of a sudden.

I nod my head and turn back to the keyboard. Catherine, meanwhile, gets up and excuses herself to go to the bathroom. This pisses

me off, that she's deserting me, but I don't say anything. I turn to
the next song. By now it has begun to dawn on me that I don't
remember how any of these goddam numbers go. The terror is
snowballing. I make one last effort to try and at least fake my way
through a song, and what comes out lacks the essential quality of
what distinguishes a song from any yammering nonsense. I sweep
the rest of the lyric sheets off the piano, get up, pour myself about
three fingers of Remy Martin in a snifter, and glug down half of it in
a couple of swallows. Nobody says anything. Nicky Stulz coughs into
the sleeve of her oriental dress. Her husband looks pained. Wolf
gamely attempts a smile. Simon is expressionless.

"Guess that set fell kind of short," I quip. Claire titters and looks
momentarily embarrassed for it. Suddenly, a new inspiration seizes
me, a way to save this lame act! I knock back the rest of the brandy.
"Short intermission," I say, and head back to the piano. I sit down
at the bench with a portentous determination that evokes early Lib-
erace, I lay my hands on the ivories, and start womping out my
number 1 hit single from 1966, "Rebecca's Window," an irresistable
rave-up guaranteed to send the folks in the audience. And they do
seem, well, intrigued with the performance, except for Stulz, who,
I happen to notice, is copping a glance at his wristwatch.

"Past your bedtime, Abel?" I ask between chorus and verse, without breaking stride.

"No," he mouths the word, smiling politely.

"Good, 'cause you can sleep on this," I mutter and point down
between my legs. "Just kidding," I tack on quickly, as if I have
included a Don Rickles imitation to prop up the act, which is growing more manifestly abysmal with each passing second. "Welcome
to the Lead Balloon Lounge," I joke. I'm so wired, there's no stopping me. I finish "Rebecca" and segue right into "Fugitive," out of
habit from our old touring playlist. I am, perhaps, two lines into the
song when an appalling screech is heard from another part of the
house. I stop playing. The others shift to the edge of their seats,
their heads lifted to this keening. The screech repeats itself and
suddenly we are all up in a mad rush through the halls, pantries,
kitchen, and finally to a back bathroom where, like some lurid photo
out of the *National Enquirer*, the doorway frames a tableau of Catherine collapsed around the toilet while the maid presses hands to
ears and wails in wide-eyed horror.

In the first seconds there is, likewise, a confused rush among per-

sonalities to assume command. I don't know if Catherine is dead, or
what. It is quite unreal to a man in my condition. I am simply numb.
Amid all this confusion and unreality I hear various cries, shouts,
orders, and curses.

"Lift her up!"

"No, don't move her!"

"She might be choking on her own vomit!"

"Pull her out of there!"

"What's that?"

"Christ—!"

"A needle!"

"A syringe!"

"She's breathing!"

"Call a doctor!"

"No, wait!"

"Call an ambulance!"

"Do *not* call any fucking ambulance. Here, help me."

"Can you hear me, Catherine?"

"She's still conscious, I think."

"Get her on her feet."

"Will somebody please call an ambulance—"

"No! Shut up already with the ambulance. She's conscious.
Where's Minnie—?"

"I'm right here."

"Is there any more of that coffee left?"

"Yes sir."

"She *is* conscious!"

"Help me walk her around."

"I still think we ought to call an amb—"

"For a heroin overdose? Don't be a schmuck."

"Well—"

"Is that what she's on?"

"You saw the needle."

"She doesn't seem like the type."

"Sandy thinks they're all supposed to look like Sonny Liston—"

"Sssshhh."

"That's right, Catherine, one foot in front of the other."

"Coffee's hot."

"Let's see a cup of that over here, Minnie."

It must have been a couple of hours, really, before Catherine was coherent, and even so she was still good and goddammed stoned. I straightened out considerably in the meantime, myself, not having the inclination, or the opportunity, really, to slip off to another bathroom and blow more cocaine. It must have been close to three o'clock in the morning when they poured Catherine into the front seat of the Rolls. We were not invited to stay at Simon's overnight, though you may be sure there were plenty of beds left, even with the Stulzes and Wolfs as house guests.

"She'll be all right," Simon said coldly. "Let him drive her home."

"Can he drive? Can you drive?" Nicky asked.

"I can drive."

"He's all right."

"At least follow them, Simon. Make sure they get home all right."

"Okay, I'll follow them."

It was a hairy ride home. I felt mentally okay, but my coordination was lousy. It was still drizzling out and I crept along the slick, winding roads at around twenty miles an hour. Catherine was singing idly to herself, singing one of the new songs, actually. I suddenly recognized the tune. She'd had it in her head all along. Simon's headlights trailed us all the way back, then up the long, dirt driveway. He helped me get Catherine upstairs to the bedroom. Then I walked him back down to his car. It was idling, rain cutting through the twin headlight beams and blue exhaust smoke curling around the tires. We didn't say a word to each other until we got all the way back to the car.

"Are you still using?" Simon asked in a perfectly normal tone of voice, like he was asking if I wanted to play eighteen holes in the morning.

"Still. . . ?" I played dumb, right?

"Yes. I'm asking if you're still shooting smack. Your wife's shooting it. Are you?"

"No," I said, as if his accusation was not only unfair but illogical. All of a sudden, he whipped me around bodily with my front up against the window. Using his superior weight, he kept me firmly pinned there while he went through my pockets. He found the plastic bag of white powder, of course, then wheeled me around violently and grabbed a fistful of my shirt. I was dying inside.

"What do you call this shit?"

"It's cocaine," I told him meekly, knowing he'd never believe it.

"You sure about that?" he said.

"I swear to God, Simon, it's not smack."

"Good. Then you don't need it."

He undid the rubber band and dumped about a thousand dollars worth of coke into the wet gravel where it instantly went into solution and vanished. Then he flung me aside, threw open the car door, and got in.

"I don't think you need me for a manager anymore, either," he said. Then he slammed the door and drove away.

# CHAPTER 10

*Strange desire*
*Faithless heart*
*To stand in the light*
*Of a falling star*

—"Never Like a Miracle"

It was Byron's idea to go over to St. Johnsbury for some dinner. We took his car, the green station wagon. Inside, it had the impersonal look and feel of a car owned by a corporation and given to an employee to use in the routine performance of his duties. It was tidy without being especially clean. My side of the seat had a film of dust over it.

It was still raining hard as we drove west through the countryside toward the Vermont border and daylight was failing rapidly at that hour in the foul weather.

"Spring, the smell of the woods," Byron said quietly, "it reminds me of the accident."

"He fired *you*," I said, still marveling at the recognition. "Simon fired *you!*"

"That's right," Byron said, glancing my way with a shy, pained look that would not become a smile.

"How could he do that?"

"My contract had run out."

"It ran out? Simon let it run out?"

"That's right. He let it run out and then he walked."

"You didn't know it had run out?"

"Rick, when you count up all the things I didn't know, or wasn't aware of at that time, well. . . ."

"How could he afford to walk?"

"You mean moneywise? Please. Simon was a wealthy man long before I sailed into his life. He enjoyed his money and he knew how to spend it, but having another million more or less in the bank wasn't going to affect his style of living one bit. Anyway, I didn't sleep a wink that night I ruined their dinner party. Starting about nine in the morning I tried to call his house, but the maid kept on answering and saying he couldn't come to the phone, blah blah. Finally, I got so mad that I decided to go over there personally. I took one of the cycles, the Vincent. I'm not sure why I took the bike instead of a car. The reds I was taking probably had something to do with it. I also had some inclination to ride straight up to the stable and take care of Richmond."

"Richmond? What did he have to do with anything?"

"Lots."

"That stuff from the summer before?"

"That's right. The drugs. The carrying on. He knew every goddam thing that went on in that house. We were ridiculously careless. Maids would see things. They must have passed it on to Richmond and Richmond filled in Simon."

"But why?"

"Why—? Sears, Simon owned Richmond Petty, lock, stock, and barrel. He owned his soul. And Richmond hated my guts."

"Because you were doing precisely what had destroyed him—"

"Right—"

"And getting away with it."

"Oh, worse. I was screwing Simon's wife! My goddam wife was screwing Simon's wife!"

"So he blew you in."

"Yup. He told on me. I'm sure of it."

"So you were going to—what? Punch him out? Kill him?"

"Who knows. But he wasn't the main reason I went over there that morning. Simon was. I was going to beg Simon not to throw me out of his life. Anyway, it's all academic because the last thing I remember was riding down that big curving hill into Tamberlane Village proper. I woke up 36 hours later, in a manner of speaking, in Riply-Varden Hospital in Kingston, rigged up in traction with a crushed left leg, a dislocated shoulder, six cracked ribs, and a fractured skull. To complicate matters, I started going through Seconal withdrawal. They didn't know what the hell to make of my EEG."

"So that's where all those rumors about brain damage came from that first week you were in the hospital."

"I suppose. Where do you want to eat anyway?"

St. Johnsbury was eerily quiet at this hour, the gloom of a New England mill town decades after it had outlived its purpose. Over most of America the day shift was wheeling homeward in the spring rain, except here, where, from the looks of things, the last day shift ceased around 1965. Past the center of town, among a block of oxydizing wood-frame houses, and next to a tropical fish store, we saw DiNaldo's Neopolitan Cuisine, the chief virtue of which was that it was open for business.

"Can your stomach take this?" I asked Byron.

"Hey, I'm right back at 99.9 percent. Sure."

We parked and entered the cinderblock structure. An elderly couple, both gaunt and chinless with faces like large birds, sat ignoring each other in a booth over plates smeared with red sauce. Christmas lights strung along the moldings burned spiritlessly above them suggesting that this was a land where holidays had catastrophically ceased years ago. Byron rubbed his hands together and said, "Smells great! I love eating out, don't you?"

"Crazy about it," I said.

A waitress showed us to a booth across the room from the old couple.

"Did I ever tell you about this French joint my parents used to take me to, and the frogs' legs?"

"Yes. You did."

"Oh. Bet you can't get 'em here. But hey, this is fun, huh?"

"Very festive," I agreed.

"We ate out a lot today."

"Twice."

"For me that's a lot. It's almost like being a member of the human race again." He picked up his menu and began reading it. I put my hand over it to get his attention back.

"You think about that a lot, don't you?" I said.

"About what?"

"Rejoining the human race."

"Naw. That was just a figure of speech."

"You do, though. I know you do. We could discuss it sometime if you like."

Byron looked up at me, shrugged his eyebrows, and sighed.

"I don't even look like myself anymore," he said. "Who would believe it?"

"You look more like your old self than you think. In my opinion that wouldn't be a problem."

"Maybe not," he said quietly. "But you know what would be a problem? Figuring out who the hell I'm *supposed* to be. Peter. Byron. Joe. I don't know. I just don't know."

"You could be Peter Greenwald if you want."

"You think people would be satisfied with that? Forget it. They'd figure out who I was in a second and there I'd be, right in the middle of some ridiculous circus. 'Here I am, folks! Just stepped out of my life for a while.' "

"It could be managed in a reasonable way."

Byron exhaled noisily.

"Hey, what's so wrong with the way I live anyway, huh? It's not such a bad deal, you know. You ought to try it sometime. You do what you want to do and go where you want to go."

"And what do you want to do?"

"Nothing."

"Where do you want to go?"

"Nowhere."

"You sure about that?"

"No."

The waitress reappeared and Byron flinched. He consulted the menu hurriedly and she took our order. He watched her return to the kitchen.

"Pretty girl," I remarked, wondering how he would react to it.

"Not bad for around here," Byron said.

"Can I ask you a personal question?"

"You want to know what I've been doing for dates all these years, right?"

"You must think about it."

"I think about it a lot."

"Is that where it stops?" I was nervous about pressing him on the subject, but he looked more ruminative than upset.

"No," he admitted. "It doesn't stop there. You really want to know what I've been doing?"

"Yes," I replied, falling for the bait. He leaned forward and cupped his hand beside his mouth.

"Every now and then I whack my weasal," he whispered.

The waitress materialized behind me with our steaming plates and I was the one who ended up feeling flustered. Byron seemed to enjoy my discomfort immensely. He thanked the girl, tucked his napkin into his collar, and attacked his eggplant parmigiana with the zeal of a little kid, taking comic delight in the long rubbery strands of mozzarella. My spaghetti and meatballs were, frankly, repulsive, the pasta mealy and overcooked, the meatballs redolent of something like unto the contents of a gym locker. I was so hungry, though, that I nearly cleaned my plate.

"Isn't this fantastic?" Byron said. "We ought to come here more often."

"Good, huh?"

"You bet." He buttered a Saltine and popped it in his mouth. "I forgot how much I like to eat. God, in the old days I was always on a diet. I'm telling you, it was brutal. I was whacked out on sheer hunger half the time."

Byron picked up the check and paid it. The rain had finally stopped. It was night now. The center of town was deserted. A few electric signs blinked absurdly in the windows of storefronts facing the vacant town square. The darker countryside beyond it was even more forbidding, and the thought of all the things Byron had given up to hide here for so many years was almost unbearable.

"That summer after the crash was when I first met you, right?" Byron asked.

"Yes."

"Tell me something, just between you and me and the doorknob, what was your impression of Catherine. Be honest."

"She was . . . intimidating."

"She wasn't any shrinking violet, that's for sure. What else?"

"She was very beautiful. I remember the first time I saw her, she had a scarf around her head and big hooped earrings. She looked like a beautiful pirate."

"Hey, I think you're right about the scarf. You have a great memory. What else?"

"I thought she was . . . nuts."

"Crazy, huh? How come?"

I strained my memory.

"Well," I said, "remember that first session, we were alone. . . ?"

"Yeah. . . ?"

"And then your wife, Catherine, came home. You introduced us. She kissed me. . . ."

"Yeah, so. . . ?"

". . . on the lips."

"Showbiz."

"Yeah, maybe. But then she sat down in this chair behind the sofa you were on. We continued our conversation, you and I, but she started making faces at me and gesticulating every time you said something and acting really cuckoo."

"She did that? Behind my back?"

"Yes."

"Well, no wonder you thought she was a little weird," Byron said and nibbled on his lower lip. "Simon detested her. I guess you've gathered that by now."

"I assumed they weren't members of a mutual admiration society."

"He hated her for corrupting Claire. That's a howl, huh?"

"Maybe, deep down, he desired her."

"Maybe. Others did."

"Do you think they ever . . . you know."

"I doubt it. I don't think he ever . . . had her. He might have been the only one."

———

I thought Byron was going to drop me off at the cottage and then go home, but when he turned off the engine and asked if I had any tea in the house, I realized that he intended to stick around for a while. I was nearly cross-eyed with fatigue, but how could I kick him out?

Meanwhile, the fire in the woodstove had burned down to embers and we could see our breath in the lamplight. Byron saw to the stove while I made a pot of Earl Grey, good and strong. I drank it with a lot of sugar. Byron stoked the fire expertly and soon I began to feel restored.

## The Life of Byron Jaynes—Tape 8

*Simon never came to see you in the hospital?*

No, that's not quite true. He came two or three times in the beginning, when there was some question about me ever recovering, the convulsions, all that stuff. I wasn't really conscious though and I have no recollection of him being there, but Catherine told me he came.

*The two of you never talked it out?*

I don't think there was ever any question of what Simon had made up his mind to do. As far as he was concerned, I was a hopeless junkie and my wife was a junkie *and* a degenerate. No, he dropped me cold.

*Marva Faith had a habit off and on for years, and Simon never dropped her.*

Marva never hurt him like I did.

*You were like a son to him.*

I don't know. All I can say is I never had much luck with fathers or with father-figures. I tried to work out a lot of that stuff on *Oedipus Forgiven*, later on.

*But he wasn't forgiven. You weren't forgiven.*

Of course not. That's the whole point. It was only a wish. Anyway, I lay there in the hospital getting more and more famous just for being a convalescent. People found out that Simon and I were no longer . . . together. I was approached by a lot of opportunists who wanted to take over. All they did was make me determined to show everybody that I could jolly-well handle my own affairs and prove that Simon Lewisohn wasn't so indispensable. I resolved to become my own manager. I hired Albert Franks, an economics professor from Beal College, to tutor me in the rudiments of handling money. I had nothing else to do, lying in bed for three and a half months. It was the highlight of my day. I found a new lawyer and a CPA. We had all my accounts audited and it turned out that Simon had been scrupulously honest down to the last dollar. I had assets amounting to over three million bucks.

Of course, I never did put an album together that year, but then again Jerry Zuckerman's rosy predictions for the future hadn't panned out either. Bobby Kennedy got shot, not nominated, the Vietnam War got worse, not stopped, and that new era of good feeling that Jerry looked forward to so misty-eyed just never came to pass. Instead, we got Tricky Dick. And my dad. Nixon made all his cabinet appointments before Christmas. My father, Morris Greenwald, was named deputy attorney general in charge of the criminal division of the U.S. Department of Justice. All his fancy footwork finally paid off.

*Did he visit you in the hospital?*

No, he didn't.

*Did he know you were hurt?*

He would have had to be deaf, dumb, and blind not to. Look, he knew long before the accident that Nixon was going to run and he wasn't going to do anything to screw things up for himself. And associating with the likes of me was just the kind of thing that might have screwed things up. He sent a card, though. A card!

*But they must have known you were his son. They have procedures, security checks—*

They knew. Nixon knew. But the story was that we weren't close. And I hadn't done anything embarrassing enough yet to keep my father out of the government. Besides, nobody outside politics or the press really gave a shit who the *deputy* attorney general was until later, when my father headed up all those antiwar prosecutions. But back then, in the fall of '68, nobody was very concerned about our being related except him. Anyway, I called him at his office to congratulate him when I heard the news about his appointment. It was partly an excuse to contact him again, to let him know that I still existed, and partly to show him that I was interested in his life, even if he did ignore mine. Parents and kids are so goddam perverse. I gave my name as Byron Jaynes to his secretary and my father took the call immediately.

"Congratulations," I said.

"Thank you. How are you, Peter?"

"Aside from almost being killed in a motorcycle crash, fine."

"Did you get my card?"

"I sure did. It was very, very thoughtful of you." That was a good conversation stopper right there. Neither of us said anything for a really long time. "Hey, when are you moving to Washington?" I finally asked.

"We're looking for a house now," my father said, and didn't elaborate.

"Did you see me on the cover of the old *Rolling Stone?*"

"It was brought to my attention. Yes."

"Someone had to bring it to your attention?"

"I don't subscribe, Peter."

"Sure. Well, what'd you think?"

"It was a good likeness, that painting of you."

"What'd you think of the interview?"

"I didn't read the interview."

"Not even to see if you were in it?"

"I wasn't in it."

"How do you know if you didn't read it?"

"Sheila read it."

"She write you a memo on it?"

"No, we discussed it."

"You ought to read it sometime when you get a chance."

"Maybe I'll do that, Peter."

"Were you relieved that I didn't spill all our family secrets?"

"I don't know what secrets you're talking about, Peter. You really do have an active imagination to go along with that sharp tongue of yours. If you're trying to provoke me, you're wasting your time—"

"I'm not trying to provoke you, I'm—"

" 'Did she write you a memo—?' Come on, pal."

"Well, you should have read it yourself."

"I wish I had time to read a lot of things."

Another one of those spooky pauses followed. The truth was, I didn't want to let him off the hook quite yet.

"So what does this new job of yours entail?" I asked.

"Same thing, really, on the federal level."

"Groovy. You going to Julie's wedding?" I meant Nixon's daughter. She was getting married to Eisenhower's grandson that month.

"I don't know, Peter."

"Can you wangle me an invitation?"

"They'd love that," he cackled. He wasn't totally devoid of a sense of humor.

"Tell the president-elect I'll entertain for free, no charge. Hey, he's got another daughter, right? What's her name?"

"Tricia," my father said wearily.

"Yeah, Tricia. Hey, what if Tricia and I got hitched? You'd be family. You wouldn't have to look for a place to live in Washington. You could move right into the White House. You've got to get me an invitation to this wedding."

"Aren't you already married, Peter?"

"Hey, that's right. Tell you what I'll do, though. I'll get divorced."

"I've got to go now, Peter. But do me a favor, will you?"

"Sure. What?"

"In the future, give my secretary your real name. My calls are logged and—"

"And my real name is Byron Jaynes. I changed it in the goddam probate court so I wouldn't embarrass you, remember?"

"Thank you for calling, Peter—"

"And thanks for visiting me in the hospital, you douchebag!"

Click.

What a pair of ballbusters we were!

Of course, just because my father didn't come to visit me didn't mean I was totally abandoned and bereft. Catherine was around a lot in the beginning. Rego and Gary came. Even Bobby called several times from California.

This isn't a generally known fact, but I asked Rego if he would like to join me in a new band after I got better. It really bothered me when he turned me down, not because I was being spurned, but because he always had such good instincts about where things were headed. I took it as a bad omen.

The truth was, I was surrounded by bad omens, not the least of which was Catherine's behavior. You know, up until that night at Simon's, I'd never known her to mainline. And she didn't mainline again for a long time after that, so I should have been more suspicious about what it meant. Not that she could have told me if I had asked her. She wasn't what I'd call an introspective person.

*What did you think her OD meant?*

At the time I thought it meant she had moved up to a higher level of heroin addiction. It wasn't until I came home from the hospital months later that I realized her OD might have been a different statement.

*Why?*

Because when I came home, she wasn't mainlining anymore. It was only that one time, at Simon's house, that she did it.

*But she was still using heroin, after you were discharged from the hospital.*

Yes. But she gave herself intramuscular injections, not intravenous—she was always a skinpopper.

*Do you think she OD-ed on purpose?*

Of course. That's what I'm saying.

*So Simon would boot you out of his life—?*

Right!

*But why would she want him to do that?*

You tell me.

*Jealousy?*

That's an obvious choice. But no, I don't think so.

*I don't know. Sheer perversity?*

That's right. The overwhelming need to fuck things up! She didn't have to turn Claire onto smack the summer before. That was totally unnecessary.

*But I still don't get the motive. Simon—*

Hated her.

*And obviously she couldn't stand that—*

No, no! That's exactly what she wanted.

*To be hated—?*

To be a bad girl.

*I don't believe that. We all crave approval—*

Do you think we all want to *be good?* We all want to *do good?*

*It's not the same thing as wanting approval—*

Right! It's not the same thing. And you want to know something else? Some people don't give a flying fuck about being approved of, either, Rick. They want *attention*, pure and simple. And some people don't care if they do good things or bad things to get it. Catherine liked to be a bad girl and she liked to fuck things up, but she wasn't like that all the time—nobody is—and it took me years, and a lot of heartache, to figure out her game.

When I was in the hospital, I had no control over her. I couldn't even tighten the old purse strings because she had turned 21 that fall and two trust funds devolved on her, so she had an income of her own. She would vanish into the city for days at a time. I didn't know if she was sleeping around or not. All I knew was that, being in traction, I wasn't much use to her, and I suppose I resigned myself to the possibility. What could I do?

*Divorce her.*

I didn't want to divorce her. I wanted to possess her. Don't you understand? Weren't you ever in love with someone? You're married. You must know what it's like. Sometimes the harder a person makes it for you, the more you desire them, until you reach such an extreme pitch of emotion that all your original, good reasons for loving that person become lost.

Anyway, I had Keough back on my payroll that fall and winter, helping me out with a lot of things, and he would see her out at night in the city, making the rounds of the clubs and parties. He'd see her with men. She was hanging out with Ronnie Barron and his crowd of morons at Ondine. I let it be. Then, one snowy afternoon just before Christmas, when she'd been gone for days, I was sitting alone in front of the fireplace, killing a bottle of Johnny Walker. I heard the heavy thunk of a car door closing, her footsteps sharp on the marble floor of the entranceway.

"Hello, stranger," I said across that huge space from the hearth to the hall.

"What. . . ? Oh, hi," she said, looking fatigued and distracted.

I was reclining on our big sofa with my bad leg up. I could watch her traverse the whole distance from the entranceway and I think that made her nervous. She dragged her coat behind her, a long red fox coat, but she put it on again and slouched into an overstuffed easy chair near the hearth.

"Take off your clothes and stay a while," I said. "I mean your coat."

"It's cold in here."

"I miss you, Catherine."

She looked down in her lap and shrugged one shoulder. "I guess I need other people more than you do, Byron. You used to like to go out."

"I was never crazy about it. Besides, it's not possible anymore."

"What's so impossible about it?"

"People don't know how to act around me. Sometimes I wish I was Joe Dork, some ordinary guy working for the power company."

"You're not, though."

I could tell she was already losing interest in the discussion. Frankly, we'd had it more than once before.

"Hey, want to see something?" I said excitedly.

"Sure." She looked up.

I got off the sofa and started limping around.

"See, no cane even. I can bend it a little, too, now."

"Fantastic," she said with slightly forced enthusiasm. She was pretty wasted, I could tell. "I'm really very proud of you." She got up and began trudging toward the staircase. At the bottom of the stairs, she looked over her shoulder and said, "I'm exhausterated." Catherine often created her own vocabulary.

I followed her upstairs to our bedroom. She was leaving a trail of garments strewn down the hallway. The room was a shambles, clothes everywhere, mostly her stuff, empty glasses, magazines all over the place.

"You going to bed?" I asked.

"I guess I am," she said.

"It's four o'clock in the afternoon."

"So what?"

"You could stay up for a while."

"What for?"

"I don't know. We could chat."

She turned on a lamp next to the bed. It was a beautiful piece of mauve-colored frosted glass shaped like a giant lily. Outside the leaded windows it was already twilight. Catherine shivered and hurried into the adjoining bathroom. On a table next to the sink was a small autoclave, a sterilizer like the kind your dentist has in his office. Catherine opened the lid and carefully laid various tools of the trade on a white linen towel. Next she took an antique enameled box out of the drawer below and, with a silver-and-blue enameled spoon—like the kind you'd see with an old-fashioned salt cellar— she measured out one level scoop of pale-brown powder. Her fastidious preparations were such a winning combination of the modern and the medieval. She lit the wick of a little glass alcohol lamp, dropped some water into her silver cooker—cunningly adapted from an old candle-snuffer—and held it over the flame by its long handle until the heroin crystals dissolved. Then, working with the expertise of a true professional, she rested the cooker in a stand that had been a silver napkin ring and filled a small stainless steel and glass reusable syringe with the cooked liquid.

"Hold this." She handed me the needle. "This place is like a mausoleum."

She reached for a green and white kimono that hung from a hook on the door. Then she marched back into the bedroom and began clearing the muskrat fur bedspread of books and magazines, including the spiral notebooks I used for ideas, poems, and lyrics. Finally, she lay down on the furry spread with her face in a pillow and her backside up and hiked the silk kimono until flesh was exposed. On each cheek where the large muscles of her ass joined the thighs were dozens of blue-black bruises about the size of a berry. It was more bizarre than gross, really. At the same time, I couldn't help noticing the inverted V of flesh and tawny hair visible between her legs.

"What are you waiting for?" Catherine said.

"Just a second."

I opened the button of my jeans and coughed loudly as I pulled down the zipper.

"Don't cough on the needle, please," she said testily.

I dropped the needle on the carpet, seized both cheeks with my hands, parted the flesh athwart the aperature, and thrust homeward. Catherine groaned and tried to escape, but I girdled her belly with clinched hands and held her close to me until she stopped struggling. When I was finished, she collapsed beneath me and I lay on top for a while.

"You're crushing me," she eventually muttered into the pillow.

"Forgive me."

"Could I please have my injection now."

"You just had it."

"And what a treat it was. Get the needle, Byron."

I picked it up off the carpet and brought it back to her on the bed. She swept some damp strands of auburn hair out of her face and took it from me.

"Squeamish?" she asked.

"I don't feel right about it anymore. Never did, really."

"It's a riot the way you can act morally superior when you sit downstairs in the middle of the day draining whisky bottles."

"You arrived at cocktail hour."

"I see. Well, it's my injection hour." She rolled over on her side, drew up one leg, and jabbed the needle into the fatty tissue below the hip. Then she placed it on the night table and got under the covers. The way she took her junk—popping—it took several minutes for the stuff to start taking effect.

"Keough says he ran into you at the Blood, Sweat and Tears party."

"Oh, did he?"

"Yes, he did."

"It seems like I run into him all over town these days. Is that a coincidence or do I just imagine that he's spying on me?"

"He's not spying."

"Everywhere I go, it seems like he turns up."

"He's a very sociable person."

"I wish you were," she said and sighed and looked at the lily lamp. I reached for her hand and squeezed it between both of mine.

"Am I a terrible disappointment to you?"

"I thought it would be more fun, is all."

"Why do you keep coming back?"

"Different reasons."

"Like what?"

"I don't know. Instinct. Curiosity. That empty feeling."

"What was it this time?"

"Exhaustion."

"Never love?"

"Love is mixed up with that empty feeling I get."

"Where do I fit in?"

"You're my husband," she said drowsily. "Hero of the multitudes." She chuckled once. Her eyes closed. She looked like the
fairy princess of the storybooks falling asleep on her enchanted mattress, her red-brown tresses fanned out against the pale linens. I
found myself envying her sheer nerveless bravado, as if it were a
virtue, something worth cultivating. I kissed her on the forehead,
turned out the light at her bedside, and was about to leave the room
when she mumbled, "Do something for me, will you, Flash?"

"Sure," I said. "Anything."

"Turn up the heat."

She flopped over on her side and pulled the covers over her head.
I left her there and went back downstairs.

*Had you begun drinking heavily at that point?*

Rick, I was drinking heavily, on and off, before I ever left Beal
College. Except for those two stretches when I was using smack,
and then the time I got strung out on downs, I always preferred
alcohol. Liquor is so comfortable, so legal. And it ran in the family.

*You drank scotch.*

Yes. Like mom used to. But don't get the wrong idea. I wasn't
sitting around the house that winter like Ray Milland in *The Lost
Weekend* sucking on whisky bottles and watching rodents chew
through the wallpaper. If someone told me I was developing an
alcohol problem after what I'd been through with narcotics, not to
mention having my leg crushed and two operations and all, it would

have seemed ridiculous. And, oddly enough, during the fall and winter of my convalescence, with Catherine absent so much of the time, I actually got a lot of writing accomplished. In February I was ready to record *Oedipus Forgiven*.

*Country Byron*.

Country Byron, exactly! You know, more horseshit has been written about that record than any other part of my life. For instance, the *Rolling Stone* review, when it first came out—

*I wrote it.*

That was you?

*Since I'd just interviewed you a few months before, they figured I was the leading Jaynes expert on the staff. Yeah, I wrote it.*

Well, my boy, that was some piece of Talmudic scholarship, that review of yours.

*It was a style back then. We used to write the, quote, "important reviews" like they were doctoral dissertations.*

But that Country Byron touch was hilarious—the idea that this wild and flamboyant young minstrel had quit his lowdown ways and retired to the simple yeoman's life close to the soil—

*"The elements," I think, was the exact term I used.*

Whatever. It was great. It was especially ironic because when that review came out—the record was released in early June of '69, right?—I was on the road again and coming apart at the seams. But I'm getting a little ahead of myself here.

When I went down to Muscle Shoals to record *Oedipus* in February, I had no intention of making any so-called landmark album to turn the whole tide of rock music back to its simple agrarian roots— or whatever bullshit was said about it. I went down to Alabama scared stiff and all I wanted to do was cut a record. I wasn't sure I could even do it anymore, it'd been such a long time. I went down there without a manager or a band. I couldn't use the same guys from *Childe Byron.* Cleanth was on the road playing behind Joe Cocker with Leon Russell. Harvey was busy in California. Tommy was dead, for Godsake.

Meanwhile, the whole technology of recording had changed drastically in the two years since *Childe Byron.* I didn't know anything about it. Though it's true, I did arrive with all the songs written, the sessions down in Muscle Shoals, from my point of view, took place in an atmosphere of total desperation. I didn't know any of the guys who played behind me. Keough rounded them up in the twelve hours after we got down there, and we had literally no rehearsal time. It was just, *boom!* into the studio. The reason the arrangements sounded so simpleminded—

*Pristine—*

Pristine? Shit. . . .

*Everybody thought you did it that way on purpose.*

That's hilarious. When we packed up and left there a week later, I almost dumped the masters in the Tennessee River. I thought the stuff was horrible. I thought I was about to become the laughing-stock of the industry. I was convinced after I got Jerry Zuckerman's reaction—not that he was the best arbiter—but the way he hemmed and hawed about it, I was pretty sure I had at least a commercial disaster on my hands. Keough was the only one who thought it was any good, in his own solid, quiet way. And if it hadn't been for him, *Oedipus Forgiven* might not have been released at all. I might have thrown in the towel right there, and none of the rest . . . oh well, it's foolish to hypothesize because the record *was* released, and nobody was more surprised than I was by the reaction it got. I couldn't understand what all the fuss was about.

*It was a great album, Byron. It was simple and moving at a time when the music was getting overly complicated and pretentious— the Who's* Tommy, *for example.*

I don't know. You were in a better position to judge, maybe. That was your job, right? I mean, I was so down on the album I was going to title it *More Songs from a Depressed Young Man.* Keough talked me out of that one, though. I was flabbergasted by the early reviews and it shipped surprisingly strong.

*You kept track of sales?*

I had to, Rick. I didn't have anyone looking out for my interests anymore. In any event, Gemini started flogging the hell out of it— big ads, hype all over the place. It was like my return to the record racks was the biggest thing since Elvis came home from the army.

Before that, when I still thought it was going to bomb, Jerry had tried to talk me into a limited tour, and I shot down the idea immediately. I mean, I was petrified. But then, after the favorable reviews rolled in, I changed my mind. We got together and planned it, big halls and stadiums only, commencing at the end of June and running into early fall.

I had to put together a touring band in very short order. Who could I get? I couldn't use those guys from the *Oedipus* sessions because they were strictly country musicians and couldn't have played any of the other material from the earlier albums. So we ended up with the most improbable collection of misfits you ever saw on one stage together: Buddy Breathwaite, whose statutory rape conviction was on appeal in New Jersey—he was always the example that managers would dredge up to impress upon you the dangers of fornicating with groupies. He was on drums. For a bass player we got Duane Crocker, who had the distinction of being asked to leave not one, but *two*, of the most successful rock and roll bands of that time, the Scoundrels and Blind Dog's Mother, because of ego problems—his was overgrown. On keyboards we got Dodie Cotton, who had a chip on his shoulder about the size of the RCA Building, and finally, when all my attempts to get Michael Bloomfield and then Todd Rundgren, failed, I resorted to poor old Stephen Spagnola, who had become a genuine legend in the industry, but who was now *so* withdrawn and introverted that he actually hadn't worked since the Romantics came off their tour in late '66 and I disbanded them. He was even living in the same crummy apartment on West 4th Street, though he had plenty of money. My motives weren't purely altruisitc, but I thought it might do him some good to get out on the road again.

Anyway, I put them all up in my house in Tamberlane, except

Dodie, who demanded special accommodations, and we rehearsed for a week straight. They might have been a bunch of pains-in-the-asses as human beings, but one thing about working with professionals: they get their chops down fast. The night before our opening date, I was feeling pretty optimistic. We sounded quite decent. Even with Spag back it was a very different sound than the old Romantics, tougher, twitchy, like a finger on a trigger. I knew it was going to throw the audiences off balance at first, because they'd come out to the concerts expecting to hear Country Byron and *whammo*, it'd be loud and wild, not what they were expecting at all. But I was confident that they could be won over.

I was confident about a lot of things all of sudden. But my marriage wasn't one of them. I came down to the city the night before our scheduled departure. It was the night Judy Garland died of an OD. Catherine told me she was pregnant.

*She had some sense of timing.*

It was me just as much as her. I was letting it slide, Rick, letting it slide. But then, after *Oedipus*, when spring came and things started looking up for me for the first time in more than a year, I began to ask myself: why put up with this crap anymore? Becoming physically intact again had a lot to do with it. You know, when you feel weak and busted up physically, it's next to impossible to feel strong mentally and emotionally. So I let it slide. But in the spring I started thinking about the possibility of a divorce, and soon it seemed inevitable. The baby threw me for a loop.

I met her over at the Pierre, where she'd been keeping a suite during her constant city sojourns. Her parents had gotten rid of the pied-à-terre on 72nd Street a long time ago. It was one of those gluey, superhumid 90-degree evenings when you felt sorry for anyone who had to live in New York. But inside, the hotel air conditioning was turned up so high that I started shivering outside her door. I was scared too, I suppose, knowing what I was going to ask her, probably even more scared that she might agree to a divorce without an argument.

The door swung open and she threw her arms around my neck. She squeezed me hard and then let go. Her face was taut and pale. To be honest with you, the first thing I thought was that she was going through withdrawal or something. She held onto the front of my shirt so tight that a button actually popped off.

"Oh, Flash," she said in this choking little voice, "I'm pregnant!" She clutched me again. Her eyes were all bloodshot and her nose was red too, from crying or blowing it.

I didn't know what the hell to do. Here I was, all set to pop the question in reverse, so to speak, and all of a sudden she's pregnant and in a state.

I put my arm around her, she grabbed me around the waist, and I helped her wade through the clutter of clothes and empty shoeboxes and Bonwit bags in the bedroom. I don't know where I got the idea that she should be in bed, but from the way she was carrying on, being pregnant seemed tantamount to having some terrible illness. I helped her under the covers and pulled up this padded chair beside her. For a long time she stared up into the ceiling with the back of her hand pressed against her forehead and her other hand wringing a Kleenex.

"I guess you'll have to get an abortion," I finally said.

She turned to me, her reddened nostrils flaring, and said adamantly, "No! I'm going to have this baby."

"Great. A junkie baby."

"I'll get off it."

"Does he get off it too, then, this baby? And live?"

"I'll go to a clinic, that place in Connecticut where Marva went."

"Is there anything to drink around here?"

Catherine pointed to a bottle of Jack Daniels on the writing table. It reminded me instantly of Ronnie Barron, but I poured myself a glass anyway.

"I thought you'd be a little more excited about the prospect of becoming a father," Catherine said.

"Just because you're pregnant doesn't mean that I'm becoming a father."

"Well, you are."

"How do you know for sure?"

"I do. A woman just does."

I came back to the chair and sat down again.

"What about Ronnie?"

"It's over," she said. "That's over with."

"How far are you along?"

"What does that matter?"

"I want to know, that's all."

"About ten weeks."

"Can you still get an abortion—?"

"I'm not getting one, and that's that."

Finally, I couldn't help it anymore. I started crying right there in the chair. "What's the use, Catherine? It's not working. Don't you understand?"

"It'll change."

"Nothing's going to change."

"I'll change. I will, Byron. Oh, I'm such a fucking brat I can't believe myself sometimes. But I'll change. Things will get better, you watch. A baby! Think of it, Byron, you and me being parents!"

I thought about it all right, and the idea terrified me. Suddenly I was on my feet, pacing up and down the room, tears streaming from my eyes. Catherine was crying too. What a pair of prospective parents we made. I'm sure Doctor Spock would have renounced all his theories in a minute if he got a load of us, two prime products of it, in that hotel room. Finally, I couldn't stand it any longer. I sat down on the bed right next to her, took her face between my two hands, and said, very emphatically, very clearly, "I don't want a baby. I want a divorce."

"Well, you can't always get what you want," Catherine said right back in a tone of voice that seemed amazingly bloodless for all those tears and theatrics.

"What possible good could it do for anybody if you go ahead and have this baby?" I asked, trying to elevate the depressing discussion to something approaching the adult level.

"It could do *me* good, Byron," Catherine said quietly. "It could save my life."

"Save your life—? You mean, either you have this baby or commit suicide?"

Catherine's face contorted again and this terrible soundless crying followed, as if her life was so miserable that not even the simplest animal expression of pain could communicate it. I didn't know what to do, so I just sat there and stroked her hairline with the back of my fingers. Finally, she bit down on the knuckle of her index finger and a sob came out, like punctuation, ending the spasm. Then she looked away, toward the wall.

"Not suicide," she said. "I don't know."

"What then?"

She looked back up at me, and there was real fear in her eyes.

"Sometimes I feel like I'm sliding down a long, slippery tunnel, Byron, and I get so scared. I'm afraid I'm never going to make it to thirty, and it scares me so bad—I can't stand it anymore."

"You could try some self-control."

She laughed, not maliciously, but as if I had said something truly hilarious.

"You could," I emphasized it.

"You should hear yourself saying that."

"Okay, we could both use a little more self-control."

She laughed harder. "A little—?"

"You know what I mean."

"All my life I've been looking for someone to make a few clear rules so I could tell what game I was playing," she said. "Is that asking so much?"

"No, not for a child. A child needs that. But—"

"Daddy was incapable. Mom. The two of them made me sick."

"Well, you're grownup now, Catherine, and there's nobody but you to say what you can and can't do."

"There's you. You're my husband."

"You want me to tell you when to be home at night? What you should indulge in?"

"Just act like you care."

"Catherine, I've never tried to make those kinds of demands—"

"You should—"

"—May I finish?"

"Okay, finish."

"Because I'm sure you wouldn't stand for it."

"I would if you were strong enough."

"Strong enough for what?"

"To make me."

"That's the whole point," I raised my voice in exasperation. "You have to do it yourself. You have to make yourself."

"That's why I want to have this baby."

"If your parents couldn't control you, and I won't, do you think a little tiny baby can?"

"Yes. I do."

"How can you possibly arrive at that conclusion?"

"Because I'll be its mother," she said, clutching herself. "I feel like this is my last chance, Byron," she said, her voice breaking and the corners of her mouth twitching.

I got off the bed and went over to the window. We were up on the twelfth floor. Looking down on Fifth Avenue made me dizzy and I pulled the curtain closed.

"Okay," I turned back to her. "You can keep the baby," I said, as if the decision was mine to make.

"I'll be good, I swear, Byron."

"Find out where this clinic is where Marva goes to clean herself up."

"It's in Connecticut, I told you."

"Okay. We're opening in New Haven tomorrow night. I'll drive you up in the morning and check you into this place—"

"You don't have to—"

"I do," I corrected her strenuously. "And I'm going to."

"Okay. You don't have to yell."

"No, I have to do that too. You want to be controlled? Okay, this is part of being controlled."

She sat up in bed, wiped her eyes with the sleeve of her nightgown, and smiled.

"My hero," she said, without a trace of sarcasm. "My husband."

So the next morning I trundled her up to the Ainslinger Clinic in West Canaan and signed her in. The place was chock full of middle-aged women who reminded me of my mother, and I was overwhelmed with regret that I'd never known enough to put her in a place like this. Maybe Catherine was right, I thought. Maybe it would paste us back together. It certainly couldn't hurt for her to get cleaned up. It wasn't until I was onstage later that night in the Yale Bowl, singing in front of a live audience for the first time in almost three years, 60,000 people, that I remembered there was a good chance the baby wouldn't even be mine.

# CHAPTER 11

On wings the horseman's chariot
Sails off empty into the sun
Apollo is at ground zero
With tickets for everyone

—"Apollo at Ground Zero"

I woke up freezing on the sofa with all my clothes on and my jacket thrown over me. Though it was cold as winter inside the house, outside the spring sun was shining warmly and the birds were singing like mad in the budding maples. Blood-red trilliums were in bloom down by the pond, where I stripped naked and washed in the frigid shallows with a cake of soap left on a rock from the previous fall. Then, lathered from crown to calf, I flung myself flat out into the water with such a subsequent contraction of the vascular tissues that visions of the coronary care unit flashed before my eyes. I was numbly toweling off when I heard the crunch of gravel up above and saw Byron's station wagon pull into the vaguely circular drive. He emerged from the car with both arms around a supermarket bag.

"Hey, good morning!"

"Same to you."

"Do you like pancakes, my boy?" he shouted as I gathered my clothes.

"Sure do," I replied.

"Then ye shall have 'em!" he cried and limped energetically to the kitchen door, guffawing like Robert Newton in the old film version of *Treasure Island*. When I caught up with him inside, he was rooting through the cabinets, grabbing mixing bowls and egg beaters and humming cheerfully to himself. I noticed he was wearing faded blue jeans and the very same satin shirt embroidered with moons and stars that he was photographed in for the cover of *Oedipus Forgiven*. It was eerie to see that holy relic of the Aquarian Age on his back. For all his talk about being careful, he seemed to be growing more reckless, more brazen, by the day. I didn't say anything, of course, not wishing to start a quarrel, but went upstairs to find some clean clothes to replace the ones I had slept in. When I returned, the woodstove was stoked, the house was filled with the smell of fresh coffee, and Byron was flipping the last batch of griddlecakes onto a platter heaped high with them inside the oven. He gestured to the table, all set, with napkins and utensils jammed artistically inside two coffee mugs.

"You're pretty handy in the kitchen," I remarked, buttoning my shirt.

"Any numbskull can fix flapcakes," Byron retorted, and set the steaming platter down between our two places.

"I'm impressed."

"Hey, what do you think of this idea: what if I rode down to New York on one of the motorcycles, parked it right in front of Rockefeller Plaza, and went up to Gemini Records?"

I'm afraid I looked at him blankly.

"Wouldn't that blow their ever-lovin' minds?" he said.

"Is this something you've actually been thinking of doing?" I inquired.

"It's just a fantasy. What do you think about it?"

"Something tells me this is more than a fantasy."

"Either way, wouldn't it be wild?"

"I think it would rank among the more bizarre incidents of all time," I told him frankly.

"Well, I wouldn't want to be bizarre," he said with a frown. "Your flapcakes are getting cold."

I drowned them in syrup and dug in. We ate silently for a while.

"Were you really thinking of doing that?" I eventually asked him. "Riding down to New York?"

"Of course not," Byron said, as if my taking him seriously was more outlandish than the idea itself. He lifted a forkful and gazed longingly out the window at the robins probing the greening grass. "Let's see, what happens after I land there?" he mused. "Do they send out for drinks? Do they make me wait in the reception room while they torch the bookkeeping records? Do they take a valium? Do they call the newspapers? I mean, what happens then? You get what I'm driving at?"

"I agree. Your showing up cold would cause an incredible amount of confusion for them and very likely a lot of unpleasantness for you."

"But what's the alternative. A press conference? I don't think I could take that circus atmosphere. I mean, what the hell would I do?"

"Look, Byron, let me be honest with you. If you were to . . . go public, there's probably no way you could avoid a period of . . . intense interest. They'd be all over you for a while, the media, everybody. But I think we could minimize a great deal of the aggravation with some careful planning."

"It's not like I'd be out to give everybody such a big thrill. It's a question of leading a life, right? What if there were a person, like you, who was authorized to speak for me at a press conference and everything?"

"Without you being present?"

"That's right."

"You'd have to produce yourself sooner or later, so I'd say all that would accomplish is to postpone the things you're afraid of." I could see that my response depressed him, so I hastened to add, "I think when you get right down to it, people would be very happy to know you're alive and well, and I think you'd be surprised at how quickly the noise would die down, how soon you could resume living as normal a life as you do now."

I knew as soon as the words left my lips how inapt they were.

"God help me," Byron said.

He got up from the table, poured himself another mug of coffee, and drifted into the other room, leaving me there feeling foolish again. Eventually, I also got up and found him out on the screened-in porch, where Allie and I slept the previous summer. Byron was setting up the tape recorder on a rickety table between two white wicker chairs.

"It's warming up out," he observed.

"Going to be nice today," I agreed.

"You know, the past may have some shitty things about it, but one thing is a great comfort."

"What's that?"

"That you live through it. That you somehow survive to remember it. However grotesque or unhappy it may have been at the time, you're sealed off from any further hurt. I think that's why we cherish even the horrible experiences. Some things still bother me, it's true, but for the most part I've enjoyed talking to you about the past."

"Thank you," I said, still feeling awkward and even unsure now that my thanks were an appropriate reply to what he'd just said.

"It's funny, though," he continued. "I feel more comfortable with the past than with the future. It hasn't been that long since the future even started to feel real to me."

"I know," I tried to reassure him. "You're doing okay, though."

"You think so?"

"Yes," I said. "I think everything's going to work out all right."

"Who knows," he said wanly. Then, with a burst of animation that took me by surprise, he slapped my knee and said, "You lucky, lucky boy, today I'm going to tell you all about my adventures at what they called the Woodstock Music and Art Fair."

"I was there."

"You were? No shit? I don't remember seeing you around."

"I'm surprised you remember any of it from the condition you were in."

"I know," Byron agreed. "I was a mess."

He clicked on the tape recorder.

## The Life of Byron Jaynes—Tape 9

I should backtrack a little here. We went on the road that summer starting in June. Oh, man! What a terrible year that was, 1969! What a horrible summer! What a disastrous tour! We had one good night: that first one at the Yale Bowl in New Haven. After that, everything unraveled faster than a golf ball with the cover torn off. It started with Dodie.

He refused to stay in the accommodations that Keough had arranged for the whole band. That is to say, Dodie would not subject himself to the depredations of honkie Holiday Inn personnel. He demanded that we book him into "black-owned" hotels wherever we went. This was, of course, a somewhat outrageous demand, but the sonofabitch had us over a barrel. He was relentless. When he found out that the motel we booked him into in Portland, Maine's, teeny little ghetto was owned by a man named Goldberg, he threatened to walk.

"Ah ain't stayin' in no Genocide Hilton, you dig!"

The place we finally found for him was the spare room of the sister-in-law of the shop steward of the musicians' union local 203.

It got worse.

Soon he was demanding that all his backstage snacks be prepared according to Muslim dietary laws. This was at a time, you understand, when the more outrageous your personal politics or religious beliefs were, the hipper you were considered to be.

"Dodie, man," Keough tried to reason with him in our dressing room under the stands at Soldier's Field, Chicago, where 75,000 people were waiting for us to come onstage, "we can't be running a kosher kitchen just for you. If you don't want a ham sandwich, eat something else. Have some cheese or fruit. Fruit's allowed, isn't it?"

"Kosher kitchen, shit!" Dodie said. "It's the vibes, man. Just havin' that filth around in the same room! I don't know if I can play now."

I heard what was going on across the room. You couldn't help it.

"Don't play then," I said.

"You tellin' me not to play?" He looked at Keough. "Is he tellin' me?"

"He's not telling you anything," Keough tried to calm him down.

"I'm calling his bluff," I said. "I'm tired of his goddam whining."

"I got a contract, motherfucker," Dodie said smirkingly, as if he had me covered.

"I bet he's got a license to be an asshole, too," Duane said, not completely under his breath either, and Buddy started cackling in that obnoxious way of his.

"You can just kiss my ass, you dumb cracker," Dodie said right back, and before you knew it the two of them were mixing it up, with Breathwaite not being any help, egging them on from the sidelines, and Keough and me trying to get between them. It ended up with Dodie walking out and Duane spraining the first two fingers of his right hand so he could barely play his bass anymore. And this was only the second week of the tour, right?

Now, I'm not trying to make excuses, because it was wrong for me to go off the deep end. But the whole time the band was disintegrating on the road, I was getting more and more upset about the situation with Catherine. I'd call her up at Ainslinger and she'd sound so cheerful.

"Byron, I'm clean! I feel so good! And the baby—he's growing so big. Oh, Byron, we're going to have such a beautiful baby!"

"I'm real proud of you, Catherine."

"I have the most wonderful shrink, Dr. Meeker. He's not even thirty yet, so I can trust him."

"Great."

"He knows all my secrets and he still likes me. I think I'm halfway in love with him."

"That's nice."

It was diabolical. She wouldn't let you forget about other men for a minute—even when she was supposedly getting her head together, right?

I was drinking much more than I should have as the summer wore on. The concerts were not up to par. Dodie couldn't be replaced. Even your magazine said my tour was a disappointment after putting out such a fine album. But I didn't start missing shows until the weekend of Woodstock, when my life began to veer very sharply out of control.

They had approached me through Gemini in the spring about appearing at their festival, the so-called Woodstock Music and Art Fair, and I'd turned them down flat. It sounded like just another rumdum promoter's scheme to me, and the Gemini people agreed. Remember, this was at a time when everybody and his uncle was throwing a, quote, "festival" trying to make a fast buck. It got so that when you merely mentioned the word in the company of professional musicians it instantly conjured up images of rubber checks, worthless contracts, and vanishing gate receipts. Anyway, back in May when they approached me, I didn't want to have anything to do with it. We were scheduled to play Seattle and then San Francisco the two nights Woodstock was being held.

*What persuaded you to change your mind?*

Mr. Walker.

*Pardon me. . . ?" Which Mr. Walker?*

Mr. Johnny Walker of the black label.

*Oh, I see.*

As the summer wore on, you began to hear rumors about this Woodstock Festival, that it was actually going to be a very big deal. They had an awful lot of top acts signed up—Butterfield, Creedence, the Dead, the Airplane, Sly, Janis, Hendrix, the Band, blah blah blah. It's hard to recall just exactly what was going through my head because I was on the sauce, but I guess I had a premonition of everything spiraling downward for me personally and professionally, and I saw this Woodstock festival as a chance to stave it off, maybe even redeem myself. So, after the show in Seattle, early in the morning of August 16th, I slipped out to the airport and caught a flight back to New York City.

You could tell from reading the headlines in the New York papers that the festival had turned into an *extremely* big deal. And it was a horror show from the point of view of someone trying to get there. Like a lot of people, I had logically assumed that the festival was going to be held somewhere around Woodstock. But I found out from the road manager of Iron Butterfly, in the VIP lounge at Kennedy, that the site was actually located down in Sullivan County, in some rinky-dink town called White Lake. And the latest reports said that traffic was tied up all the way down to Rockland County on the New York State Thruway. As the *Times* said, the southern Catskills region was becoming the "biggest parking lot in history."

Now, this guy who was Iron Butterfly's road manager—I never did catch his name—was really pissed off. The festival promoters had sent a couple of limousines to the terminal to pick up his band, but he was afraid they wouldn't be able to get through that gigantic traffic jam to the festival, and, frankly, on the basis of the news reports, I thought he was right. He was on the phone for about half an hour with these jokers up in White Lake. They were giving him the runaround, and he was saying that for the lousy couple of thousand dollars his band would get, it wasn't worth the aggravation. He demanded helicopters to airlift his boys and their stuff to the festival, but whoever was on the other end wouldn't go for that because Iron Butterfly wasn't scheduled to go on until Sunday, so you could see they were jerking this poor guy around. Anyway, I could tell I wouldn't be able to hitch a ride with them.

But while he was still hassling, Seabird's plane got in from Boston. Christy White came sweeping into the VIP lounge in green satin shorts and one of those little white sleeveless undershirts that barely kept her big boobs contained, and with a bottle of Drambuie hanging in her hand. She started squealing when she saw me. I think she was half-plastered too.

"Byron, what are you doing here?"

"Gonna be a s'prise guest," I told her. Meanwhile, her road manager, Steve Reese, was quickly apprised about the transportation difficulties by the Iron Butterfly guy.

"Come on, we'll hire our own damn helicopter," Christy said.

"It'll cost as much as they're payin' us," Steve told her.

"Aw, who cares," Christy said. "It's only money."

"Want to let them in on the deal?" I dipped my head at the Butterflies. They looked exhausted and depressed.

"I can't stand their music," Christy said. "In-A-Gadda-Da-Vida? Shit!"

"Not so loud. . . !"

"I mean it. Yccchhh!"

"There'd be too many for one chopper anyway," Steve informed us, and he knew about those things because he'd been in Vietnam.

Poor old Iron Butterfly never did make it up to White Lake. We all—Christy, her band, Steve, and me—caught a limo across the borough of Queens to LaGuardia Airport, where we heard a few charter choppers remained to be hired, and found one for $2000, one way, to the Holiday Inn in the little town of Liberty, where most of the performers were being put up. It was the pilot's third trip there that day.

Approaching the vicinity of the festival from the air was one of the wildest goddam things you ever saw. It was like one of those "Twilight Zone" episodes about the day the earth stood still. Every single road, from the big four-lane highway, Route 17, down to the narrowest dirt lane, was jam-packed with automobiles, and none of them was going anywhere.

"Take it down lower!" I said to the pilot.

"You ever hear of the FAA, sonny boy?"

I took a C-note out of my pocket.

"Take her down lower," I said, and he snatched the bill out of my hand.

"Yes, sir!"

The chopper pitched forward and our stomachs flew up into our throats. The pilot was really hot-dogging it now.

"This good enough for you?" he said, and laughed insanely. You could see Steve devour practically a whole roll of Tums in a few minutes. Swooping down lower you could see that not only were the cars stopped bumper-to-bumper for miles in every direction, but alongside these lines of inert machines were little ribbons of flesh and denim, all wending in one direction, tens of thousands of them.

"Lower!"

"Fuck you, kid."

"Nice talk." I stuffed another C-note in his pocket.

"I bet this is weirder than Nam," Christy said.

"Nothing was weirder than Nam," Steve mumbled.

Down on the ground, all these kids were waving at us, giving us the V-for-Victory sign. We were so low, you could see the shadow of the chopper under us. We followed this one dinky road for miles, cruising over the heads of the faithful pilgrims. Then the road curved. There was a small hill a thousand yards ahead, the pilot eased the nose up, we swung around, and there before us opened an enormous natural bowl in the earth jammed with a quarter of a million people.

"Jesus, Mary, and Joseph," Christy said, and her face went pale.

The pilot laughed, enjoying himself thoroughly.

"Wish I had me a couple of fifty-millimeter cannon," he quipped.

"What's your name?" Christy asked him.

"Earl Withers."

"Well, you shut the fuck up from now on, okay, Earl?" she told him nicely and patted him on the shoulder.

"Yes ma'am," he said and burst out laughing again.

The chopper banked into a left turn and we circled the festival. It was hair-raising to see that mass of bodies below, churning like one big mindless organism. The sound system they had rigged up was enormous, two gigantic stacks of speakers and scaffolding. The stage looked as big as a dime down there. Imagine Yankee Stadium filled to capacity and then multiply that number five or six times. The thing just completely blew your sense of scale. What was your impression?

*I got there Thursday morning, and I was afraid if I even returned*

*to my motel for a shower that I'd never get back, so I slept overnight
on the floor in one of the production trailers. I watched the area fill
up slowly over that two-day period. For me the shock wasn't so sudden. The fear built up by increments.*

But it scared you?

*Fuck yes. Down on the ground you got the feeling of an event
completely out of control. The backstage area reeked of fear. And
the people in charge seemed more freaked out than anybody—well,
not Lang, but his partners, particularly John Roberts. Lang was
enjoying the chaos. In fact, he was tripping. Roberts, on the other
hand, was tearing his hair out, especially after they trampled down
his fences and he had no choice but to declare it a free concert. It
was very ominous. I was sure some kind of catastrophe was in the
works. It was only a week after the Manson murders, and I guess a
lot of us had mayhem on our minds.*

That happened the week before? Charlie Manson?

*Some week, huh?*

Hey, for a guy in your line of work, it must have been sublime.

*I was fucking terrified, Byron.*

I was too awe-struck to be terrified just then, up in the helicopter.
I remember something Randy Orloff kept saying over and over again
as we circled the festival: "This is the peak! This is the peak!" he
kept saying to nobody in particular, but we all knew what he meant.
Woodstock was turning into every rock and roller's wildest wet
dream: the whole generation at your feet while you sing your sad
little song. That was it, the pinnacle, Mount Everest, the top. Even
if we couldn't put it into fancier words, all of us grasped that this
was going to be the event that defined the age. There was such a
specific epochal sense of living in a time and place like no other,
there at Woodstock. This vast clustering of bodies was going to sum-
marize it all. In a strange way, I think we knew it had to be downhill
from there. A lot of us were going to start dying soon.
Earl made one final sweep of the festival site. You could see the

crowds backed up into the woods between Yasgur's farm and the road. There were a couple of ponds down there, dinky half-acre cow-wallows, and people were swimming in them. It was torrid out, in the mid-nineties.

"Hot damn!" Earl cried. "Them girls is nekkid!"

"So are the boys!" Christy yelled. "Yoo-hoooo! Hello down there!"

Steve just gazed out the door and finished his roll of Tums. Five minutes later we touched down on the temporary pad they'd set up behind the Holiday Inn in Liberty. When we got inside the hotel, it was like that movie, *Babes in Toyland*, where all the dolls come to life. Only this was like being in some enchanted record store where all the faces from the album covers begin talking.

I walked into the lobby behind Christy and her entourage, and everybody who had been hanging out in there turned to see who was coming in. Practically every head that turned had a famous face on it: there was Janis, who'd been jamming a moment before and looked upset that someone had interrupted her. I saw Grace Slick, Paul Kantner, Jerry Garcia, Phil Lesh and Bob Weir, Leon Russell—still leading Joe Cocker's backup band—Robbie Robertson, Levon Helm, Country Joe, Arlo, Melanie, Leslie West, Havens, Bob Hite, John Fogarty. And the really creepy thing was that all of them fell absolutely silent when we walked in. And you know what a comedian Christy was, right? She stops in her tracks, looks down at her crotch, and in that wonderful froggy voice of hers says, "My fly open, or what?"

But then a few people started getting up and coming over to me, not Christy, acting like I'd returned from the dead or something.

"You okay, Byron?"

"Heard about the crash, man."

"Heard a lot of bad things."

"I'm okay."

"The album knocked me right the fuck out, man."

"You gonna play?"

"I'm not sure."

"Want a smoke?"

"Want a drink?"

"Want a toke?"

"Want a snort?"

"Want a hit?"

You see, I wasn't really personally acquainted with most of those people, especially the West Coast crowd. I knew Levon and Robbie from when they lived up near Tamberlane, and Arlo, who lived just across the Massachusetts border, had been to a few of Simon's parties. I knew Christy and her band pretty well. But as far as the rest of them went, I was as much of a fan of theirs as anybody, like Janis, for example.

There she was, this frowzy, not really attractive, hurt-looking, Texas-swamp-country hoople with bad skin, pin teeth, dirty-looking hair, all gussied up with strings of cheap baubles and bracelets and three-dollar rings, like some hoople's idea of what it means to be a sophisticated lady, and she's swilling some low-rent beverage like Southern Comfort straight out of the bottle, and smoking one cigarette after another, and her voice sounding like somebody took a belt sander to her vocal chords, and, finally—this might be a matter of the pot calling the kettle black, but—she carried such a sense of doom around with her that you could practically see it, like the ball and chain she sang about. But for all her blemishes and shortcomings, Janis wasn't fooling around. She was living out that part with total conviction, and you had to admire her tremendously for it.

A lot of people think Janis had a great voice, you know? She didn't have a great voice. She had a unique capacity for abusing her voice, for giving live demonstrations of voice abuse, you might say. Her performances weren't singing so much as a form of punishment. But it was exquisitely controlled punishment, up to a point.

That weekend, her voice was already shot to hell from jamming. But the music didn't require great voices or we all would have sung like Nelson Eddy and Jeanette MacDonald, right? The only thing you really had to put across was the fundamental idea that you meant what you said, and when Janis Joplin sang about pain, brother, you believed that she meant every frazzled note of it.

Now, while all these people swarmed around me, Janis remained on her sofa across the room, looking very chagrined that somebody had stolen the spotlight from her. But I was so electrified to see her that I went right over to where she was sitting and introduced myself. The whole crowd followed me over. I'm telling you, it was weird.

I held out my hand to shake. Frankly, I didn't know what else to do. I never went in for that phony-baloney social kissing bullshit with strangers. But Janis just leered down at my hand as if to shake it would be some odious and barbaric formality from a bygone century that she'd heard about but never actually seen in practice.

"Byron who?" she said loudly, pretending she never heard of me, and a lot of the others tittered. She was clearly happy to be back in the center of attention again. I wasn't insulted, you understand. It was pretty comical, to tell you the truth.

"Byron Jaynes," I told her, playing along.

"Well, tell me something, mister suave and romantic Byron Jaynes: do you like to fuck girls?"

She was going for the shock effect, and she was succeeding.

"I'm married," I said, not trying to act huffy or put her down, but in lieu of some snappy rejoinder, making a mundane statement of fact.

"Married?" Janis said skeptically. "That's not what I hear."

"What do you hear?" I fell for the bait.

"I hear that your old lady's about as hard to get as a haircut."

The people around us started coughing into their sleeves, looking like they wished they were somewhere else. I was certainly stunned, but you know how I get when somebody tries to pick a fight with me.

"Funny," I said, "I hear the same thing about you, Janis."

"Honey, I'm *easier* to get than a haircut," she said, reaching up and winding her finger around a lock of my hair, which I was wearing down to my shoulders then. Everybody started laughing relievedly again, and a few of them clapped. But it still stung me that she made that remark about Catherine in the first place. I don't know what Janis knew about my personal life, from rumor or hearsay or what, but that crack of hers was like a proclamation of what was already an open secret: that Catherine was making a fool out of me. And it hurt.

A lot of people probably thought they were witnessing some amusing hip repartee, but I'm telling you, Rick, I was so humiliated I didn't even want to be there anymore. Luckily, Christy and Levon, who were actually friends of mine, took me by the arm into the bar. Soon we were seated in a dark corner drinking whisky, and once again you could hear Janis wailing in the lobby. She was singing Reuban's song, "Ain't I Too Terribly Bad."

"She didn't mean nothin'," Levon said, but he knew what Catherine was like and how I felt. "Ain't this a hell of a party, though?"

The whisky was blunting the jagged edges of everything again. It was some scene, all right. We were jammed into that Holiday Inn like one big family, snowbound in the middle of the summer. Janis and I were like the siblings who couldn't stand each other. As long as there was a wall between us, we were happy.

There was no way to get in or out of the place except by helicopter, and practically everyone you saw was a hippie, so you could tell where people got the idea that weekend that we were really taking over the world. Then, later in the afternoon, the mood changed. People started to get cranky and burned around the edges. Tempers grew short.

First of all, a big brouhaha erupted about the bands getting paid. I didn't give damn, personally, because I was there on a lark, but some others were pissed. Word was sifting around that the promoters had run out of money and not to trust the checks they were issuing. The Dead's road manager was the one who called them on it. He insisted on cash or a certified check or his band wouldn't even get on the helicopter. Then you were hearing reports from people who'd already been out to the festival site about what a scary situation it was turning into, how half a million kids got rained on the night before and were now bogged down in a huge mud wallow, about how there was no food for them to eat, how some really evil acid was bumming thousands of people out, how the Port-a-Johns were overflowing—in short, how conditions were perfect for some colossal rock and roll riot. And so a lot of the performers were getting very nervous about going out there under any circumstances that night.

Meanwhile, everybody just kept drinking and snorting and carrying on. It was so stiflingly hot outside that you didn't even want to leave the building and get a breath of fresh air. We were literally cooped up. People were eating huge meals out of sheer boredom, cleaning the place out of lobsters and steaks. The bar ran out of champagne around six o'clock and people started grousing about having to make do with wine and whiskey. One thing that didn't run out was the cocaine. There was some character that everyone referred to as "Bogie," short for "Bogota Bob," who was part of some band's entourage from San Francisco, and I swear he must have arrived with five pounds of blow.

Several hours after my tiff with Janis, I'd been drinking steadily, and I'd borrowed a couple of grand from Christy to buy some of that blow, and I mean to tell you, I was wired. I was back in the lobby noodling around on the guitar with Jorma Kaukonen of the Airplane, a wonderful acoustic guitar player, and we were playing some old Leadbelly tune, "Red Cross Store Blues" or "T.B. Blues" or something like that, when who should walk in the door fresh from the helipad but Ronnie Barron, Catherine's shithead paramour.

He was done up to perfection by his moronic standards: his blonde hair was really long, down to the middle of his back, and tied up in a ponytail so everyone could see that long, lantern-jawed horse-face of his. He had on a pair of jeans so tight they looked sprayed on, and patched with so many velvet and satin embroideries that it must have taken a crew of twelve Belgian seamstresses a month to get the job done. Those long skinny legs of his were jammed into a pair of calf-length cavalry boots, making him look seven feet tall instead of six-three. He wasn't even wearing a shirt, just a kind of choker made out of tiny beads and gamebird feathers strung together, a perfect Age of Aquarius adornment—in other words, the kind of pretentious garbage I wouldn't be caught dead in. In each hand he carried a guitar case. You remember how he had these handmade guitars that cost about ten grand apiece and he never let the goddam things out of his sight. The topper, though, was his glasses. He was sporting a pair of those trip glasses with all the facets cut on them like a dragonfly's eyes—they used to sell them in head shops, remember?

As soon as he came in, half a dozen women, some other guys' girlfriends, who knows, started buzzing around him, like flies to a big piece of shit. He put down his instruments, slid the trip glasses up on his forehead, and surveyed the scene. I mean, this guy was pulling out every theatrical stop in the book to give himself a dramatic entrance, and I think he was a little miffed that the rest of us didn't drop what we were doing and run right over and kiss his cavalry boots. In fact, Jorma and I didn't even stop playing.

But that doesn't mean I wasn't aware of him. I was intensely aware of his presence. A few moments later he started sauntering over in our direction. The idea of him even laying one of his big mangy paws on Catherine made me absolutely hysterical with loathing. And then I thought of the baby. It all happened *that* quickly. I got up, swung back the guitar, and let him have it over the head. Unfortunately, it was a really nice custom Martin and it belonged to Jerry Garcia, I think, but the goddam thing splintered into a million pieces. I wouldn't have done it if I wasn't so wired, but I couldn't stand the sight of him. And I wanted to humiliate him the way he had made a fool out of me. Anyway, that's why Ronnie Barron never made it to the festival. They put him on the next outbound helicopter to Middletown and he regained consciousness in the hospital. It was only a moderate concussion. I guess I'm lucky that I didn't get into trouble over it, but everybody else hated his guts too, and when his lawyers came around sniffing for witnesses months later, nobody could remember exactly how he had hurt himself. He never did find those two guitars of his again, either, or so I heard.

Anyway, Christy and Seabird were catching a chopper out to the festival a short while later, and since the idea was for her to bring me on as a special guest near the end of their set, I went with them. It was around eight o'clock. The sun was going down over the mountains in one of those fantastic Frederick Beal Catskill sunsets, salmon-colored streaks of clouds against a barely blue sky. The great festival bowl was in semi-darkness. You could still see that big churning organism down there. Closer to the stage, where Canned Heat was pumping out "Goin' Up the Country," you could see the fierce lights shining on individual faces. Farther back, campfires blazed in the woods.

Though it was the second time I had flown over the festival, a whole different tide of emotion filled me now, inspired, no doubt, by all the cocaine I had stuffed into my head. You'd hear the music pouring out, and see those tiny, pale faces turning up to see you hanging in the sky, and the beautiful pink light of the heavens glowing beyond it, and you felt all the glory of being a true God descending to the adoring multitudes. I closed my eyes for a moment and took a deep, deep breath, enjoying every false kilowatt of that illusionary power. Then we were on the ground.

The backstage area looked like a combination of a masquerade party and a concentration camp. You knew at once that the place was in the grip of chaos. For one thing, nobody on the festival staff even came up to greet us on the helipad, to tell us where to go or anything. The performers' pavilion, the big tent behind the stage where we were supposed to congregate and socialize while waiting our turns to go on, had been hastily converted into a psycho ward for all the drug casualties that they didn't have room for in the original hospital tent. It was a scene out of *Marat/Sade*, a babble of private nightmares, kids in disgusting mud-caked jeans laying on stretchers or on the plywood floor moaning, blurting out unconnected names, fragments of sentences, kids wandering, blundering around, grabbing the volunteer doctors by the sleeves and saying they were dying, that they were going crazy, talking to themselves, talking nonsense, singing along with Canned Heat one moment and bursting into tears the next. There was a terrible mixture of aromas pervading the area, the sweet smells of pot and incense that failed to overpower the ranker odors of vomit and shit, and somewhere in between them the smell of steaks grilling.

Outside the tents, hundred of people were milling around in the stark semi-darkness, performers, many festival techies in their red Woodstock T-shirts with the guitar neck and dove logo. Some of them were bustling around with equipment, loading keyboards and Leslies and what-have-you onto the elevator cage at the rear of the stage. Others were just standing around, grooving on the music, sharing joints, hanging out with the stars. Beyond this and the dozen-odd production trailers, where the technicians had lived and worked for weeks, was a triple chain-link fence to keep out the plebians, who you could see roistering darkly on the other side in the streaky light. It was back there, among the trailers, that I ran into Janis again.

She wasn't scheduled to go on until much later, after Christy and Seabird, and then the Dead. The promoters were hoping to keep the music going all night long so everyone's attention would be focused on the stage and keep their minds off making trouble—you know, roving bands of drug-crazed youths on the loose and all that. Anyway, I was passing among the trailers, trying to locate something in the way of an alcoholic beverage, when I saw Janis through the open door of one of them, and she hollered at me to come in. I went cautiously over to the door.

"Honey, I'm sorry I talked that trash to you before," she said, and apologized so strenuously that you had no choice but to make up. Besides, Janis had a bottle of vodka in one hand and a bottle of tequila in the other.

Canned Heat, meanwhile, had finished their set and come off-stage. In the lull between acts you could hear this British voice wafting out over the loudspeakers.

"The blue acid is not poison," it said. "You are not going to die. It's badly manufactured. If you have taken some of the blue acid, you are going to be okay in a few hours. Just lay back and try to dig the music, man. . . ."

"How can you call half a million people 'man'?" a guy in the trailer said in disgust.

"That's what we are," another man said, "*Man*."

"Except for me," Janis said. "I'm *Woman*."

"You wish," the first guy said.

"Fuck you, Andy!" Janis screeched and threw an ashtray at him.

"No, he means you wish it was you and half a million guys," the second guy tried to explain.

"How do you know?" Janis said. "How does he know?"

"Forget it."

"No. I'm not talkin' to you ever again. Get out of here sumbitch. Go on, git!"

Andy and the second hippie left dolefully. Janis angrily crushed out a cigarette on top of a beer can.

"Let's you and me have a serious little drink together, Byron Jaynes," she said, and that is exactly what we did. Outside the trailer, this monumental uproar went on while we traded shots of tequila and vodka and blew line after line of Bogota Bob's face-freeze. To tell you the truth, I barely remember a goddam thing that happened after that.

*Do you remember being on the bridge?*

The bridge. . . ?"

*The ramp they had built over the road to get to the stage from the backstage area.*

No. I don't really remember it. I've heard different versions. They all make me sick.

*I was there. I saw you on the bridge.*

Okay, what's your version?

*It was around midnight. Seabird had been on for over an hour. Christy finished singing "Albatross." The audience cheered. The applause went on for a long time. It would start to die out on one side and then well up in another direction. Christy said, rather quickly, into the microphone, "We have a special treat for you tonight. Would you give a warm welcome to an old friend, Byron Jaynes." There was a strange lull for, oh, two or three seconds after that, as though that enormous crowd was one great stoned individual. Then they cheered wildly. And then I saw you up on the bridge without any clothes on. John Moore was—*

John who?

*One of the guys in charge: the Englishman. He was holding a pair of jeans, yours I guess, and imploring you to put them on. Some other staff people were holding your arms. You were screaming at the top of your lungs.*

What was I saying?

*Oh, "Let me go!" Shouting maledictions, being wild. A rather sizable crowd had gathered down below the bridge to watch.*

I remember one thing.

*What?*

I was playing strip poker with Janis—that's right! And I heard Christy introduce me over the speakers. That's why I came out of the trailer.

*Anyone could see how drunk you were. When Moore couldn't get you into your pants, the festival staff people began to panic. You didn't go out on stage, obviously. Christy, thinking you hadn't heard her intro, said it again, only slower and more clearly this time. The crowd cheered again, but not quite so enthusiastically this time, and when you failed to come out, the cheering died down fast. Another one of those awful lulls followed. Neither the audience nor the performers seemed to know what to do. Meanwhile, you were hollering and trying to break free, only now they had three very large guys holding onto you. The festival people were arguing: "Let him go out there if he wants to!" "He's too drunk." "Let him go out and make an asshole out of himself!" "Those kids will tear him apart." "Those kids will tear us apart if we don't send him out there."*
*While they were arguing and struggling with you, a chant started to build out in the crowd: "We want Byron! We want Byron!" Seabird started playing the introduction to another song behind Christy,*

*who leaned up to the mike and said, "He was here just a minute ago." Half a million people booed. She was in a jam out there, but everything she said to appease the crowd was backfiring. Essentially, it was like holding a banana out in front of a 1000-pound gorilla and then not giving it to him. In any event, the band was playing "Make It Better" and Christy wisely decided to stop talking and start singing, hoping, I guess, that the music would soothe the savage beast. But they kept up the chanting and the booing and before she could finish the first verse, Christy stopped and said, "What do you want me to do? I don't know where the hell he is!" And the chanting, the shouting, the booing grew louder, more insistent, more terrifying. We were all close to pissing in our pants. Finally, John Moore did the only logical thing that remained to be done. He ran up on stage, took the microphone away from Christy, and said, "I'm sorry to tell you all this, but Byron is not going to be able to play for you tonight."*

*The chanting, booing, and shouting stopped at once.*

*"Byron's here," John told the vast audience, "he's backstage. But, unfortunately, he's had too much to drink and he's passed out—"*

*"Bullshit!" the cry rang out from several directions. This too became a chant. At that point I had ridden the freight elevator up to the stage level. I was standing on top of a stack of monitors where I could see both you, down on the bridge, and the whole forestage, including much of the audience. John was holding up his hands with the palms out trying patiently, and bravely, to calm the crowd.*

*"It's not bullshit," he told them with the authority in his voice of a teacher standing before the largest kindergarten class in history. I looked back toward the bridge and they were carrying you off unconscious. You were still naked. They had you up on their shoulders, like a corpse. One of your arms dangled, your head was lolling over, long hair hanging down. In that baleful light you looked like Christ pulled down from the cross—*

You can cool it with the Christ comparisons, Rick.

*Sorry, but. . . . Anyway, John told them it wasn't bullshit, that you were too drunk to perform. He apologized to all the kids on behalf of you and the festival staff. "We still have a lot more music for you," he said. "The Dead, Janis Joplin, Sly, the Who—" and a great upwelling of cheers drowned out the rest of the list.*

How soon they forget.

*Yes. Well, it's a good thing they did, I guess. Anyway, after that I lost track of you.*

We both did. I woke up back in the Holiday Inn, on Sunday sometime. I felt like Prince Andrei after the Battle of Austerlitz. I didn't have the faintest recollection of how I got back to the hotel, but I sure didn't want to leave there and return to the outside world. I was holed up for days. Then the outside world came right to me, in the person of Billy Keough. He showed up on Wednesday after the festival. There was a knock on the door. I hadn't ordered anything so I yelled at whoever it was to go away.

"Open up, Byron. It's me, Billy."

"Oh, shit," I muttered to myself and hauled myself over to the door, dragging the bedclothes with me. He had sort of a cracked smile on his sad Irish face that you couldn't help but interpret as an utter failure to be of good cheer. "Oh God. . . ." I mumbled and staggered back to bed.

He entered the room cautiously, as if the carpet was mined, and then pulled a chair over to the bedside.

"Care for a drink?" I asked him.

"Sure," he said, and I knew I was in for the business, because Keough never liked to drink before evening. I handed him the bottle and he took a slug, drawing in air through his teeth.

"How'd you know I was still here?"

"Oh, the grapevine."

"I think I fucked up pretty bad this time, Billy."

"I just wish you'd told me where you were going before you split."

"You would have tried to talk me out of it."

"That's right, Byron. I would have. Those were big dates we blew: San Francisco, L.A., San Diego."

"I never did like California."

"A lot of people in California buy your records."

"Well, that's nice."

"Anyway, the promoters are pretty hot. I told them they'd have to take it up with you."

"Oh, great!"

"If you had a manager, it'd be different."

"You're my road manager."

"I'm not going to get involved with contract disputes."

"Then refer these guys to Max," I told him. Max Goodsen was my attorney. "Can't we put out some story that I was ill or something?"

"Can't. It was in the papers already."

"What was?"

"That you were here."

"Did it say what I did?"

"Said you were too drunk to go on. That's all." Billy said, shifting his weight uncomfortably in the seat. "See, the problem is we're receiving more cancellations down the road."

"*They're* cancelling me? The promoters?"

"That's right."

"Shit. Where?"

Billy took out a small spiral notepad out of his back pocket. "So far, three: Houston, Mobile, Baton Rouge."

"Goddam crackers. Where the hell am I supposed to be now?"

"Tonight? Santa Fe."

"Goddam rednecks. . . ."

"You've got to get this tour back on track, man, and show these bozos that you can be depended on. Also, Duane and Buddy say they're going to walk if they don't get paid right away."

"Well, pay them, for Godsake."

"We've been paying them out of the gate receipts. But without those California dates—"

"Call Max and tell him to have a cashier's check for five thousand delivered to us wherever the hell we're supposed to be after Santa Fe."

"Spag too."

"Okay, seventy-five hundred."

"And the roadies."

"Okay."

"And me too, Byron."

"Okay. Tell Max twenty," I said calmly. "I take advantage of your good nature, don't I?"

"It's a free country," Billy said. "Guess I missed one hell of a party, though, huh?"

"It was big, all right. But I bet twenty years from now nobody will remember that everyone here was fucked up, soaked to the bone, or scared half to death."

"They're calling us the Woodstock Generation now."

"Really?" I said. "Well, it figures they'd name us after some place we never really were."

Before we left the hotel, I called Catherine at the Ainslinger Clinic and they told me she'd been discharged the previous Thursday. When I called the house in Tamberlane, someone picked up the phone on the fourth ring, but it wasn't Catherine.

"Who's this?"

"It's . . . I'm, like . . . I help out."

"Are you the maid?"

"No. I'm . . . the helper."

"The helper?" I said to myself. "May I speak to my wife, please?"

"B-Byron! Just a sec."

"What time is it?" Catherine asked, sounding as if she just woke up.

"I don't know. What time is it, Billy?"

"Is Keough there?"

"Yes. He says it's two-fifteen. Who was that?"

"Who was what?"

"That girl. On the phone."

"The maid. Where are you?"

"I'm in the town outside of where the festival was."

"Still? Oh, Byron, I saw that mention of you in the paper. What happened?"

"I got loaded."

"Shame on you," she said, and I had an odd feeling that she actually meant it. "When they let me out on Thursday, I almost came down."

"To the festival?"

"Yeah. I guess it's a good thing I didn't come, huh?"

Just then I realized that she would have had no idea beforehand that I was going to be there. I thought of that goddamed horse-faced Ronnie Barron, and the beautiful sight of Garcia's guitar splintering over his head.

"It was a good thing you didn't," I agreed.

"I'm so big, Byron. I wish you could see me. It's so strange."

"I wish I could see you too, Catherine."

"You can even feel him moving around in there."

"Hey, great."

"And guess what else, Flash!"

"What?"

"I'm clean!"

"I should hope so, after six weeks in the clinic."

"I haven't felt so good in . . . years! Oh, won't you come home for a night. Please, Byron. I'm aching to see you."

"Okay."

"You will?"

"I will."

"Or I could come down."

"No! I've had enough of this place."

"I can't wait to see you, darling."

"Me either. Just sit tight."

I hung up and started rummaging around for a shirt, but I couldn't find one anywhere in the room.

"How's Catherine?" Keough asked gingerly.

"She's home. They cleaned her up," I said. He knew about her habit. I didn't tell him every personal tidbit about us, but he knew about Catherine and her drugs.

"It would've been nice for you to see her," he said, just nervously enough for me to infer the real meaning.

"I'm going to see her. Right now."

"You can't, Byron."

"Don't tell me I can't. I'm going."

"If you go up there, Byron, you're going to blow Santa Fe too."

"Fuck Santa Fe!" I said angrily.

"You can't afford to!" he yelled back just as loud. "I've got a charter waiting for us at Newark Airport. It's an hour and a half down there. Maybe two if we hit any traffic. Another four hours in the air to Santa Fe. We're talking about an eight-fifteen ETA. There's no time, my friend."

"Where's my fucking shirt?"

"I'm sorry," Billy said.

"I just told her I was coming."

"You'll have to call her back and tell her it won't be possible after all."

We glared at each other across the room. No matter how much I carried on like a little kid, I knew he was right. Of course, I wasn't quite through acting like one.

"You call her," I said calmly.

"She's your old lady, Byron."

"Fine. But you call her and explain to her why I can't come."

"I'm not going to get in the middle of this thing."

"Hey, you're already in the middle. You put yourself there."

"Look, I'm telling you," his voice rose again, "that if we're not in Santa Fe—if *you're* not in Santa Fe—by nine o'clock tonight, this tour is going to be in big trouble. So why don't you quit playing fucking games with me and yourself."

"You think I'm playing games?" I asked him.

"Yeah," he said. "I'll be down in the lobby, waiting."

"At least find me a fucking shirt, will you—" I yelled as he slammed the door on his way out. I lurched back onto the bed and pulled a pillow over my head, trying to make the world go away like a child would do. Eventually I reached for the phone again.

"Oh, it's you again," she answered it cheerfully.

"I'm afraid I can't come after all," I told her and explained about Santa Fe and the cancellations, blah blah. I could tell she was pissed off from the way she was breathing into the phone. "Maybe you could fly down and join us for a couple of dates," I suggested.

"I'm pregnant, Byron!"

"I know that—"

"It's out of the question."

"You don't have to make up your mind this instant—"

"Why did you have to pick now for this dumb old tour?"

"I didn't know you were pregnant when we set it up. I can't break any more commitments."

"What about your commitment to me?"

"What about it?"

"You tell me," she said.

"Okay: I'm out here trying to make a goddam living."

"That's ridiculous. You've *got* money. I've got money. We're wealthy people, Byron."

"I've got a reputation."

"You're getting one—"

"As an artist."

"As a drunk."

"Look who's talking!" I said.

She decided not to escalate. It was already incredibly depressing to me. But I think I hit a sore spot with her too.

"Okay," she said. "It's not for me to judge."

"That's right, Catherine."

"I'm just mad that you'd change your mind so fast like that. It's cruel, Byron. I can't help thinking you did it on purpose."

"I didn't do it on purpose. Look, we have a cancellation in Houston, September 1st. I'll fly back then for a visit, okay?"

She didn't reply.

"Okay, Catherine?" I asked her again.

"What if you change your mind again?"

"I won't. It was a mistake and I've already apologized."

"I'll see you in September, then. Good title for a song, huh?"

"I do miss you."

"Sure. Think of a name for the baby."

"I'll do that, Catherine."

"Bye."

"What?" I said, thinking she had said half of my name, but then the dial tone came back on and I realized she'd said half of "goodbye" instead.

I never did make it home on September 1st. I called her the night before to tell her when I would be arriving but she wasn't home. That brainless hippie girl, Debbie, the maid, or "helper," or whatever she was, answered and said that Catherine was down in the city. And though it might have been a perfectly innocent sojourn, I got it into my head that she was up to her old tricks again down there, and I retaliated by not going home. To tell you the truth, I don't know what freaked me out more—the possibility that Catherine was carrying some other guy's bastard or the prospect of becoming a father myself, and I suppose not going home in September was a way to avoid facing it. Drinking was another.

*Were you drunk that night in Gainesville?*

Technically, no. But I was drinking steadily through all those southern dates. I wasn't falling down, puke-in-your-shoes drunk, just well fortified. I got up and played every night and behaved myself. They weren't great shows but nobody complained. Gainesville shouldn't have been any different, except for those clowns in the audience that night.

The concert was held in a minor-league ballpark. Oddly enough, I had good vibes about it when we showed up for the sound check. It was a cute little bandbox of a stadium, with a nice old-timey feeling of what the sport must have been like in the early 1900s before it got big and overblown. The stands were freshly painted dark green. The field was real pretty, with thick, short grass, a red clay infield, and crisp white foul lines. In fact, I felt bad knowing what the audience would probably do to the field. The risers for our stage were set up in center field. The stands held 15,000 and they were figuring about as many more on the field itself. It was a fairly small house by our standards.

Later on, we were out in one of the bullpens waiting for the warm-up band to wrap up their set. We couldn't use the locker rooms under the stands because there was no way you could get to the stage from the dugout through that crowd in the infield. I didn't care. I wasn't a prima donna about dressing rooms. It was a beautiful southern autumn night—quite warm and comfortable. When the Allman Brothers were finished and the applause died down, you could hear katydids and frogs in the swamp behind the right-field bleachers. We usually waited half an hour after the opening act before we went on to give the audience a break. That night, being in the bullpen was like waiting in a foxhole during World War II—a handful of men lost in their own thoughts, their faces lighting up as each man drew on his cigarette. I didn't have anything to say to Crocker or Breathwaite by then. And they were sick of each other's company. Spag was sitting next to me making noises that were halfway between what a jazz musician might hum to himself and what an autistic child might make. A brilliant, copper-colored moon was rising over the third base side of the stands.

"Do you believe in reincarnation?" Spag asked.

"No," I said.

"Why not?"

"I believe we pass this way but once."

"Sometimes I feel like I've been here forever," he said wearily. "I'd like to come back as a subatomic particle. Move fast. Zip zip zip. Be weightless."

"What do you think you were in a previous life?" I asked him, a little amazed that we were having this conversation at all.

"I'm not sure. Maybe a bird. It would've been nice to be a bird."

"Birds have short lives."

"We all have short lives," Spag said, "compared to the ages." He gazed up at the moon and went back to that secret center of himself. A few moments later, Keough came back to the bullpen with five local cops as security guards and escorted us to the stage.

I spotted the guys who started all the trouble early in the set. There were a dozen or so of them, about fifty feet out in the crowd, ugly overweight southern agrarian types, your typical redneck yeoman congenital morons. They just stood out. They were drinking beers—the official moron beverage of choice—from an endless supply of bagged six-packs they'd hauled in with them, and it was obvious that they were bothering the people around them.

About a half hour into the set, while I'm singing "Never Like a Miracle," one of the quieter numbers, I see and hear a string of firecrackers go off, the kind where you light one and the whole pack of fifty explodes in about two seconds. This blue-white cloud of smoke wafts over the infield. There's some shoving going on. I happen to be playing acoustic guitar on this song. I stop my singing, but keep on fingerpicking the D chord. When the smoke clears, I can see that the rednecks are really enjoying themselves.

"Now that you've got my attention . . ." I try to joke with them over the mike.

"Fuck you!" one of them yells.

"Your place or mine?" I say, and the people near the front who can hear both ends of this exchange get a big kick out of it. There's laughter and applause. I resume the song.

Meanwhile, I glance over to the side of the stage. Keough is talking to one of the cops. The cop nods his head and laughs. Keough points to the morons out front. They're still screwing around, bothering other people. Two of them, a big fat guy with a hat made out of squashed beer cans and a skinnier kid, are dancing the redneck Watusi in a little area cleared by their buddies. I decide to try and ignore them.

I wrap up "Miracle" and walk back to get my Fender. There's a scotch bottle right beside the guitar stand, and I'm picking it up when I hear a much louder explosion this time. I drop the bottle and it breaks. The applause stops at once. I turn around again. For a moment the whole audience, including the people way off in the grandstands, is absolutely quiet. Buddy plays a drum roll and punctuates it with a cymbal crash. There's some laughter and scattered applause. Another blue cloud is floating over the infield. I look over toward the side again. Keough is still arguing with that cop. The other cops are passively watching the crowd. Suddenly a sputtering trail of smoke arcs out of the audience and lands on the stage. It bounces a couple of times and stops, not ten feet from me, against a taped-down cable. For a second I see very clearly the bright red hull of a cherry bomb and the sputtering green fuse. I stand there like a dolt, in thrall, really, and watch it blow up.

Duane comes right over. "How much longer are we going to put up with this bullshit?" he asks.

"Nobody chases me off a stage," I tell him. "Especially not a bunch of redneck morons." Unfortunately, this is a pretty good description of Duane Crocker himself, and I think he knows it. He backs away.

I put my hands on my hips, my ears ringing, and saunter up slowly to the mike.

"Would it be asking too much for security to remove the shit-heads who are throwing explosives up here?" I ask calmly. The crowd is booing and jeering—not at me, I realize—but at these jerks who have succeeded in stopping the show. The cops don't move. They pretend to be scanning the audience, looking for the perpetrators supposedly, but they don't leave their positions.

"You don't see who I'm talking about?" I say into the mike. "Okay," I start pointing. "That shithead down there with the beer-can hat, that one with the blue jacket, the one with the yellow shirt. . . ."

The cops still don't move. I march off to the side of the stage—there aren't any wings, properly speaking, you understand, these are just portable risers—to where Keough's still arguing with the cop.

"What the hell's the matter with these cops?" I ask him.

"They're afraid to start a riot," Billy says.

"We don't want to be responsible for no riot," the cop supposedly in charge of this unit says.

"That's exactly what you're going to get if you don't get rid of these shitheads."

"Oh, yeah," he retorts. "Who goan' start it?"

I return to center stage feeling very insecure about what's going on here, like I don't quite understand it, you know?

"Sorry about the interruption," I say into the mike, "but we've got some, uh, unruly elements up front here who want to play Vietnam War or something. And I guess I'm supposed to be the Viet Cong, right?"

A big laugh.

"Hey, Byron," a voice cries up at me.

*Oh no . . .* I think.

I look out there and this one shithead is being hoisted up in the air by three of his buddies. His pants are down, his backside is facing me, and when they get him up in the air, he bends over and shines his asshole at me.

"Hey, that's real clever," I say, then unwisely retort: "That's a terrible case of acne you got there, buddy."

"That's what you can kiss," one of them shouts back.

Okay, now I'm really getting sick of these idiots. The cops won't lift a finger. I unzip my jeans and pull out my joint. I realize it was foolish. I was going for the shock effect.

"You can just honk on this," I tell the morons.

"What you say?"

"I said, YOU CAN SUCK MY DICK!"

Then, surprise, surprise, the police leap into action. They swoop out on stage, bundle me between them, and haul me off the back of the risers, through the bullpen, and into a police cruiser that happens to be waiting on the service road just beyond the back of the bleachers. They slip on the cuffs and shove me into the back seat, a cop on each side, and we drive off into the sinister southern night. On our way around the stadium, I hear what sounds like a riot going on.

And that's how the great Gainesville bust of '69 happened.

They managed to screw around long enough on the arraignment to make sure that I'd have to spend the night in their crummy jail. Then, around noon the next day, they finally set bail and Keough sprung me for fifty grand. The charges were indecent exposure, public lewdness—the verbal stuff—and incitement to riot, a felony. They even threw in resisting arrest because I called the cops "a bunch of jerkoffs" in the squad car. The so-called riot was nothing more than a few seats being torn out of the grandstand.

Of course, it would come out much later that the whole thing was a set-up—that these troublemakers were hirelings of a stupid organization of semi-professional morons called the Alachua County Decency Committee. The cops were in on it too. The idea, evidently, was for them to provoke incidents of indecency so they could then swoop in and stomp it out and be heroes. I don't have to tell you how typical this kind of brainless vigilantism was back then.

Anyway, the following night our date in Jacksonville was cancelled when the city council hastily passed an ordinance forbidding, quote, "gatherings of over 500 persons for the purpose of musical exhibitions," meaning no more rock concerts. By this time I just wanted to get the hell out of Florida, so we caught a plane to Atlanta, and by then it was splattered all over the papers. There was a wire service photo of me onstage taken, quote, "only moments before the alleged incident," the caption said. The grainy, distorted image showed a dazed-looking, indignant figure with sweat-soaked long hair scowling at some indeterminate point over the photographer's left shoulder, one hand on the mike stand, the other reaching for his fly—

—————

"Is that the end of the tape?" Byron asked. His upper lip glistened with perspiration. The afternoon sun shone hotly through the screens and the bud-tipped branches that surrounded the porch.

"Yes, that's the end of it," I answered him. "Want to go down to Dottie's Lunch?"

"What for?"

"Some lunch. It's almost two o'clock."

"Do you have any more cassettes?"

"Yes."

"Then let's keep going."

"We can do it after lunch—"

"I'd rather keep going, Rick. It's connected."

"Okay," I said. "How about a little coffee though? Or some tea?"

"No. Not for me, thanks."

"Okay," I said, and got up to fetch a fresh cassette off the desk in the living room.

"Where are you going?"

"To get a new tape," I said.

—————

## The Life of Byron Jaynes—Tape 10

We were in Atlanta when I first heard on the evening news that my father was under pressure to resign his job. I was only halfway paying attention in the hotel room when I heard David Brinkley say ". . . a top Nixon administration lawyer whose effectiveness may have been compromised by the antics of his son, the rock star Byron Jaynes, blah blah. . . ."

Now, don't get the wrong idea, I was never a fan of the Nixon administration, but in my opinion this was one example of how the goddam press created a big issue out of practically nothing just to throw their weight around and hurt somebody. Forget about Watergate for the moment. This was way before that. They used my weakness and stupidity as an excuse to knock off my old man. What I did in Gainesville had nothing to do with him. He hadn't taken anybody's dirty money or broken any laws. It was totally unfair—

*Wait a minute. You're defending him? Morris Greenwald, the Scourge of the Left?*

Frankly, Rick, I didn't give two shits about the left. I met a lot of so-called revolutionaries during those years and, believe me, you never met such a bunch of hypocrites in your life. You know what most of them wanted? To get their pictures in the paper.

*That's just not true, Byron. I knew quite a few radicals myself, and many of them were sincere, idealistic people.*

Maybe the ones you met. The ones I knew all wanted to be rock stars, only they couldn't carry a tune. I mean, what were they doing hanging around someone like me in the first place when they should have been up in a garret writing a manifesto? I'll tell you why they hung around me: because they were the biggest bunch of moochers and freeloaders you ever saw. "Power to the People!" I never heard such horseshit. It should have been "Power *over* the People," because that's what these operators really wanted: to dictate their version of morality while they fed from the golden trough—which is exactly what they accused the establishment of doing. Don't tell me about the left—

*And don't tell me you weren't against the war—*

Who said I wasn't against the war?

*You seem to hate everyone who was trying to stop it.*

Hey, I was trying to stop it. You were. We were all trying to stop the goddam war. Sure I was against it. You want to know something crazy? I bet even Nixon was trying to stop the war. In my opinion, Rick, an idealist can be more dangerous than a cynic.

*Come on, Byron—*

I'm serious. Look, I didn't mean to get going on a whole political tangent. The point is, Morris Greenwald was my old man, and the press used me as a club to knock his head off with and it worked, and I didn't feel good about it at all. Can't you understand that? If he had to go down, let it be for some mistake that he made himself, or at the hands of some political adversary, but, God, not because of me. And then to have you idiots in the so-called underground press applauding me for bringing about his downfall—that really iced the cake.

Anyway, I'm not entirely sure what was going through my mind the night I went to see him in Washington, but I guess you could boil it down to a last-ditch effort to undo all the damage and make things right. We were next door, in Baltimore. After Atlanta the tour was in pitiful shape, with one cancellation after another: Charleston, Raleigh, Norfolk, Richmond. The papers wouldn't drop the goddam story. It was too juicy. I was back at the hotel in downtown Baltimore—one of the few dates left standing—when I saw the item on the six o'clock news: they had called my father back from Chicago where he was supervising the Black Panther prosecutions. They said Mitchell called him back "for consultations," but it was obvious they were getting ready to cut him loose.

I didn't even know my father's address, for chrissake, so I called up my parents' old friends, the Havermeyers back in Westchester. Boy, was Frank surprised to hear from me! He kept calling me "Pete," though I'm quite sure he knew who I was. But he didn't mention it once, or all the trouble I'd created for my dad, or anything going on in the real world. It was like we were suddenly back in 1962 and I was calling to find out if he needed a caddy for his Thursday golf game.

"Gee, it's been great talking to you," he said right after he gave me the address. "Good luck, Pete." Then he hung up, as if it wasn't altogether kosher for him to even be on the phone with me. It made me very nervous. Being nervous made me want to have another

drink. Having another drink convinced me to go see my father without further delay.

I put on a fresh shirt, tucked the scotch bottle inside my black
velvet sport jacket, and skulked down the hall to the elevator, pray-
ing that none of the other guys or Keough would catch me leaving.
There was no way I could justify skipping out on a show like that.
But, of course, I did it anyway.

It was about a 45-minute drive to Washington. The cab driver
was an older guy who didn't know Byron Jaynes from Horatio Horn-
blower, which was fine with me. I just sat quietly in the back, nip-
ping at the bottle and watching all the famous buildings and
monuments roll by, lit up against the dark sky as we crossed the
heart of the city over to Georgetown, where my father and his new
wife lived.

The cabbie stopped in the middle of a narrow, tree-lined street
of two- and three-story town houses. The one with my father's number on it was typical—white-painted brick, a flight of stairs up to a
bright-red door with polished brass fixtures, and blue shutters. A
light was burning in a bay window, but the shades were drawn.
Then I noticed somebody lurking beside a tree on the sidewalk across
the street from the place. I told the cabbie to pull around the next
corner and I got out. I waited there about five minutes, then turned
the corner onto P Street and snuck up on the guy beside the tree.

"Who are you?" I asked him.

He wheeled around, a young guy about my age but dressed in a
suit with an open raincoat on.

"I'm a reporter," he said.

"For who?"

"The *Star*," he said.

"What's your name?"

"Mark Nagel," he said, and dug a press card out of his wallet.

"What are you doing here, Mark?"

"Trying to get a story."

"Want a drink?"

"No thanks."

"Mind if I do?"

"No, go ahead."

I took a hit off the scotch bottle.

"Do you know who I am, Mark?"

"Yes."

"You know, Mark, sometimes in this world people have problems, family problems. I'm sort of having some right now, you know?"

"I know," he said sympathetically.

"I realize you're only doing your job, but would you do me a favor and pretend you didn't see me come here tonight."

"I don't know, man," he said, trying to sound more hip than he looked, but basically still being apologetic.

"Really, Mark, as a personal favor, huh? I'd really appreciate it." To make myself abundantly clear, I took out a couple of $100 bills and tried to press them into his hand.

"I don't want your money, man," he said acting sincerely chagrined. "No, come on, I can't take that."

"It would mean a lot to me, Mark."

He started backing away from me and my money, making a little circuit around the tree. Finally, he stopped and let out a deep sigh.

"I'll just split, Byron, okay. I don't want your money."

"Hey, at least take this, huh?" I proffered the scotch bottle. Poor Mark just kept on backing down the street. "Next time I'm in town, I'll give you a personal interview, okay? I'll spend the whole day with you, whatever, okay?"

"Sure, Byron."

"I mean it."

"Sure."

"Okay, then, see you Mark."

He flicked his hand forward as an attempt to wave good-bye and walked backward about halfway down the block. I waited until he disappeared into the murk. Then I planted my bottle next to the tree, crossed the street, and climbed the stairs to my father's front door.

Sheila answered the bell, first opening the door a crack to see who it was, then letting it swing wide open while she stood there in a visible state of shock. Otherwise, you'd have to say she looked very demure in her gray wool woman lawyer's outfit and peach-colored blouse. But there was a conspicuous bulge in her tummy and all of a sudden I realized she was pregnant too. She was around thirty then, a tall, red-haired thoroughbred of a girl, but with eyes that seemed to perpetually squint at you, as if everyone in the world were a defendant who she couldn't wait to prosecute.

"Is my father here?" I asked before even saying hello—not to be nasty, but I was anxious to state my business without seeming to get personal with her or dragging her into it, which I should have known was unavoidable anyway.

"I'm sorry," she said trying to be cool and collected. "He's not here."

"Hey, I saw him on the news, landing at the airport. I know he's here."

"He's in town," she admitted. "But he's at a meeting right now."

"Where? With Nixon?" I asked excitedly. It was stupid, I know, but aside from all our personal difficulties and who we had become and everything, it was a thrill to have your old man in conference with the president of the United States, even if this particular president was a shithead. The liquor must have been getting to me.

"He's at the department," Sheila said dryly, then stuck her head more fully out the door and peered up and down both ends of P Street. "Would you like to come in?" she asked nervously. I got the feeling that she was far from enthusiastic about inviting me into the house, but that she was even more paranoid about us being spotted together on her front doorstep.

"Thank you," I said. She led the way into the living room. It was decorated with pieces of American primitive and folk art. On one wall was a big green-rusted copper weathervane shaped like a swan. On another hung a trio of scary-looking Indian masks. The furniture was very fine old American stuff, and carefully selected too, you could tell. But all in all the place seemed rather austere, certainly nothing like our old place in Bedford. It didn't contain a single item that I associated with my father and our former life together as a family. The only thing that evoked his presence at all was a subtle trace of scents.

"Would you like to sit down?" Sheila asked. I didn't hear her and she had to repeat herself. Then we were seated, about as far away from each other as possible in that particular room, the way they had the chairs and sofa set up. It was chilly in there too—that time of the fall when the nights are turning crisp but you still don't have the furnace switched on yet. I looked longingly at the fireplace, which was neat as a pin and obviously out of service. You could hear an old-fashioned clock ticking loudly from the hall.

"I don't mean to pry," I said, "but are you going to have a baby?"

Sheila looked down at her stomach and then back at me. "Yes, we are," she said gravely.

"I am too—I mean we are, me and my wife, Catherine."

Suddenly Sheila perked up and a smile sneaked over her face. It was a nice smile, actually, and it completely changed her face. As things turned out, this baby theme was just the right icebreaker. Sheila asked when Catherine was due, and I told her, and Sheila said she wasn't that far along herself, and we were chatting like a couple of normal human beings for a while. She even offered me a drink—she had just come home from her hot-shot job with the Federal Trade Commission—and I asked for a scotch.

When she returned with the drinks, though, her demeanor had cooled again noticeably.

"I'm afraid I don't know what to call you," she said.

"Call me Byron."

She held her glass with both hands and peered down into the drink as if the right words might be found floating down in there with the ice cubes.

"This wasn't the best time for you to come," she said.

"When would be?"

"I don't know," she said, looking up, showing that she appreciated the difficulties such a thing presented, and pleading with her eyes for me to understand her side of it. "Not while Morris is in office," she finally said.

"But the problem is now."

She sighed and nodded her head, gazing into her drink again. "And he may not *be* in office anymore, as a matter of fact," she said quietly.

"Is that it? Are they firing him tonight?"

She nodded. Her mouth was set and even, her lips drawn real tight. "I think so. Yes," she said.

"Who? Nixon himself?"

"Not in person."

"Does he ever talk about me, my father?"

"On occasion."

"What does he say?"

"He doesn't understand your generation."

"He seems to understand you okay."

"I'm thirty-one," she said with a quick sardonic smile to indicate that she had proved her point.

"You're certainly not part of his generation, though," I said. She shifted around in her chair as if it were suddenly uncomfortable.

"I guess I'm caught in the middle," Sheila said.

"I don't mean to put you there."

"No, just age-wise."

"Oh, yeah. Sure."

"But I've heard you on the radio," she added, "and I like some of your songs."

"Hey, really? No kidding?" I was quite flattered, to be honest. "Which ones?"

She didn't know any of their names, just a few snatches, a lyric here and there.

"Better not let Morris catch you listening," I joked around.

"Don't worry," she assured me. "I listen in the car, on my way to the office."

"Hey, the papers would love that, huh?"

"I won't tell them if you won't," she said with a connoisseur's delectation for the inanity of the press. This was at least one area where musicians and government officials might agree. I was feeling okay about talking to her, but then her spirits seemed to flag again. "I'd offer you another drink," she began, "but . . . I'm not sure I should be encouraging you to . . . to remain here."

"You're not encouraging me. I'm here, that's all."

"No, I mean . . . please don't be offended, but it might be better if you weren't here when—"

"Do you want me to wait on the front stoop?"

"No," she said, dismayed that she was failing so completely to persuade me to make myself scarce.

All at once we both noticed unusually bright lights swerving against the drapes from outside on the street and we heard male voices. Sheila got up, went to the window, and peered out. I got up and likewise took a peek.

"Shit," she said.

A TV news crew was setting up their equipment right on the sidewalk at the bottom of the stairs. They were checking out their portable floods and running cables to a panel truck.

"I hope you're satisfied," Sheila said, and I was taken aback by the anger in her voice after our pleasant conversation.

"Hey, don't blame me. I didn't call them."

I returned to my chair and sat down, which was a way of demonstrating my determination to stick around, I suppose. Sheila, meanwhile, paced up and down the living room, worrying about a situation over which she no longer had any control.

"You're probably sorry you let me in here in the first place, huh?" I said, trying not to be flippant but to sympathize with her predicament and not have her feel so rotten.

"I'm sorry you ever came to Washington," she said, her arms crossed and sort of hugging herself in the chill. You could hear a car door slam outside, then a gaggle of voices. Sheila quickly stepped into the hall.

I don't know whether to get up or not. The door opens. White light floods the hall. The door slams, muffling the yammer. Heated whispers. Footsteps on the hardwood floor. I get up, finally. My father strides around the corner and stands framed in the entrance to the room, tall and erect in a beautifully tailored gray pinstripped suit. Only his face betrays the depth of his emotions. His skin is ashen, close to the silver-gray of his hair, or maybe it's just the stark light refracted from the TV equipment outside. His jaw is quavering though, as if he's grinding his teeth, and his eyes radiate that special spellbound hatred you associate with large, gravely wounded animals in the moment when they're confronted with the cause of all their misery.

"Hello, dad."

My father continues to stare at me, like I might be a figment that can be driven away with strenuous concentration. Sheila is wringing her hands beside him.

"He wouldn't leave," she says.

"Of course he wouldn't leave as long as someone's pouring free booze," my father says in a voice so strangled in the attempt to control its volume that it's painful just to hear it.

"He thinks I'm still in high school," I explain to Sheila.

My father reaches up and loosens his tie. He turns and walks stiffly down the hall, to where I can't see, the dining room maybe, the kitchen, whatever's down there. Sheila follows. I can hear vehement whispering, but can't make out a word of what's being said. It goes on for quite a while with big spooky pauses between bursts. I think about getting up and splitting, ask myself if it's worth it to stick around, wonder if it can possibly accomplish anything, change anything. I don't know, but I have to try. I sit down again and wait. Soon I hear his footsteps in the hall again. He stops for a moment in the entrance, establishing that I am, in fact, still on the premises, and then makes for the very chair where Sheila had sat and passed the time of day with me. He sits down resolutely, looking more collected than when he first stepped into the house. He crosses his legs and picks a piece of lint off his trousers.

"You must be happy now that you've gotten what you wanted," he begins quietly, but in a tone of voice dripping with that humorless sarcasm that is his trademark.

"I'm not happy," I tell him.

"Well," he continues more expansively, "you've humiliated me. And destroyed my career. And ruined a man's chance to serve his country. Isn't that precisely what you've wanted all these years?"

"That thing in Florida, do you think I did that on purpose just to—"

"Oh, absolutely."

"I didn't."

"Oh, you mean your . . . putz pulled the zipper down all by itself and escaped without your permission? Come on, Peter."

"I don't know if there's any way I can explain it so you'll understand. It was a mistake—"

"I'll say it was a mistake!" he roars.

"But I didn't do it to hurt you."

He is suddenly on his feet.

"You make me sick!" he spits out the words. "You and all those clowns out there like you. I want you out of here, out of my house. Come on, get up!"

You know that feeling of mental nausea? It's like being sick to your stomach, only inside your skull, like your brain wants to vomit, but can't so it chokes instead. That's what I felt like sitting in that chair.

My father takes a step forward.

"Come on, Peter," he says in a threatening tone of voice. "You can go out the back door."

"I'm not going out the back door. I'm not going anywhere until we finish this discussion."

"The discussion is finished, pal."

"No it's not."

"Up!"

"Up your ass!"

He lunges forward now as if to seize me, physically, but even with my bum leg I manage to get out of the chair and around the back of it, evading his grasp. Sheila is watching the whole thing from the entrance to the foyer. Her face is white with anxiety.

"Will you tell him to calm down, for Godsake," I plead with her.

"Go upstairs, Sheila—"

"Morris—"

"Do as I say!"

"I am not a little girl!" she shouts and shakes the hair out of her face. "Both of you stop it! Stop it!"

"Tell *him* to stop it," I implore her. "The sonofabitch is attacking me!"

"I want him out!"

"I'm trying to apologize, don't you understand?"

"I don't care! I don't *care!*"

"Morris! Stop shouting!" Sheila screams.

"Do they let you act this way in a court of law?" I ask.

"You worm! You rotten, miserable *worm!*"

"I hate you!"

"Get out!"

"Stop!"

My father crouches like he's actually going to spring over the chair and try to strangle me. I circle halfway around and grab a heavy, deep-blue vase off the mantelpiece. I brandish it overhead. My father freezes. Sheila screams. The yammer of voices outside is insistent.

"I hate you!" I scream again and rear back and peg the vase against the wall. It explodes over a mahogany lowboy. My father finally lunges. I push the chair right into his knees and he stumbles over it. A cry of pain. I rush to the front door, throw it open, and step into the lurid glare of the TV lights, momentarily stunned. The door closes neatly behind me. A bolt is thrown.

Man, I was shaken, standing there on the top step of my father's house. I was stupified by the total failure of it all. But looking into those hypnotic lights, the strangest sensation came over me, a feeling of light-headedness, giddiness. My blood felt carbonated. I raised an arm to shield my eyes from the glare.

"This way, Byron!"

I looked down to the left.

"Hey, Byron, over here!"

"How 'bout a smile . . . put your hand down . . . that's right . . . thattaboy!"

The Nikons clicked and the autowinders whirred. I stepped down to the sidewalk and a bunch of microphones were thrust at my face.

"We understand that your father handed in his resignation tonight," a reporter said.

"Good news travels fast, huh," I quipped morbidly. There's some sardonic laughter.

"What'd you two have to say to each other?"

"There's always so much to talk about whenever dad and I get together."

"We heard some shouting and—"

"Well, we're a boisterous bunch."

"They say you two don't get along very well."

"Who says? Who's *they?*"

"That's what the rumor mill says, Byron."

"Oh, yeah. Well, how come this fabulous rumor mill doesn't know the real reason they fired my dear old dad?"

"What's that, Byron?"

Suddenly these guys were poised on the balls of their feet, pens and pads at the ready, microphones outstretched.

"Don't you guys know? I was supposed to marry Tricia. The whole thing was all arranged. It was me who broke off the engagement."

There was a stunned silence. Then, when the reporters realized what titillating copy I was creating for the morning news, they started poking each other in the ribs, and guffawing.

"No kidding," I went on. "Nixon took it out on my old man, who's almost singlehandedly been saving this great country of ours from all these radical hippie slobs."

More laughter. There were tears in my own eyes.

"I hope the motherfucker doesn't bomb my house. Whoops. Can you bleep that word out? I don't think I could stand another bust this week. Hey, one of you geniuses want to give me a ride to the airport?"

Almost all of them volunteered. I picked this guy from Reuters. The British love scandal. The whole way across the Potomac to the airport I spun out this incredible tale of secret White House romance and sexual profligacy between me and the first daughter. The reporter would frequently try to interrupt with a ". . . but seriously now, Byron . . ." and I just kept heaping on the old bullshit, afraid I'd burst into tears and never stop if I allowed myself to be serious for a second.

At the terminal, I called Keough back at the hotel in Baltimore.

"Where the hell are you?" he yelled.

I told him.

"Great," he said.

"The tour's over, Billy."

"I'll say it's over. You know something. You really piss me off."

"I piss everybody off," I said and started blubbering, right there in the booth.

"Are you okay, Byron?"

"Yeah, yeah, sure. . . ."

"It's only that—"

"I know, Billy. I'm a fuckup. What can I say?"

"I wish just once you'd make it easy on yourself, man."

"I will. Next time."

"Are you sure you're all right?"

"I'm fine," I insisted, but he knew I was coming apart.

"Where are you going to now?" he asked.

"Home, I suppose. I want to go home."

"What about your stuff?"

"Give it to the roadies."

"Are you absolutely sure you're all right?"

"Hey, my plane's loading. I'll call you in a week or so, okay?"

"Sure, Byron."

"I'll tell Max to continue your salary."

"It's not the salary—"

"Hey, everyone's got to eat. I'll be in touch, Billy."

And so I went home. Home. It was never really quite that. I went to the place where Catherine was. Tamberlane. I still get queasy at the thought of it.

*You should see the town now.*

Yeah? What's it like?

*Boutiques from end to end. They sell handmade things and gourmet cooking equipment and posters of you.*

---

Byron switched off the Sony and stared broodingly into his lap. The minutes ticked by and I began to worry about his state of mind. He seemed to be working out some abiding problem and I was afraid to interrupt. The afternoon sun was uncomfortably warm on the back of my neck. It no longer reached the wicker chair where Byron sat, though, and a shudder eventually brought him back from his inward-searching silence.

"What is it with the human race, Rick?" he asked.

How could I answer him? As I stumbled mentally over one cliché after another. Byron sighed and pushed the tape recorder back on.

## The Life of Byron Jaynes—Tape 10 (Cont.)

I could hear the gunfire coming up the long curving driveway in the limo. For some reason, probably because I was drunk, I went right inside without any regard for danger.

Like Simon's house, I had installed french doors opening onto a terrace beyond the living room. Only our house was perched way up on a hilltop, and from the terrace we had a view of the Hudson Valley, looking northeast across the river toward Beal College and the Taconic mountains. Anyway, I entered the house. It was October, but Catherine had the doors thrown wide open. She stood out on the terrace, extremely pregnant, wearing a floor-length night-gown with a wool and leather varsity jacket that said "Bearcats" embroidered across the back. A blonde girl dressed in jeans and a fluffy sweater was bent over a machine down on the flagstones.

"Pull!" Catherine said.

The machine spat out a clay pigeon. Catherine mounted the gun fluidly, with her weight forward, swung on the floating target, and gave it both barrels. A dusty little smudge appeared against that brilliant fall sky, and then vanished. She turned her head slowly my way, and you could tell she'd known I was there all along, watching her. She had an expression on her face that was supposed to be something more than a simple smile. With a quick, deft, knowing jerk, she broke open her shotgun and pulled out two smoking shells from the breech.

"Nice shooting," I said.

"Oh, Byron," she said in such a tumultuously breathless tone of voice that it gave me goose bumps. She hung the shotgun in the crook of her arm and placed her other hand on her swollen belly. My insides turned cold. In that instant I saw how she was carrying my fate, and it scared the daylights out of me.

*If you saw it that clearly, why did you stay?*

Isn't it, by definition, something you can't run away from. Or it wouldn't be fate, right? You'd give it another name. Anyway, once I felt that, it seemed like all I could do was stay there, close to it, close to her, and watch it with fascination. Staying drunk helped. The weeks at Tamberlane passed like a fever dream. Reality barely penetrated our little Cloud Cuckoo Land. I submitted with the same sense of surrender that a harried fugitive must feel when the dogs are finally on him.

Then, one snowy night in December, Catherine began to squeal with the pains. She'd made a plan beforehand.

She knew this guy and his wife from Tamberlane Village, a young couple, our age. The guy was one of those mysterioso deracinated opportunists that the Age of Aquarius spawned by the thousands. He called himself "a healer." His wife was supposedly a midwife. The guy named himself Suliman. He wore a turban, smoked dope almost continually, and talked about life in the most appealing, absurd generalities. He was a handsome devil too, with a black beard. His wife was named Ranya. Both of them had heavy midwestern accents, with a real flat A. Both had B.O.

I tried to convince Catherine to have the baby in the hospital, but she was determined to do it the way she'd planned. Suliman and Ranya set up about a thousand candles downstairs around one of the bearskin rugs we'd brought down from Big Slide years ago. Catherine lay in the center of this now, naked, whimpering with the pains, her skin glistening with sweat. Suliman chanted and played finger cymbals. Debbie, the "helper," sat at Catherine's head with a bowl of ice water and wet towels. I knelt on the other side, essentially superfluous, a bottle of whisky close at hand. The pains were coming at constant intervals now and Catherine's cries were becoming one long scream. Her fingernails broke the skin of my palm.

"Pant, Catherine!" Ranya shouted. "Like a dog!"

Suliman's idiotic chanting grew louder.

"Push, Catherine," Ranya said.

Catherine took sharp little breaths. Each exhalation was a pained grunt. She arched her back. Both Debbie and Ranya helped hold her legs up. I never saw such an expression of agony on anyone's face before. I felt weak just looking at her. Things spun around. I heard a sharp slap, another scream, higher, another voice really, and Ranya was hoisting this red-smeared, black-haired creature aloft by his tiny legs. I fainted.

I came to about fifteen minutes later. The bearskin rug was vacant. They were all gone. It took me a while to locate them. Mother and child had been removed upstairs to the bedroom. I went up to them.

Catherine was under the covers, her eyes half-shut with an exhausted smile on her face. Debbie and Ranya were swaddling the baby on the bed. Suliman was dancing some foolish oriental jig of thanksgiving. They gave Catherine the baby.

I came over and sat down beside them.

"Say hello to your old man," Catherine said wearily.

Every father will tell you the same thing. You see this wrinkled little critter all wrapped up in blankets and it just blows your mind. I reached down and touched his arm, his cheek. He was so soft. He had dark hair, too, like me.

"Did you think of a name?" Catherine asked.

"Jesse."

"Jesse. . . ?" she said skeptically. "That's kind of cute, don't you think: Jesse Jaynes."

"What do you suggest?"

"I like Jeremiah."

"How about Jesse Jeremiah?"

"I like it the other way."

"Okay, Jeremiah Jesse." Anything to avoid more conflict. *Anything.* "Hey, Suliman. . . ?"

He interrupted his astral rapture for a moment.

"Yes, Byron."

"Have you got a dime?"

He searched the pockets of his corduroys.

"Aha! Here you go, Byron."

I returned to the bedside and pressed the dime into Jeremiah Jesse's warm little hand.

"What's that all about?" Catherine asked.

"A tradition," I told her.

The baby didn't know how to grasp an object yet, though. The dime sailed out of his flailing little hand and bounced on the carpet.

A week after the birth of the baby, Max Goodsen called and asked if he could come up and see me. When he arrived, around noon that day, I was sitting in the wintry sunshine on the terrace, wrapped in my old wool cape, wearing an otter fur cap, sipping whiskey as I watched the shadows of clouds playing over the broad valley below.

Max sat down on the low stone wall at the edge of the terrace, huddled up in his chesterfield coat, gray flags of hair fluttering in the wind under his Russian-style lamb's-wool hat. He looked tired but pleased with himself. The reason for his visit, you see, was the trouble in Florida. I'd been trying to ignore it for months, but they wouldn't let me anymore.

"I think we've found a way out of this thing," Max began. "We're going to plead you. The court has proved a bit more tractable than they originally indicated."

"How much?"

"Fifty thousand."

"Not too greedy, huh? The pigfucker."

"You can easily afford it, Byron—"

"It's the principle of the thing. What if I say, 'Fuck you, come to New York and get me?' "

"Then they could come up to New York and get you." Max turned up his collar and stuck his gloved hands in his coat. "They can compel you to return. We could fight extradition, but in the current climate . . . well, I assure you we'd lose."

"All that just for waving my weenie, huh?"

Max sighed.

"It's that riot charge, actually. It's a felony. Look, we can fly down there next Tuesday, grease the judge, go to court after lunch, he slaps your hands, *bing!* four o'clock you're back on the plane to New York. It'll do nothing but good for you to have this thing over and done with, Byron."

"I know."

"And I'll tell you something else: it'll make an impression with some of these yo-yos who cancelled concert contracts last fall. We'll show them what a fine young man Byron Jaynes is, willing to face up to the consequences of his behavior."

"Willing to buy his way out for fifty grand, you mean."

"They won't know that."

"I hate giving them the satisfaction. It's legalized blackmail."

"It's also a one-time thing, Byron. Once this case is disposed of, that's the end of it. They can't come back for more. For $50,000 you learned a thing or two about the way the world works. Kiss it good-bye and forget it."

So Tuesday we flew back down to Gainesville. Max had a meeting with the judge's bag man at a place called the Headhunter Lounge out in Orange Heights. They had a regular three-ring circus set up for us at the Alachua County Courthouse: reporters, TV crews, the whole miserable rig.

The judge came in from his chambers, a hardened, hairless old man wearing half-glasses which allowed him to look over the lenses at you imperiously without straining his neck muscles. His name was Ambrose Heade. He was 74 years old and what he might do with $50,000 I couldn't begin to imagine.

The proceeding was brief: "Mistuh Goodsen, yo' client is charged with blah blah blah and blah blah blah and how does he plead?"

"He pleads guilty, your honor."

"Mr. Jaynes, please stand up and face the bench. You have duly pleaded to blah blah and blah blah and I hearby sentence you to the county penitentiary at Waldo for a term not less than 120 days and not to exceed six months blah blah take you into custody now. Is there anything you would like to say at this time, Mistuh Jaynes?"

I was dumbstruck. Max was bright red. He was repeating something under his breath and gripping the defendant's table with both hands. At first I couldn't make out what he was saying with all the commotion in the courtroom. Then I recognized the words: "Suspend it! Suspend it!"

The blood drained from Max's face. He turned to me, positively stricken.

"He's not going to suspend it, the sonofabitch!" he said.

I looked up at Heade. His hands were crossed primly and he was smiling. The deputies moved in and clamped the cuffs on me. The gallery was packed with middle-aged Floridians and they whooped their heads off at the verdict. I felt like I was in another country.

---

Byron punched the stop button and slumped in his seat. Spring peepers filled the violet semi-darkness around us with their shrill music. For a long time the two of us sat out there listening to it all, and it was all right.

"We came a long way this afternoon," I finally said.

"Almost to the end," Byron replied. "What a night! Listen to that life out there."

"Makes you wonder how they ever survive the winters."

"One at a time," Byron said, and there was enough twilight left to make out his shy smile.

We sat quietly a while longer but soon I felt another one of nature's calls and excused myself to take care of it. I had just washed my hands upstairs when I heard the engine of his car fire up, and by the time I made it to the kitchen door, his tail-lights were receding down the driveway.

"Goddam you, anyway, Byron Jaynes," I shook my fist into the cheeping darkness, realizing in the next moment that I wished him nothing of the kind, and ashamed at my limitless vanity. "Patience," I corrected myself, looking up at the emerging stars. "Have patience. And have mercy."

# CHAPTER 12

*Nothing lasts*
*It's all temporary*
*Why not let the past*
*Become a simple memory*

—"Jesse's Song"

Sleep failed me utterly that night. I traced the interminable hours on my wristwatch, waiting for the darkness to lift and for Byron to return. By ten the next morning there was still no sign of him, so I got into the rented Plymouth and drove hurridly out to his place. He had just showered and finished dressing when I got there, and compared to my frazzled state of mind he seemed positively serene. He was dressed in faded jeans and one of the dueling blouses from the old days. The shirt was somewhat yellow and frayed at the cuffs, but seeing him in it evoked such an instantaneous sweep of longings and regrets that my eyes grew misty and a lump formed in my throat.

"You all right?" he asked.

"Fine," I said and followed him into the kitchen. "I didn't know if you were coming to my place or what. You split so suddenly yesterday."

"I tried calling you," he said, glossing over the question of his hasty departure, "but your phone's disconnected. That's very anti-social of you, my boy. Here, hold onto these." He handed me a box of chocolate donuts and proceeded to fill a big stainless-steel Thermos with boiling water, tea bags, and honey.

"I can't have it switched on right now. I'm supposed to be in California."

"Hey, who else would call but me?" he asked playfully. But before

I could answer, he took me gently by the arm and led me out the back door. "What a beautiful day!"

In all my fatigue and anxiety I had failed to notice that it was one of those spring mornings when all the latent energies of the earth burst into color and motion at once. Swallows were winging for bugs in the yard between the house and the barn. Narcissus were blooming beside the woodshed. The air was filled with insect clacking and birdsong and the smell of thawed earth.

"Shall we go to the top of the world?" Byron asked, gesturing with a jerk of his head to that rock outcropping in the high meadow where we had first talked so many months ago.

"Okay," I agreed. Byron's hillside was a solid mass of golden dandelions. He hummed abstractly to himself as we climbed. When we reached the outcropping, I was breathless. A vein throbbed in my neck. And I remained dizzy for quite a while afterward, not from the exertion, which had passed, or the altitude, which was insignificant barometrically, but from an abiding feeling of restless expectation. Byron poured a cup of tea from the Thermos and placed it between us.

"You don't mind sharing, do you?"

I didn't. We ate our donuts silently, enjoying the view and the fine, mild weather, and eventually Byron hooked up the microphone to the tape unit.

"Ready, Freddy?" he asked.

"Yes."

"Okay, then. One more time, let the good times roll!"


## The Life of Byron Jaynes—Tape 11

You might not understand this, but going to jail was one of the best things that ever happened to me. When the shock passed of being double-crossed by that two-bit judge, I realized that I actually welcomed the prospect. It's true I was a little worried about what kind of jail they were going to stick me in—I saw *Cool Hand Luke*, right?—but I ached to be taken out of circulation for a while, that was really it. Fortunately it turned out to be nothing like the Hollywood version of a Down South prison. No chain gangs, no slave-labor draining swamps, no striped pajamas. It was a clean, hygienic one-story building about the size of your average suburban elementary school. It even smelled like one inside: that sweet-rancid aroma of linoleum and canned spaghetti. My cell was comfortable and the bedding was clean. The only special treatment I got was that I wasn't allowed any contact with the other prisoners. I wasn't officially in solitary confinement, but that's what it boiled down to, and it turned out to be all right with me. I wasn't even allowed in the mess hall.

For almost four months, then, I was by myself, except for the guards. I had no booze, no drugs. It was what I wanted. It was what I needed. And to think that on the outside the underground press was trying to make a martyr out of me. . . . The ironies never end, do they?

*Are you trying to tell me you were happy in jail?*

I'm trying to tell you that I was changing in there. It was change or die. No, I wasn't happy. I was grateful. People would come to see me. Max. He was half crazy with self-reproach. I tried to tell him it was all right, I didn't blame him, and not to be so hard on himself. He had just never seen anything as treacherous as what Heade pulled. Forget it, I told him. It was a treacherous age we were living in. Keough came down to see me many times. There were others whose visits I declined. I didn't want to clutter up my head with their good intentions.

*What about Catherine?*

I was about to get to her. No, she didn't visit me. At first I brooded over it, couldn't understand it. Then it hit me: not only was it perfectly consistent behavior for someone virtually incapable of facing reality—Catherine—but also it allowed me to think long and hard about finally freeing myself from her. In the quiet of my cell, I thought about how close I came to divorcing her the summer before, how I'd allowed her to flim-flam me with all that jive about saving herself, and how the baby would force us to live like normal human beings, and I finally saw how things would never be like that, never be right, never be healthy. Our life together certainly didn't become any healthier in the weeks after the baby's birth that winter, before I surrendered in Florida. And so I made up my mind.

Keough couldn't keep tabs on her in the meantime. She hated him for being my spy—which he was, of course—but with me in the slammer, he had no access to the house in Tamberlane and he didn't know what was going on there. As the season turned, though, the winter ended up north, she began showing up in the city again, Keough said, doing the clubs, the parties, the scenes, just like before. He heard things about her from reliable sources. I wasn't surprised to learn that she was back into the old smack again, either. I realized it was inevitable. But it wasn't until she cracked up the Bentley with the baby in it that I made up my mind she was unfit to be a mother as well as a wife. Keough flew down and filled me in on the accident the same day it happened. She was whacked out and ran a red light on Main Street in Tamberlane Village. The kid was on the front seat, just lying on it swaddled in a blanket, no safety seat or anything. It was a miracle that he only broke his arm. And Catherine? Not a scratch. It was amazing, like the way she went through life itself, breaking all the rules and always getting away with it.

I got out of Waldo two weeks after the accident, after serving four months' time minus ten days off for good behavior. It was April 20th, 1970, and the sixties had ended while I was inside.

There were hundreds of people, young people, waiting outside the prison gate the day I was released. The warden wouldn't let Keough bring a limousine onto the prison grounds, so I had to walk the gauntlet of my admiring, stalwart supporters with their beads, beards, and foolish banners. And though I realized they were sincere in their naïve idolatry, it made me sick to be the object of it. I didn't want to be anybody's symbol of anything anymore. I had resigned from my generation.

With the plane trip and all, it was close to six o'clock in the evening when we finally pulled up the long gravel drive at Tamberlane. The woods were so beautiful to me after being surrounded by nothing but cinderblocks and linoleum for 110 days. The buds were bursting into leaf up there. I really had no idea what I was going to find at home, but the first thing you couldn't help noticing was the half-dozen strange cars parked in the driveway: two identical brand-new Volvo station wagons, a Ford Econoline van—painted with day-glo swirls—and a Corvette Stingray. These, plus my old white Rolls-Royce and my blue Rolls convertable. Catherine's Bentley was presumably in the shop.

Keough and I looked skeptically at each other.

"Looks like there's a party going on," I said.

We went inside.

You could barely recognize the place. Over the big stone mantel-piece someone had installed a huge "God's Eye," one of those things where you take two crossed sticks and wrap a bunch of colored yarn around until it makes all these groovy rings—exactly the kind of schmucky aboriginal fetish our generation went in for. This one was huge: six feet across at least, which is how come you noticed it right off. But it was by no means the most shocking thing.

*That* was what a goddam pigsty the place was: clothes, hookahs, papers, food wrappers, records, kids' toys. I did have a kid, of course, but he had hardly attained the level, at five months, where he played with Lego blocks and plastic dump trucks. A movie projector was set up on a side table and there was a sheet pinned to the wall where my big Beal used to hang. The painting had been taken down, as a matter of fact, and was leaning against the wall right beneath the makeshift movie screen. There was a puncture hole right in the center of the canvas like somebody had stuck a pencil through it.

I waded through all this garbage to the french doors. I could see two women and a grimy three-year-old child out on the terrace. There was also a goat staked out on the grass in the back and a little shed that someone had slapped together for it.

When Keough and I stepped out there, the two women just turned and froze. To tell you the truth, my first impulse was to reassure them that we weren't burglars or rapists or anything, but then I realized they froze up like that because they recognized me, and by then my charitable instincts were fading. The women were young. Both had on long skirts. One was wearing a South American pon-cho. The kid looked like one of those Dorothea Lange photos of a Dust Bowl baby, except it wasn't quite that malnourished.

"Where's my wife and child?" I asked them.

They looked blankly at me.

"Do you ladies speak English?"

"Yes," one said. The other shook a blonde forelock out of her eyes.

"What's going on here?" I asked, generally indicating the whole spread.

"Nothing," the first girl said.

"People living," the other said.

"People living in my house, you mean."

The child whined and the blonde girl picked it up. From another part of the house I heard someone put a Crosby, Stills and Nash record on a stereo. We left the two women on the terrace and waded back through the living room to the kitchen wing. In a small bedroom off the hallway originally planned for the maid, some hairy beanpole of a guy was lying on a mattress reading *The Lord of the Rings*. We stuck our heads in the room. It smelled. He lowered the book, his eyes bugging out.

"H-Hello, B-B-Byron . . ." he said in a timid, phlegmy voice.

"Who the fuck are you?"

"I'm Elliot," he said, trying to force a smile.

We moved along to the kitchen. There were four more women in there, in similar homespun hippie garb to the girls out on the terrace, and a sort of Hassidic-looking doofus wearing a pork-pie hat and thick wire-rim glasses. He was sitting at a butcher-block table weighing out lids of grass from a couple of kilo-size bricks and packing them in Zip-Loc baggies. He stopped what he was doing and grinned nervously. The girls had been kneading bread and making a big pot of some vegetarian goulash.

A very jittery, guilty look came over all of them when they saw us standing there.

"Are you hungry, Byron?" a girl asked lamely.

"Want to smoke some?" the guy asked and held up a baggie.

"Where's my wife and kid?"

"Jeremiah's upstairs," another girl said.

"We're taking care of him," a third volunteered.

I left the kitchen, wended back through the hallway, and took the stairs two at a time. In one of the upstairs bedrooms a bearded man was playing with—or entertaining—three children, about five years old, with a hand puppet made out of a sock. Farther down the hall I could hear a television set. My heart started pounding. The door to our bedroom was open. Inside, lying on my bed, was that shabbyass charlatan, Suliman. Beside him was Debbie, Catherine's "helper" or maid or whatever. Suliman was watching the evening news and smoking one of those unfiltered French cigarettes that smell like burning garbage. Along with his usual B.O., this made for quite an aroma. When he saw me, though, his face turned a whiter shade of pale—if I may borrow a phrase—than his goddam turban.

"Where's Catherine? Where's the baby?"

"Oh, hello, Byron—" he tried to sound casual.

"Where are they?"

Debbie, having less success at hiding her nervousness, got up off the bed and went over to the bathroom. "He's right in here," she said throwing the door wide open.

"What the fuck are you doing keeping him in the bathroom?"

"It's warmer in there," Debbie tried to explain.

I went in and picked him out of his crib. He had a cast on his arm that was about half as big as he was. I held him in the crook of my arm while he clumsily tried to rub the sleep out of his eyes with one little hand. Then we saw each other. He smiled.

"Where's his mother?" I asked.

"She's, like, in New York," Debbie said.

"How long has she been down there?"

"I don't know," Debbie looked anxiously to Suliman.

"A few days," he said.

"Who are all these people?"

"These people? Here, you mean?"

"That's right. Who the hell are they and what are they doing here?"

"They're . . . friends!" Suliman said, as if the concept possessed some irresistible charm he had just discovered in the process of thinking it up.

"They're not *my* friends," I corrected him.

"Perhaps if you got to know them better—"

"I don't want to know them better. I want them out. I want *you* out—"

*What happened to Suliman's wife? Didn't he have a wife, the midwife?*

Sure. Ranya.

*Yeah, what happened to her?*

Who the fuck knows? Maybe he dumped her. I didn't care and I didn't ask. Anyway, I told Suliman to clear out. He just sighed and crossed his arms and stayed right where he was—on my bed—as if I might calm down and let them stay if he showed some astral patience.

"What about the baby?" Debbie asked.

"Your services are no longer required, if that's what you mean."

"Byron, do you realize that you are utilizing only the top 25 percent of your lung capacity, the way you breathe?"

"No. And I don't give a damn, either. Get out of here."

"You're not aware then, Byron, how closely related breathing is to the emotional state?"

I went over to my closet and rooted around inside briefly until I found what I wanted: one of the canes I'd collected during my convalescence. It was a nice, stout, English walnut walking stick with a silver head in the shape of a griffon.

"Is this what it comes down to in the end?" Suliman asked portentiously. "The threat of violence?"

"Yes," I said. "Get out or I'll brain you."

Suliman finally bestirred himself grudgingly. He stuck the pack of Gauloises in the breast pocket of his cheap, lime-green Dacron shirt and got off my bed.

"You know, Byron," he said in that superior tone of his, "I used to consider you a person of high karmic attainments. Now, I'm not so sure."

"Don't sweat it. I believe we pass this way but once. Now, get out."

It took them a couple of hours, actually, to get all their kids, pets, livestock, and other assorted effects out of the place. Before they left, Suliman prevailed upon me for some cash so he could put up his "holy ashram" in a motel for a few nights until he found a new place for them to despoil. He asked me to "consider the children." I gave him $500 and told him never to darken my doorway again. I didn't find out until the next day that he'd gotten into my personal things—how could he resist it?—and looted one of my local bank accounts to the tune of $27,000—including the price of those two new Volvo station wagons.

In the meantime the phones weren't working, because, as things turned out, Suliman and the gang had run up a bill of over $1000. In their little astral world, things like phone bills were paid by magic. The phone company had cut our service. So I sent Billy down into Tamberlane Village to call up and arrange a nurse for the baby and someone to start cleaning up the house. And when he returned, I asked him to go down to the city, find Catherine, and bring her back.

"What if she doesn't want to come?" he asked, reasonably enough.

"She doesn't have any choice," I said.

"How can I force her?"

I peeled off a bunch of $100 bills.

"Find someone to help you," I told him.

Keough ballooned out his cheeks and nodded his head, agreeing reluctantly to my ham-fisted instructions. I don't mean to make excuses, but I was just so far beyond the point of fucking around that it wasn't funny anymore.

The nurse arrived about ten. The baby had been crying before then, and I couldn't find any formula, or even bottles. I think one of Suliman's harem-mates had been breast-feeding it. Anyway, she had to drive back down to the village and get the stuff. Eventually we got the baby squared away. I fell asleep on the sofa downstairs.

It was much later when I heard them come in the front door: Keough, Doug Pattin, a six-foot-six second-string ex-New York Jets cornerback who had been Reuban Shays's bodyguard on and off, and Catherine.

She needed Pattin's assistance to stand up. It looked like wherever they found her, she'd gotten herself together very hastily. She had on jeans and a silver shirt with one tail untucked. Her hair was a mess, all tangled and knotty and uncombed. Her eyes were barely open and you could tell it was taking an extraordinary effort for her to keep awake.

"Hello, Catherine."

" 'Lo, Byron."

For weeks and weeks I'd dreamed about this moment, lying on my bunk in a muggy jail cell, projecting all the furies of my hatred, jealousy, and disappointment onto the blank ceiling, replaying the scene ad nauseum until I knew every minute gesture, every nuance of inflection—and now that the longed-for moment had arrived, I knew from looking at her that life itself would prevent that scene from ever being played. Not that I didn't try.

"Would you guys please excuse us," I said to Keough and Pattin. This would have been a nice opening for the big scene I had in mind, but it didn't really apply here because, you see, Catherine couldn't stand up on her own. Billy and Doug just kind of looked at each other, and then helped her over to that sectional sofa we had in front of the fireplace. Catherine curled up there in a position that looked like a question mark. The others left the room quietly. I sat down on the section facing her and watched her for a while. Upstairs, a toilet flushed.

"Can you hear me, Catherine?"

"Mmmmmmmm. . . ."

"I'm divorcing you."

"Mmmmmmmm. . . ."

"And I'm going to take the baby away from you."

"Mmmmmmmm. . . ."

"You'd better get yourself a lawyer—"

There wasn't any point in going on. She didn't give a flying fuck about anything. I got up, went to her cautiously, and knelt down on the rug beside her. Asleep, she was as beautiful as ever, cheeks satiny in the dim light, tangled auburn hair fiery against the pale skin, the smell of jasmine. I placed my hand against her cheek. It was warm. She didn't feel me, though, didn't stir.

"You broke my heart, Catherine," I whispered in her ear and the tears poured out.

I staggered blindly up the stairs. Keough was in one of the numerous guest rooms getting ready to sack out. Outside, through the diamond-shaped, leaded windows, gray morning light was starting to glow.

"Billy, we have to go back to New York," I said, and his whole face drooped. He was sitting on the edge of the bed, one leg in his jeans, one leg out. It was the last thing I ever asked him to do.

I got my passport from the other room, roused the nurse, and helped change the baby for the ride down.

"Jesse," I whispered to him. "Your name's Jesse now."

The others filed wearily out to the white Rolls-Royce. I remained behind a moment in that great soaring downstairs room. The God's Eye stared emptily over Catherine, still asleep on the sofa. I limped to the french doors and threw them open. The sun was a peach-colored wafer in the thin clouds above the Taconic hills, miles and miles east of the river. "Good-bye," I whispered through the tears, looking back at Catherine and then at the beautiful valley coming to life on a spring morning. "Good-bye to everything." Then I walked around the big stone house to the driveway and got in the car. It was the last time I ever saw Tamberlane.

We flew to England that very afternoon, Jesse and I, and arrived at Heathrow at one o'clock in the morning their time.

I must have read every baby book they sold at Kennedy Airport on the flight over. The decision to go on to Scotland was really spur-of-the-moment. I wanted to go somewhere remote where the people at least spoke English. I didn't have any idea what I was going to do. I tried not to think of the future. Luckily, the Scottish people have a deep sense of their own privacy and were careful not to meddle with me, though I was recognized by a few kids in Edinburgh. I wasn't traveling incognito or anything.

We found a cottage outside the village of Balqfeldy on the shore of Loch Orrin. They called it a cottage. It was actually a 400-year-old manor house. We used only a few rooms downstairs. I hired a Scottish nanny, Mrs. Peebles, sixty, white-haired, a spinster. She was both kind and sensible in her starched way and I could listen to the sound of her voice for hours. She was not able to give Jesse a mother's love, but a lot of people would be better off without a mother's love, in my opinion, I'm sorry to say. Still, the three of us came to comprise a staunch little family there in the Trossachs.

At first I missed America horribly. I'd gaze out the window through the rain at the gray loch and the brooding blue hills behind it, and I'd try to pretend it was that stretch of the Hudson where Beal is. My head felt like a radio sometimes, receiving broadcasts from a bygone era—"Bye Bye Love," and all that—and I suppose, in a way, I was going quietly crazy there for a while.

In June the rain finally stopped. I began to venture outdoors. Mrs. Peebles had rigged up a backpack for me to carry Jesse in and I took him on long walks around the glen. There were lovely woods alongside the River Orrin on the way to Loch Tay where we'd stop and watch the salmon in the deep pools. Jesse would toddle around on a blanket with the silk-lined tam-o-shanter on his head that Mrs. Peebles made for him, and I'd read him stories about Robert the Bruce. It made me laugh to think about myself as a Jewish baby in the New York suburbs a quarter century earlier, watching Loony Toons on TV with Arlene. Anyway, it was a peaceful, enchanted place, this part of Scotland, for a child to gather his first impressions of the world, and though part of me regretted that his little bones were not being formed of American clay, I was grateful that we had a refuge.

The summer was mild and unusually dry for that part of the world and toward the end of it I was able to think about the future in a limited sort of way. For five months I had evaded a lot of responsibilities. So in September I sent a long letter to Max asking him to go forward with the divorce and try to settle with all the people who were still suing me from the '69 tour, so if I ever wanted to resume performing again in the States it would be possible. I had no immediate plans to return there, though. I was writing some songs and I needed to work a lot of things out.

No, I wasn't quite ready to go home, but I didn't want to remain in Scotland through the fall and winter, when it can get mighty dreary, and I had the urge to try a few things in the studio, not an album, necessarily, but just a few tracks—what had it been, almost two years since I cut *Oedipus Forgiven?* So we packed our little entourage up, Mrs. Peebles, Jesse, and me, bid farewell to Balqfeldy, and made a leisurely drive down to London, where I took a suite at the Grosvenor House, around the corner from the American Embassy, of all things.

And we lived there happily through the fall. Some Gemini people put me in touch with Dee Burnette, George Martin's ex-assistant who had worked on *Sgt. Pepper*, and he gave me the run of his new studio. I accumulated enough material for a couple of albums as the weeks went by. It was all just me, though, solo. Dee suggested bringing in some different musicians. That was when I finally began to decide to come home. I wanted to find some guys to play with, but Americans, guys I could depend on for more than one album, more than one tour. I wanted to feel that old electricity of a band again.

I asked Max to scout out a place for Jesse and me to live, somewhere close to the city, but outside it—and not in the Catskills. He knew I could never return there again. He located a secluded house out in Amagansett, right on the beach, that he thought I might like. We were going to spend Jesse's first birthday, and Christmas, in London. After that . . . well, that was the plan. Then Catherine showed up.

*There's a certain amount of confusion about the, uh—*

The murder—?

*The whole chain of events.*

Like what?

*Well, like, how did she get the baby out of the Grosvenor House, away from the nurse?*

She sent a basket of puppies to Jesse as a gift. No indication as to who it was from, so they couldn't send it back. The hotel didn't permit guests to keep pets in their rooms, so the chief clerk called Mrs. Peebles. I was away at the studio. Mrs. Peebles left the baby in his playpen for a few minutes and the door unlocked. Catherine had found out what suite we were in beforehand, apparently. When Mrs. Peebles came down to the lobby, she took her cue.

*She brought Jesse directly back to her hotel?*

That's right. And sometime between then and four hours later, when they found the bodies, Catherine shot my boy full of heroin and then OD-ed herself. Anyway, that's the best reconstruction they could come up with. On the other hand, some things had to be left confusing.

*Left confusing? By whom?*

By me.

*After Catherine and Jesse were found dead?*

Yes, afterward. After I took him back to Scotland and . . . put him to rest. After I decided . . . what I decided. It's no simple matter to make yourself vanish off the face of the earth, you know. A lot of delicate wheels had to be set into motion. I had to liquidate some of my holdings very quickly and quietly. My personal wealth at that time was about five and a half million dollars. I only needed a portion of it. I was able to dump a bunch of bonds and money that was tied up in mutual funds directly through a broker, without Max's intervention. I didn't want him the least bit involved. I had the money sanitized in the Bahamas and transferred to accounts in Canada under the name of Joseph Doaks. It was about a million and a half altogether. I've been living on the interest for over ten years. Actually, I've been living on a good deal less than that, so it must really be piling up.

*What happened to the rest of your money?*

Oh, I didn't have any grand plan for disposing of it. I didn't have the time. I just didn't want my father to get his paws on it, so I left lump sums to Keough, Rego, Gary, and Spag, and the rest to about eleven different charities. Most of it was going to be tied up in probate anyway. All this financial finagling was simple compared to the next part: making myself disappear.

I returned to London once again. It was a good thing for me that they had socialized medicine, because if British doctors made a decent buck I never would have been able to pull this thing off. Dee Burnette had introduced me to some club owners in Mayfair, people who knew people who knew people who could get certain things done.

*Underworld people?*

I guess you could call them that. For a large sum of money, they put me in touch with a certain physician. He agreed to furnish me with a phony death certificate and also a dead body roughly my age, sex, and coloring. Only the physician and the undertakers would ever see the actual corpse and the undertakers were mob-owned too. I was impressed with how businesslike and trustworthy they all were. Sometimes gangsters are more honorable than the guys who lock them up.

*It sounds to me like you're describing a whole chain of individuals who knew what you were planning to do.*

It was a chain, all right, but only the physician at the end of it knew what my ultimate intention was.

*And he kept it to himself all these years.*

I guess he did. He was in his sixties then, so he may not even be alive anymore. And he was well paid to keep mum. Very, very well paid.

*How much, Byron?*

Over half a million dollars. Anyway, it was all arranged. The quote "body" was quote "discovered" by my quote "personal physician" in the bathtub of my hotel room. He attributed my decease to quote "heart failure." The right palms were greased in the city magistrate's office so that the question of an autopsy was delayed until the casket was six feet under St. Clement's Churchyard, and by then the legal process for obtaining a disinterment was so lengthy and elaborate that they just let it slide. When you really got down to it, nobody gave a damn whether I died of a heart attack or an overdose. In any case, long before then I had already departed England, quite incognito with a shaved head, for Berndorf, Austria, where I had my nose bobbed. Nobody in the clinic had any idea who they were working on. Before the last shovel load of English soil was tamped over Bryon Jaynes's grave, Joe Doaks was landing in Halifax, Nova Scotia.

*What kind of passport were you traveling with?*

American, made out for Joe Doaks. Hey, after procuring a stiff and faking my death, the passport was easy, if you could afford it. Anyway, when I got off the plane my face was a complete mess. I had the goddam bandages on my nose from the surgery, and two black eyes from where they had to break the bone, plus I was a skinhead. I was totally unrecognizable.

*Why did you come here? To Cardiff?*

Well, Rick, I wish I could give you a fascinating explanation, but it was quite accidental, really. I landed in Canada and bought a car up there. I needed time and space to think, so I just got behind the wheel and started driving.

I drove all over the Maritimes and then dropped down into New England, staying in motels, eating in roadhouses. I had to get used to this new identity, figure out what I might do. In the beginning, you see, I had a lot more illusions about actually being able to create a brand-new life for myself. It took a while before I realized it could never happen, that I had made myself a permanent fugitive, like the character in my own song. Believe me, when you see your name listed in the "Milestones" column of *Time* magazine and your puss on the cover of *Rolling Stone* with a black border around it and the dates "1945–1971" underneath it, one tends to develop a sense of having no future, and since Joe Doaks had no past, there was nothing left but the road.

And that's where I stayed for months: on the road. It became an entire world unto itself, safe, familiar, and yet ever-changing. You develop a kind of tunnel vision which affects your imagination as well as your eyes. I must have covered every little capillary of roadway in New England during those months of wandering. Then, one spring afternoon a lot like this one today, I was driving down this dirt lane and saw the "For Sale" sign stuck in the weeds, and I knew instantly that this was where I was going to get off the merry-go-round. I knew that this hillside and this house were waiting for me, and I felt it as strongly, as surely, as you know that somewhere on this planet there is a plot of earth waiting to receive your bones. The place hadn't been lived in for years. I bought it and moved right in.

I had no idea for how long. Before I knew it, a couple of years had passed. I can't tell you what a tremendous relief it was just to be left alone. Then, one day I read in the paper that my father had died. To be honest with you, I had repressed those memories so successfully that I doubt if his name or face even entered my head three times after I fled England. It was part of that tunnel-vision thing. But after his death, I don't know if I thought about anything *but* the past for the next several years. Rego and Steve Spagnola were next, dying within six months of each other, and Simon followed them in '76. I was obsessed, living in a continual panic, trying desperately to wring some meaning out of what had happened to me, to make sense of events that really defied the emotional order I was trying to impose on them. It was like trying to catch ghosts with a butterfly net. I don't know if a person is equipped to judge his own sanity, but by any standard I was acquainted with, I must have been around the bend for quite a while. I'd stay awake for days on end, go for a week without eating, soil my clothes. It had to end. It did. I simply gave up.

It was the peace of surrender. I slid into a comfortable fog of acceptance. It wasn't entirely negative. I started doing things, working on bikes when it was warm, building little boats in the winter. I read a lot. I lifted weights, ran up and down the hill. It was a life, after all. Then, one day, I was buying groceries in the Top Shopper and I saw you.

*You saw me? You knew who I was? Right from the start?*

Yup. I knew exactly who you were. And I knew it was all over. And here we are.

———————

Byron slowly squeezed the "stop" button and the tape recorder clicked off.

"And so ends the final installment of *The Mummy's Tomb* starring Joe Doaks, Little Ricky Sears, and Anwar Sadat as the Dead of the Ages. What are you going to do with your tapes, my boy?"

"What are you going to do with yourself, Byron?"

"I'm going to take me down to the bunkhouse yonder and set a spell. And you are not invited."

"You'd rather be alone for a while?"

"Well, since you are not invited and I have no other visitors, then I suppose that means I'd rather be alone for a while. Yes."

He stood up and stretched. It was midafternoon. The temperature must have been up in the sixties. The first bees of the season prospected lazily among the year's first flowers.

"It's still early, and such a nice day," I said. "Wouldn't you like to go for a walk somewhere. Down the dirt road, maybe."

"Some other time, huh?"

"How about tomorrow?"

"Sure. Tomorrow."

"What time?"

"Whenever you feel like it."

"Shall I call you?"

"Yeah, that's a good idea. Call me."

"It's such a beautiful day," I repeated to myself. Byron looked at me. His dark, expressive eyes were never so filled with sheer emotion than at this moment, and never was the precise nature of this emotion less scrutable. "Are you all right?" I asked him.

"Never better," he said in a brittle voice. "Let's go."

This time he didn't gallop down the hill ahead of me, but kept back with my pace, stopping now and then to pick up some bright little weed, examine it closely, mutter its name, and toss it over his shoulder.

"How about some Italian food tonight?" I suggested when we reached the barbed-wire fence.

"No," he said almost inaudibly.

"I thought you liked it. You had such a good time."

"I did like it."

"So, let's go tonight. We could have a small celebration."

Byron recoiled at the suggestion, but soon his face softened into that shy, boyish grin that reminded you so much of another time and place. He shook his head, put one arm around my shoulder, and guiding me toward the Plymouth in the driveway, said, "Sears, Sears, Sears. What am I going to do with you?"

"You don't have to do anything with me," I retorted, half sick with frustration.

"No, I suppose you're right. A guy like you, you can take care of yourself, lead a nice normal life. I admire that."

"I'm not so hot—"

"Hey, can't I just admire you? You've been a great comfort to me in my old age. A comfort and a true friend. Thanks for everything."

He took my right hand in both of his, pumped it once, squeezed it, and then let go, opening the door to the car for me. I got in. He swung it shut. I rolled down the window.

"See you tomorrow," I said.

"Not if I see you first," Byron said with another smile. "G'bye, Rick."

He turned and started limping up the driveway. I fired up the ignition. Through the rear-view mirror I watched him disappear around the back of the house.

––––––––––

I returned to the cottage in such a state of melancholic agitation that I wanted to jump out of my skin. I tried a nap, but sleep was a maddening mirage on a parched interior landscape. A plunge in the pond cleared my head for a little while, but the two fingers of vodka I drank afterward to drive out the chill ended up perturbing my mind all over again. Twilight found me huddled miserably on the porch, staring blankly at the darkening opposite shore, and agonizing over what, if anything, to do about Byron.

The taping was over, the literal thread that tied us together. And the way he ushered me away from his house earlier scared the hell out of me. I was also aware of my increasing inability to separate my own emotions from what I imagined his to be. That very morning, for instance, when I raced out to his place in a torment, only to find him utterly composed, had taught me to be skeptical about such leaps of empathy. And now, was I projecting some new exigency? I didn't know. But I felt lost and frightened for both of us.

When I couldn't stand it any longer, I drove down to the village and called him from the booth outside the Top Shopper. His phone rang five times before he picked it up, and then he didn't say anything.

"Byron. . . ?" I said loudly, afraid he might have just taken it off the hook.

"Yeah, it's me," he finally replied, and in such a timid voice I could barely hear him.

"Are you okay?"

An empty interval, then a sound that was either a cough or a choked sob.

"Where are you?" he asked.

"In the booth outside the market in Cardiff."

I heard that muffled, choking noise again and this time I was fairly sure he was sobbing.

"Do you want me to come out there?" I asked him.

"No!"

"You sound upset."

I could hear him trying to gain control over his breathing. "What I told you today. . . ."

"Yeah. . . ?"

"About Catherine. . . ."

"Yeah. What about Catherine?"

"What I told you!"

"You told me a lot about Catherine."

"About her death! Her *death!*"

I waited for him to explain, but another torturous pause followed.

"Yes, you told me about her death, Byron."

"It's a lie," he wailed. "I killed her."

I felt such a violent transposition of my bodily organs that I had to seize the side panels of the phone booth to remain standing.

"You didn't kill her, Byron," I corrected him stupidly.

"How do you know? You weren't there."

"Neither were you, Byron."

"No. I was. That's what I'm trying to tell you. I was there, in the room."

"When she died?"

"I was there, Sears. I killed her. I knew she was in London. She called me at Burnett's studio. She said she'd come for Jesse. 'You can't have him, you irresponsible bitch,' I told her. 'That's what you think,' she said. 'I've already got him.' "

Byron sobbed. I couldn't have been more painfully aware that fifteen miles of copper wire was all that connected us to each other. "Go on, Byron," I pleaded with him.

"She said she had him. 'What the fuck are you talking about, Catherine?' I said. 'I'm at the Connaught, Room 402. Why don't you come over and say hello. Jeremiah's dying to see his old man.' She hangs up.

"I call Mrs. Peebles at the Grosvenor. No answer. I split the scene immediately, afraid something terrible is going on. Even with the beard I grew in Scotland, a cap, and a heavy winter coat, I'm scared to death someone's going to recognize me. Got to get into the hotel without a scene, without being seen, in case there's trouble. I get an idea: the old backdoor routine. I buy a big bunch of flowers on Curzon Street. Hurry over to the Connaught. They've got this con-cierge-type guy behind a screened-in booth at the delivery entrance, checking stuff in. I scope it out. Man is ahead of me with a parcel. 'Fortnum & Mason, 312, Mrs. Fuller,' he tells the guy in the cage. I'm a good mimic. I can do accents and all. Anyway, I hang loose a minute, then step up to the cage. '312, Mrs. Fuller,' I say and hand over the flowers. 'May I use the WC?' I ask. 'Awroit, lad.' Few minutes later, I slip out of there, up the fire stairs, fourth floor. . . ."

"Go on, Byron."

"It's so terrible."

"Go on."

"I get up there. Door to the suite is unlocked. There's a parlor, then the bedroom. Two beds. Catherine sitting on one. She looks up at me. Big doped-up smile. Spike in her arm. Jesse on the other bed. Sleeping . . . ? He's so still. He's . . . he's blue. He's turning fucking blue! I tear open his little sweater . . . heart's not beat-ing. . . !"

(Byron sobbed wildly now.)

" 'Oh, Catherine . . . Oh, Catherine!' She's boosting with the spike now, drawing blood in and out, pumping it in and out. 'What have you done, Catherine. . . ?'

"I try blowing air into Jesse's lungs. Nothing. He's dead. 'There,' I hear Catherine mumble. I turn to her. She's starting to nod. I pull the spike right out of her arm. Works right on the night table. I cook up all the shit she's got. Fill the needle. Draw it right in. Hold it in front of Catherine. Grab her by the back of her head and show her the needle. 'Take it!' She does. Slowly, slowly, she finds the vein again. Needle in. Plunger down. She falls back on the bed. Muscles twitch. I watch the stain spread darkly on her jeans, hear her breath rattle out. It's over. I stay with them both for a while. An hour, more, less, I don't know. Then I just leave. Go back downstairs and out. Nobody notices anything. Two blocks to the Grosvenor. Mrs. Peebles's beside herself. They've stolen Jesse! Scotland Yard swings into action. Four hours later, they find Catherine and Jesse at the Connaught. 'She killed the baby and took her own life,' they say. It's over, Rick. It's all over. . . ."

He hung up.

---

You could see the glow in the sky more than a mile down the dirt road, and when I got there the house was fully engulfed in flame. I pulled up where the weeds ended and the woods started and rushed out of the car. Even at that distance the heat was as warm on your skin as a sunlamp. Something dark leaped out of a ditch at me and my heart flew into my throat, but it was only Whitey, Byron's little black cat. It was crying. I scooped it up in my arms and put it into the car. Then, above the whoosh and crackle of the conflagration I distinctly heard the whine of an engine. I raced up the weed-choked lawn to the driveway.

The soaring pastures behind the barn were lit an incredible orange, like an empty, hellish version of Woodstock. The barn door was open, and though the building itself was not in flame, I could see fire flickering within. I ran up the driveway. An engine raced in the barn. The motorcycles.

"Byron. . . !"

He was stark naked except for a pair of workboots and he was limping rapidly around the inside of the barn, like some demented imp, pouring kerosene on the floor and walls and lighting it, and flinging lighted rags up into the loft. The red Triumph motorcycle stood just inside the door, its engine running, handlebars vibrating, and yellow-white headlight cutting through the pall of smoke.

"Byron. . . !"

He wheeled around and saw me.

"Get out, Rick!" he screamed.

The heat on my back from the flaming house behind me was so intense I was afraid my shirt would burst into flames.

"Leave it!" I yelled back at him, thinking that he'd already done an expert job on the house and the barn would surely be engulfed soon too. But he seemed intent on torching every structural member. "Come with me!" I pleaded to him.

"Get out!" he raged.

I couldn't stand the heat anymore and retreated back into the driveway, expecting him to follow any second. But, instead, I watched with horror as he drew the sliding barn door closed from the inside. I ran back up, seized the door by its huge wooden handle, and threw it back open again. The barn was filling with dense smoke and flames. He was mounted astride the bike, revving the engine, going nowhere. Exhaust from the tailpipes billowed up into the loft mingling with the smoke of the burning barn.

"What are you doing?" I screamed.

"It's over. Don't you understand?"

"You didn't kill her, Byron. She killed herself. You want to think you killed her because it gives you an excuse not to face your own life."

The idea seemed to rock him like a blow. His eyes glazed and his body shook as though verging on a rapid and momentous transfiguration. There was a roar and I turned to see the roof fall in upon the house. The heat and the smoke were suffocating.

"Live, Byron!"

His back arched wildly and an elongated howl poured out of him that must have been the summation of all the bitterness, terror, gall, and sorrow husbanded in his ten years of exile. I lunged for him, trying to wrestle him off the machine, but he gunned the throttle, kicked the shift lever into gear, and suddenly shot past me into the flaming night. I stumbled out after him and lurched over to the driveway. He was down at the end of it, revving the Triumph and spinning his rear wheel in the dirt, apparently trying to decide which

way to go. Then he saw me and yelled something, but in the din of
his engine and the conflagration I couldn't make it out.

"Wait!" I cried.

"Hey, don't you think I've waited long enough?" he yelled back.

"At least put some clothes on."

"Sears! Sears! You're beautiful, you know that?" His shoulders
heaved as though in some sort of spasm, and then I realized he was
laughing.

"Where are you going?" I tried to stall him.

"I don't know. Away."

"Away where?"

"I don't know, Sears," he hollered and laughed again, wiping the
tears from his eyes. "Do you know where you're going? Do any of
us know?"

He goosed the carburetors and the bike bucked forward.

"Let me follow you—"

"Can't. . . ."

"Byron!"

This time he cranked the throttle wide open. The front wheel
lifted slightly off the ground while his rear wheel spewed a great
roostertail of gravel over the weeds.

"Hang on, Byron!" I shouted, wiping the tears from my own eyes.
He vanished down the dirt road in the direction of Haverfield, his
gearbox singing above the roaring flames. Three sharp explosions
shook the barn and yellow fireballs shot out the door as the gas tanks
of the other cycles began to blow. In a little while the Town of
Cardiff pumper truck arrived on the scene, but by then there was
nothing left to do except watch the remaining walls and beams col-
lapse into cinders.

# EPILOGUE

Among the innumerable ironies, surprises, alarms, and, shall we say, heavy changes, wrought by Byron Jaynes's reappearance in the world, not the least of these was his arrest that night in the crossroads hamlet of Haverfield by deputies of the Coos County Sheriff's Patrol. Because he was innocent of clothing, not to mention helmet, license, insurance, and registration, and because he was "incoherent," as one of the deputies put it, he was taken to Mary Hitchcock Hospital in Hanover for observation. Imagine their surprise to find out that this "36-year-old white male" claiming to be "the late Byron Jaynes" actually was the genuine article. It took some doing on Byron's part, but after 48 hours the evidence, both medical and personal, was overwhelming and they had to believe him. Shortly after he was released from the hospital, the police charges were dropped and then Byron's real headaches began.

Predictably, the press wanted to devour him as the news of his existence crackled out to the rest of the world. I did what I could to help out, acting as a sort of unofficial press secretary and personal assistant. For a start, I installed the two of us in a suite of rooms at the redoubtable Hanover Inn where I organized the initial press conferences. It was interesting to be on the other side of a news event for a change.

It took two days, while he was still being detained in the hospital, to get hold of Allie by phone, and when I finally did, and told her that I was not in Hollywood but rather in New Hampshire with Byron Jaynes, Allie must have thought I had finally lost my mind. In fact, there was a series of increasingly manic calls that long night, but it wasn't until she was at work twelve hours later, and heard the news come over the radio, that she had the slightest inclination to believe me. And less than an hour later, she was headed north on the New England Turnpike in the Saab. The first time Allie met Byron at the hotel, she had trouble relating to him as something other than an extreme oddity of history, but soon the skeptical side of her nature gave way to the warm, quick-witted woman she was and found a friendly foil in Byron. During that first, frantic week in Hanover when the world wouldn't let Byron alone, she was the only one who could really make him laugh and feel relaxed.

Billy Keough was a great help too, flying in from the West Coast as soon as he heard the astonishing news, and the reunion between him and Byron that beautiful May evening on the inn's front portico could comprise a chapter in itself. But this is really the end of the story.

After a week of "the Ringling Brothers number," as he termed it, Byron flew off to Keough's place in Santa Barbara to rest and also to see another part of the country after his long seclusion, and in June I received a letter from him.

*Dear Rick,*

*People have been very nice to me here, but I don't know if I'll ever get used to California. I have to keep reminding myself that I can pick up and go anytime I want to, though I'm not sure where. I guess there's plenty of time to figure that one out. Billy has got himself a ranch, sixty acres, right off the Pacific. I can't tell you what a thrill it is to walk along the ocean after such a long time away from it all. The security is okay, but the phone rang so continuously the first two days after I got here that they had to change the number. Then, somehow, they got their mitts on the new number and we had to change it all over again. You newshounds are incorrigible.*

*Speaking of the press, the stories I've seen are exactly what I expected, meaning mostly ridiculous. Your old rag managed it with some dignity, but did you see that spread in* People: *"Rock Van Winkle?" Sweet Jesus! My favorite, though, was the head-*

*line in the* National Enquirer: *"Byron Jaynes Returns—Is There Hope for Elvis Too?"*

*My eyes are still black and blue from the operation. I suppose I could have left my nose the way it was, but I couldn't look in the mirror without remembering the farm and all the years there. I hate to admit it, but I feel occasional yearnings for that strange life apart. It gets into your blood. Back on the farm there was never any question of where do I go now, because I was always there. You get to be around my age and all you want to do is go home. Now there's none to go back to, and a hell of a job making a new one, a real one, one that is worth having and will last. But you know what? Something has begun to dawn on me out here. I'm a lucky guy. And I'm grateful for everything, Rick, with all my heart.*

*As ever,*
*Byron*